Pamela,

Thank you for supporting my dream!

Best wishes,

And the Walls
Came Tumbling Down...

The Secret Life of Senator Jack

by
Vernadine A. Merrick

Eloquent Books
New York, New York

.

Eloquent Books
An imprint of AEG Publishing Group
845 Third Avenue, 6th Floor—6016
New York, NY 10022
http://www.eloquentbooks.com

ISBN: 978-1-60860-213-1

Book Design: Bruce Salender

Printed in the United States of America

Acknowledgments

This book is dedicated to my sister, Valdasia Merrick. Her talents have been an inspiration to me. Her encouragement has been unmatched and her editing skills invaluable. To my sister Valynda Mitchell, you're my confidant, lifelong buddy and unwavering supporter. Thank you for pushing me forward through the dark times. Thanks also to my extraordinary father, a person always willing to safely stand beside me in case I should fall, and who has provided me unconditional love. I thank my beloved mom, though she is no longer with us. She taught me to dream and lived her own dreams with vigor and might. I love you Mom. To my dear friends Marta Guida, Antoinette Brown and Lisa Shasteen, I say thank you from the bottom of my heart for your support and enthusiasm for my writing. You are like sisters. My brother, Hank E. Merrick, deserves my gratitude for showing me, through example, that vision must be driven by dedication and hard work. Also I give thanks to the support of my wonderful sisters Vuncia Council and Vaneese Merrick Adams. To my nieces and nephews, Latifa, Ronnie, Cole, Jemila, Darlisha and Maraya, thanks for bringing me such joy. To all my wonderful friends and family, I say thank you!

Prologue

It was a cold windy day. It was the sort of day you wished you were home snuggled by a fire with anybody who was willing to hold you close. However, here I sat, in a deserted park on a cold hard bench. Waiting... I was waiting on God knows what was on the other side of this meeting. I was perspiring as if I were in the midst of a Louisiana summer.

Ridder knew he had me. He was one of those detectives that smelled blood and tracked the scent until the prey was caught like a deer with headlights shining in his eyes. I knew my deepest despair would only make his conquest even more rewarding, capturing the high-powered senator - the mover and shaker of D.C. I was the first African-American to ever make it to the Senate from Massachusetts and rumored to be in serious line for the White House. The thought of my future tied to any-one's whim made my hands run cold. *Interesting how you can be burning up and bitter cold at the same time.* I waited for what seemed like an eternity.

"Have you been waiting long?" he said. I turned to see a middle-aged man, with an expression of sobriety and caution written on his face. He was a 'brother' too. Chocolate and lanky was the best way to describe him. His posture carried the weight of the world, but with a certain grace and stature.

I decided to be honest, "Not too long. Let's head to Winston's Café and get out of this weather." We strode in complete silence. I studied my environment as if it were the first time I had been to D. C. The smell and sight of D. C. was always intoxicating. There was only one word to describe it - power. It was the sexiest city I'd ever encountered. Again, I marveled how a poor boy from Ohio ended up as a senator from the State of Massachusetts. Not just any senator either, but one to be feared and revered.

We arrived at Winston's Café just before the cold heavy rain began to fall. Winston's was one of those trendy cafes that most people go to for the ambience or just to be seen among the politically elite, rather than for the food or drink. Its walls were the warm color of rich burnt orange. The restaurant had granite gray-topped tables with black iron chairs scattered about and an equally hard looking black and white marble floor. Soft music played in the background and well-lit, colorful modern paintings adorned its walls. It was a Sunday, so the usual wall-to-wall crowd was nowhere to be found. We chose a very private table in the corner.

"I'm glad you could meet me," Ridder said.

"Did I have a choice?"

"We always have choices, Senator."

We sat in silence as the waitress took our order. "Just coffee will be fine," I said. Ridder looked up at the perky blond waitress. "Coffee as well and one of those delicious looking cinnamon rolls you all are so famous for. Thanks." "Yes sir," she winked, smiled and walked away. How he knew what this café was famous for was beyond me. Ridder certainly didn't fit the profile of the crowd who were regulars here. But then again, appearances could be deceiving. *I should know*, I thought bitterly as I sipped my coffee.

"So tell me, Ridder, how will this story play out?" I said.

"You tell me, Senator Montgomery, or should I say Senator Baker." He was both formal and sarcastic. We burrowed into each other's eyes trying our best to size up the other to make the best next move. It was life and a game of chess at the same time. My move. Ridder had declared checkmate.

It was a strange time to ruminate on the past, but here I was, the walls of my life tumbling down around me and I was

in reflection. I thought of my pretty, tall, slender, mocha colored wife, Suzanne and how she would react. I married the
princess, the daughter of the multi-million dollar attorney from
Atlanta. It was sad that I didn't really care what the ice queen
thought. *Our marriage was nothing but an appearance, window dressing and duty.* I thought about my mistress Nicola.
How I adored her. As always, a tinge of guilt overwhelmed me
as I thought how I chose power over love. *Nicola was magical
with her sassy ways; smooth textured ebony skin and sultry
eyes. Even if I had the chance to make it right, would she want
me after this?* Then I thought about my beautiful, properly
reared children. *How would this affect them, to know that their
father was a murderer and a fraud?*

As dark thoughts swirled around in my mind, I somehow
drifted back to the days when I was a simple, but mischievous
boy from Cleveland, whose only unique trait was the identical
twin brother named Jack and a father who loved me, but had
just plain given up.

$\partial\!\!\!/\partial$

Chapter 1:

Growing Up in Cleveland

Cleveland in the late 1960s was one of those northern cities that was hit hardest by the riots when Martin Luther King, Jr. was slain, perhaps because its people were angrier than most anyhow. Between the constant snows, the soot from the factories, hard blue-collar labor, gray skies greeting you on most mornings and feelings of despair floating through the air, most people were looking for a channel to express their rage. Martin Luther King, Jr.'s assassination provided the perfect outlet. In a matter of a few short days, a dreary city became even dimmer. I was only ten then, but I felt the rage deep within my spirit. It's funny how nine years had passed since that dark day. At nineteen, that boy seemed no more than a memory.

My deep-seated indignation in those days came from other things. I don't know if it was because I never knew my momma or that my daddy, though living, seemed like a ghost to me. They said his spirit flew away with my mom's when she died on the operating table giving birth to us. Yet, sometimes, it appeared that his spirit would return when he laid eyes on my brother, Jack. Maybe it was the abject poverty that surrounded us that ignited my fury, swallowing up all hopes and dreams with its unending appetite. However, I knew my torment stemmed most from that 'perfect' brother of mine. He looked like me, almost to the point where I would get this strange sensation that I was looking into a human mirror. It made my skin crawl just thinking about it. That's where it stopped.

Jack was the apple of Daddy's eye. He did everything right. I remember when we were at the state fair. We were nine then. This old, elephant-skinned, battered woman with bosoms that reminded me of two creamy pillows was selling the most delicious looking fruit I'd ever seen. Papa had left us to get tickets for the rides. I turned to Jack. "How about we go over there and get us some apples?" I said with a wicked smile. He looked at me miserably, "We can't, Papa didn't give us no money." "Who needs money when they have hands and feet," I said. Any other boy our age would have jumped at the chance to prove his manhood and have some fun while doing so, but not 'Mr. Do Gooder' Jack. He furrowed his forehead like he always did when he was disturbed by something and stared at me like I was the devil himself. "Joe, how could you suggest such a thing? You know Papa would have our back sides if he caught us doing something like that." I said with complete exasperation, "Jack, how can we get caught? Who will catch us, that bent-over woman?" He again regarded me as if I was a complete stranger, "No, Joe. It just ain't right." Jack walked away to find Papa, leaving me standing there.

Then I burst out into laughter at the complete soberness of his expression. You'd have of thought I was asking Jack to kill our math teacher or something, not that at times I didn't want to kill that old bat. She'd purposely call on me in class for yesterday's assignments, knowing damn well I hadn't done it. I'd make a joke about it and the class would burst into laughter. Mrs. Rhiner would turn up her nose in distaste and mumble under her breath, "Why can't he be more like Jack." She was always trying to shame me into my brother, the bitch.

Jack and his serious forthright expressions, those facial contortions of his were the best way to tell us apart - maybe the only way. My aunts still mixed us up. Hence, they were always careful to get us everything the same and let us speak first about events in our lives. My Aunt Jean asked Papa one day, "John, how is it that you can so easily tell Jack and Joe apart?"

Papa smiled sheepishly and answered, "One has the sweet spirit of the only woman I ever truly loved." That would have been Jack. He continued, "The other is just like me back then, a rebel without a cause or a care." No more needed to be said. I still, until this day, don't know why those words Papa uttered hurt me.

At twelve, I finally convinced Jack to play a trick on Papa. Boy, was that some work. We switched identities. I was 'Mr. Do Gooder' Jack. He became me. I could tell he was struggling with his role as Joe. It's hard to be smooth when you're so square. And I was smooth… Sometimes you're just born with the gift. "Man, you gotta do better than that Jack. You're so wound up," I said.

Papa came home from work. He looked tired and distracted, as he normally did. I still don't know how he could work at that steel mill for twenty years, doing the same dirty menial job day-in and day-out. He never complained though. No one would know how much being a low-wage maintenance 'gofer' ate him up inside. His eyes died a little more each time he came home from that job. I remember when my Aunt Eulie took us to Papa's work site because she didn't have time to drop us home without missing her hair appointment. Papa was almost off by then anyway. Those white boys treated Papa like he was just above spit, ordering him to do this and then that. Papa never questioned anything either. He just did what he was told. How can you respect a man like that?

"How was your day at school, boys?" Papa asked. He always asked the same damned question when he dragged himself in the door. In fact, that was the first thing to come out of his mouth, even before hello. "You first, Jack," Papa said. Jack always got to go first. Here would be my grandest performance ever. I hopped from the sofa where we were watching the cartoon "Speed Racer" and munching on potato chips, eager to please. I then said with enthusiasm and complete admiration for Papa that I did not feel, "School was great. I tried out for track today and made the team." Jack had told me that earlier. "I also aced my math test Papa. I got a ninety-eight." Papa stared at me for what seemed about a minute, shifting his feet like he did when he was uncomfortable. It was as though he was attempting to look through me. Then he said slowly, "That's good, Jack. I knew you were a fast kid. Just don't let those grades drop because of some sport. Do I make myself clear?" I replied yes, dropping my eyes because I could no longer look at him. "I want you both to be somebody, and you will if you apply yourselves," Papa said with understated passion in his voice. "That was your momma's dream for both of you. I want you to command the respect I never had."

Papa turned to Jack. "How about you Joe, anything new at school?" I could hear the hope, yet frustration when he asked Joe the question. Jack sat there on the couch, trying to compose himself. He was attempting to look tough, cool or something. He came over to Papa walking like a 'white' boy. Lord knows I would never act like that. Even before Jack rose to meet Papa that furrowed brow began to form. Jack shrugged nonchalantly, "School was okay, Pops, same as yesterday. I didn't ace the math test, but I did pass." Jack proceeded to walk pass Papa, but felt a strong, powerful lion's grip on his left arm. Jack swung half-circle, slightly off-balance. Papa and Jack were regarding each other face-to-face. Papa said in a controlled, low and strangely penetrating voice, "Jack, now really tell me how your day was." I could see Jack physically tremble. Perspiration poured down his face. He squirmed to get out of Papa's grip.

Papa released Jack's arm, but continued to survey his son disappointedly. That was the first time I ever saw him look at Jack that way. Those gazes were usually reserved for me. Jack could not meet Papa's stare. He continued to survey his tattered shoes. Finally he said, "School was fine Papa. It was true what Joe told you. I did make the track team." He then began to yell, "It was Joe's idea to trick you Daddy!" Jack lowered his voice and his shoulders slumped. Tears began to stream down his face. "I'm sorry, Papa."

Papa turned to me with knowing, livid eyes. "Joe, if you want to act like a punk, leave Jack out of it. You are both grounded for a month, no friends, no phone, no TV," he said flatly. Unfamiliar fear shot through my entire body. I stood frozen, incapable of moving. When I found my legs, I shot out of the room, and out to the backyard like a man running for his life. At the time, I didn't know I would get a lot of experiences like that. *I was always running, just different faces behind me.*

I don't think I remember ever seeing so much fury in Papa's eyes. *This time I really screwed up,* I thought remorsefully. I don't even know why he was so vexed. It was just a practical joke, one of my many. Probably his outrage stemmed more from me involving his 'precious' Jack. *I hated him and Jack sometimes!*

Once out back, I ran to the huge worn oak tree posing in the center of the tiny yard. It was the place I went to think. I stood by the tree and cried. It was more like whimpers. My breath got shallow and my chest heaved in and out. My shoulders were rolled up tight and my fists were rolled up to match. Then after what seemed like an hour but was only a few minutes, I stopped. I felt even worse for crying because 'real' men don't. *Maybe I was becoming a loser like my brother Jack.* After that day, I promised myself I would never cry again. I kept that promise, at least until that dreaded day. Sometimes life takes you in circles.

Again, I thought, *it's all Jack's fault. If he hadn't behaved so poorly, Papa never would have found out. It could have been the prank of a lifetime.* Instead, there I was, leaning my face into that old tree with one arm draped above my head, feeling less of a man. I felt a hand rest on my shoulder, and I knew it was Jack.

"I'm sorry, Joe."

"Leave me alone, you chicken shit."

"I don't know what to say. I tried to pull it off. Daddy knows us too well."

Not turning to face him, but somehow knowing his eyes were pleading for forgiveness, I said, "Leave me the hell alone." I then turned to look at him just in time to see Jack shudder. I wanted him to see the extent of my rage. I knew why Jack flinched. He never used curse words and he didn't like it when I did. Knowing that I made him uncomfortable gave me a twisted sense of pleasure. Jack faced me with deep grieving in his eyes. I didn't want to care how he felt, but, somehow, I always did. *It was like he was a part of me that I couldn't shake. He was the conscience that I lacked.* "Just leave me alone, Jack," I said without much conviction. Jack didn't though. He leaned against the tree with me, and we were enveloped in a peculiar silence that reminded us of our nexus. We were connected, and we both knew it.

After we shared the moment of regret, Jack took off on the used bike Papa had bought him as a Christmas present last year. He rode it often, but especially when he needed to get away. Jack practically begged Papa for a bike. *He was always different than the rest of us,* I thought in reflection. *No one much cared for bikes in this neighborhood. It was considered 'not cool.'*

Our punishment lasted for a month, though not for me. I'd sneak out of the house to hang with the 'boys' in the neighborhood to all hours of the night. Even though we were twelve, we'd smoke cigarettes, drink the liquor gotten from big brothers and play craps like we'd see the older kids do. We were trying to be men. I remember wanting to be grown so bad that one day I actually made the prayer to God. I told Him that if He would just let me be eighteen a little faster, I would behave in church and not sneak out during service and play hooky in the parking lot.

At school, I wasn't much better. I hung out with the 'tough' crowd. Even the teachers themselves feared my friends, Ronny, Rico and Leo. Somehow hanging around them made me feel more powerful. I usually didn't participate in their bully tactics with the other kids. *I was above that. Yet their foul mouths, constant pursuit of girls and pleasure appealed to me.* For the most part, I was bored with school. It was such a waste of time. I skipped half my classes and still would get a C or a B on exams. I sucked up the information like a sponge. My friends would wonder how I did it. They would be 'hangin' out with me and they'd fail. I never let anyone know that I secretly loved knowledge. *The more I knew about any subject, the more invigorated I'd feel.* That was probably the only thing I shared with Jack.

Jack and I didn't spend much time together at school. He was always attending class. The teachers just loved him, always the pet. He never missed an assignment, and, without fail, had the right answers. He got straight A's too. Jack took brown nosing to another level. *What a jerk.*

Jack was equally popular with the kids. He was as good of an athlete as he was with academics. He was on the track team, football and basketball teams. Jack was a star in each. I'd sometimes go to the games and watch him with pride, sprinkled with a lot of resentment. To top everything off, he was nice. Jack never said a bad word about anybody. He motivated his teammates and took up for lesser kids. Unbeknownst to Jack, he had a few enemies. Most of them were just jealous. I secretly protected him. If I ever heard anything bad about Jack, I would have my 'boys' beat up the kid after school. That usually did the trick. *Why I did that I never knew.*

Papa basically raised us himself. My three aunts, Jean, Eulie and Sadie, helped me out as much as possible. They would bring us Sunday dinners. They'd take turns taking us school clothes shopping and would make sure we had some fun at amusement parks, movies and ice cream shops in summer. I felt extremely close to them. However, Papa did the bulk of rearing us.

People used to whisper at church, inquiring why Papa never remarried. One time, he told my nosiest aunt, Aunt Sadie, that it was none of her business. In his mind, no woman could compare to the woman he had in Charlane. I swelled with pride when I heard him say that about my momma, even though I never knew her.

However, there was one woman Papa did react to. He even dated her for a short time. Her name was Lidia Ruly. Jack and I were thirteen, at the height of my thirst for independence. Ms. Ruly was always at church in one of those great big church hats that looked like it had a garden of flowers attached to it. Her skirts swayed in the wind. Her hips moved like a music box wound up and just released. Her lips were always red, like candy apples. When she smiled, the contrast of white teeth made you think of the leading ladies in Hollywood. Boy, was she pretty. She had the biggest tits I'd ever seen. I sometimes had to will my hands not to reach out and touch them. There were a lot of men who fantasized about Ms. Ruly, but she had her sights on my daddy. I think she was attracted to the way he looked in his Sunday suit, but maybe she liked him because he was one of the few men who paid her little to no attention.

Ms. Ruly would smile coyly when she would see Papa at church. "How are you today, Deacon John," she'd say, batting her eyes ever so slightly. Unconsciously, Papa would poke out his chest and respond, "Just fine, Lidia. Thank you for asking." This went on for quite a while. And then, one day, he asked her out to dinner, just like that.

Ms. Lidia, as we started calling her, was none too crazy about children. She made that clear to us whenever Papa was not around. She tolerated Jack, but my pranks and sassy talk, as she referred to it, rubbed her the wrong way. Ms. Lidia lasted with my Papa for about nine months. I was worried, as was Jack that they would end up married. Jack had his own reasons for not liking Ms. Lidia. Mostly, I believe it was because he wasn't sure of her motives, not that Papa had any money or anything. Jack used to say that Papa's biggest treasure was his heart. It was worth more than gold. Papa had grown more spiritual as he got older. He was a long way from that mischief, hardheaded boy of his youth. Jack wasn't sure Ms. Lidia wouldn't crush that heart the minute something better came along.

One day, Papa called us into the kitchen to talk to us over dinner. This meant it was serious. He began with trepidation, clearing his throat, "Now, I know you boys have gotten used to Ms. Lidia and I spending time together. She has become a part of the family, so to speak. However, I am sad to say that she and I will no longer be together." That is all Papa said, no other explanations given. He waited for our reaction. We said nothing. Both Jack and I tried not to show our elation. *Thank you God!*

Later, Jack and I heard rumors that Ms. Lidia's ex-boyfriend moved back to town. It was said that Daddy caught them in the 'act.' Though if Papa did, he never said anything about it to us.

That was Papa's way. Ms. Lidia did get married to another man shortly thereafter. I remember seeing them together at a church picnic after they got married. The man looked like a younger version of Papa. He was more prosperous though. I'd see Daddy time-to-time stealing looks at them.

At age thirteen, Jack and I took off on completely different paths. With Jack's academic excellence and athletic prowess, he got a full scholarship to Smith Academy. It was the best private school in Cleveland, if not North Ohio. It was where all the rich white boys attended school. *These were probably the kids of the parents who talked down to Papa at work.*

At thirteen, I was "running" for one of the most powerful bookies in the neighborhood. At fourteen, I started selling small time drugs like marijuana in the Martin Luther King Middle School I attended. When I was fifteen, I moved on to heavier drug trafficking, including crack and cocaine. I also began at that age screwing every woman I could seduce with my syrupy lines and soft brown eyes. If I never said it, Jack and I were handsome men. We stood 5' 11' even at age fifteen. We were lean and muscular. Our nutmeg colored features were strong and chiseled like African royalty. We got our looks from our dad, though his were somewhat withered now. The softness of our eyes I'm told came from Momma. Those eyes were able to do wonders for me with the ladies. *Because of those soft, expressive eyes, I got more 'sweet spots' than should have been allowed for a boy just out of puberty.*

By eighteen, I had a reputation as 'The Man' that could get you anything you desired to get you high and the player who could make you forget why. I was very proud of my reputation. By eighteen, I no longer cared when Daddy looked at me with deep sadness in his eyes. I told myself, "He has Jack. That's all he cares about anyway."

Chapter 2:

Jack

My first day at Smith Academy was the scariest day of my life. Papa's chest swelled with pride as he dropped me off, but my heart was in my stomach. Daddy spent his entire paycheck on the uniforms for school. He also insisted that I wear the proper shoes. "No son of mine is going to be the brunt of anyone's jokes," he said. Little did he know I didn't fit in anyway, even with the proper attire. I was as different from them as I would have been if I had just come off a slave ship from Africa.

The first semester was onerous. I had no friends. One Jewish boy in class talked with me on occasion. It was probably because he was an outsider too. It was strange. Above all, I felt out of place because Joe wasn't there. When we attended the same school, I hardly saw Joe, but I always felt his presence. Just knowing he was somewhere in the vicinity made me feel 'safe.' Joe didn't know that I knew he was my guardian angel. *Any form of angel in reference to Joe was ironic,* I thought. I heard through the grapevine more than once that Joe and his friends beat up a kid because they talked bad about me. Sometimes my brother was a mystery to me. He was always so 'tough' on the outside, but I knew there was a caring soul deep down within him. *Why he chose the path he had, I never knew.*

Yet at Smith Academy, I knew there would be no one trying to physically harm me. Battles at this proper school were fought with words, alienation and snobbery. You were put in your place by not being invited to eat lunch with the group or by being the last to be chosen for a game of rugby in gym class. Sometimes you'd hear through absent chatter that there was a party over the weekend and you were not invited. The worst was when a boy would purposely ask you what your father did or where you lived, knowing you wouldn't make the cut. The reactions were always the same - awkward silence, so the gravity of your response could sink in to you and his friends. A knowing smile would cross the classmate's face and he'd look sideways to his friends. The other boys would snicker, say something patronizing, and walk away. *This was the worst of all.*

I endured all of this and more with a resolve I never knew I had. *It was worth it just to see the pride in my daddy's eyes when I would get off the bus from school.* Sometimes he would eagerly greet me at the door, savoring every word I'd say about what I learned in school that day. I'd find myself improvising, just to make him even happier. I sometimes thought he listened more attentively to me than the preacher on Sunday. For that I felt pangs of guilt. *If he only knew how many things I didn't tell him about the all-powerful Smith Academy.* I omitted the isolation, the loneliness, and the tension that my mere presence stirred up in my classmates. I kept all of that in for the sake of Papa.

Things got better as time went on. I didn't speak much outside of class, for fear of the negative attention that was sure to come. My academic performance spoke for me instead. I always participated in class. I couldn't help myself. One thing Joe and I had in common was the love of knowledge. Joe didn't like to admit it. I openly embraced my passion.

Smith Academy, with all its negatives, was the only place I wanted to be. Its teachers were finer than those at Martin Luther King Middle School. The books were full of rich stories, complicated equations and symbolic meanings. I could not get enough of them. I even asked many of my teachers for supplemental books, so I could learn more. I was like a sponge. Smith Academy was the never-ending pool of wisdom. And because it was an all-boys school, the academic focus was even keener. Many of my classmates grumbled about it being a same sex environment. I loved it. Girls were a mystery to me anyway. I felt awkward and uncomfortable around them, like my tongue was in my shoes. I never knew what to say. Plus, the pretty ones made me feel peculiar and out of control down below. I didn't know what to make of it. Joe on the other hand, had a way with women. *How he did it I'll never know.* They would flock to him like a magnet to metal. Joe mystified me in so many ways. *How did he learn about women? We both grew up without a momma...*

As time went on, I built a reputation at Smith Academy as one of the smartest kids there. Unlike Martin Luther King Middle School, it was a 'good' thing. Peers at the Academy looked up to you, not down at you for having brains. The teachers who at first ignored my raised hand in class, now called on me even when I didn't volunteer, and I always had the correct answer. I knew my stuff. By half way through the school year, I had an interesting popularity. It was one built on respect, not liking. No one rushed to include me in his or her social activities, but they did ask me to help them with their demanding assignments. That gradually allowed them to get to know me as a person. From there, I slowly started to get to know people on a social basis.

By the time two years went by, I was even known by upperclassmen. One of the few other men of color was a guy by the name of Dirk Patterson. Though we were the same race, we were almost as far apart from one another as I was from the white kids at Smith. Dirk was fair, very good-looking and in the tenth grade. His mannerisms and speech sounded like no other black kid I knew. If you made yourself not think about his mocha-colored skin, you could easily mistake him for white. However, Dirk had a smoothness about him that did set him apart. He was confident and cocky, like my other classmates, but he also had a depth of spirit and compassion that made you realize he had his own untold stories. I met him at my first upperclassmen party. I knew I had arrived when I got the invitation. While I was no longer the new kid on the block, I still was only in the ninth grade. There was no greater badge of acceptance.

The party was at Rick Stanton's house. Rick was one of the most popular students at Smith Academy. He was in the 11th grade and was the starting quarterback for the school. He was good academically, with looks to match. The girls from the sister school, Miriam, would come to our games just to get a glimpse of him. It was sickening how they drooled over him, but Rick's dark Italian looks were hard not to notice. The strange thing about Rick was that he was one of the nicest guys you could ever hope to meet. Whenever I crossed his path, he would always smile and say hello. This was even before my reputation preceded me. It was like he went out of his way to be nice, as if to say, "Hang in there; I know it's not easy." Somehow you knew Rick's confidence came from within and was not built on his accomplishments or talents.

Rick personally invited me to his party. One day, clear out of the blue, I passed him in the hall, and he stopped me. "Jack," Rick said in his deep tenor voice, "I'm having an end-of-year bash at my parents' house. I'd be honored if you could come." I was totally caught off guard. We were on conversational terms by now, but I was not even close to being in his league. I finally managed a response. "I'd love to come," I stated in a slightly intimidated voice. Rick seemed genuinely pleased. He smiled a broad, perfectly white-toothed smile, his blue eyes twinkling as he ran his hand through his dark sable hair. I smiled back in return.

I couldn't wait to tell my fellow classmates. When I did, they were duly impressed. From then on, I became one of the most popular boys in my class. I liked the status, but I kept my head. I never forgot the way it was in the beginning. And I still would never be able to do simple things that they took for granted, like inviting the guys over after school, vacationing for the summer in Hampton, or working for 'Daddy' at his company or law firm for the summer. These were things that they never brought up to put me down anymore, but it didn't matter. They were the ghosts I kept quietly hidden in the closet. I successfully pretended I didn't notice the differences.

Papa had Aunt Sadie take me to Rick's party. She had the nicest car and would fit in better than anyone in the family. Aunt Sadie made a point of keeping up on the latest fashions and projecting an image her bank account didn't quite agree with. I think it was her way of living the dream. Anyhow, Papa really didn't want to take me. He'd never admit it, but he was intimated by the prospect of driving through Shaker Heights. Papa said with a funny look on his face that I could not read, "A colored man in a raggedy car driving through a rich neighborhood like that was sure to get stopped." *Daddy was probably right.*

I bought some new clothes just for the occasion. I watched how my classmates dressed when I went with them to social events out of uniform. I caught the bus after school one day and went shopping downtown at one of the fancy stores. I didn't like the way I was treated there, but I had a goal in mind. Stanfords' sales assistants practically ignored me, that is, with the exception of one salesman. He somehow always ended up where I was, watching me. He was watching me as if his life depended on it. There was, however, one salesperson smiled at me when I entered. I went to him, explained the occasion, and he helped me pick out an outfit.

Saturday's party came up fast. I'd been thinking about it all week. It was a warm, breezy spring day in May, when the flowers were in full bloom. I donned my clothes. I looked up after putting on the last shoe to find Joe at the door watching me with a smirk on his face. It was obvious he didn't approve of my attire. I admit it was a little on the preppy side, but I dared not take a chance of not fitting in. Joe came to me, then slowly circled around me when I stood up, inspecting me with eyes that grew colder every passing second. "Jack, you look like a punk-ass, preppy, stick-up-his-ass white boy," Joe said with a mirthless laugh. My forehead furrowed. "Leave me alone, Joe. You're just mad no one ever invites you to parties," I shot back.

"Jack, what happened to you, man? You've changed so much in the last two years. I hardly know you, man. You dress like a white boy. You sound like a white boy. You even act like one. I told Papa not to send you to that stuck up school." I stood there, the rejection I felt from Joe building into a crescendo of anger and resentment. *Joe was 'cooler' than me, even as a youngster.* I was always overshadowed by his presence. I never fit in at Martin Luther King Middle School. I never fit in with Joe's friends and had few of my own.

For once, a group was willing to take me into their fold, and here he was trying to spoil it for me. I turned on Joe with a vengeance. "You are just upset, Joe, because people treat me with the respect that you will never have from the doped out, drop-outs you call friends." I was sorry the minute the words came out of my mouth. Joe regarded me for at least a minute in utter disbelief and thinly veiled anguish, and then he slowly left the room. I looked into the mirror, seeing the polo shirt, khaki pants and loafers, not recognizing the handsome young man looking back at me. I picked up the slip of paper with Rick's address and left the bedroom. As I descended the steps, I could hear Aunt Sadie pull up. Her high heels clicked on the pavement as she came to the door.

"My, my, my," she said as I came toward her. "You look like a younger version of the man I knew one day would rescue me." Aunt Sadie laughed her beautiful, melodic laugh that came directly from her soul. She was dressed in an exquisite floral dress that probably cost her half her secretary's paycheck. Aunt Sadie did what was necessary to maintain her image. "Now if I could just find an older version of you," she said. Papa grinned from ear to ear, sitting over on the couch smoking a cigarette and drinking an off-name beer. "Sadie, when are you going to give up that silly dream of yours? You going to wake up one day and be an old maid. You better grab one of these neighborhood boys that are still drooling over those pretty legs of yours. They won't last forever," Papa's head rolled back with laughter. Aunt Sadie just shook her head, smirked at Papa and forcefully turned her back on him.

"Are you ready honey?"

"Yes, I am."

"Good. Give your daddy a hug goodbye, and let's be gone." Aunt Sadie sashayed out the door.

I agreed. I was embarrassed giving my dad a hug at my age. I was almost fifteen. But Aunt Sadie loved displays of family affection and would have been mad at me if I did not comply. Plus, Papa looked eager to hug me. He had that same look of pride on his face that he had when he dropped me off on my first day at Smith Academy. "Have fun, Son. You look like the man I always wanted to be," he said in a stoic voice. Untangling myself from his embrace, I turned around to see Joe resting on top of one of the worn out living room armchairs. His eyes were like black ice as he scrutinized me. I said nothing to him, but opened the front door to leave. "Have fun, Jack," Joe said softly. I turned to see a look of sincerity on his face. "Thanks." It was as if he had given me the keys to a brand new, fire-red Ferrari. I could never explain it, but Joe's approval was more important to me than anyone's, even Papa's. *I knew it was going to be a good night.*

Aunt Sadie drove through a neighborhood that seemed like it was from another planet. The houses and lawns were more magnificent than any magazine had ever depicted. There were people walking their dogs and jogging at dusk. *That would never happen in East Cleveland. Everyone looked so polished, thin and glossy.* And these were only the people who were casually dressed on the streets. Yet they did not prepare me for those at the party.

We pulled up to Rick's 'house' as he described it. It was nothing short of a mansion. It was red brick with four huge white columns in front, massive windows and an enormous flow of steps that led up to the front door. Two concrete, regal lions stood guard at each end of the stairway. The driveway was circular with a sprawling lawn before it. The landscape consisted of unimaginable flowers bursting with vibrant colors and scrubs done up in fancy shapes. Aunt Sadie and I sat in the car, immobilized. We were unprepared for this. We suddenly felt shabby.

"Let's go," Aunt Sadie said, after what seemed to be an eternal few minutes. She sighed and got out of the car. "I wouldn't be able to dream up a house this spectacular, Jack," she said with awe and longing. We climbed the enormous staircase in silence. I timidly rang the doorbell, fear crossing my face. *This was worse than my first day at Smith Academy,* I decided. It brought home the sharper differences between them and me.

An elegant, yet casual, middle-aged woman opened the door. Time had taken its toll, but she was still quite incredible, very slim and regal. She reminded me of an older, feminine version of Rick. "Hello, you must be Jack. I'm Rick's mom," she said. Her eyes danced with merriment, warmth and genuineness. *Now I knew where Rick got his disposition and good looks.* I didn't know if I should have been uncomfortable with her knowing who I was before I introduced myself. I assumed Rick had described me to her. *I wonder what he said.*

"Hi. I am Sadie," my aunt extended her hand to Rick's mom. "Victoria. Very nice to meet you, Sadie." I thought *Victoria is such an aristocratic sounding name.* "We'll take very good care of him. I promise," Victoria said to Sadie. The women appeared to have a good rapport. Aunt Sadie hugged me and told me to have fun. She descended the steps with a grace that was her own. *Aunt Sadie would have fit in well with this crowd*, I thought. *If only she had been born into a different family.* A momentary sadness came over me. The touch of Rick's mom's hand on my shoulder, guiding me through the front door, snapped me back to the moment.

The entryway was gigantic. A chandelier with at least a thousand crystals hung from the ceiling. There was a Chinese vase almost my height and a grandfather clock in one corner. Each was placed at just the right angle to display their magnificence. There were antiques made of gold and oil paintings and overstuffed furniture everywhere you turned. It was simply luscious, an exquisitely arranged masterpiece. "They're all downstairs. Follow me," she said, as if not noticing my eyes widening as I viewed my surroundings. As Rick's mom led the way, I followed closely behind. I was not sure how my legs, which were at this point numb, kept up. She opened the door to downstairs. "Be careful with the steps. Have fun. Let me know if you need anything." And she was gone.

The music was loud. The place was crawling with people, the 'beautiful' people. I can honestly say everyone there was striking. The women wore skimpy, but very upscale, sophisticated clothing. They were all sleek, looking like they had just stepped out of a high-fashion salon. The men were preppy and casual like me. I was relieved to find I had guessed correctly. Just about everyone there was white. However, I was surprised to find two black women, a black guy and one Asian guy. The black women looked like sisters. They also closely resembled the white girls there, except a darker hue. They were tall, slim with long flowing hair and possessed rather narrow features to be black. They were also glossy. I could not take my eyes off of them. I did not know whether it was because they were so stunning or whether it was because I did not think of black women in this context. They had high style, cool sophistication and casual, sensual self-confidence. *Aunt Sadie was the closest woman I knew to meet these standards, and she could not begin to come close to these two.*

Rick saw me and came over. "Jack! I am so glad you could make it," he said, with a beer in his hand. I stared at the drink. *Rich people seem to have different standards* I thought. My daddy would kill me if he saw me drinking alcohol. Even Joe never brought it into the house. Here, just about everyone had a drink or a bottle in his or her hands. I inspected my surroundings further. People were shooting pool in one corner. Some were dancing in the middle of the room. Others were making out on the couch. *They were making out!* I forced myself to continue perusing the room as if I didn't notice.

"Come, Jack, let me introduce you to some folk," Rick said, apparently more than a little buzzed. He took me around and introduced me to some people, at least the ones not totally preoccupied with pool, dancing or making out. For the most part, people were friendly. There was no evidence of the snobbery that I assumed would be there on the first introduction, but then again, I had been invited to Rick's party. I situated myself in a corner when Rick went away to tend to someone else just coming in. I felt self-conscious and out of place, but very, very intrigued. I noticed the black guy sitting with his legs crossed, a drink in his left hand. He would periodically give attention to the white girls that enveloped him at all sides and then he'd examine me further. He nodded at me when I met his gaze.

After a period of time, the well dressed, clearly upper class 'Negro' strolled toward me. I immediately stood a little taller. I don't know why. Maybe I didn't want to display my intimidation. He obviously fit in here, not just with the clothes, like me, but with the entire package - mannerisms, attitude, everything. "Dirk Patterson," he said, extending his hand to me. Dirk was even better looking and more intimidating up close. "Jack Baker," I responded, thinking how unsophisticated my name sounded compared to Dirk Patterson. "So you are the renowned Jack, underclass whiz kid of color," he said, smiling with a mixture of pride, wonderment, interest and disinterest. I really didn't know what to say; "Yes, that's me. Or at least I've heard that is my trademark," I said as I rubbed the back of my head to shield the fact that I was ill at ease. We stood in silence. "Nice party," I managed to remark after awhile. I said it mainly to fill the air.

"I'm going to get another drink. Do you want something?" Dirk said as he was rising. My decision had to be quick. "Sure," I said with contrived comfortableness, "I'll have a beer." "Any particular kind?" Dirk asked with a little bit of impatience. "No, it doesn't matter." *Papa would kill me*, I thought, as I stood there in anticipation. Dirk came back with two beers, unfastening his cold German beverage with unbridled anticipation.

We began talking about school. We talked about the limited number of blacks attending Smith Academy, people we both knew, sports and other topics. Dirk and I were the same and as different as a cow and a lizard, but we were forming camaraderie that evening that would last a lifetime. Dirk was much more relaxed about life than me. I thought *that must come with privilege.* Most people at Smith Academy had that relaxed attitude. He was funny in a dry way. He had strong beliefs about some things, like equal opportunity and the right to succeed. Dirk, to say the least, was an enigma and magnetic. Obviously the women in the room thought so, black and white. They looked irritated that he was spending so much time with me.

Finally, the two stunning, honey-colored sisters came to break up the fun. "You two seem to be enjoying yourselves," said the one in the hot pink, bust-dipping dress, with a pretty pout. Dirk kissed her on the cheek and turned to me, informing me her name was Sophia. "And this," he said as he went to hug the other girl, more conservatively dressed in a navy pantsuit, "is Sasha. They are glued at the hip." I was glad to have had the drinks because I was able to compose myself, appearing more self-assured than I felt. "Hi, Sophia and Sasha," I said, as I nodded to each. "Are you two sisters?" They laughed in unison. "No," they said. "Everyone thinks that. We aren't quite sure why." I made no comment. *Some things are better left unsaid.*

Needless to say, it was the best party I'd ever been to. I danced with Sophia and then with Sasha. I even danced with a few of the white girls. Rick came to check on me once more, but by then I was conversing with a group of guys on the football team, getting the inside 'scoop.' The drinks kept flowing, and more people were making out. I could not participate in that though, even with the invitation of a pretty brunette. *It didn't seem right to be 'necking' with someone I just met.*

By midnight, Aunt Sadie came to pick me up. I was sorry I gave her such an early time. Dirk gave me his number and told me to definitely call him. I did. Sophia gave me her number as well. I never used it. *She was much too different from my real-*

ity of women. Though nice, she was too ingrained into a culture I was only beginning to learn and accept. I was stuck in two worlds, and neither made sense any more.

The most in depth learning experience for me at Smith Academy came from social interaction with the rich boys. What I learned from them no textbook could have taught me. I went through the biggest metamorphosis of my life hanging out with these guys. I didn't even realize it. However, Joe surely did.

Chapter 3:

Growing Apart

There was never any greater feeling of distance between us than when Jack went off to college. Though we shared a bond that could never be broken by circumstances or distance, this stretched the limits. By the time Jack set foot on the Ivy League campus, I had chosen a path so crooked and unyielding that I could no longer turn back. The meanness and hardness of the streets were my reality. My friends of elementary school had followed me into the life, but didn't fare so well. Leo was in jail for stealing a car, caught red-handed. Ronny was no longer with us. He got shot during a drug deal that went bad. And Rico, or what's left of him, spent most of his days in a heroine daze on the corner of 9th and Vine Street.

During our high school years, I watched Jack change into a different person. In many ways, I admired the person he had become. *I would never have let him know it.* I also resented the hell out of him. Simply put, he made me look bad. Not that I wasn't a no good son-of-a-bitch in my own right, but when compared to Jack, which everyone seemed to do, I had no redeeming qualities. I could never explain to anyone the choices I'd made. I think it was the thrill that kept me addicted to the 'life,' at least in the beginning. By the time the allure of power, manipulation and suspense lost its seduction, I had created a world so intense I was no longer the 'Master' of it.

How could I ask anyone to understand or sympathize? It was of my own doing. I had the right role model in Papa. I had but to look at his life as the example of what not to do. Papa was a young man who also chose the wrong path and regretted it. I could hear his incessant preaching, without his even uttering a word. It had become a tape played over and over in my mind. "What's wrong with you, Joe? Why are you wasting your life? Don't go down the same path I did. Make something of your life." A look by him or a disgruntled remark would start the tape rolling.

Jack tried to no avail to talk some sense into me. Unlike Papa, who had given up, Jack kept trying. "Joe, what are you doing? Can't you see you are destroying your life," he'd say with deep hurt and concern in his eyes. "Joe, not only are you destroying your life, you are taking others down with you. How can you not see that? Don't you care that people are dying and lives are being destroyed from your doing." These were the only times I could remember when Jack would raise his voice at me.

I did all I could to hide it, but it hurt me that Jack was losing respect for me. He never said as much, but I was too smart a person not to realize it. My world was like a wedge between us. As Jack grew into Smith Academy and all its trappings, the divide grew in proportion. *If only I could tell him I hate who I've become, hate the world I built with my own hands, despise those who now follow me like I am a God who can give meaning to their lives. How can I explain this to Jack, much less to Papa, without losing my manhood and ultimately my pride?* No matter how I wanted to speak the words, "I was wrong; you were right, Papa and Jack," the words would get stuck in my throat. It wasn't as if I could change things. I had made too many enemies and owed too many favors. I had gotten in bed with the devil, and I was now hers. *How do you say you were a fool?*

If I knew how to get out of the mess I created I would have done so yesterday, I meditated. I'd had friends O. D. on drugs that I sold them. I'd had sisters sell their bodies to get more of my 'white magic.' Brothers were dropping like flies from turf wars. *How could I feel good about that?* I knew right from wrong. I knew good from bad. I knew the difference of respect built on integrity and accomplishment versus that built on fear and adversity. *What have I become, I asked myself? How did I get here?*

At first, it seemed like a game to me. I was able to manipulate people. I was my own boss. I didn't bother to think about the consequences of my actions. I told myself that if people were stupid enough to try drugs, it was their problem, not mine. The fact that users were looking for a quick fix to their sense of hopelessness and despair was not my concern. I told myself I was a 'provider' not a 'pusher.' The sheer danger of it thrilled me to no end.

To find others to persuade with my logic and follow me into the life was easier than I thought. For some reason, I always had power over people. I once told my friend, Rico, "I could get a person to follow me into hell if I wanted to." I laughed then. Little did I know it was a self-fulfilling prophecy. *Life was pure hell.* The gravity of my actions hit me greatest when my own 'boy', Rico started doing the cocaine he was supposed to be selling for me. He then progressed to heroine. I watched as one of my closest friends faded away into darkness. He was one of the few from the streets I trusted. His mother never spoke to me after that. She blamed me for his demise. I blamed myself.

Rico never knew his daddy growing up, so he latched on to anyone willing to take on the role. In his mind, I best fit the bill. In the beginning, I was honored to take on the responsibility. I viewed Rico as my younger brother. It was nice having someone looking up at me. Jack and I were the same age, yet I always felt like he was light years ahead of me. However, as time went on, I feared I was hindering Rico. Rico picked up all my bad habits and then some. By age thirteen, he was drinking heavily, swearing like a sailor and smoking marijuana all day - every day. The kid I knew since fifth grade was barely recognizable. I was responsible for his demise, and the sense of loss and guilt was, at times, unbearable.

I reflected back on how we became friends with a sense of sadness and longing. It was a blistering winter day in fifth grade. I was acting out something awful in my classes, making loud rude comments and gestures to my teachers, playing practical jokes and cursing non-stop. To put it simply, I was bored and became my own entertainment. Rico was my biggest fan in English class. When I played a practical joke on Mr. Wiggins by putting glue on his chair one day, all the kids laughed. Rico laughed the loudest and the longest. Subsequently, we both got sent to the principal's office. I had never seen Mr. Wiggins so furious. He threatened to see that we were expelled from school. We did get suspended.

That day I got to know Rico as a person and not just a fan. We sat in the principal's office for what seemed like an hour. Waiting… We were both terrified. Principal Green had a reputation of taking no 'shit' off his students, and I knew if I got thrown out of school even for a day, Papa was going to be furious. I was curious to know why Rico appeared even more panic-stricken than me. He was shrinking in his chair as time slowly passed by and shaking uncontrollably. I asked, "What are you so terrified of?" "My momma is going to kill me," he said with a stutter.

"All Momma talks about is how important education is to getting out of the projects. She is going to pulverize me when she hears about this. Momma whips me every time I bring home a failing grade, which is often. Papa used to always say, before he finally split for good, I was a dumb son-of-a-bitch like my Momma. I guess I am proving him right." Rico slumped over as if to hold back the tears he was too embarrassed to shed. The bond between us at that point was instantaneous. I knew how it was to feel the rejection of a father. Though I still had my father, he never approved of me. I also sympathized with only having one parent, feeling like you were missing out on something. It was as if you were always attempting to fill an empty hole inside, like a piece of you were missing.

We spent the remainder of the time waiting on our sentence, plotting how we were going to hide the suspension from our parents. Rico's momma worked two jobs, so his situation was going to be easier than mine. He was also the only child. He would just need to get home in time to erase the phone message from the school and make sure he went through the mail every day for the written notice. I, on the other hand, would have to do the same, but with a little more maneuvering. Jack usually took the messages and got the mail. I was never home much to worry about those kinds of mundane matters, even as a youngster. Jack was mildly curious as to why I was all of a sudden so interested in taking messages and picking up the mail, but he was glad to pass off the duties so he could hit his books faster. As a result, Jack didn't really probe into it. *Can you imagine that?* So, Rico and I were successful.

We had the best time playing hooky those three days of suspension. We hung out on the streets, went to the movies and had ice cream and soda afterward. From then on, we became the best of friends. Rico looked up to me, even though we were the same age. We did everything together. In some ways, I felt closer to him then I did Jack, or at least I felt more comfortable. Rico and I could relate to each other in ways Jack and I couldn't. It breaks my heart every time I see him on the corner in a daze. I get tears in my eyes thinking about my friend. The sense of loss never lessens. These days, Rico doesn't know or care who I am. Deep down inside I cannot help but feel that I failed him.

Remorsefully, the money came easy and quick. Though that was the least of my drivers toward the 'life,' it didn't weaken the case. I liked nice things, expensive clothes and cars, but I was not too concerned about them. I knew I would make money in any vocation I chose. It might have taken longer with some other endeavor, but I knew I was meant to be on top and surrounded by cold hard cash. I was always destined to live large and meant for greatness.

Throughout my drug-dealer career, I kept my thirst for knowledge. Jefferson High School wanted nothing to do with me, but they couldn't find a justification to get rid of me. My reputation as a dope dealer was well known in the 'hood.' I made passable grades in spite of it. They were actually excellent grades for a person that rarely attended class. I kept a B average despite my 'extracurricular' activities. Also, unlike many of the other kids dealing at Jefferson, I never conducted business on school grounds. This was something for which the administration was eternally grateful. I did that as a way of showing respect for the institution of knowledge. In return, they tolerated me until graduation.

The women that came with my image were also heady at first. They were gorgeous, sexy and down right freaky at times. Like me, they were drawn to an image of danger. However, I must admit, I enjoyed all the 'sweetness' I got. Much of it was based on my powerful kingpin image, although my good looks probably didn't hurt. Yet, this too got old after awhile. In fact, I started to degrade the very women I initially could not get enough of. I began looking at them as parasites with no respect for their own bodies and no interest in their minds. A few I kept around because they were especially good at their trade. One girl named Tina I found quite pleasing, until I discovered she was also doing my 'homie,' Chuck. That was probably the last time during my adolescence I felt anything for a woman.

I didn't know it then, but I longed for the women Jack dated in his senior year at the Academy. There were very few he mentioned and even fewer he brought home, but the ones he did date were usually pretty and very wholesome. A couple of Jack's women were from the neighborhood. I remember this one girl named Veronica. He started dating her in his mid-year of senior year, and went out with her through the end of the first year of college. Veronica actually lived three blocks down from us. Everyone called her Roni. She had also received a scholarship to attend a private school. Though the school she attended was not as impressive as Smith Academy, Denison was a very good school in its own right. Unlike the Academy, Denison was co-ed. Also unlike the Smith Academy, they appeared to be more interested in having a diverse student body.

Jack and I used to play with Roni when we were young. I remember when we were seven. Roni went running home crying after I put a worm down her dress. I thought it was the funniest thing. Papa yelled at me and put me on punishment. Roni, along with her big fat older brother, came back that day, and he punched me in the stomach until I apologized to her. Out of fear of getting my ass totally whipped, I told Roni I was sorry. I wasn't though. I would have done it again just to see that expression on her face. I never knew her eyes could get so wide. Jack watched the entire episode and, afterward, told me I should be ashamed of myself. Even then, he was protective of Roni. "Mind your own business, Mr. Goody-Two-Shoes," I said with great indignation. "You never know how to have fun, Jack."

Roni was a very attractive girl, with brains to match. She was brown with big luscious dark brown eyes, a petite frame, and a stylish persona. Her hair was done in an ear-length bob that was all the rage of the time. Her legs were shapely and very sturdy. I couldn't help watching her walk, especially when she wore those trendy mini-skirts. I told myself, "Even if she was Jack's girl, there was no harm in looking."

I suspected Roni had a crush on both of us as we were growing up, but the tenderness Jack displayed won out in the end. I would not have known what to do with a woman like that anyhow. As life went on, the more I was incapable of respecting women. Sex was all I could give or rather take. Roni definitely deserved more. I was glad she and Jack had discovered their feelings for one another. Even though it brought a strange kind of longing when I saw them together. These feelings were uncomfortable, so I would periodically disappear when she came around. Plus, Roni would often look at me with a kind of regret, similar to Jack's gazes. It made me uneasy. Somehow, knowing they cared made matters worse. Roni was such a sweet girl.

I really thought Roni and Jack would make it in the long haul, maybe even get married. They were so compatible. Jack would talk on the phone for hours with her. They discussed everything. Roni knew things about me that she only could have learned from Jack. The two of them were inseparable. They would do their homework together, sneaking stares of love at each other. It was sickening, all the touching and what not. Yet, like many relationships, when the persons are young and great distance is between them, they don't survive. *Maybe if Roni hadn't chosen a school all the way in California...*

Papa also thought they would make it. He overwhelmingly approved of Roni. "Joe, why don't you find a nice girl like that?" he'd say with exasperation. "A good woman can often straighten your life out boy. That's what happened when I found your momma. I still wonder what she saw in me," he'd go on. "Those trashy women you pay attention to are doing nothing but using you." I wanted to say to him, "As if I don't know that Papa. It's a two-way street." I never said too much during these talks by Papa. I didn't know how he would react.

Jack and I were like boats held together by a rope, but drifting away from each other. Jack was drifting toward shore. I, on the other hand, was drifting out to sea. When Jack wasn't cuddled up with Roni, he was hanging out with a guy by the name of Dirk Patterson. Dirk came to the house to visit Jack a couple of times. I remember the first time he came over. You could tell he was in shock as he perused our living room. He sat on the couch looking at the furnishings in total dismay. Jack had run up to get out of his school uniform and change into something for the football game, so I had the opportunity to observe Dirk while he was unaware that he was being watched.

I had just come from the kitchen where I had made a peanut butter and jelly sandwich for my after school snack. Papa wasn't home yet from the factory. I was headed toward the living room to view reruns of "The Jeffersons." For some reason, I still liked that show, even though it was outdated. Dirk was sitting on the couch inspecting his environment with this ridiculous expression on his face. Our eyes locked. He quickly got up and extended his hand. "Dirk," he said tentatively. I think he got up so fast because he was embarrassed that I caught him in his snobbery. If not snobbery, at least it was an act of 'classism.' I shook his hand anyway. "Joe," I said without much enthusiasm.

"Jack told me he had a twin brother, but I was not expecting you two would look this much alike," he said, making conversation, but also showing true amazement. "People often say that," I stated nonchalantly. I was on full guard with this white/black 'boy.' *So, this is why Jack sounds so white these days,* I thought. I sat down in front of the TV and pulled out a cigarette. It was clear from the distaste on Dirk's face he did not approve of me smoking. "Those things will kill you, man," Dirk said, trying to put lightness to his words he apparently did not share. I wanted to laugh at how he said the word 'man.' "Why even bother to try and be cool," I wanted to blurt out.

As much as I tried to dislike Dirk for all his upper class breeding, I actually was fond of him. I begrudgingly had to admit he was a nice guy. Even though he was clearly uneasy in such 'low end' surroundings, Dirk went out of his way to make conversation. We talked about the rerun on television. We discussed the Cleveland pro football team that year. We even joked about a few of Jack's idiosyncrasies, particularly how he was not able to laugh at himself and how his forehead furrowed when he was troubled or concerned.

Just as I was telling Dirk the story of when we were kids and was trying to switch identities to fool Papa, Jack came down. "What are you two talking about that's so funny?" Jack asked in paranoia. "Nothing, man," I said. Jack would not have thought it was amusing. He was extremely private and serious. "You two enjoy the basketball game," I said, while getting up to head toward the bathroom, leaving before Jack asked too many questions. "Thanks. It was nice meeting you, Joe," Dirk said as he opened the front door to head toward his sports car parked outside. Dirk seemed to say it in earnest. It was also clear that he sincerely liked my brother Jack. *That alone was enough for him to make the cut.*

Dirk came over maybe once or twice more throughout the school years, but mostly Jack went over to his house. Jack told me Dirk's house was not a 'mansion' like Rick Stanton's, but it was quite impressive. There was no doubt in Jack's mind based on Dirk's parents' home alone that he came from serious money. Plus, Dirk's dad was well known about town as one of the top trial lawyers in Cleveland. According to Jack, Dirk would sometimes brag to him that Cal Patterson, his father,

"Made most white attorneys tremble in the courtroom." Papa met Dirk during one of his few visits to our house. As with Roni, he thoroughly approved of him. *It's funny, come to think of it; Papa never said anything nice about my friends.*

Jack graduated from Smith Academy with honors. In fact, he was the school's first ever-black valedictorian. He gave a very powerful speech about excellence being colorblind and the need for opportunity to be the same. I think most people were stunned and jittery with the topic of the speech, but it was so well anticipated and delivered from the heart he received a hearty standing ovation. No one could deny the truth of his words. Papa and I both swelled with pride. I hugged my brother after the ceremony for a long time. We both had tears in our eyes. It was one of the few times I was willing to show my vulnerability. Roni came up behind us and put her arms around us both. Dirk even made it back from his freshman year to see Jack graduate. He hugged Jack with affection shared by brothers.

When I graduated from Jefferson, it was without the same fanfare. I didn't care. I was just glad to graduate. Papa and Jack were there to see me walk across the stage. Roni even came along. Papa and Jack did show much of the same pride I experienced at Jack's graduation. This was the first time I ever remember Papa looking at me with undiluted respect. He hugged me and kissed me on the forehead. I was affected more than I wanted to admit. Jack and I hugged with the same intensity as at his graduation, though there might have been even more meaning with this embrace. Jack's unspoken body language said volumes. He obviously was hoping this would be a new start for me. I wish I could have not disappointed him. I wanted nothing more myself, but I was not that naïve.

Chapter 4:

Colliding Forces

Jack went on to Yale to study political science. He decided on a pre-law major, following the footsteps of Dirk's dad. I thought Jack would make a fine lawyer. He was very persuasive when he believed in something, and he was remarkably passionate about justice and standing up for the underdog. A part of me felt that Jack himself was an underdog in many ways. At Smith, he was one of the few without. Like me, he was without our mother. And his sensitive, compassionate spirit made him an anomaly among men. This was especially true in the neighborhood we lived in. I knew it couldn't have been easy for him.

I will never forget the day Jack was packing up his things to leave for school. Though we all knew it was coming, no one seemed prepared. I think Papa was the least prepared. He walked around in a stupor for days after Jack left for school. When Papa and I dropped him off at the dormitory at Yale, Papa hugged Jack so hard and for so long I thought he was going to do permanent damage to Jack's ribs. He kept saying, "My boy, my boy, my boy..." Connecticut was a long way from Ohio.

Papa said very little to me on the long trip home. The first several hours on the road, he stared off into space. *Given his state, I wondered whether it was safe for him to be at the wheel.* I inconspicuously found my seat belt and put it on. Papa got through it though. About mid-point in the trip, Papa just started talking. First he said a few words and then got quiet again. By the time we were three hours from Cleveland, he was telling stories of when we were growing up; talking about Momma; and commenting on the landscape as it whizzed by. We even stopped to get a bite to eat. That was probably one of the few and last times I remember spending a pleasant day alone with Papa. *Maybe he figured I was all he had left.*

Pleasantries lasted between Papa and me until the end of the trip, not a second longer. The minute I got back to Cleveland, I was back on the 'job.' And now that Jack was out of the picture, Papa had all of his focus on me. With Jack there, Papa chose to ignore my indiscretions. *Maybe Papa was simply ignoring me*, I thought with contempt. Now, he no longer had that luxury. To put it bluntly, shortly after Jack went away to school, Papa and I were at war.

Papa criticized the hours I kept, the friends I hung around, the women I dated, even the words I spoke. Nothing I did or said pleased him. It was more than I could take. As a boy, it was painful. As a man, it was intolerable. We yelled at each other on a constant basis. A few times it actually got physical. I remember Papa slamming me up against the wall as soon as I entered the house. I later found out he had witnessed me dealing dope to someone while coming out of the neighborhood grocery store. He knocked me up against the wall so hard, my head thumped against it, making a loud noise. It took a few seconds to get my bearing. "You are a disgrace to me!" Papa fumed through clenched teeth and a deep, enraged, baritone voice. "I didn't raise my children to destroy others," Papa said as he raised his hand to strike me. Somehow, just then I got my wits about me. I pushed Papa away so strongly that he fell into the lamp next to the sofa. The lamp crashed to the floor and split into a thousand pieces. Papa and I both stared at the glass in dismay. It symbolized the level to which our relationship had deteriorated. Jack was the glue that had kept us together. Through him we were able to form a connection to each other. Without Jack, that connection was severed.

As if Jack were aware of his need to keep the family together, he called on a regular basis from school. It wasn't the same though. Jack would talk with Papa for hours when he called. What they talked about that long, only God knows. Papa would ask Jack a lot of questions about classes, the Alpha Phi Alpha fraternity he was thinking about joining, the girls on campus. It was as if Papa were living his life over through Jack. When Papa would get off the phone from one of those marathon phone sessions, he would be in the most buoyant mood. *He never ceased to amaze me.* It didn't seem right a man having so many regrets in life, nor being that attached to his son or anybody for that matter.

I enjoyed talking to Jack as much as anyone, I thought, *but I don't go around drooling over his life.* In fact, Jack and I never talked for more than fifteen minutes at a time on the phone, I realized as if in revelation. It was strange. We had nothing really to say. The void between us was an ocean wide on the phone. There were way too many pauses and periods of silence when neither one of us was comfortable. So many times I wanted to tell Jack how proud I was of him. I wanted to tell him I loved him. I didn't know how. Even worse, I felt relief when we hung up.

Life was moving on a fast track for Jack and me, but going in opposing directions. As Jack was learning the ways of a 'Yale' man, I was becoming my own man. The house was growing too small for Papa and me. I wanted and needed my own space. I didn't want to answer to anyone, least of all Papas. Not that I did, but I didn't want to feel bad about that either. I made plans to move in with one of the women I 'grooved' with on a regular basis. Her name was Lequisha. I knew Lequisha would put up with me. She obviously was in love with me, silly woman. *It would feel good to have someone take care of me,* I determined. I'd wait for the moment to break the news to Papa.

One rare morning, Papa and I were in the kitchen together having breakfast. It seemed like the perfect time to break the news. Papa was to work second shift at the factory that day, and I was late getting up from a particularly wild night with a pair of twins and a bottle of Hennessey. "Morning, Papa," I said through bloodshot eyes and a head throbbing so hard it felt as if I had tap dancers performing on it. "Mornin', Joe," he muttered under his breath.

"You look as if you had a rough night, son."

"I did."

"When are you going to do something constructive with your life, boy, instead of just partying?"

"Don't start on me, Papa."

Then I blurted it out. "That's why I'm moving out this weekend, Dad."

"You're doing what?" Papa said, caught totally off guard.

"I'm moving in with Lequisha. I need my space, Papa," I replied in complete defiance.

"The only thing you need is some sense in your head. I don't think you moving in with her or anybody else is going to give you that. I don't bother you, son. We hardly ever see each other," he said with a look of hurt and frustration on his withered, handsome face.

"I'm surprised you even care, Papa. But I'm old enough to make this decision on my own, and it's what I want to do," I shot back. "Fine, son. Do as you please, but don't come running back here once she throws your ass out. And why would you think I wouldn't care, Joe?" Papa said in an elevated and highly agitated voice. I had never heard that tone from him before. It took me aback a little, but I recaptured my stride. "Because the only son you ever cared about is Jack." I didn't mean to let the words roll from my lips with the level of venom that was attached to it. Papa stood there, frozen. He put his head down, pulled away from the counter where he was pouring himself coffee and began to walk out. As he left the room, he grunted something about, "You do as you want, Joe. You always have." *Why couldn't you deny my statement for me,* I thought as I stood, torn between anger, hurt and resolve. *I'm out of here! It should have been sooner,* I reflected as I threw my fork across the room.

Once moved out, I stayed with Lequisha for three months before finding my own place. I learned that it's hard to see other women when you are living with someone. Besides, Lequisha felt she had some right to pressure me into a serious relationship because I was staying with her. I was having none of that. Bitches. They're always plotting and conniving to get what they want. *Not with me though,* I thought, as I looked around to collect my things from Lequisha's small, but cozy apartment.

I settled in a flat in East Cleveland that was nice, but not conspicuously so. The updated one bedroom apartment was clean and efficient. It was in one of the better sections of East Cleveland where people were not living in the projects but weren't able yet to live in an 'upscale' neighborhood. It was an area filled with hardworking, decent folk. Children played without fear of being shot. Homeowners kept their tiny yards in front of their modest homes trimmed and tidy.

The neighborhood was only eight blocks away from where I grew up, I thought. *Yet it might as well have been on the other side of town. Why was Cleveland such a checkerboard?* I vowed to keep my business away from the area. It seemed that no one around there knew who I was, I realized with incredulity. *Anonymity was nice. I almost felt like an upstanding citizen.* Even the neighbors smiled and said hello to me. While the option to move to a true upscale neighborhood was certainly in reach with all the money I'd stashed away, the neighborhood held an air of familiarity and comfort.

Though home life had turned the corner to a more serene place for me, which was anything but true on the streets. The drug trade was more dangerous than ever. This was especially true once the new 'homie' moved into the neighborhood. Once Puto moved into my territory, turf wars became an everyday occurrence. Puto either didn't know this locale belonged to me or he didn't care. Neither was a good thing, for Puto that is.

There would be no sharing or carving out territory. He would respect me or he would pay.

Puto was a dark Hispanic, with smoldering gray eyes that were hardened with time and rage. A mixture of pain and coldness spilled from his sternly set features like smoke pouring out from under a door of a burning building. Rumor had it that he came all the way from Florida and brought some of his 'homies' with him. That didn't intimidate me though. In fact, I found the challenge invigorating. *I was the top dog in this neighborhood, and he was about to find that out.*

To the Hispanics in the community though, Puto was their savior. They rallied around him in total awe. Before he came, most people dealing in dope, not connected to me, did so in back doors on a small time basis. This included the Hispanic population. With Puto hitting the horizon, they were emboldened. Word began to spread that there was another major trader in town. To make matters worse, he was said to be cheaper because he had the inside track with an extended clan in Florida. Puto was taking my clients from right under my nose.

I admit it took me a while to react to the threat. Business was booming as the economy slowed once again and people were losing their jobs and dreams. I fed off the downtrodden. Those with lost dreams and broken promises were my biggest clienteles. It seemed that the deeper the financial woes, the more they turned to me to forget them. I never concerned myself that the outcome of their solution would be greater financial disaster and deeper woes.

So, in the midst of a thriving trade, with more business than I could handle, I brushed off Puto as an annoyance that would eventually go away. That was a grave mistake. It seemed that, one-day, I looked up and half my business was annihilated. Some of my recruits were no longer peddling for me. My bosses were asking questions about the corrosion of my business that I could not answer. People no longer feared and respected me in the way I was accustomed to. I was becoming impotent and did not even see it coming. That, most of all brought out the hurricane in me, *me, naïve?*

I could not let it continue. I had built a lucrative empire, and I would be damned if I was going to let some 'wetback' destroy it. One day, I let one of Puto's boys know that I wanted to meet with him face-to-face. Roberto got back to me that a meeting on Tuesday at 2:00 P.M. had been arranged at the old playground on Kenard Street. I was to come alone. *To hell with that,* I thought. I will have a couple of my boys with me to back me up. As it was, I was meeting him on his 'turf' and initiated the first contact.

Tuesday was here before I knew it. It was a bitter cold day in February. Cleveland's winters were always brutal. At least no more snowstorms were predicted for the remainder of the week. The playground was a winter wonderland from earlier snows. I saw a husky man - one foot on a park bench, leaning forward while smoking a cigarette. I knew it was Puto. The battle had begun.

Puto straightened up as I approached. He turned on me with smoky-gray rock eyes and folded arms. My boys lurked in the distance. They were behind trees, well out of sight or at least I thought. "I thought you were to come alone," Puto said as he stomped out his cigarette. "I am alone," I said in an equally defensive and frigid tone. "If you are alone then why are there loaded men hanging out behind trees?" He caught me off guard. How did he know? Puto must have his own men staking out the area. Maybe they provide him with signals that only he can understand. I stood my ground anyway. "There's nothing for you too worry about - unless there's something for me to worry about," I said with all the indignation I felt. *How dare he come into my territory and start making demands, much less questioning me about my actions. Doesn't he know who I am?*

Puto stood there silent for a while, as if contemplating his options. He must have decided it was not worth fighting over. I visually watched him relax his position. He unfolded his arms, his shoulders dropped slightly and he tilted his head, studying me, sizing me up. I couldn't read the expression on his face. That disturbed me. I prided myself on dissecting the minds of others. It gave me an indescribable power over them. I met Puto's stare, refusing to be the first to look away or back down.

Puto spit on the hard icy earth. "You called this meeting, so let's get on with it." I shuffled my feet side-to-side, unaware that I had picked up one of my father's traits. I knew why I had called this meeting, but I was unsure how to begin. I decided the easiest way was to get straight to the point.

"Ever since you moved into this neighborhood, you've been taking my business. I want it to stop," I ushered this edict in my most threatening, street savvy voice. Puto examined me for what seemed like an eternity. Then, he burst out in a tumultuous mirthless laugh and began lighting another cigarette. "You do, hun?" He replied in a voice filled with sarcasm and venom. "Why on earth should I do that? You don't own these streets. I don't see your damn name written on anything, anywhere." Puto was plainly infuriated now. His free fist was balled and shoulders were tense. My own animal instincts were kicking in, alerting me of entering dangerous waters. I struggled to keep my temper from rising; especially since it was evident both of us were armed.

"It's not a matter of me owning these streets. I was here first. I have cultivated this market for the past five years. It's mine." My voice was too low and calm. I was getting concerned, because this was always a sign that I was about to explode. Of course, one would have had to know me to understand this. To Puto, I was just another enemy that needed to be squashed. He was unaware, but about to find out just how dangerous I could be.

Puto took another draw on his thin long cigarette and blew the smoke out slowly. He then turned his complete attention on me. "I have no intentions of leaving nowhere." He was undoubtedly prepared to take me out right there on the spot. After living and breathing these streets for over two years as 'top dog,' I could sense a true threat. However, I knew I needed to back off in the short run because, if nothing else, *Puto had backup.* The amount of backup almost certainly outnumbered my two men by a factor of three. I chose to reiterate my position and let the warning stand.

We both stood just over 6 feet. I stepped closer to Puto, leaving only about a foot between us, and as a result, we were eye to eye. "Puto, let's just say you have been warned," I said between clenched teeth. "Your warning doesn't mean shit to me, you two-bit punk-ass 'coon." Puto spit the words out with unbridled pleasure. He obviously wanted a fight. I felt my hands instinctively go for my 'piece.' Puto reached for his. The air between us heated up a thousand degrees. "Spic, you don't know whom the hell you are dealing with, but you best believe you are about to find out," I said with all the hatred churning within my very gut. I turned and strode away in a carefree posture to let him know who the boss of this terrain was.

That was the last time Puto and I met face to face, but both our presence after the conversation amplified. There wasn't room for two of us. It was a divided neighborhood. Not only were people still dying from overdosing on our 'wares,' but also now we were wasting away from fighting amongst ourselves over the prey. If you were in the 'business' you had two choices, Puto or me. Chances were, either one was a deadly one. I slowed down his penetration of the neighborhood, but it came with a price of blood. Men were dropping like rats enticed with cheese and poison on both sides of the fence. It distressed me, but in my mind I had no choice in the affair. More than anything, it was a matter of pride. *No one took me out or called me a 'coon.' No one.* I was the Kingpin around these parts.

I began using my coastal connections to lower rates. I, too, had risen to the level where I had contacts in Florida. I found that by interacting directly with smugglers, you could decrease prices as much as thirty-five percent and still maintain a healthy profit. *If only people knew how cheaply they were giving away their souls,* I reflected solemnly. I dropped the price by twenty percent and still made more money than God. Imagine that. I started nurturing my contacts by making trips to Miami at least every other month. A side benefit of these visits was the most beautiful bitches you'd ever want to lay. My new-found partners would line them up for me when I came to town. Hispanic, black, white, Asian, whatever your heart desired. Connections do have their perks. *With women like these, I could almost forget how I used to crave the earnest innocence of the women Jack dated.*

Chapter 5:

The Bloodhound

Things were finally getting back to normal, or at least I thought. Puto appeared to be put in his place. Business was booming. My reputation was as robust in Miami as it was in Cleveland. I was again to be reckoned with.

No one would have known that, under the placid surface, turbulence lay deep within the ocean depths. What appeared to be a retreat by Puto was merely a retraction in order to sharpen his sword. The real confrontation was about to begin. In hindsight, if I could have gotten pass my ego, I would have suspected that my conquest was only short-lived. When it appeared too neatly packaged, it usually was a cover for rot. I was too cocky to believe that the fight for my life literally was just around the corner.

It went down not on my own turf, but on a hot steamy day in June over 1,000 miles from my hometown. Miami was one of those cities that attracted all types, from the 'beautiful' people to 'low lifes' looking like they just crawled out of some gutter. Many times, the two groups intermingled, and it was hard to distinguish the two. Each sector fed off the other. Money was the common denominator. It was the juice that poured into the well-tuned engine. To be in Miami is to be in the middle of a drama without a beginning or end. *The combination of Miami's sin, thrill and risks was like nothing else.*

As I got off the plane, the exhilaration of Miami and the sense of peril poured through my veins once more. This trip was one of my biggest deals ever. I planned to get two kilos of cocaine from the Colombian trafficker at a price way below market value. What made the deal even sweeter was that it was being taken right from the stash slated to go to Puto and his crew. I smiled knowingly every time I thought about it. Payback was delicious.

I was able to get the 'poison' cheap because Puto had infuriated one of the smugglers by shorting him on funds for a supply of marijuana not delivered on time, or so I thought. At least, that was the story I was told. I was too anxious to swallow the big fish to carefully examine the festering waters below. I thought about what a fool I had been only after the fact. Nothing in my life had been given to me so easily. *Why would this have been any different?* It's amazing how your senses dull when you want something so badly. I will never forgive myself for taking off my armor before the battle was completely won. My instincts were kicking in now in high gear, and every muscle vibrated with a sense of treachery.

This time when I landed in Miami I found a nearby place to eat and retired early. Tomorrow would be a long day. I'd spend the day connecting with my Florida crew to get the money in place for the big deal that evening. Normally on my trips to Miami, I wouldn't get down to business until the second or third day into my visit. I would get off the plane, check into my favorite Marriott hotel and shower and change for dinner in South Beach. South Beach was the epitome of the finer things in life. It represented good food, delectable women, spirited nightlife and overall intoxicating seduction of everything illegal or immoral. Silvers was my favorite restaurant. It wasn't the most expensive restaurant on Ocean Drive, but to me, it offered scrumptious delicacies, a quiet and relaxed atmosphere and warm, friendly, dedicated service. Best of all, Silvers was where I met Irma.

Irma was the best lay I'd ever experienced. Her curvaceous, café latte figure and long legs perfectly wrapped around my body like a piece of a puzzle needed to complete me. Irma was the stereotype of Cuban heat. When I first met her, she was sitting at Silvers bar, downing a Whiskey Sour. She stared straight ahead as in a trance. One of her hands was running through her long, kinky, chocolate treads with aimless repetition. Her beautiful legs were crossed and totally revealed in her short, black linen skirt. I sat across the room soaking in her beauty when she suddenly faced me and matched my stare in defiance. Her hazel-green cat eyes were cool and confident. She must have seen me checking her out in the mirror behind the bar. I walked over.

"Hi," I said in my sexiest, most charming voice. She scrutinized me with a sultry, pouting smile, "Hello," she responded. "I'm Joe," I said extending my hand to her. I wished that I had taken more care in my dress that day. I had on a white short-sleeve shirt and khaki shorts, along with braided brown sandals. It wasn't the most sophisticated outfit I'd ever worn, but it did suit the climate. Irma's eyes surveyed me from head to toe. She must have approved. She held out her delicate hand and met me half way in a shake, "I'm Irma." Her expression had a tint of mischief in it. I sat down next to her, moving the chair as close to her as possible. "You are one gorgeous woman, Irma." I meant ever word of it. The steam of her sensuality was stirring my loins. I was mesmerized by the fullness of her burgundy lips and elegant neckline. *Irma was even better looking up close than from a distance.*

That night we must have talked for hours. Irma was an enigma to me. I found out she was an attorney and engaged to be married to a guy named Mario. She had been married once before. Looks, brains and mystery were a powerful combination and I could not help but surrender to her charms. *Why was she even talking to me if she's engaged to be married?* I later found out she had just had a major argument with her fiancé. That same night we made love. I knew I probably was nothing more than a way for her to pacify the wounds left by Mario's stinging words. As Irma explained it, Mario was as controlling as he was incredible. He was also extremely jealous. She told me this again with a twinkle in her eyes. *It was probably a strange time to bring that up,* I reflected, having just plunged deep within her.

Though Irma remained engaged, we saw each other whenever I was in town. I never felt guilty for sleeping with her. As far as I was concerned, her relationship with Mario was something she needed to deal with, not I. Irma was more than a sex partner; she became a close and dear friend. We kept the other parts of our lives away from each other. When we were together, it was just the two of us. I suspected Irma knew I was involved in illegal activities from the questions she asked. However, she never inquired deep enough to make the reality of my endeavors concrete in her analytical mind. It was as if she didn't want to know. We would talk for hours after lovemaking. I was careful not to let myself fall in love with her. I did unconsciously give up all the other women I used to see during my trips to Miami. I convinced myself that these actions meant nothing.

My mind was swimming in the thought of Irma all the way from the plane to the rental car. I forced myself to snap out of it. *There would be no enjoyment of Irma on this trip. It was strictly a business trip. Maybe I would taste her sweetness on my normally scheduled run. I was in town for one thing only.* The deal was to go down tonight around 8:00 P.M., just in time for the sunset and relief from the suffocating heat and humidity known only to Miami. It was downright unbearable. In a futile attempt, I wiped my brow to only see sweat replaced before I could lower my arm.

I surveyed the old junkyard as if for the first time. Cars once the symbol of power and position, crushed beyond recognition. Tires were piled in heaps, and trash scattered the landscape to finish off the scenic appeal. Waiting on my contacts to appear, I lit a cigarette and took a hefty draw. With every passing minute, my patience grew thinner. I was like a cougar spotting prime prey, anxious to pounce and be done with it. *The thought of heading home to claim my crown made my toes curl with delight.* My face was flush with the thought when the three strange faces approached me. I dropped my cigarette and squashed it out. Hairs on the back of my neck rose, alerting me to significant threat.

"Where are Johnny and PJ?" I asked as I waited for them to reach me. They walked in silence, nearly floating toward me with haunting purpose. There were obvious signs that something was awry. Three men approached instead of the usual two. They were not the regulars who met me. One was wearing a long trench coat in the dead heat of Miami. Not a one of them seemed to have business on his mind. I stood fully erect, aware that I did not have my normal backup in place. It's never good when you let greed and glory blind caution and competence. *What was I thinking?* The only backup I had was a pistol at my waist and one near my left ankle. Like the American Express slogan, I never left home without them.

The husky, tall one in the trench answered gruffly when he arrived one foot away from me, "They were held up." It was obvious he was lying. The words came out too quick and smoothly. His eyes were menacing, two dark unbreakable pieces of coal. He spread his chest unknowingly as if he were preparing for battle. "I'm Dyke. This is Tito and Louie." The other two nodded their heads in acknowledgement. There was no half grin, no handshakes, not even the politeness of eye contact. They stood like statues. One was bulky, bald and black. That would be Dyke. The other two were comprised of a Hispanic with slicked back oily hair and a truncated stature and a blonde gold tooth Caucasian that reeked of alcohol and looked like he hadn't bathed in a week. I didn't know which one was Tito or Louie since neither met my eyes when they were being introduced.

Suddenly I longed for Johnny and PJ. I was a friend to neither of them, but at least they were familiar. We would exchange a few words about the weather or a game before getting into the transaction at hand. It was just enough to put everyone at ease and reestablish the level of trust needed for a mutually beneficial partnership. After the goods and 'dead presidents' were exchanged, we would all shake hands and depart. It was all done very efficiently, allowing less chance of being detected by unwanted intruders.

"Where's the dope?" I said in my toughest street voice. Dyke cocked his head, with an eerie smile lingering on his lips. He finally answered in a deep, intimidating voice to his partners, not responding directly to me. "He doesn't have a clue, does he?" Dyke said with a gesture to his boys. They chuckled in an almost choreographed response. The Hispanic spit on the ground as if to add special effect. Dyke continued, this time directing his response to me, "Puto said you were a clueless, puffed up, self-indulged asshole." During the two seconds it took for everything to sink in and for me to regain my composure, the two thugs were standing so close to me that I could feel their breath on my cheeks and smell the alcohol permeating through the pores of the white creep. "Frisk him," Dyke barked out the order. There was no doubt he was in charge.

They quickly and professionally raced over my body, taking out the pistol at my waist and the Swiss army knife in my back pants pocket. I thought they had my little pistol at my left back ankle, but they just missed it. I let out my breath in relief. It was my only hope with three enemies and an unexpected position of weakness. "Puto is behind this?" I uttered weakly, in total disbelief, but somehow knowing it was true. "How did he know?" That was even a dumber question. "You fool," Dyke sneered before he punched me in the stomach. Then Dyke hit me so hard in the face I lost consciousness. As I trailed off, I heard him say, "Count the money. See what the cunt brought, and then let's waste him. He should know nobody messes with Puto."

I was lying there with blood dripping out of my mouth and nose with one eye swollen shut. I knew they thought I was still unconscious. My mind was reeling. My pride was hurt from being set up and not seeing it coming. My body ached for obvious reasons. Only survival instincts were breathing new life into me.

How do I get to my pistol without them becoming aware? I thought hard and feverishly. It was a matter of life and death. I knew counting the $500,000 in cash was keeping them occupied. People had a way of losing focus with sex and money. *I decided surprise and speed were my only advantages.* All three of Puto's 'hired help' were leaning over the bag, counting the cash. From what I could make out, the Hispanic was suggesting they keep a little for themselves and tell Puto I tried to cheat him on the deal. The others quickly denounced the thought. They were completely in fear of Puto.

Squatting over the bag of money, Dyke's big, broad back was the easiest target. He was also the leader. Taking him out would make dealing with the other two simpler. I knew I would only have one chance to get it right. If I missed, it was over. Life never feels so precious until you are close to losing it. I found myself praying to a God I was not sure even existed. I turned my back on the idea of God when I was eight. My rage at my existence was even more intense back then. *If there were a God,* I thought, *he wouldn't let me live like this. I needed God now though, in the worst kind of way.* I prayed with fervent purpose.

My body was drenched, and my stomach buckled from where I had been punched. However, in one swift movement I grabbed my pistol and shot squarely at Dyke's back. It was deafening silence. The others looked up in disbelief. Dyke did not move. I thought I had missed him and braced for the worst. It's strange the things you think about when you're near death. I thought *how I wished I had told Papa how much I loved him. I wished that I had kept my promise to visit Jack at Yale during his first year.* Just as my mind wandered further, Dyke toppled over. He trembled slightly, placed a hand over the blood oozing out of his chest and let out his last breath. I closed my eyes to thank God before regaining control of the scene.

The two remaining punks instinctively reached for their hardware. "I wouldn't do that if I were you," I said in utter defiance. My wrath at what had just transpired, the thought of my being taken for a fool by Puto, and my physical anguish all made me a worthy foe. I could tell both were contemplating what to do next. "Drop your weapons, and I'll give you each 50G to forget this ever happened." "Make it 100G and you have got yourself a deal," the scrawny, alcohol induced Caucasian muttered. "Okay," I said in a tone of pure indignation. How dare these lowlives negotiate with me? However, I wanted this nightmare to end as fast as possible. "Drop your weapons," I yelled again at them. They were obviously used to following orders. Neither of them hesitated.

"Take 100G each from the bag and bring it to me." I commanded.

"Why should we trust you?" the Hispanic spat out in a heavily accented voice.

"Because I could have shot you by now if I wanted you dead. It serves no purpose."

Both men stood for a minute to digest their options. They slowly reached into the bag, counted out the money and came forward. It was probably more money than they would own in their lifetimes, much less in one lump sum. I double-checked the amount to make sure I wasn't being cheated further. I also frisked them to see if they had stashed any more away or had additional arms.

In a menacing voice I asserted, "If either one of you breathe a word of this, I will have one of my men track you down and kill you. Is that understood?" They both gave a worried nod. "If someone asks you, as far as you know, Dyke got the money, and I was killed with my body disposed of in the sea. I will take care of Dyke myself." They stood gawking at me in utter disbelief. The Caucasian was visibly shaking. "I suggest the both of you leave town in a hurry. If anyone finds that kind of money on you, you'll have a hard time explaining it. Now get the hell out of here!" First they started walking away, and then took off running. *They were going to need to find a sack for the money fast,* I thought, *but that was their problem.* I had enough to worry about. I knew I should have wiped them out, but I didn't have the stomach to do so. It was a grave mistake.

After the two left, I turned my attention to Dyke's body. There was a puddle of blood surrounding it. His eyes were still open. A chill ran down my spine just staring at those glassy, vacant eyes. The gravity of what I had done was finally sinking in. In all my years as 'Mr. Tough Guy,' I had never murdered an individual. I roughed up a few. And if someone stepped out of line or another faction needed to be taken out, it was one of my 'boys' who did the dirty work. I never was even there to witness the event.

Dyke was a heavy man. Dead, he couldn't even assist me. It was a mixture of adrenaline, terror, fury and desperation that I found the strength to drag him the 50 yards needed to reach the automobile compression equipment in the junkyard. I attempted to haul his body onto the conveyor belt without success. I decided to leave his lifeless frame tucked inconspicuously amongst the machinery and debris. I then retraced the trail of blood with some old rags I found, using water and soap from the restroom in the tattered building on site. It wasn't a great job, but it would suffice. At least it would have to until I could get out of town. I suspected not too many people would be worried about Dyke, least of all the police. *Dyke probably had a rap sheet as long as the Declaration of Independence.*

I was drained as I left the junkyard. I would also never be the same. It was an eerie feeling to have someone's blood on your hands. I didn't like it, to say the least. It didn't matter that I was defending myself either. *Why was I in this game in the first place?* The tape of Papa began to play in my ears.

My next thoughts were how to get out of Miami and back up to Cleveland unnoticed. This time, not only did I need to go back to Cleveland, I needed to go home. I was suddenly a frightened boy running back home to Papa. I didn't care. The strength I needed now only Papa could give me. I dialed those ever-familiar digits.

Chapter 6:

Forever Lost

"Papa," I was crying into the phone. "Joe? What's wrong, son?" My cracked voice was as much of a surprise to me as it was to Papa. "Oh my God... Papa, I have made such a mess of my life." My hands were shaking so bad, I could barely hold the phone I used both hands to steady it. I attempted to contain the hopelessness I felt, but my voice would not obey. My thoughts were spilling out of my mouth with no restraint. "Papa, I killed a man today," I blurted out in anguish. There was silence on the other end. For a moment, I believed I lost him.

My father's voice was deep and tortured when he recouped and responded. "Son, I knew it would come to this. Come home," Papa said in a voice so low and calm that I strained to hear him. I stood frozen in my tracks. I had expected every reaction from Papa but this. *Where were the lectures, the self-righteous indignation, and the anger?* "Papa, I am so sorry. I don't know why I chose this life. I should have listened to you. I should have been more like Jack. If only I could do it over again." My voice was hoarse and packed with emotions I did not realize were still a part of me. I rubbed one of my eyes, feeling the warm tears streaming down my face.

"Come home," Papa repeated. "I'm going to ask Jack to come home for a while as well. He doesn't have to take that summer job in New York. I think it is time we're together again." I could hardly argue with him. I felt guilty and selfish for wanting to interrupt Jack's life, but I needed to see him. Jack had always been my Rock of Gibraltar. Even when he went away to college, I would call him during times of isolation and defeat. Jack and I never had much to say when we talked, but just hearing his voice was enough. "Okay, Papa. Call Jack. I'll try to make my way back up to Cleveland unnoticed."

The enormity of my situation weighed on my shoulders. I could not risk taking the plane back to Cleveland. I also dared not return the rental car at the airport. Yet, driving that car around was a danger in itself. I needed to evaluate my options. Irma was the only one I dared to trust in Miami. I dialed her cell phone and got her voice mail. "Irma, this is Joe. Call me as soon as you get this message. It's urgent," I said in a voice that I did not recognize. I found a nearby hole-in-the-wall bar to await her call. I looked around to see if I were being followed and parked the car in the alley behind the establishment. Entering the bar, I found a dark corner in the back and I ordered a scotch.

I knew if I was ever to get out of town alive, I needed to act fast. Anxiously, I waited for my cell phone to ring. Irma had the type of voice mail that would automatically alert her home phone to the call. I sucked down my scotch like it was water, waiting on the soothing burn to follow. It never did. I ordered a second drink. Just as it arrived my cell phone rang. Irma Rodriguez's name appeared in the phone window. "Hello," I said with a composure I did not feel. It ate me up inside to entangle her in this mess, but I had no choice. "Joey, baby," she said in her usual sultry, yet girly voice. "You didn't tell me you were here in town treading my waters." I could tell she was pouting with disappointment. *That was when Irma was her sexiest, and she wasn't even aware of it*, I thought offhand.

"Irma, you know I never miss a chance to see you, but this trip was unexpected," I said trying to conceal the trauma I was feeling. "You know how much I enjoy seeing you." The thought of her warm body had the power to distract me for a moment, but not for long. It was time to get to the issue at hand. Time was swiftly running out. "Irma, I called you for a reason." All the tension I felt when talking with Papa was stirring up once again in the pit of my stomach. "Joe, are you alright?" Irma's voice was full of concern and alarm. "No, I'm not." There was no sense in pretending when so much was on the line. There was a brief period of silence as the gravity of my response sank in. "What is it Joe?" Irma's voice took on the professional tone she must use when talking with clients. I could tell her analytical mind was bracing for the worst. I would not disappoint her.

"Irma, I'm in a terrible bind and I need your help. I was trying to think of a way to get out of town without your assistance, but I couldn't come up with one." Again, I was feeling lower than a pregnant pig's belly for involving her in this. I reminded myself that I had no choice. "What's going on Joe? Why aren't you free to leave town? Why are you trying to leave so soon after getting here?" Her voice had raised several notches, and her pitch was getting higher. I didn't have the time or patience to answer all the questions or deal with her panic. I kept my statements to a need-to-know basis. I felt Irma would be safer that way.

"Irma," I said impatiently, "Let's just say a deal went sour. They received the consequences for their actions, but I expect retaliation. The retaliation could be death." I could hear her take in air on the other end. "Oh my Lord! I knew you were into some shit you shouldn't be in, but I had no idea it was this deep. Joe, what the hell are you doing?" I had crossed the line with Irma. First, I had never heard her swear before. Second, I never heard her raise her voice. Third, I had never ever experienced her being so furious with me. *Yet I had to remain focused,* I thought, *darkness will soon set in and it will be in-*

creasingly more difficult to maneuver through the city to escape.

"Irma, I know I need to explain things to you, but there's no time. Can you pick me up?"

"Where are you?"

"I'm in a bar. Ironically its name is 'Joe's Bar.' It's on 5th and Calhoun Street. Do you know where that is?"

"I know the area. I'll find it."

"Hurry. It will only be a matter of time before they realize something is wrong. Once they do, my time in Miami alive is limited."

"I'll leave now."

"Be careful Irma. This neighborhood is filled with low lives. Lock your doors."

"Joe, that is the least of my concerns. I'll be there as soon as I can. I love you."

"I love you too."

And I meant it. All the emotions I denied for so long were not worth burying any longer. However, I was surprised she felt the same way. *Why weren't we together?* It seemed like that would have been the logical next step for two people in love. That contemplation was a luxury I could ill-afford right now. Making my way to the front of the bar, I paid the bartender and peered out the window. I saw a couple of burly men haul their bulky bodies out of a black Escalade. They were obviously scouring the neighborhood. It was clear the hunt had begun.

Fifteen minutes later, but what felt like several hours later, Irma's navy blue, black top convertible BMW came to a screeching halt in front of Joe's Bar. Before she could swing out of the car, I was out of the dive, racing toward her like she was the mother I never knew. The two 'gentlemen' in search of me turned to witness the event. Without delay, they returned to their vehicle, hopped in the truck with amazing agility and took off behind us in pursuit. My heart was racing.

At first it looked like we were going to outsmart them. Irma grew up in Miami. She was familiar with all the side streets and neighborhoods. Irma's machine was agile and fast, but the SUV behind us was a force to be reckoned with. It was like a lion, powerful and swift, and in hunt of its prey. I constantly looked behind in amazement at their ability to keep up. They were professionals. I knew it must mean they wanted me very, very dead. A chill ran down my spine. "Irma, you need to drive faster if we are ever going to lose them." The tone was harsh as I barked out the order, "Faster!" "Damn it, Joe, I'm doing the best I can!" Irma screamed out as if she had lost her mind. I thought she had snapped completely for a moment. Her face was contorted and flushed as she glanced over at me. Her eyes were glass reflections of unadulterated terror. What happened next caught both of us by surprised. It was no longer a game of cat and mouse.

Just as I was about to apologize for yelling at the person who was saving my life, a bullet came crashing into the front pane. It missed my head by two inches. Irma screamed, covering her mouth with both hands and let go of the wheel. The car swerved right. It was heading directly for a utility pole when I instinctively gripped onto the wheel and took control. "Irma, I need you to stay with me here. I want both of us to come out of this alive. The only way that will happen is if you stay in control of the car." I found composure I did not realize I had within me. I knew that if we both panicked, we were as good as dead. I wanted to live. I wanted Irma to live. *If we get out of this,* I thought, *I will ask her to be my girl.* To hell with Mario; somehow my words reached her. Irma took back hold of the wheel and drove on with new purpose and fervor.

"Irma, see if you can get us to I-95," I said with a command I did not feel. There were no more shots, because we were weaving in and out of traffic and cutting through alleyways. Yet I knew it would be a matter of time before they called for backup. Only their egos had probably stopped them up to this point. *I need to get us out of the city as soon as possible.* "Joe, you sure you want to do that. It's Miami at night and there's always a lot of traffic. It's going to be slow going and lots of people." "Irma, that's exactly what we want. They will be hard pressed to shoot at us with so many witnesses. We can slide between cars until we get to Route 1 and then get off there."

"I know dirt roads leading from Route 1 that can get us all the way to Georgia," I said. "My father once shipped us down here during the hottest summer I can remember. We were eleven when we went to visit Uncle Ray who lived about an hour South of Tampa. Uncle Ray died a few years ago in back woods of Florida known as swampland to most. Uncle Ray was a recluse and was happy to travel roads unknown to most people. I never knew these roads could someday save my life." Irma turned to face me with a strange and eerie expression, "Joe, this is no time for reflection." With that statement, we both regained focus.

Irma maneuvered through traffic, taking rights and lefts until the I-95N ramp was visible. We both released a sigh of relief when we saw it. I checked behind us to see the Escalade right on our heels. Traffic was backed up to get on the highway. We felt trapped. "Take the red light and get onto the ramp's shoulder. We have to get on!" Irma was climbing the ramp as best she could when a series of shots ravaged the car. "Duck!" We both slumped down in the car. Irma rose up to dodge a truck when the bullet hit. It went straight through her forehead and through the window. Her head fell forward with a thump onto the steering wheel. *Only high-priced professionals or fools would shoot someone in broad daylight in the middle of traffic.* I was stunned, completely frozen and unable to move.

The car was wiggling around like a fish just pulled from a pond. It nearly missed two other vehicles when I pushed Irma to the side to take over the steering wheel. "Irma, hang in there!" I irrationally shouted at her with sheer adrenaline, "I cannot lose you! I love you, baby. I love you." My stomach was in knots and my palms were chilled and clammy. Tears streamed down my face in buckets. My head was spinning so fast, I felt dizzy. Somehow my will to survive kicked in full gear. I had just lost the first woman I ever loved. It would not be in vain. Stepping on the pedal until the car hummed into high motion, I bullied my way from the ramp onto the highway. I couldn't shake them though. I traveled in and out of traffic for about two hours and exited onto Route 1 going north. For a second, I thought I'd lost them. However, five minutes later they were back on the trail like bloodhounds given a new scent to track.

I was determined. Once I got onto Route 1, I achieved my goal. Much of Route 1 was a one-lane road with passing sections. I took risky moves and passed four cars at a time. I passed as frequently as possible. *It could have been a thrill, driving on the edge like this, if it were under different circumstances.* After the fifth such driving acrobatics, I actually lost them. *Thank goodness for heavy traffic.* I did not see them when I turned off Route 1 onto Lehman Road in search of the dirt roads to freedom. I felt comfortable I had lost them. I pulled to the side and hid the car behind an abandoned barn. It was fifteen minutes before it truly felt like the coast was clear. Five miles down on Lehman Road I turned onto an unnamed dirt road. I was on my way home to Cleveland.

Once the immediate peril had subsided, I calculated all that needed to be done. For the last two hours I had been practically sitting on a dead person driving a car. I would be heading into a den of lions back home, unless I went on the offensive. My mind was racing. I decided to bury Irma's body in a swamp near my deceased uncle's shack. I'd get rid of her car with the body. *There is nothing more conspicuous than a black man driving a BMW convertible in the South.* Hopefully, my uncle's rusty red pickup truck could still be cranked into action. Uncle Ray also used to boast of stashing cash in an old sock. I'd check that out before heading on the road. Money, other than the $100 dollar bills needed for the deal, was starting to get low. *That size of bills would be too conspicuous,* I concluded.

I rolled into Uncle Ray's place with visibility quickly vanishing. It was rundown when he was alive, but I was stunned to see the deterioration that had taken place. Half of the tin roof had caved in, and the walls on his house were barely standing. There were old car parts and trash scattered throughout the yard. Even the sturdy twin oak trees to the side of the house seemed faded and worn. Cobwebs covered the truck. I felt for the keys under the driver's mat where Uncle Ray always kept them. Some things never change…Bingo! Now if the retired truck started I would know that God was shining down on me. Forcing my hand to stay steady, I turned the ignition. Nothing. I turned it again, pumping the pedal as I twisted the key. Nothing. I felt the sweat increasing on my brow. Saying a prayer to God, I gripped the key and forced it right. The engine puttered and choked and finally started. *Thank you Lord. I'm going to owe you big time.* I let the engine run, too afraid to turn it off. I transferred the remaining drug money to the truck.

I decided to rummage through the dilapidated house for that sock of money. I turned over every item in the house unsuccessfully. I was about to give up when I spotted an old spice chest sitting in the corner of the kitchen pantry. I sifted through the chest of drawers. No luck. I moved the chest to the side and found a small hole in the floorboard. After searching around in it with my right hand, I located the pouch. It was bigger than I imagined. I dumped the money on the kitchen table. Uncle Ray had managed to save $5,000! I decided that I would use what I needed to get me back to Cleveland and give Papa what remained. After all, Uncle Ray never had any descendants. It was rightfully Papa's. And I knew this money would not be traced when spent to get back home.

Feeling numb from what I had to do next, I walked over to the navy BMW. It was as if someone had painted it a rich red inside. Blood was literally everywhere. Irma was still slumped to one side with her two feet hanging over the driver's seat. All the color had drained out of her lovely face, except for the crimson hole in the middle of her forehead. Her magnetic hazel-green eyes were wide open. I pulled her up straight and then sealed her eyelids shut. I began to cry, a whimper at first. Before I knew it, a rainfall of tears soaked my face. My body felt strained and heavy. My shoulders were tense and heaving. I was once more against the oak tree back in Cleveland after my Papa had scolded me for switching identities with Jack. Only, this time, Jack was not there to console me. I stood there staring at Irma's lifeless body, thinking *how much I needed Jack now.*

· · ·

"Jack, this is Dad," Papa said with a steady and strong voice. "Papa," I replied with a groggy, half-sleep grunt. I pulled my alarm clock to face me, "Papa it is one o'clock in the morning." "I know son, but something terrible has happened. I want you to come home." The control in Papa's voice had faded away, replaced by remorse. I bolted up from the bed. "Papa, what's going on?" "Son, I'd rather discuss this in person, but it has to do with Joe." Concern turned into alarm. My worst fears were confirmed when I pressed Papa for details. Papa could never tell me no. "Joe had a drug deal go bad in Miami. He's murdered someone. I suspect they're after him by now. I am hoping to hear from him soon. He must have his cell phone turned off, because I haven't been able to reach him. I told him to make his way back here the best way he can." Papa finally broke down and cried into the phone.

My knees felt like they were going to give out beneath me. There was no doubt Joe and Daddy needed me in Cleveland. As much as I wanted to work the internship at the top law firm, Sheffield, Levert & Evans, it was out of the question. Family comes first. "Papa, I will catch the first plane out." "Thanks, Jack." Papa's voice was so low I could barely hear the response. "I love you, son." It was strange hearing Papa say those words, even though I always knew he felt them. "I love you, too, Papa. Be strong for Joe. He needs you now more than ever." "I know." I gingerly hung up the phone.

I felt so many emotions toward Joe - fear for his life, anger for what he was doing to Papa and me, guilt for not being around to keep him from going so deep into the 'life', and sadness that it had come to this. Yet, I knew Papa's phone call was inevitable. *Thank goodness the firm had given me a month's pay in advance,* I thought, picking up the phone to make reservations with Delta Airlines. The next flight with available seat-ing was at 7:30 P.M tomorrow evening. I'd explain to my boss this morning that I'd had a family emergency and needed to go back home. I'd take the flight tonight. If I had just made it to Friday it would have been two whole weeks on the job, I recapped with disappointment and longing. Just one more day… *Of course, I'd have to give the money back*, I thought distractedly while packing my limited garments. At least I wouldn't have to worry about breaking a lease. The small rundown efficiency in New York was paid for weekly.

I sat on the plane next to an elderly white gentleman in his fifties who looked like he was on his way home from a long business trip. His face was rather pale for this time of year, eyes watery and slightly pink from lack of sleep. His suit was wrinkled with signs of constant travel. Normally I would have tried to make conversation to be sociable, but not this trip. I unpacked the sandwich I had bought while in the airport, pulled out my John Grisham novel for later reading and peered out the window.

Neither the book nor the food could distract me from my thoughts. I was worried about Joe. I was also deeply concerned about Daddy. No matter what Joe believed, I knew how much he meant to Daddy. I could hear the hurt in Papa's voice. Knowing Papa, he probably blamed himself for Joe's predicament. *It was going to be a long journey home from New York to Ohio,* but the time and the solitude would do me good.

• • •

I opened the door of the BMW and sat on top of Irma, who was still behind the wheel, as best I could. I started the engine. The car purred. Wasting no time, I put the vehicle in reverse, and then in first gear, and headed down the road toward the swamp. It was only five miles, I recalled, but, that day, it seemed like thirty. I raised my watch and realized only ten minutes had passed since I brought the car to a stop at the edge of the misty, pea soup waters. *Swamps were spooky places,* I thought getting out of the car.

I took a deep breath to help prepare for the task at hand. I then peered into the car at Irma, trying to etch her face into my mind forever. This was the type of girl Jack would date, I realized. *Yet she chose me, and look what happened to her.* My first and probably only love, and I killed her. Tears were streaming once again down my face as I leaned over and released the brake. Just before the car overcame inertia, I took out my revolver and placed it in the glove compartment. "I won't be needing this any more," I said with conviction, "I'm through with the life." I put the gear in neutral and pushed the car from the rear until it descended into the murky water.

I stood there, gripped by the car's downward motion and the loss of the only woman I ever loved. Forcing myself to snap out of it, I turned my back to the scene and walked away. I pulled out my cell phone and flipped up the lever. The first call would be to let Papa know I was okay.

"Papa." "Joe!" I could here the relief in his voice. I knew how much I was hurting him. "Papa, I just called to say I'm alive and en route to Cleveland. I'm still a long ways away. I suspect I won't arrive home until very late tomorrow or early morning the next day. This is even with driving straight through." "Just be careful, son. I talked with Jack; he is flying home tomorrow and should also arrive in the evening."

"Thanks Papa."

"For what Joe?"

"For loving me in spite of me."

There was a long silence before Papa answered, but it was worth the wait. "Joe, I have always loved you… you and Jack." Papa's voice was heavy with emotion, "Joe, I love you as much as I love Jack. It's just different. You remind me so much of myself." Papa couldn't go on. He finally managed, "Hurry home. Your old room is waiting on you." My heart sang in spite of myself. *There I was, in the midst of a surreal drama, and I was as jubilant as a five year old, because my Papa said he loved me.* I pondered my father's statements with the first smile on my face in days. I was still smiling when I dialed the number on my cell.

"Cisco," I said, all warm feelings erased. It was back to business. I was a CEO orchestrating an empire on the streets. Cisco was the second in charge. "Joey? Is that you," he said with his usual respect, but this time with a hint more substance. "Joey, the word on the street is that you were taken out by some of Puto's men. One of Puto's men got drunk and squealed. We thought we found out about it too late. I've been calling you on your cell, but you never answered." There was a worried tone in his voice that he tried to conceal, but I'd known him too long. Five years is too much time to pass together without sensing the other's position. My other 'boys' fell with drugs, the wrong women, jail time and betrayal, but not my boy, Cisco. We had an unspoken bond.

"Cisco, I turned off the phone to take care of other shit. I'm thrilled to hear about the talk on the streets. What you heard was true, man. Puto set me up. However, the act did not play out as scripted. Let's just say I'm here to talk about it." The fury was rising in my voice as I contemplated the day's events, but I stayed in control in order to carry out my plans. "Cisco, matters are life and death now. I need you to take Puto out." "You want me to do what?" Cisco's alarm was valid. Puto was a force to be reckoned with. He always surrounded himself with protection. *Puto was a paranoid son-of-a-bitch.* The mission, should Cisco accept it, was not going to be unproblematic. Yet I was determined to cut off the head of that poisonous snake. It was my only chance at survival. Otherwise, Puto and his 'Cleveland crew' would be waiting to give me a homecoming I would never forget or remember. *Surprise was my only defense.*

Cisco was willing to go along. As it stood, he had his own Puto vendetta. Puto had strung Cisco's younger brother out on crack-cocaine. One day, Cisco came home to find his brother James had O. D. It was like a part of Cisco died along with his brother that night. However, I never remember him talking about it after that day. Again, I felt a wave of shame that so many people were dying for nothing. I snapped back to the matter at hand. "Joe, what do you want me to do?" Cisco repeated. We talked about the plan for about one-half hour. I could feel Cisco's enthusiasm escalating. *It was possible for it to work if done just right. That was for sure.*

We decided on a strategy that would catch Puto thoroughly off guard. By now, we were sure word had gotten back to him that I was still alive. His henchmen probably dialed him with the bad news as soon as they lost me on Route 1. *He'd be awaiting my return.* Cisco and I opted to use one of Puto's own men to take him out. It took us awhile, but in the past, we were able to finally recruit Josea to our camp. Josea came unwillingly, but his own intense hatred of Puto led him where he didn't want to go. *He was the perfect tool for our plan.*

It was rumored that Josea had been one of Puto's most loyal men for over a decade, even during the Florida days. Things began to go sour when Puto brought someone from the outside in to be his number two man. If it had been blood, maybe Josea would have understood. Unfortunately for Puto, Tomas was not. No one knew quite why Tomas got 'top billing' with Puto, least of all Josea. I found out later through a tight-lipped rumor mill that Puto had gotten Tomas's sister pregnant. She had lost the baby after Puto slapped her around in the midst of an argument. Upon the news, Tomas descended on Puto with the intention of murder. As a way to save his skin, Puto offered Tomas the number two slot in his growing empire. Tomas accepted. However, this bit of information I kept to myself. *What Josea didn't know wouldn't hurt him.*

I only found out about the story when I happened to overhear a cousin of Tomas' talking softly one night about it at a liquor store. Call it fate. I nurtured Josea's resentment toward Puto in spite of the information. He was the ideal mole. I knew, someday, he could be useful, and that day was here.

Josea still knew all Puto's dealings and was privy to information only the 'inner circle' knew. Puto was totally unaware of the enemy he had created in one of his biggest allies. Josea said that Puto would be visiting one of his favorite 'whores' on Seymour Avenue tonight. That would be a just right time to take him out. Few ever interrupted these occasions. Interruptions in the middle of his visits with Rena were not taken lightly. If the reason for the distraction wasn't good enough from Puto's perspective, you were definitely going to pay, sometimes with your life. This was especially so if he were intoxicated. Hence tonight, Puto would be fairly unprotected and his people low-key. The plan was a go.

. . .

I stepped off the plane wanting a new body. After two hours on a fully booked flight, every muscle ached, and my head was thumping. I remembered why my feet were once again landing on the ground of Cleveland's airport, and my forehead began to furrow. Any moment Papa would arrive to get me. *Why couldn't Joe see that his life was leading up to this? What made him want to choose this path?* All the emotions I felt when getting the news from Papa flooded back - anger, guilt, worry and remorse. I was so deep into my concerns that I didn't notice the rain pounding me from the pitch-black sky. Thunder roared and lightning lit up the heavens. Even though I was getting drenched, I went out to the curb to search for Papa. Papa was there waiting, conveying all the images his voice conjured up on the phone. Papa shifted his feet ever so slightly as he always did when he didn't have the answers. He appeared burdened with worry, and he had aged greatly since the last time I saw him.

"Hello, son." "Papa!" We held each other longer than usual, but these were unique circumstances. We were holding each other for support, love and affirmation. *How did we fail Joe?* "You look well, Jack," Papa said with a forced casual tone. "You do too, Papa." I kept up the façade in order to give us both time to acknowledge the gravity of the situation in our own way. We got into the worn, gray sedan and drove home in silence. As Papa pulled out of the lot, I noted that late spring had finally made its presence known with the first major thunderstorm of the year. *Mother Nature was a little slow on the draw this year.* I stared out the window in despair.

After about twenty minutes, Papa pulled up into the tiny driveway. We got out of the car and headed inside. Papa carried my modest suitcase in for me in complete silence. The living room looked in total disarray. *The house was aging along with Papa. Its height of glory had clearly passed a long time ago.* "I thought Joe would have been here by now." Papa continued, "He said he'd get here shortly after dusk. That was over five hours ago." I couldn't tell whether it was raindrops or tears streaming down Papa's face. Papa sank into the chair next to the TV, holding his stomach as if in discomfort. "Papa, don't worry. Joe will make it back. I'm sure of it. If nothing else, he is a survivor." I put my hand on his shoulder in comfort. "Papa, I'm concerned about what this is doing to you. We will get through it together." I came in front of Papa and grabbed his hand attempting to be strong for him. He had been through so much.

"Jack, Joe never believed I loved him." Papa was literally wailing between his words. "I have always loved him. Why couldn't he see it? He is my son." Papa continued, "I shouldn't have put so much pressure on him to be like you. The truth is, I did want him to be more like you, Jack. Joe is so rebellious, stubborn and thickheaded, just like I was when I was a kid. I too got caught up with the wrong crowd when I was his age, but your momma saved me." *I don't know what to say to this,* I thought. *Papa is bearing his soul to me, and I can't handle it.* I cradled Papa in my arms. I was at a loss for words. I recouped my composure, "Papa, its okay. You shouldn't blame yourself. Joe is a man now. He's made his own decisions since we were boys. We both attempted to talk sense into him. Sometimes you have to learn through your own experiences. I feel culpable too for not being there more for Joe, but in the end, they are his choices." My voice was soothing and low as I held Papa and rocked him back and forth.

Standing there in the dingy living room that had not changed since I was a child, I began to feel suffocated. The mood in the house, my own feelings, Papa's confession, all of it was too much for me. *I have to get out.* "Papa, I'm going to go for a bike ride. I need to clear my head." "Jack, it is after midnight. It's raining and it's dangerous. I could barely see two feet in front of me driving home. Maybe you should wait 'til morning." "Papa, if I stay in this house a minute longer, I will break something. I really need to release." I didn't realize how loud my voice had gotten. I believe the intensity of it is why Papa stared at me with concern. "Be careful, son." Papa kept any further reservations to himself as I crossed the room, heading for the front door. "Jack." I turned to meet his weary eyes. "I love you, son." "I love you too, Papa." He anxiously watched as I closed the door behind me. I went to the back porch. I unlocked my old bike and took off down the street. The rain had not let up.

The warm heavy drops pounded on my face the minute I hit the main road. It was cathartic. My heart and stomach were so knotted up I could barely breathe, but the fresh air was starting to work its magic. The warmth of the rain helped to melt away my tension. *You could almost tell it was spring from the warmth of the drops,* I mused. Deep in thought, I rode with a purpose not fit for a stormy night. Focused on resolving the turmoil surrounding my brother, I failed to realize I was crossing the street with the traffic light still green. Calhoun was only three blocks from the house, and yet a major intersection. It was also a busy Friday night.

It all happened in an instant, and in slow motion. The driver hit the brakes, skidding on the slippery pavement unable to stop the wheels of mortality. I snapped out of my trance in time to witness the end of my promising future. In an instant, destiny had been changed forever. I lay bleeding profusely on the ground before I went unconscious. The bike lay crumbled to non-recognition twenty feet away. The middle-aged gentleman rushed out of his dark green Cadillac to see how badly he'd damaged the man he had just hit. A sinking feeling spread across his countenance as he took in the extent of his handiwork. "Oh my God, oh my God..." The driver covered his mouth. "Call 911!" He screamed at the small crowd that had formed. Suddenly he remembered his cell phone. "I need someone quickly. I hit a man." "Calm down sir, I need to gather information. Where are you located?" the 911 dispatcher recited. "I'm at Calhoun and I don't know what…I think it says Render Street. Hurry or he will die." Panic had given way to hysteria. The scene became pure mania. A fire truck was the first to arrive. An ambulance and police followed soon after.

Jack lay there motionless, taking his last and final breath. Jack's face began turning a brownish-gray. The police were yelling, trying to keep the spectators away from the area. Paramedics were attempting unsuccessfully to resuscitate the body. Jack's body rose slightly as the electric stimulation tried to revive him. Nothing. After several attempts, they covered him over, put him on a Gurney and placed him in the ambulance. Police then turned to question the distraught driver about events leading up to the accident. An eyewitness corroborated the story of the driver. It was an accident. It was Joe's future.

· · ·

Josea and Cisco drove to the Lakeview apartment complex on Seymour Avenue. They taxied to the back of Rena's building with the lights turned off and quieted the engine. They had spotted two of Puto's men in the front of the building in a black Mercedes. They were drinking beer and smoking dope. Josea recognized one of them as Tomas. Clearly, their guard was down. *Lucky for us,* Cisco thought, *Rena lives on the first floor. That's not too smart for a single woman.* Josea and Cisco completed their black attire by putting on black gloves and ski masks. They pulled out their firearms, attached the silencers and stepped out of the car. *This was going to be a piece of cake.* Josea's blood was boiling with excitement. Revenge was sweet, and his only regret was that it took him this long.

After surveying the area to ensure all was clear, both men sleekly moved toward Rena's apartment. *I never did like the bitch,* Josea reflected. *What Puto saw in the whore, only God knows. She wasn't even that pretty. Some things will just have to remain a mystery,* he concluded. Cisco turned to Josea,

"Josea, you take care of the girl. Put her away as soon as we go in. We don't need any screaming bitches alarming the neighbors. I'll take care of Puto." Disappointed, Josea reluctantly agreed to the strategy. *I deserved the pleasure,* Josea thought to himself.

It all went so methodically it was almost eerie. Puto and Rena were in the bedroom screwing. *The dumb 'cunt' left one of the windows open.* Josea and Cisco used it to enter. Stepping into the green and white kitchen, the two killers tiptoed to the bedroom. Moans of pleasure were seeping from the corridor leading to her bedroom. *They were easy targets.* Rena was positioned on top of Puto, legs straddling his hips. She twisted her head towards the unexpected movement in the apartment. *Lights out.* Josea shot her squarely in the back. *Nice aim,* Cisco noted with admiration. She slipped to the side of Puto and fell onto the bed.

Puto immediately sprang up, trying to reach his 'pack' on the dresser. "Puto, this is for my brother." Cisco said as he raised the gun and fired into Puto's chest. He then came up to Puto's bleeding body lying on the bed and aimed for his groin. Before Puto's face could fully contort into a scream, Cisco moved the gun up once more and shot him in the head. Puto went limp. Blood was everywhere. The white sheets turned crimson.

Cisco and Josea climbed through the window they had earlier entered. They moved quickly to the unassuming, burgundy-colored car. Cisco turned to Josea, "Josea, I think we should take out Tomas and his pal. I don't want them raising their ugly heads when they find their leader is gone or trying to retaliate." "Excellent idea." With arms raised and silencers still intact, they circled the building and approached the Mercedes from both sides. Tomas and Enrique were busy drinking and laughing. They barely had time to react before it was over. "Let's get out of here." Moving as fast as possible, both men got back to the car. The engine purred, and they rolled out of the complex and into the darkness unnoticed.

When they were far enough away to feel comfortable not to be connected to the scene, Cisco pulled the vehicle aside. He dialed his boss' digits.

"It's done."

"Wonderful. Any complications?"

"None. We also took out number two, just in case."

"Good job. I can always count on you, man. I'll see you back in Cleveland."

I closed my cell phone with assuagement. For the first time since the junkyard, I felt hopeful I would live. *When I get back to Cleveland, I am going to turn over a new leaf,* I committed. *I'm out of this life. I will turn my empire over to Cisco. No one was more deserving of it,* I reflected. *I should have enough money to live comfortably for a while. Good thing I was never one of those guys who spent my money on the goods themselves, women or being the 'big man in town.' Maybe I'll even look into community college.*

I was making good progress. I took the back roads up to Georgia. Once near Macon, I picked up I-75. I kept to the speed limit, careful not to get pulled over for a moving violation. *I need to call Papa.* It took a lot longer than planned to get through those back roads. *Papa was probably worried.* I was just in Knoxville, Tennessee, and it was 5:00 P.M. At the rate I was going, I wouldn't be in Cleveland until early morning. I opened my cell phone.

"Papa."

"Joe. How are you? Where are you?"

"I just hit Knoxville, Tennessee. I probably won't get there until 2:00 A.M. or thereabouts."

"That's fine, son. Just be careful."

"I will, Papa. It will be good to see you and Jack again."

"I know, son. I just wish it were under different circumstances."

"So do I," I said under my breath as I hung up the phone, "So do I."

It was two o'clock in the morning when the front door lock turned. Papa ran to open the door to face me. Our eyes met for what seemed a minute. "Son." Papa grabbed and held onto me so long I thought my ribs would break. I could no longer breathe. "Papa, I can't breathe." He let go of me with a trace of a sheepish grin. "I'm so glad you're alive." I was at a loss for words. *What do you say to a father that has stood behind you, even with murder?* A few more awkward moments passed in silence. "Are you hungry, Joe?" "No, Daddy. Just tired. Where's Jack?" "Jack went for a bike ride. He said he needed to clear his head. I'm a little worried though, because it's been at least a couple of hours." "Papa, you worry too much. I can understand the need to get some fresh air. I feel like the walls are closing in on me too," I said, sinking into the sofa. I felt way pass my years.

Papa sat down in the chair across from me. "Joe, are they going to come after you now that you're home?" He looked so concerned and heartbroken. *How could I have been so careless with those I love so deeply? Why didn't I recognize how much my lifestyle was hurting them? I was so selfish. Did it take a murder to realize this? I had no answers.* "No, Papa. I took care of it on this end." I could tell Papa wanted to ask more, but restrained himself. Some questions are better left unasked. I rose from the sofa and headed for the kitchen, "Papa, I think I will make something to eat after all." Papa followed, "I have some cold cuts and bread in the fridge. You can make yourself a sandwich. Let me put on coffee for the three of us. I have a feeling it's going to be a long night." "Thanks, Papa."

I busied myself making a sandwich, and Papa made coffee. We both let the task at hand consume us to avoid what needed to be said. I finally came up to the plate, "Papa, I know I've made a mess of my life." Papa put the unused coffee filters back in the cabinet before responding, "That you did, son. I am hoping that the events of the last couple of days have taught you something." Papa looked exhausted and old. *Had that much time passed, or had I aged him? Maybe it was both.* "Papa, I've learned a lot these past days. I believe I was coming to this conclusion slowly anyhow. The streets are no longer for me. It carries so much death and violence. I asked myself is the money and false sense of power worth it? Papa, it's an empty life."

Papa looked at me as he did the day I graduated from high school. It was a mixture of pride, love and wonderment. My chest tightened with emotion. *What was I trying to prove out there?* The thrill of the streets had died so long ago. I was faced with death and destruction on a daily basis. Papa came to me. *We hugged again for a long time. It was good to be home and not just in Cleveland.* "Joe, I have waited for these words since the day you left this house. Tonight, I feel like the richest man on earth." Just as we were pulling from the embrace that meant so much to both of us, the doorbell rang. We looked at each other. *Who could be visiting at two something in the morning?* Papa nervously headed to the front door. I felt my pocket to make sure I still had my weapon on me. I did.

Papa opened the door and was surprised to find two policemen. Deep apprehension crossed his face. "May I help you, officers?" I could hear a slight tremble in Papa's voice. I peered at the door from the kitchen, making sure I remained unnoticed. "Are you John Baker?" "Yes." Papa's voice shook a little more. "Can we come in?" Papa moved to one side to let the officers in. One of the officers was short, black and portly. The other officer was white, medium height with reddish hair. "Have a seat, gentlemen." The officers removed their hats and sat on the sofa. Papa sat across from them in the chair. I was not able to see his face.

The black officer's tone was somber and official. "We just came from an accident scene where a young black man on a bike got hit by a vehicle. We believe that person is your son. One of the eyewitnesses recognized him. Do you have a picture of your son?" Papa gripped the armchair to keep his composure. "I doubt it's my son. When did it happen?" The white officer responded, "A little after midnight." The black officer repeated the question, "Do you have a picture of your son?" Papa didn't answer, but reached in his back pant's pocket for his wallet. He was moving like a man in a trance. I watched as Papa showed the officers a photo from his wallet.

The black police officer examined the photo and passed it to the white officer. The white officer nodded in affirmation. The black officer's voice softened. He appeared humbled by the need to give bad news. "What is your son's name?" Papa sat stone still for what seemed an eternity. "His name is Joe, Joe Baker." Papa's voice did not flinch. My mind was reeling. *What was Papa doing? Why in the world would he say Jack was I? Was Jack okay? He had to be seriously injured for the officers to come by.*

The black officer cleared his throat before continuing, "Mr. Baker, I am sorry to tell you the accident was fatal. Your son died. From all indications, it was an accident. We have written up a report that you are welcome to come down to the station and review. We will need you to identify your son at the morgue tomorrow." Papa took a long time to respond. When he did, his voice was unrecognizable. "I'm sorry, officers. You must have the wrong person. My son did not die tonight. Now, if you will excuse me. I appreciate you stopping by." Papa rose and so did the officers. They all went to the front door. The black officer turned after stepping outside, "We are truly sorry to have to give you this news." Papa responded this time in his natural voice, "Good evening gentlemen." He closed the door behind them.

I came from the kitchen to see Papa's face ashen. He was leaning against the wall by the doorway, staring into space. He focused his eyes on me. "Joe, do you know anyone that can break into Dr. Cantelli's office before morning? We need to have yours and Jack's fingerprints and birth certificates switched. I will also need to have someone else change the dental records of you two." I stared at Papa in disbelief. "Papa, what…" "There's no time for that now, son. Just do it!" Papa sat back into the chair he had earlier vacated, his arms cradling himself like he were a baby. He began to rock. I went to the phone and made the calls. *When you're in the 'life', it's not difficult to find folks willing to do the deed if the price is right. Thank goodness I still had $300,000 left of the dope deal money.* It would go a long way. Minutes later I got off the phone, and the wheels were in motion. It had only cost me $250G's. I would use the remainder of the blood money to pay for my school plans and living expenses and a down payment to buy Papa a house in a safer neighborhood.

Chapter 7:

Rebirth

The night Jack died still flashes in my mind. Sometimes, I wake up in a cold sweat, my bed soaked with perspiration and tears dripping from my eyes like a leaky faucet. Other nights I just toss and turn, unable to sleep, heart palpitating and swearing I can hear the ghost of my brother. The sad thing is that the ghost is as forgiving, warm and compassionate as Jack. *How dare he let me off so easy? I want to be tormented, told what a loser I am for shortening the life of the one that deserved to live.* Papa and I never talked about what happened that night. And that was the eeriest thing of all. It was like it never took place. The only clue of its existence was the vacancy in Papa's eyes. I remember every detail as if it were yesterday.

Just after the policemen left, I was on the phone with my boys. I called Spider. He was about as good as they get for break-ins and theft. I told him to enter into Dr. Otterman's dental office and switch the records of Jack and me. No questions asked. We agreed on a price and hung up. Then I called Rodney. He was also an infamous thief. Unlike Spider, he paid for his actions with jail time, lock-down for five years. Rodney was into forgery and computer hacking. *Perfect.* Rodney agreed to crack into the Hall of Records database and swap

Jack's and my birth certificates, along with the hard copies. By morning it was done. I was now Jack. *It all was so uneventful that I almost forgot the turbulence in my spirit. Almost.*

Papa rose the next day, got dressed and went down to the morgue. He told me to stay home. He didn't want to make for public record that Jack had an identical twin brother. He wanted no suspicions. *Papa was a little paranoid, but then again, you can never be too cautious.* Jack and I were truly identical twins, at least to the undiscerning eye.

Papa searched for his keys as if in a trance. His stony face was devoid of expression and any animation. Papa's suffering was so visible that my heart skipped a beat just gazing at him. I crossed the room as Papa was feeling between the cracks of the sofa. "There," he said as he felt the familiar metal pieces. I rested my hand on his shoulder as he straightened up. "I'm sorry, Papa," I said with an emotion I didn't realize I had. The words seemed so inadequate. I was wrecked with feelings of loss, self-contempt and repentance. As I touched Papa's shoulder he flinched and sharply pulled away. *I deserved that,* I thought.

Papa turned around to face me. Unable to apologize for the knee-jerk reaction, he pulled me into his arms. He began to cry. It was a whimper at first, and then he began wailing like a baby. It lasted for about fifteen minutes. I was glad to be there for him, to share the moment of loss. I was grateful that he still wanted me near him, a part of his life. I could never fill Jack's shoes. We both knew that. From that day forward, I was determined to make it up to Jack and Papa. *I am going to make something of myself in honor of Jack's memory and for him giving me a second chance at life. I will make Papa and Jack proud,* I decided with determination.

I fiercely held on to Papa as he released a volcano of pent up emotions. "I love you, Papa." Twice I spoke these words within a week's time. "I love you too, Joe. We will get through this together, for Jack's sake." I shook my head in affirmation, too devastated to utter a word.

Papa gathered himself together and set out for the morgue. He was gone for at least two hours. The morgue was on the other side of town. I stayed in my room in his absence, deep in thought. Thoughts of the time I pretended to be Jack suddenly popped into my head. *I was good at playing Jack back then. I wondered how I would do now. Jack's personality was so much more complex than before. Plus, he was living in a world that was completely unfamiliar to me. On top of that, I had changed in ways I wasn't even aware of. My language had taken on a street vernacular. My view of life had become overly cynical. I trusted no one.* It was a daunting task ahead of me. The gravity of my situation began to sink in. I had nineteen years to learn the ways of the streets. I had one summer to learn the ways of a Yale man. *Was I up to the challenge?*

When Papa came home from the morgue, he was the walking dead. His eyes were hollow stones. His skin was ashen. Papa had deteriorated further in a span of two hours than I had seen him age in over ten years. I could barely stand it. I knew part of Papa's reason for living was Jack. I would hear him bragging about Jack's achievements to his friends. "Jack is showing them what a colored boy from Cleveland can do at that 'hot shot' school. My boy's on the dean's list again. Jack is dating one of those high society girls. I told him to be careful...." Papa would go on and on, especially with his best friend, Scottie. It used to get on my nerves. *You wouldn't have thought he had another son.* My name was never mentioned.

It was the end of May when Jack died. That gave me just three months to learn a new way of life and shed the skin of my past. I was at a loss on how to begin. *I surely couldn't use my environment as a guide. Looking through magazines was like peering through a window of an expensive shop with no money or appearances to enter. Charm school was out of the question. Attempting to hang around a bunch of rich kids to find out how they conducted themselves was ridiculous. Why on earth would they want me around?* I thought hard and long. One idea that kept ringing through my head was Dirk. Dirk had called several times trying to speak to me, or should I say Jack. His father had read about Joe getting hit by a car in the newspaper. Apparently, Dirk and Jack still talked on a regular basis. I had been avoiding Dirk's calls. There was no way he would believe I was Jack.

I concluded Dirk was my only ally. He knew Jack better than I did. He was closer to Jack than I could ever be. However, to get Dirk to help me came with a huge risk. I would have to tell him everything. *Could Dirk be trusted? Would he come to the aid of someone who had just about killed his best friend?* I was asking him to be an accomplice to my life. *Would someone from the other side of the tracks want to get entangled with the law for me? His father was an attorney after all.* Dirk himself was in pre-law at Stanford! This would take some evaluating. Yet, I knew my options were limited. *In reality, what alternatives did I really have?* I would talk it over with Papa. Lately, Papa seemed like the wisest man on the face of the earth. *It's funny how a set of events can change the perspective of a person.* I used to view Papa as out of touch and old hat. Now, he was full of wisdom and direction. I consulted with him on all important matters.

Papa was sitting in front of the TV, asleep. His head was cocked back, and his mouth gaped open. His breathing was heavy, and his arms had fallen to both sides. They were resting lazily on the worn sofa. Papa appeared so peaceful that I hated to wake him. However, this was important, very important. "Papa." I shook him gently at first and then harder when I didn't get a response. "Papa!" I raised my voice and deepened my tone until he regained cognizance of his surroundings. Papa shook his head as if shaking away cobwebs from his mind. He straightened his frayed glasses and peered up at me. "What is it son, that you can't let an old man take a Sunday catnap?" Papa appeared extremely irritated until he examined my sober eyes, then no words were required.

"Papa, I need your advice on something." Papa sat up at full attention "Yes, son." I was suddenly at a loss for words. I hated to bring up Jack's name. It was always an uncomfortable subject for both of us. Yet I had no choice. *Here goes...* I sucked in my breath, sat down in the chair across from where Papa was sitting and began. "Papa," I lowered my eyes because I could not meet his gaze. "We both know that I am to take Jack's place." Even though I didn't actually see it, I knew from past experience that Papa's face had hardened like it did whenever Jack's name was brought up. I continued. "But, I'm having a hard time figuring out how to do that. It's not like Jack and I lived similar lives. I know nothing about his world." Papa sat there so still he appeared as a statue. His blinking lids were the only indication he was a living being. "Papa," I said, wringing my hands uncontrollably, "I was thinking about asking for Jack's friend, Dirk's assistance."

Papa's expression was one of astonishment. A strange look crossed his face. "Joe, what in God's name are you thinking? Have you lost your mind?" Papa stood up and started pacing the floor. He rubbed his shiny, balding head. He suddenly stopped and stood in front of me. "What will you say to him?" This was Papa's way of giving me his approval. "I'll tell him the truth. I will plead with him to help me fill Jack's shoes." I paused. "I will put my life in his hands." Papa focused on me with an expression bordering on insanity. "Son, and why exactly would Dirk want to help you?" "Dirk knows as well as I do that Jack would want to protect me at all costs. I will appeal to his love of my brother," I countered.

I picked up the phone and began to dial Dirk's number. Papa sat in the background leaning forward, preparing for the conversation that would go back and forth through the wires. *This would be the hardest thing I'd ever done.* The phone was ringing. I took a breath, held it, and reminded myself that *I had no recourse.*

Chapter 8:

Ridder

Ridder sat at his paper-laden bulky metal desk in the midst of the noisy, dingy beige-colored police station thinking, *is this all there is to life? Nine years on the force, and what do I have to show for it,* he thought bitterly? Pushing the chair out, Ridder stretched his long lanky chocolate legs, crossing them while at the same time folding his extensive arms behind his head in reflection. *I should have made lead detective by now. If only I had not made the big 'screw up.' Now I'm here shuffling papers and reviewing petty criminal cases and drug lord scuffles. Nothing I did could have deserved this shit.*

Ridder began digesting the stack of files in front of him. "Same crap, different day," he said under his breath. By 10:00 A.M., Ridder stood up to stretch and get his second cup of coffee. A file caught his eye. The name was Puto Sanchez. *I put that petty thug away four years ago for dealing crack. I remember it like yesterday,* he thought. "Puto, I am only going to ask for two years if you promise to get your sorry ass out of town when you're released and crawl back in the hole you came from in Florida." Puto, cold as ice, agreed to the terms. *So the bastard never left.* Leaning over, Ridder flipped open Puto's file. There was a close-up picture of his face, blood streaming down one side. There was a black hole in the middle of Puto's forehead. His ebony marble eyes were fully open and lifeless. *Goodness. Somehow, he never got used to these photos.*

Ridder left and returned to the file with a cup of fresh coffee. *So the son-of-a-bitch got what was coming to him after all. I told him to leave town,* Ridder thought, trying to suppress a wry smile crossing his face. *Sometimes justice is served.* Reading the file, he began mulling through Puto's life. Ridder prided himself that, ever since he'd joined the force, he'd always had a sixth sense for foul play. *Something was wrong here.* Ridder pondered why the case felt awry. *There was nothing out of the way about it.* Apparently, Puto had gone to the top of his game, he noted with an observer's interest. Before he died, he was the head of the largest Hispanic gang in Ohio, the 'Black Angels.' "Not bad for a low-life thug," Ridder said under his breath. *The homicide appeared to be someone taking revenge in a drug world where revenge was the soup of the day, so why the funny feeling,* Ridder thought. He glanced through the file a little while longer before moving to the next one.

Puto's file indicated Puto was shot in the head at his girlfriend Rena's house at approximately 1:30 A.M., the Friday morning of May 27th. He was in the middle of the 'act' when he died. *Lucky bastard,* Ridder thought. *That sure as hell wouldn't be my fortune. I can't even seem to get laid while I'm alive. Maybe if I weren't working all the time I'd have a chance to meet someone,* Ridder concluded in passing. Flashes of his ex-wife suddenly crossed his mind.

It was the day Samone left him. Samone was packing her bags in a hurry, screaming at the top of her lungs. "You self-serving, controlling asshole!" she yelled. "I'm tired of you, Ridder; your job and your no-good friends," she continued. "I cannot wait any longer for you to one day realize my existence." Once she finished packing her bags, she raced into their daughter's room and began placing Adelle's items in a suitcase. "I'm out of here, Ridder." She snatched their crying daughter and the suitcases and went toward the door. She suddenly turned, "I'll be back for the rest of our things." Her pretty face contorted with anguish. Adelle stared at him with longing, distrust and hurt. That's what disturbed him the most. "Daddy, I'll miss you," she sniveled, tears streaming down her angelic face. Adelle then ran up to him and hugged Ridder tightly. His chest constricted. Samone pulled Adelle away and dragged her to the front door of the tiny apartment.

How did he fail her and Adelle? Ridder knew he was not the husband or the father they needed. He had no clue how to change. That was nine months ago, *and it still hurt like it was yesterday. Seven plus years with a person grows on you.* Ridder remembered the first day he met the sexy, lithe, urbanely chic, Samone. They were both coming from work, standing at the bus stop to return to their respective spaces of possession. She was seemingly unaware he was checking her out. Samone was dressed in a stylish deep wine-colored suit. Her hair was cropped short in an afro-centric' natural style. Her skin was dark and smooth. Her lips matched the color of her suit. Long, sensual and shapely legs sprang from the modestly fitted skirt. She was simply stunning. Suddenly, Samone caught him staring at her. Their eyes locked. She smiled the most beautiful smile and shyly looked away. From that moment on, Ridder was bewitched.

Ridder walked over to Samone and started talking about only God knows. They continued the lively conversation on the bus. She told him she was an executive secretary for the Senior Vice President of Marketing at Rockwell Corporation. He told her he was a policeman. He could see her body flinch ever so slightly. Ridder was used to that reaction whenever he confessed his occupation. For the first time, however, Ridder was concerned that being a policeman would keep him from what he wanted. Samone quickly recovered. By the time she got off at her stop in a nice, inner-city neighborhood with lots of trees and children, Ridder had gotten her 'digits.' He called her that night. They went out to dinner two days later. It was the start of a long journey together. Adelle came into their world three years later. The little bundle was a complete mystery to Ridder. Her constant crying and baby noises intimidated him, but he grew to love her in a way he did not know was possible.

Ridder forced himself back to the present. He felt compelled to return to Puto's file. It suddenly hit him why the case was slightly off. *Puto was shot, along with his lover. Normally gang members try to only take out their target.* There was a code in Cleveland territories that neither side 'rats' to the police, so there was never a need to 'take out' any witnesses associated with the other side's camp. *In the normal scenario, Rena would have lived.* This was especially true, since she was a woman. *The killer must have shot Rena first and then targeted Puto's trapped body.* Ridder picked up the photo of Rena. *Now, that was a gorgeous woman. Who would have known Puto had such good taste? She wasn't the typical type of beauty, but alluring nonetheless.* Rena had a bullet hole coming through her chest as if shot from behind. Ridder concluded, *only a paid killer would shoot such an electrifying woman. From the setting of her mouth, it looked like she didn't even get a chance to scream. Maybe she knew the killer. There were no signs of breaking and entering.*

Ridder shook his head. *No, that wasn't it,* Ridder decided. *While odd, having someone pay to kill another person in 'that' world is not too difficult or uncommon. There had to be more to it. Maybe I'm just tired or been at this game too long,* Ridder considered. Perhaps there was nothing to his discomfort that time off would not cure. Unable to let it go, Ridder began searching the news database. He begin by entering in various dates. *If I don't find anything worthwhile, I'll move on,* he thought. There were several stories that came up, some of interest, but none sparking any connection to Puto's death. There was a million dollar home in Shaker Heights that burned down to the ground because the owner lived on the county boundary, so neither of the surrounding fire stations knew whether it was their jurisdiction. A woman was arraigned for smothering her six-month old baby to death. There was also a small story of Puto's death. And the stories went on.

Ridder decided to enter one day before Puto Sanchez's fatal accident into the computer search engine. There were more news stories; they were much of the same. They started blending into one another. Ridder was about to give up when an event on that day caught his eye. The story headline read "Notorious Drug Dealer Hit by Car and Dies." Ridder's heart began to race. The article detailed the accident of Joe Baker being hit by a vehicle on the same morning Puto died. The collision must have happened in just enough time to make the Saturday paper. According to the story, Puto and Baker would have died within hours of each other. *Was it a coincidence that two of the city's top rival 'kingpins' died on the same day?* Coincidental events without purpose were rare in Ridder's book. "I smell a rat rotting in the basement," he said loud enough that a co-worker looked over from his computer. Ridder acknowledged Mike's curiosity, "Nothing, man, just feeling a hot lead." Mike nodded and turned back to his computer, shaking his head in the process.

In the back of Ridder's mind, he couldn't help but realize that, if he found a story in this, it might just redeem his career. *I might make lead detective after all*, he speculated. He hadn't had such a tingling feeling or thrill in a long while. Ridder delved deeper into Puto's file with a renewed sense of purpose. He was almost giddy. After careful review of the information, he decided to take a little trip to the 'neighborhood.' The drive from the precinct was only 15 minutes, but it was enough time to bring Ridder back down memory lane. Ridder began cogitating about the last time he was on the east side of Cleveland. *It was a day he would rather forget.* Feeling his heart tighten, Ridder re-experienced the day like it was yesterday, when he fatally shot a 14-year old boy, not a year ago.

It was a routine police stroll on a brutally hot early spring day. *No one had expected late April to ever get this sizzling in Cleveland.* Yet here it was, 89 degrees and humid as hell. People were on edge. Turning the corner onto Martin Luther King Drive, Ridder and his partner Tony were confronted with teenagers in a brawl. They pulled up beside the boiled-over activity. The shouting and physical entanglement coming from the group was so intense they didn't even notice the men in the black and white vehicle with blue flashing lights pulling up beside them. This put Ridder and Tony on further guard. Sirens and cops usually spell the need to cool down, but not here. By the time Ridder and Tony got out of the car with their weapons pulled, there were at least four teenagers fist fighting with knives drawn. They were sporting gang attire with opposing colors.

The fight was taking place in the middle of a neighborhood basketball court. There were two basketballs, one on each side of the littered concrete square. Apparently they were arguing over who would have time on the court. Sometimes Ridder wondered *why humans found it so difficult to solve the 'little' things in life. Was basketball worth getting bloody over? Would either group be in any shape to play after this? No wonder I have no energy for my wife and kid when I get home at night,* Ridder mused. *Dealing with this petty shit day in and day out takes a toll on you.* Ridder and Tony went up to the group. Ridder fired his weapon into the air. *That got their attention;* Ridder smirked with satisfaction.

The teens stopped in mid-motion and turned to stare at the officers in amazement. After a couple of seconds, they composed themselves back into their 'tough guy' veneer. "What the hell!" the short dark one with braids and a prominent nose ring exclaimed in indignation. The group moved toward the cops. Suddenly, the opposing factions united to take on the 'Pigs.' Tony and Ridder exchanged nervous glances.

Tony had been on the force less then two years. He was also a 'brother', but one from the other side of town. He was born in Shaker Heights. His father was a successful banker. His mother was one of the few black women privileged enough to stay at home to take care of Tony and his sister, Antoinette. Tony went on to Case Western University and graduated in Electrical Engineering. Joining General Electric after school, he decided after a year and a half that his true calling was to 'save society' by fighting crime on the streets. Tony liked to tell the story of the day when he told his parents he decided he wanted to be a policeman. Tony had come over for the usual Sunday dinner. His mom was in the kitchen.

According to Tony, when he told his mom the news, she slid into the closest kitchen chair and passed out. His dad also didn't take it favorably. He yelled at Tony for about an hour at the dinner table. "How could you be so stupid, son? I didn't spend all that money on your education for you to become a blue-collar worker! Why would you want to put yourself in that kind of danger? No Cassing has ever held anything but a professional occupation." Mr. Cassing's face was livid. His sister, Antoinette, twirled her fork around, saying nothing. To her brother's surprise, she later told him in private that she supported his decision. "Do something real with your life, Tony," Antoinette said with purpose. "I listened to Mom and Dad, and now I'm about to marry a man that I'm not even sure I love, the respectable Doctor Arnold. It's not worth it."

Tony hugged his sister for a long time. It was probably one of the first 'real' conversations they had in a long time. Tony wanted to give her advice on the marriage matter, but he knew he was already causing his mom and dad enough grief, so he kept his thoughts to himself. Tony's parents proceeded to give him the cold shoulder for weeks thereafter. Eventually, they came around once they saw that he could be just as stubborn. When Tony completed the story, he stared at Ridder with unusual sobriety. "I'm going to make Chief of Police one day." The conviction of his statement was not expected for a guy so young and privileged. Ridder was unduly impressed. Tony and Ridder had a mutual respect for each other from that point on. They were partners in every sense of the word.

Looking very much the college kid on this day, Tony decided he would take the lead in the situation. "Stop right there," he said in his most authoritative voice. Three of the 'gang bangers' halted their movements. One teenager continued his approach. By this time, Ridder could see from the side of his eye there was a small crowd of spectators building around the event. *Entertainment at any price,* Ridder thought. "What the hell are you going to do, pig," the one punk said in a derisive tone. He appeared to be no more than fifteen. Tony ignored the boy's comments and repeated his command. "I said, don't move another step, asshole." Tony's language took Ridder aback. No matter how foul the guys language was at the precinct, they never heard Tony say more than the word 'crap.' This made him stand out more than anything else.

The kid stopped in mid-stride. In a flash, he pulled out a gun and aimed it at both cops. The other teenagers backed away. You could tell the others knew they were in over their heads. Tony aimed his gun directly at the hardened youth's face. "Drop the weapon, now!" Tony shouted while appearing to lose his composure. Ridder was compelled to jump in. "Look, kid," he said with a forced calm he didn't feel, "put down the gun, and we can forget this ever happened. I know we're all hot and bothered, but it's not too late for us to cool down." The kid then swirled his gun toward Ridder, "Shut the hell up, pig." Tony lunged forward to capitalize on a moment when the teenager was distracted. In an instant, the kid turned back to Tony with the intention to shoot. Out of instinct, Ridder pulled his trigger. He hit the boy in the chest, and the teen dropped to the ground. Ridder meant to shoot him in the leg. He later communicated this tragic fact to the investigative officer reviewing the case.

The other teens began to scatter like rats on a sinking ship. Out of nowhere, a man in his early twenties came lunging toward the policemen. He was swearing and hollering like he was insane. "You killed my little brother!" he screamed with a ferocity that could only stem from unadulterated rage. He was barely coherent. Before Ridder and Tony could react to the unexpected situation, they were dodging bullets. The lunatic and another one of his pals was shooting at them.

Ridder and Tony ran toward the bulletproof car for safety. Ridder got into the driver's seat. Tony headed for the passenger side. Inside, Ridder hurriedly turned on the ignition. Tony was opening the door when he was struck in the neck. His crimson smeared face slammed against the passenger window, and he slid to the ground. Ridder crawled to the other side of the car, cracked open the door, and pulled Tony into to the car. He raced back to the driver's side and got in, the car doors slammed locked. The crowd of spectators began pounding their fist frantically on the police unit as Ridder raced off toward the nearest hospital. Tony's breathing was faint. He was bleeding profusely. Ridder called the dispatcher to have an ambulance meet them at 4th and Bernard Street. *That was his only chance for survival.*

The ambulance was there when Ridder and Tony arrived at the designated corner. They pulled Tony from the vehicle. He had gone into shock and was shaking uncontrollably. Ridder felt so helpless at that moment. Tony was a fellow officer. He was also a friend. Ridder could do nothing to save him. Tony's passion for justice had renewed the spark back into Ridder's chosen vocation. *There was a reason he was so popular on the force.* Tony was one of the best officers Ridder had ever interacted with during his nine years on the job. *He had sound judgment, compassion and discipline in his approach.* Yet all of Tony's skills meant nothing as the monitors and machines fought to keep him alive. He died that night at St. Mark's Hospital.

The entire city was in an uproar. The black community was furious that another 'kid' had been murdered at the hands of the Cleveland police. It only helped slightly that the policemen involved were African-American. Ridder, *dared not imagine if they'd been white cops.* The police force was up in arms because one of their own had gone down, their golden child no less. Tony's parents, wracked with pain, were demanding a full investigation to determine who was at fault. They fed strident messages to the media, "Someone will pay for the life of our son." Ridder was in mourning, unable to cope with life on the force. He asked for leave while the investigation took place.

Even though Ridder was cleared of all wrongdoing, it didn't matter. Nothing mattered after that, not even the life sentence of the man who shot Tony. *Why Tony and not him? He would have made a damn good Chief of Police.* The thought would gnaw on Ridder - *if only I had covered him longer before getting into the car to protect myself.* Ridder withdrew into a place that even his wife and daughter could not find. That was the beginning of the end of his marriage and long-celebrated career. Samone had made too many sacrifices. He couldn't ask her for any more. He knew she deserved better than this, but he was unable to deliver. He started drinking heavily to escape. He lost his edge on the job. Fellow officers did their best to pull him out of it, but to no avail. Ridder was lucky to still have a job by the time it was over. He suspected his wife had eventually found comfort in someone else's arms. He couldn't blame her.

Ridder turned on the radio to help pull him back to the present and the task at hand. The harsh, blaring music poured from the car speakers. *What is this nonsense they call music these days,* he thought as he pulled in front of Puto's old girlfriend's apartment complex. He braced himself for the worst. He had purposely driven a plain car and had worn his own clothes to reduce the tension that would certainly surface from his snooping around. What he found surprised him. People were eager to talk about Puto and Rena. Apparently, Rena was a nice girl who got caught up with the 'wrong' man. The community was outraged that she had lost her life in the process. They gave all the information they had at their disposal. They wanted someone to pay for her death and were pleased to find someone cared enough to investigate the matter.

The elderly lady across the hall from Rena's place revealed through her tears that Rena wanted to get out of the relationship with Puto, but was too afraid. According to the aging woman, Rena revealed to her that Puto had surrounded himself with a new partner that was ruthless. She was terrified for him and herself. *It was intriguing information.* Also, the elderly lady exposed that two suspicious looking men were in the parking lot of the complex during the very early hours of the morning of May 27th. *Interesting.*

Something amazing then happened. Ridder questioned the young boys hanging out on the street. Their activities appeared innocuous enough, but Ridder knew all of them kept a pulse on events on their 'turf.' At first, he didn't get much. It was apparent they were suspicious of a black officer asking a lot of questions in a predominantly Hispanic neighborhood. Just as he was ready to head back to the station, a dark, waif-like Puerto Rican boy came toward Ridder. It was plain he was trying to appear 'cool' with the swagger in his walk and backward red cap. He had gold chains dripping from his neck. *Bling, bling, as the kids would say.* In Ridder's mind, *this kid wasn't very successful with his act.* "I hear you've been asking questions about Puto's death," he said in a heavy Hispanic accent. "Yeah, I have. Do you know something?" Ridder returned with equal posturing. "Maybe." The boy cocked his head left while inspecting the cop from head to toe. Ridder stood there patiently, letting this young punk know in a not so subtle way, that he was not intimidated. More than anything, Ridder played along out of curiosity as to what he had to say. It was worth the patience.

The teenager conveyed that Puto was rumored to have 'set up' a rival Cleveland drug lord to get killed down in Miami, and this was probably his payback. He didn't know the name of the guy, but he did know he was black. According to the kid, word on the street was that Puto was tired of the competition. He wanted the whole pie to himself. The kid said he heard Puto's rival died in Miami. He and his 'woman,' some high class Latino chick, both got toasted. They supposedly never found the bodies though. He only knew this because he overheard Puto yelling at one of his partners in a restaurant saying, "I want proof that the 'spook' is dead. I want to see a damn body! Don't give me shit about the body being sunk in a swamp! I should have known your partners down there were incompetent assholes. You can't send a damn boy to do a man's job!"

The kid reported that Puto's face was beet red from shouting so loud. From looking at him, the kid had thought Puto was going to take out one of his own men. The information was good enough that Ridder decided to get the kid's name. "Fernando," he responded, offering his hand, "Fernando Romero." "Thanks for your help, Fernando," Ridder said as he got back into his sedan, "Let's stay in touch." The kid nodded his head once in agreement and shrugged his shoulders, "Whatever you say man, but that's all I know." Fernando then turned and swaggered off.

Ridder's next visit was to Joe Baker's father's house. He got out of his car in front the small, run-down abode. *What a dump,* he thought. An elderly, rather stately man answered the door. Ridder noted the father seemed equally run-down, and he wasn't all that welcoming either. "Hello, John Baker?"

"Yes. Can I help you?"

"I'm Detective Ridder Jones. I was hoping to take a moment of your time."

Stiffening, the older gentleman moved to one side, letting the officer enter. Ridder instantly sensed another presence in the house. Looking around, he spotted the shadow of another person in the next room. The figure was not sharp enough to make out.

Mr. Baker walked over to the dilapidated couch. "Have a seat Mr., hum, Jones." The words were proper, but the tone had underlying rancor. *He was as frigid as the dead of winter in Siberia.* Ridder was unmoved by this though. *It was nothing more than what he expected,* Ridder surmised.

"Mr. Baker, I'm doing an investigation on the death of Puto Sanchez. Do you know him?

"I cannot say that I do, Mr. Jones." *It was clear he was lying, but why?*

"Call me Ridder, Mr. Baker," Ridder said. "I was hoping you would have a different answer."

"Okay, Ridder. Why should I know him?" Baker said with squinted eyes. *So, Mr. Baker was going to play hardball.* "Because he was the notorious enemy of your son, Joe. I believe you were aware that your son was one of the top drug dealers in Cleveland." Mr. Baker did not flinch. *He was good.* Ridder continued, "Puto Sanchez was the other one. Folklore has it, Puto was attempting to replace Joe altogether." Mr. Baker pretended he was totally disinterested. Ridder set out to change that smug look.

"I understand that your son got hit by a car and died on May 27th." *Bingo.* Mr. Baker stood up, and his eyes grew arctic. "Mr. Jones, is there a point to this conversation?" *I'm just getting into the groove,* Ridder reflected cockily. *It's amazing that you never lose the touch. It's like riding a bike.* Ridder prided himself once again. He noticed Mr. Baker had gone back to calling him Mr. Jones. Ridder had to admire his style of subtle 'frost.' "Mr. Baker, first let me offer my condolences on the death of your son." Baker stood perfectly still.

"However, I will get to my point. It strikes me as strange that both drug lords would die within a day of each other. Given the nature of my business, sir, I never believe in coincidences. Do you know what I mean?" The father did not respond. Ridder went on. "Mr. Baker, I started digging into the death of Puto and found a few things out of place." Mr. Baker finally acknowledged his words. "Like what, Ridder?" So he was back to being, Ridder. *Interesting.* The father sat back down on the couch that Ridder had never gotten up from.

"Well, I tell you, there are several things I find out of sorts. First, Puto died on a different day from your son, but it is estimated that they really died within hours of each other. Secondly, the point man that killed Puto was a professional, no doubt about it. The murder was too clean. The murderer left no trail. Not even the girlfriend Puto was 'banging' at the time survived. My understanding of street etiquette is that only the target dies. True, you hear about innocent victims in drive by shootings, but those are usually accidents. This was definitely no accident. "

Mr. Baker sat there totally composed, head slightly cocked as if listening to a juicy story. This was not the reaction Ridder was hoping for, but *maybe he would eventually break.* Ridder was determined to get something out of this visit. He continued, "Third, a young man told me today of Puto setting up your son down in Miami." Baker started shifting his feet side by side ever so slightly even as he sat, appearing nervous and listening intently. Ridder didn't know what to make of it, but found the mannerism curious. "The kid said Puto's death was probably some kind of payback. What do you think of this theory?"

"I think it is just that, Mr. Jones, a theory. It sounds like the kid wanted to have some inside information to appear 'in the know,' nothing more. Whatever the case may be, I have no more to offer to it. I am sorry that I'm not going to be of much help. If anything, I'm currently too grief-stricken to wonder about outlandish stories, theories or conjectures. Is there something else I can assist you with, Mr. Jones?" With that statement, Ridder was neatly dismissed. He stood to go. "Thanks for your time, Mr. Baker. I hope that you will be available to talk further if something of significance should arise." He made no comment. "Well, it was nice meeting you. Take care. Let me give you my card just in case you think of something." Mr. Baker reluctantly lifted his hand and accepted the rectangular piece of paper. He walked Ridder to the door. "Good day, Mr. Jones."

As Ridder went to the car, he couldn't help but conclude the visit was a complete waste of energy and time. He placed the key in the door lock of the six-year old brown sedan, and was just about to slide into the driver's seat when he looked up at a window on the second floor. The person saw Ridder spot him and quickly readjusted the curtain. However, it was not before Ridder got a good glimpse of him. Ridder stood there frozen, unable to move a muscle. It was the longest 10 seconds of his life. He had just confronted a ghost. Unless Ridder was absolutely losing his mind, *Joe Baker was peering through the glass pane staring right at him.* Finding his knees again, Ridder got into the car and headed back to the station. It was after 4:00 P.M. by the time he arrived to his final destination. Still shaken, he climbed the steps of the precinct and searched out his boss.

Vince was talking to one of the newer colleagues on the force, Susan Dayward. Vince and Susan were in an in-depth conversation when Ridder approached the two of them. Ridder knew he was being rude, but felt it was important. "Excuse me." They both looked up. "Vince, whenever you have a moment can I have a word with you?" Vince seemed surprised, but pleased. "Certainly Ridder, I will be just a moment longer. I will find you." Going to his desk, Ridder picked up Puto's file and began examining it with renewed interest. This time, he was on the hunt for anything that would support his story's theory. Vince leaned over Ridder's computer. "You still want to meet?" Ridder followed Vince into his office and closed the door behind him. "What can I do for you, sport?" *Vince had such a bizarre vernacular*, Ridder noted.

"Vince, you know you gave me a stack of files to process on recent murders this morning."

"Yes."

"Well, Puto Sanchez caught my eye, mainly because I put him away a couple of years back."

"Go ahead." Vince appeared curious, but mildly removed from the conversation.

"Well, late this morning I decided to do a little investigating on the case because there were a few items that didn't make sense." Ridder recapped his thoughts and findings of the day to Vince. Ridder had Vince's attention.

"Ridder, it definitely is an intriguing narrative, but it's not exactly concrete evidence."

"I know, Vince, but I'm telling you. I smell something foul. I'd like permission to delve deeper into the case."

Vince sat there a minute, "You said you thought you saw the ghost of Joe in the window. Well, I hate to tell you that it was no spirit. It was probably his twin brother. I recall it clearly now. There were twin Baker boys, Joe and Jack. They were identical. And I do mean identical. Only their father appeared to be able to tell them apart. They did a write up on Jack a couple of years back. It was one of those 'feel good' stories. Jack was just accepted into Yale. He had come from nothing - no mother, blue-collar father and was able to obtain a full scholarship to Yale. I think he was planning on being a lawyer one day or something like that." Ridder sat there listening to Vince, totally captivated with the chronicle.

Vince stood up and began peering out the window at the gray slate buildings across the way. He turned to Ridder, rubbing his salt and pepper beard. "Ridder, I consider this one a long shot. I know you believe the cases are linked. However, what you have told me doesn't do much to prove it." Ridder was unconsciously holding his breath. Vince kept going, now rubbing the back of his neck as he talked, "But in all honesty, it's refreshing to see you excited about a case again, any case. After Tony passed, it was like you went with him. I've been concerned ever since." Ridder felt his throat close. "Ridder, if this is what it takes for you to join the living, then go for it. Besides, it wouldn't be the first time I thought you had nothing and you turned up with a jewel. You are one of our best. I want that 'old' Ridder back. We all do." Ridder was genuinely touched. Slightly choking on his words, Ridder responded, "Thanks, boss. I won't let you down." Ridder got up to go. He hesitated and then moved to stand face-to-face with his leader and ally. "Vince, I appreciate your comments. It's good to be back on the saddle." They shook hands before Ridder headed to his desk.

Having nothing but an empty apartment to return to, Ridder decided to stay longer to map out a plan for working the case. He decided he would pay Jack, the brother of Joe, a visit. He would also return to Joe's neighborhood to talk to some of the locals. He knew he stood to gain little from conversations with Joe's 'boys', but it was worth a try. Ridder opened the file on Joe Baker written up by a fellow officer, and began reading it carefully. *Everything indicated that it was a cut and dried vehicle accident.* He read the interview of the driver with great detail. *That driver showed not a hint of intent. Though it might be worth at least talking to the man,* Ridder concluded. The bloodhound in him was back in business. It was 9 P.M. when Ridder rolled out of the empty police office parking lot in search of food.

Chapter 9:

Second Chance

I raced down the steps once the dark wiry policeman left. I could tell by the conversation I overheard between him and Papa that he was a detective. I found Papa sitting in one of the chairs in the corner by the window of the living room, staring into space. I was struck more by the unusualness of Papa in the uncomfortable chair than the expression on his face. Without moving his position or looking at me, Papa said, "Interesting conversation I had with that detective." My heart stuttered. "What did he want, Papa?" "That's just it, Joe, I wasn't really sure." Papa furrowed his brow the way Jack used to and began shuffling his feet. *Papa was troubled.*

Papa continued, "The detective asked a lot of questions, son. They were probing questions too, the kind you ask when you're on a fishing expedition. Detective Jones, Ridder, I think he went by, was quite curious about Jack." My heart, which was stumbling along a minute earlier, was now racing at the rhythm of an athlete preparing for a triathlon. I walked over to Papa. Our eyes met. I mustered the nerve to ask the question. "What did he want to know about Jack, Papa?" "Well, he never really inquired about anything specific. It was more to do with Jack's relationship with you and me. I was perturbed by the entire conversation. Somehow, I knew I should be on guard, but from what I wasn't sure. That Mr. Jones is a shrewd one. I could tell he was evaluating everything I said. I saw it in his eyes as I spoke." "Papa, did you tell him anything that might make him suspicious?" Papa's eyes grazed over me with annoyance, "Do you think I'm a fool, son? I wasn't always a godly man. I too know the ways of the street. One thing I can tell you, however, Mr. Jones will be back."

I began pacing the floor. My brow was perspiring and my shirt was soaked. The room was at a comfortable temperature, but my blood was boiling over. I stopped in mid-stride, "Papa, I think you should start calling me, Jack." Papa sat there speechless. The silence was deafening. To cover the uneasy space, I went on, "Papa, calling me Jack will help us make the mental transition. Plus, if the detective comes calling again, there will be less chance we will slip up." Papa, unable to speak, nodded his head in concurrence. "Papa, there is one other thing. Dirk has agreed to meet with me tomorrow. He was curious as to why I wanted to meet with him at a park, but he was more than willing to meet me there. I'd like you to be there with me. I need your support." Papa again nodded his head in affirmation. "We will meet him in Bolden Park once you're home from work. I know that's out of the way, but I didn't want to risk Dirk coming here."

Papa spoke in a weak, exhausted voice once he regained his composure, "Do you think this will work, son, I mean, with Dirk?" I responded feeling equally drained, "I don't know Papa, but I've got to give it a shot. I'm running out of options. I've cleaned up my language and dropped the cigarettes, but that's hardly transforming into Jack." Papa grinned, and then began laughing heartily. In between gasps of air he managed, "Joe, I mean…Jack, I didn't know what it would take to clean up your act. These alone are huge steps for you." I had to laugh myself at his remarks. *Sometimes, changes, good or bad, are necessary,* I supposed.

Papa and I spent the remainder of the evening watching TV. We looked at a syndicated rerun of "The Prince of Bel

Air" and then "This Old House." Papa found a murder suspense made-for-TV movie after that. By 10:30 P.M., he was sound asleep on the sofa. Bored, I flipped off the television and went up to my room. I lay down, but couldn't sleep. I tossed and turned for several hours, anticipating my meeting with Dirk. *Tomorrow would either be a fresh start or the beginning of the end.* I curled into a fetal position. *Dirk could react in a number of ways. He could agree to help me. He could turn me in to the authorities for impersonating the dead, or he could simply do nothing. I was literally at his mercy.* That made me most anxious. I was no longer the 'kingpin,' the person who gave an order and considered it done. That person was a lifetime ago. On Thursday, I would be asking a man I last saw three years ago, whom I barely knew at the time, for a second chance at life. As I drifted into a fitful sleep, I thought, *God, if you do exist, save me.*

The sun poured through the window. It nearly blinded me when I opened my eyes. I felt clammy, like I'd been sweating throughout the night. I showered and headed down to the kitchen. Papa had already left, so the house was silent. It was an eerie feeling. In the old days, my cell phone would be ringing non-stop from people placing orders, suppliers letting me know the 'goods' were ready for pickup or my 'boys' were calling to keep me informed of their whereabouts and the actions of competing factions. Now there was nothing. *It was almost like withdrawing from an addiction. I thrived on all that action. What now? The night Jack died, a part of me was forced to die also. The adjustment was difficult.* As I was reflecting, someone began banging on the door. It served to jolt me out of self-examination. I immediately went for the door and then hesitated. I opted to go to a side window and peer out instead. What I saw made my knees buckle. Detective Ridder Jones was on the other side.

Ridder knocked lightly at first and then harder. He rang the doorbell that was obviously inoperable. Frustrated, he peeked into the living room window. I quickly hid behind the curtain. Detective Jones then glanced over at the driveway, noting that

Mr. Baker's car was not there. He must have concluded Papa was at work, because he started descending the steps to head to his car. Suddenly the detective turned to face the house again. I could tell by his expression, he was contemplating his next move. More determined than ever, the detective returned to the door and began pounding on it. Two minutes passed without anyone acknowledging his presence. With irritation set on his brow, he returned to his car and departed.

I remained behind the curtains, feeling absolute terror. Only after I heard the car door slam and tires brushing the pavement was I comfortable exposing myself. *I cannot keep living in fear. I would have to face the detective eventually. I just needed time.* Following the incident, I went back up to my room to practice what I would say to Dirk and listen to music to calm my nerves. I also started flipping through magazines geared toward rich people, trying to imagine myself in their world. I reminded myself once more that I had never failed at anything I set my mind to and began to concentrate on my diction in the mirror. *I used to tease Jack for sounding like a white boy. My mocking him gave me the biggest pleasure. Now it would carry me to a New World.*

A few hours passed before I heard the keys rattling in the front lock. I was so paranoid that I went to the window to make sure I saw Papa's car. The vehicle sat in the driveway, showing its years of neglect. A wave of relief swept over me as I descended the stairs to greet my 'partner in crime.' "Hi, Papa," I said, as he came in the door with a bag of groceries. He must have stopped off at the store on his way home. "Hi, Jack," Papa said, with a wink and twinkle in his eye. *It was still a strange feeling, his calling me Jack, even though we had been trying it out for a couple of days now.* I didn't waste anytime on small talk, "Guess who came by, Papa?" I asked as a rhetorical question, following Papa into the small kitchen. Papa placed the bag of groceries on the table and started putting them away as he answered. "Detective Jones," Papa replied matter-of-factly. *Sometimes Papa plain surprised me.*

"Yes," I answered back. "He must have stayed at the door for at least five minutes." Papa went on putting away groceries before responding to me. "You knew he was going to come back calling. It was just a matter of time, son. I admit I was not expecting it to be so soon, but then again, if you smell blood, the natural tendency is not to let it dry up." Every day I was admiring Papa more. His wisdom and containment made me feel safe. I knew I could depend on Papa, not only for direction, but also for stamina and nerve. As we drove to Bolden Park that evening, I felt more confident than I had in days.

Dirk was waiting for us in the agreed location by the statue of President Jefferson. His back was facing us. He stood tall with perfectly straight posture. Dirk was adorned with a navy colored shirt and white linen slacks that were obviously not from Wal-Mart. One of Dirk's hands was easily resting in his pocket. He was observing the statue with mild interest and an air of cool recognition of his position in life. It was something that Dirk was unconscious of, I was sure. *Somehow, he appeared out of the ordinary, a little further along than the rest of us mere mortals.* I felt intimidated without even exchanging hellos.

Dirk turned around as he heard us approaching. He strode toward us to meet us halfway. He then practically ran up to me. "Jack! Man, it's been a long time." He grabbed my hand and then pulled me close to him for a warm hug. *It was the kind of hug that only two men that were extremely close would feel comfortable giving.* Dirk pulled back and 'onced' me over. He looked at me with approval, concern, uncertainty and elation. I was moved. As much as I enjoyed the relationships with my boys, nothing came close to this camaraderie.

Dirk moved away, still grinning, and turned to Papa. He grabbed Papa's hand and pumped it with enthusiasm and affection. "It's been too long Mr. Baker. How are you?" Papa smiled with genuine liking and respect and replied, "Dirk, I'm living, and, some days, that's an accomplishment, but all in all, life is good. How about you?" Dirk responded to Papa with the usual niceties before directing his attention back to me. "So,

Jack, what's with the way out location? And man, why wouldn't you call me back?" he said half jokingly and in a partly serious fashion. Dirk sobered and continued, "Listen, Jack, I was so sorry to hear about what happened to Joe. I know how much you loved him, in spite of your differences. Some things just happen for no reason." I looked down, unable to match his concerned, tender eyes.

Papa finally broke the silence by clearing his throat, "Dirk, there is a reason the two of us wanted to meet with you today." I interrupted. I wanted it to come from me. For some reason, I believed I owed Jack that much. *After all, Dirk was like a brother to him.* I glanced nervously at Papa before delving into the revelation. Papa's eyes were reassuring and hinted with pride. "Dirk, this is going to be difficult. There is so much to tell you. Let's find a bench with some privacy," I said. Dirk appeared confounded, but followed us as we began meandering through the park in search of the ideal location.

As Dirk was walking beside me, I noted that the handsome looks of his youth had gained refinement. He was a tad more confident and his clothes spelled of enhanced sophistication and personal reflection. There was no longer the awkwardness of his youth. Dirk had 'arrived' into his own skin. Yet with all his elegance, the intimidation I felt at a distance had dissipated. Dirk's gentle, compassionate spirit overshadowed his standing in life. His deep closeness to my brother made him fully human. The strangest emotions came over me. It was like I was a translator for Dirk and Jack's friendship. I also had a sudden urge to sincerely be a friend with this man. Most of all, I wanted, or rather needed his acceptance. *It was the closest thing to Jack's approval.* In honesty, I felt Papa had to love me even if he didn't particularly like me. That was not necessarily the case for my brother. I took a deep breath and plunged forward.

We stopped at a green painted wooden bench next to a grand weeping willow tree. There was no one in close proximity. I faced Dirk with pure determination. "Dirk, I have something to tell you. It may take a moment to sink in. What I have to tell you will literally put my life in your hands." I glanced at Papa's fretful face. Dirk interrupted. "Jack, what's going on man? You're starting to scare me. Are you in some kind of trouble? Whatever it is, I will help you in any way I can." My mouth went dry, "Dirk, right now I just need you to listen. There was a reason I did not call you back in the days after Joe died."

I was too far to stop now, even though every part of my body was telling me to do so. I was throwing the die and hoping for the best. *Please, Dirk, be there for me.* "Dirk, the loss of my brother was the most difficult thing I've ever faced. It was like losing a part of me. Words can never properly convey the sense of separation I feel." Dirk once more began to cut in. I raised my hand to stop him. "When I found out he had been hit by a car and died, I asked myself why him and not me? I was the one who didn't deserve to be spared. What happened to justice, to reaping what you sow?" Dirk looked perplexed but knew not to interject.

"So many nights I've awakened in a cold sweat. I sometimes dream that I am reunited with Jack, only to find it's only a fantasy, an ache, a longing." Dirk couldn't contain himself any longer, "Jack, I think you mean, Joe." I hesitated for only a second before reaffirming my original statement, "No, Dirk, I mean Jack." Dirk stood there motionless, letting it absorb into his psyche. He lowered his frame onto the bench for support. Tears began rolling down his face in a constant, steady rhythm. "Are you telling me you are, Joe?" Our eyes met in recognition of the truth. His face was a cloud of uncertainty. I knew it was a lot for him to take in all at once. "But the papers said Joe died," Dirk asserted. Papa jumped in, "That's because I told the authorities he did." Now Dirk was more bewildered than ever.

Papa placed his hand on Dirk's right shoulder. "Dirk, Jack died that night in the car accident. He had come home from New York only because I asked him to after learning that Joe had gotten himself into trouble in Miami." Papa took a moment before continuing. I could tell Papa was weighing in his mind whether to reveal the nature of the trouble. He must have decided against it. I was strangely relieved. To be judged by Dirk was very distressing. "Jack went out for a bike ride in that incredible storm to clear his mind. He was terribly troubled over Joe's predicament. I urged him not to go out there, but he wouldn't listen. It was like I had a sixth sense something would go dreadfully wrong. Jack insisted. He said he needed to think and clear his head.

"I won't lie to you Dirk. When I learned that Jack died that night, a large part of me went with him. Jack was my world," Papa admitted. "He was my hope for the future and the repentance of my days of the past. I prided myself that a man of my means and position in life could produce such a wonder. I lived my aspirations through his accomplishments. We also had an unbreakable bond of camaraderie I did not think possible between a father and son."

I stood there listening as Papa put into words that which I always knew he felt. Strangely, this time, I felt no resentment or anger. Papa went on, "Dirk, losing Jack that night was a hardship I was not even close to being ready to bear. Losing both sons was unthinkable. I quickly thought of a way to ensure that did not happen. I hope you can understand and forgive me. I know how close you were to Jack. He thought the world of you."

Dirk's shoulders began to heave forward and his breathing was short and labored. The anguish that was clearly there from the beginning was at a crescendo and fully audible. Nothing had prepared me for this. The remorse I experienced the night Jack died was only matched by the culpability I suffered watching his closest friend grieve. *I want to crawl beneath Jack's grave.* I desperately sought to spare Dirk the anguish I believed I caused. "Dirk, if I could bring Jack back by trading my life, I would in an instant," I said. It was all I could think to say. Dirk found his composure. He looked from me to Papa and back to me. He was visibly filled with turmoil. "Why did you tell me this, Joe? Why wouldn't you just end our friendship and move on with your life?"

I was taken off guard and couldn't respond right away. I knew my answer was crucial to gaining Dirk's support. *Every word I mouthed needed to be delivered with the utmost care.* "Dirk, there are several reasons I'm revealing this to you, but most of all, it is because I need your assistance." I decided that honesty was the only approach to the situation. I knew Dirk would see through anything short of it, and he also deserved nothing less. Dirk raised one eyebrow, an expression of surprise on his face. "What kind of help could I possibly provide you?" he said in a guarded tone.

"Dirk, you were closest to my brother. He lived in your world. There were times I wondered if you should have been the brother to him and not me. Jack spoke of you with such admiration, energy…and, well, love. I need you to show me who Jack was, how he acted around you and your friends; his desires in life, his likes and dislikes, and most of all, his aspirations." Dirk sat motionless, intently dissecting my words. I continued, "As the years went by, Jack and I grew apart. Looking back, I had to admit that much of it was my doing. I felt inferior to him. I always had. I also believed that he was too good and I could never live up to his high standards.

"Jack's relationship with Papa brought out the worst kind of resentment in me. The list can go on and on. Jack kept reaching out to me over the years, but I couldn't accept his love. The choices I made increased my bitterness. I was trapped, while Jack continued to ascend. Dirk, I can acknowledge this now, but I couldn't shake free of my own pride when he was alive. You have to believe me, through it all, I loved my brother." Tears were streaming down my own face now. Dirk was studying me, as one would examine a newborn. Papa stood in the backdrop, not saying a word.

I kept going, knowing that, if I didn't, I would lose my courage. "Dirk, to say I am not trying to save my own skin right now would be a lie. For whatever reason, I have been given a second chance at life. However, there is more to this story than on the surface. For once, I want to do something good with my life in memory of my brother, Jack, and for all the love and hope of Papa." I gazed over at Papa with all the depth of a man lying at the bottom of the cross, asking God for forgiveness and one more chance at redemption. Papa returned the eye contact as if to say 'your wish is granted, son.' "Dirk, as much as I didn't know the ways of my brother any longer, I did know the core of him. Jack wanted to make a difference in this world. He was for the underdog, for those left behind and hopeless. He desired to open his experiences of transformation and a renewed spirit to those he loved and cared for, known and unknown. And above all else, Jack wanted to make Papa proud.

"Dirk, I don't pretend to be able to live in Jack's shoes, but I am determined to not let his dreams die. I owe it to him; I owe it to Papa. There are so many people who could have benefited from Jack's love and compassion. They can now, from my own renewal. I need you to help me keep Jack's memory alive. I promise you, I will give Jack's life sustained meaning and purpose."

Dirk meditated for what seemed an eternity, staring straight ahead, focusing on nothing. His eyes were shifting left to right deep in thought. Finally, peering up at me with an expression of inner torment and understanding, he said in a tone of resolution, "Joe, I know Jack loved you immensely. He wanted to yank you from your life and said so on many occasions. However, he was unable to get through to you. No matter how well things were going for him, he always had a part of him that was heavy, laden and melancholy. I think that part was you. It would provide me the utmost joy to honor his life through your redemption. It will probably be the last thing I can ever do for him." Dirk stood. We hugged like two old army mates, finding each other after a long and bitter war. Papa came behind us and gripped our shoulders. In my heart, I knew that I had taken the first step on a long journey of transformation. "Jack, I will not let you down," I said quietly to myself as we all walked back to the parking lot. "I promise you, brother."

Dirk was true to his word. We talked everyday. He took me to social events, introduced me to mutual friends of his and

112

Jack's, and gave me a detailed history of Jack's life. He also showed me how to dress, dine and interact. It was extremely disheartening at first, but I was a fast learner. I had a little over a month and a half remaining before I needed to 'return' to Yale. *It would also be only for so long that I could hold off the tenacious Detective Ridder Jones.*

Dirk and I became friends of sorts. The relationship was tense in the beginning. It was clear that he struggled to call me 'Jack.' We both had a good sense of humor, which helped us get through the rough spots. My own sense of fun was a revelation for me. Of course, it was still not the kind of friendship I knew Dirk had with Jack. Sometimes Dirk got overly aggravated with my behavior and the fact that I didn't 'get it.' "Knock that chip off your shoulder, man," he would say in an exasperated voice. "So what. You aren't rich. Does that make you any less of a person? Jack, sure as hell didn't think so! That's partly why he was admired to such a degree. You have to let go of the baggage." I knew he was right, but it was a challenge. *'These people' seemed so carefree and expectant of life to deliver on its promise, while I had always prepared for the worst.* "Joe, I mean Jack, you have to believe in yourself in order for others to rally behind you. I cannot teach you that."

Dirk probably didn't think what he was saying was sinking in, but it was. My perceptiveness and aptitude for absorbing details amazed him, as did my ability to incorporate those details into my behavior. I even conquered Jack's furrowed forehead of worry or deep thought idiosyncrasy. One day, after I recapped all the events in sequence that Dirk had recounted to me to make sure I knew Jack's history, Dirk said - "J," as he had begun to call me to escape the Joe/Jack dilemma, "You might not act like Jack, but you sure have his brains." I chuckled with delight.

In fact, I laughed more than I ever had, hanging around with Dirk. *Life on the streets was serious business.* This was something quite new for me. The biggest adjustment of all was looking at life from an optimistic point of view rather than one of hardship, betrayal and conflict. Eventually, the change was taking hold. There was no way I would totally remove the rough edges in such a short time period, Dirk and I concluded. However, I had smoothed over the sharpest angles. That was quite an achievement in itself.

A month had passed since I had embarked on my new beginning. Dirk was heading back to Stanford for his junior year in two days. We sat outside the trendy café close to his neighborhood. I felt totally at ease with my new environment. We were sipping on Heinekens, reflecting on the strangest summer we had ever experienced. "J, I think you've made it." Dirk smiled as if he were witnessing his child receive his high school diploma. "I admire you, man. To be honest, I didn't think you could do it. I'm glad I was wrong." Dirk grinned sheepishly. "Dirk, thanks, for everything. I couldn't have done it without you." I meant that with total sincerity. We clicked our beers to salute a job well done.

"You're on your own now, J. Remember though, I'm just a phone call away. I've told you all I know about Yale and Jack's freshman year at school. I could never know his intimate relationship with Lenora, or his new friends or class experiences. I think you're sharp enough to pick it up. If I had one thing to say to you, man, it's don't give up. While you're definitely not the man I met years ago at Smith Academy, you have tenacity and a will of spirit that may serve you even better. You're tough, J. Just don't forget the soul of your brother. His was one of compassion and heart." I looked at Dirk, understanding all the esteem, liking and camaraderie Jack had for him. *He is truly amazing,* I thought. With paranoia of getting 'soft' inside, I replied, "Thanks for the tip, Dirk. We will definitely stay in touch." We both rose from the table. Dirk put money down to cover the bill. We hugged and departed. At the time, I did not realize Dirk would be an ally for life or just how lucky I was to make his acquaintance. The future would make that utterly clear.

• • •

The willowy detective must have visited Papa at least five times that month. Each time I managed to dodge him. The detective was very persistent, but not too many people are a match for Papa. Every time the investigator came by, Papa had an excuse for why I was not available. Most times, he just told him I was not there. Papa expressed to me that he could tell from the increased agitation in the detective's voice, Detective Jones was losing his patience. Papa was not the least bit perturbed. But we both knew I had to face him eventually, if for nothing else, than to close matters.

That day came two weeks before I was to return to Yale. It was a foggy, gloomy day that reflected my mood completely. The detective came knocking. This time, I answered the door. Mr. Ridder Jones appeared taken aback. I guess he expected the usual lack of response. He was caught totally off guard, but recouped quickly.

"Hello. You must be Jack," the detective said extending his hand. "Yes, I am. And you must be Detective Jones," I said equally formal. I was in absolute control. The frightened, defeated, unsure Joe was forever gone. I had seen too much and been through enough to neatly put him away as a memory of what once was. In his place was a confident, poised, resolute and unruffled young man. I welcomed the encounter with the detective. I was tired of running. I was also ready to move on with my life. This was one last thing that needed to be taken care of for that to happen. *Let's get this over with detective,* I thought with a degree of impatience. Yet nothing had prepared me for the conversation we had. Detective Jones had done his homework.

Detective Jones stood at the door ready for battle. We each sized up our opponent. The unwavering self-assurance I had a moment earlier, dissipated into thin air. I did my best to conceal the intimidation I felt. "May I come in?" the detective asked. It was nothing more than formality, because he was gliding passed me before I could respond. There was no way either one of us was turning back. "Sure, come in," I said anyway. The detective inspected the room as if it were the first time he had been in it. "Have a seat, Detective Jones," I said. He sat in the chair across from the couch. I sat on the sofa, and we squared off. "You can call me, Ridder," the detective responded, crossing his legs and pulling out a pen and writing pad. "Okay Ridder, what can I do for you? Papa told me you've come around on several occasions wanting to speak to me." I was making every effort to curtail my distaste for the man. *Why couldn't he just leave it alone and let dead horses lie?*

"Jack, I have a few questions to ask you. I am investigating the death of Puto Sanchez. I believe Joe might have possibly been connected to his death. This shouldn't take too long." Ridder spoke as he studied every inch of my face, body language and mannerisms. He was making me uneasy, to say the least. I made no comment to his statement. Obviously deciding to take the offensive, the detective continued.

"Jack, where were you the night Joe died?"

"I was here with Papa." We had rehearsed this part.

"You were here," he repeated my words in a hard to read tone.

"Yes," I reiterated with a little less assurance.

"Really, I thought you were the one lying dead on the concrete on May 27th."

I sat there in a pool of sweat, unable to move a muscle. I knew he was fishing for a reaction. I was steadfast not to give him one. However, his tactic of surprise was penetrating. I remembered to breathe in deeply as Papa trained me for just such an occasion. Matching his gaze, I said in an even voice, "Ridder, I don't understand your statement." "Don't you, Joe?" Ridder responded, obviously taunting me. I cocked my head to one side, purposely showing an air of bafflement. Ridder and I sat there in a face off that could only be mastered by two men of steel. I had no plans of breaking. The streets had taught me well.

"You see, Jack," he said in a sarcastic voice, "I've been talking to some folks. The word on the street is that Joe had been set up down in Miami by his rival, Puto. You do know your brother was a major drug dealer, don't you?" Ridder was cool as ice as he waited for yet another reaction. I was sorry to disappoint him. I said with equal poise, "Yes, I did. I tried to get my brother to alter his path, but he wouldn't listen. He told me one day that he wanted to get out, but he owed too many debts and had made a lot of enemies." Ridder ignored my comments and continued.

"I've confirmed that Joe took Delta Flight 771 to Miami at 6:50 P.M. on Wednesday evening, May 25th and was to return Thursday night the 26th on an 11:15 P.M. flight. Airline records indicate he was on the plane down, but there was no trace of him coming back. Records also show Joe was not on any earlier flights that day on Delta or any other airline.

"Let's say, for argument, Joe didn't take the plane back as scheduled because he missed it or suddenly was afraid to fly." Ridder paused for effect and to emphasize his mockery. I exhibited no emotion and continued my nonchalant posturing. Ridder went on, "The only other means of transportation from Miami to Cleveland would have been to take a train, bus or to drive back. Jack, do you know how your brother got back to Cleveland?" Detective Jones asked getting his pen and pad ready for my response. "No, I don't," I said unequivocally. Ridder wrote nothing down, but stared at me as if he were peering through me. *The bastard.* I was glad I had weighted myself down with armor ahead of time; *unprotected flesh would have been severely gashed by now*, being no match for the cunning detective. *Detective Ridder Jones is good, very good,* I acknowledged begrudgingly. Ridder repositioned his lanky body in the overstuffed chair and crossed his legs once more. He leaned back to further evaluate me before continuing.

"Jack, if Joe took any of those means of transportation back it would have taken him a minimum of 25 hours to get back to Cleveland from Miami. The twenty-five hour trip is with him driving non-stop. And driving straight for that stretch of distance is highly unlikely, unless he was using his own 'goods' in the process." The detective smiled wickedly, presenting stained teeth from too much coffee over too much time. "We have a witness in Miami identifying Joe leaving a 'Joe's Bar' as late as 10:00 P.M. on the night of May 26th with a Hispanic woman. They appeared to be in a hurry. She pulled up in a BMW sports car and swooped Joe up and took off. A black SUV was seen following closely behind.

"Tell me, Jack, how realistic is it to believe that Joe hooked up with a woman; parted from the woman; drove twenty-five hours straight; came directly to your father's house, rather than his own crib; got on a bike after such a strenuous, tiring drive, and went for a ride in the midst of a storm around midnight on the 27th?" I sat motionless, offering no response. I didn't have an answer that would suffice. I had no desire to catch the bait. "Can you tell me, Jack, how a man can be in two places at one time?" He waited and then continued, "You, on the other hand, had taken a flight from New York on Friday, May 27th on United Airlines, Flight 293 at 7:30 P.M. This would have put you in Cleveland well before the vehicle fatality."

My heart was racing. Yet my mind was moving equally fast. Papa and I had not rehearsed this part. I was going to have to wing it. "Ridder," I responded with a composure I did not feel. "Joe returned from Miami late Friday night as well. Papa said that Joe called him shortly after he landed in Miami and said something had come up and he needed to stay in Miami a little longer and would not be home until late Friday." "Did he say why, Jack?" "No," I said a tad too quickly. Ridder picked up on it. I knew he did, because he scribbled something down on his pad. "When did Joe get back into Cleveland, Jack?" "I don't know. I believe it was some time late Friday evening. Papa would know." My stomach was in so many knots it was going to take weeks to untangle. *It was time to end this conversation, fast.* "Look, Detective, I told some of my old classmates from Smith that I would meet them for a game of hoops. I really need to get going." I signaled that the discussion was over by rising from my seat. The detective did not move. "Jack, I have a few more questions and then I'll be gone, I promise."

"Do you know how Joe got home from Miami?" I knew this question was a trap, so I responded in kind. "No," I said sitting back down on the sofa. *You thought you had me didn't you, Detective, but not so.* I mentally patted myself on the back. The detective was not fazed by my response. "Did Joe tell you or your father what was the 'something' that came up down there?" "No." *That was easy.* "Just one more question for now," the detective stated. "Were you familiar with Puto Sanchez?" "Yes, but only from hearing side conversations about him from people in the neighborhood." "How much did you know about Joe and Puto's relationship?" the detective came back. Finally at the point of frustration I answered, "Ridder, I thought I addressed this question earlier. Joe, did not talk to me about his life on the streets. He knew I didn't approve. Nor was I anxious to discuss something that greatly disturbed me. Is there anything else?"

It was evident Ridder sensed my limits. He did not push pass them. "No, Jack. You have been quite cooperative. I would like to keep the lines of communication open with you." With that, he pulled out a business card and gave it to me. "If you think of anything that might be of importance, please don't hesitate to call me. I'd also like to be able to have a few follow up conversations with you. Is that alright?" *No,* I wanted to shout at the top of my lungs. However, I had managed to get through this exchange unscathed. I was not about to lose it now. "Sure, Detective," I said with an air of agreeableness. We walked toward the front door in silence. Ridder turned, "Good day, Jack." "Bye, Ridder," I said shutting the door behind him.

After he left, I leaned against the wall for support. I was drained. I went over the conversation in my mind, to make sure I hadn't made any mistakes that I would later need to retract. I couldn't think of any. I went to the kitchen, got a beer from the refrigerator and sat at the kitchen table to recoup. *If I had known it was going to be that arduous, I would have been better prepared.* That detective was going to be more troublesome than I thought. *Thank goodness I was leaving for school.* I relaxed a bit with the thought. I changed into sports gear and left the house for a walk in case Ridder was watching.

Later that evening, I recounted the conversation I had with the detective to Papa. Papa listened as if his life depended on it. *In some ways, it did.* He was certainly an accomplice to a significant cover up. At the end of my story he said, "You did good, son. He has nothing of substance. Otherwise, he'd be hauling you and me down to the precinct. I wouldn't worry too much about him. You'll be off to school in no time. I have to hand it to Detective Jones he is persistent. Any lesser man would have given up by now." Papa smiled a knowing grin. I got another Coke out of the fridge and gave Papa one. We numbed our concerns with Coke and rum and slept well that night.

Detective Jones made two more visits before I went off to school. He got nowhere with them. I was on to his tactics. In addition, my thoughts had moved on to the next frontier - school. I knew from our last conversation the detective was definitely suspicious, but he had nothing of substance. It was mostly conjectured, which we both knew wouldn't hold up in court. I was as good as a 'free' man. More than anything, I was apprehensive about leaving Papa there to deal with him. One day, I expressed these concerns to Papa. "Don't worry about me, son. I've been handling my own for a long time. I will treat the detective like I treat my bosses at work, play ignorant and only respond to what is asked." Papa laughed heartily at that one. Suddenly I felt ashamed for all those years I looked down on Papa for his occupation and the way he let those white men treat him at work. *Sometimes, life is deeper than what appears on the surface. It's important to inspect underneath before drawing conclusions.*

• • •

Yale was an adjustment, but by now I was used to adjustments. It was a legendary university. Yet it managed to create an environment that was warm, small in feel and secluded, nestled away in green hills. What surprised me most about the school was its beauty. I grew up surrounded by concrete, graffiti and monochromatic colors of gray and beige. Dilapidated buildings and unruly, unkempt people completed the picture. Here, there were vast lush, perfectly manicured lawns and old, but ornately rich well maintained buildings. At Yale, the students were diverse, but even they held an aura of significance and pulsating vibrancy. My dorm room was small and simple. However, it too reeked of heritage and inclusion. *No wonder Jack had become the person he had,* I thought with a degree of envy. He had entered a world I could not conjure up in my most imaginative dreams.

I knew the gods were favoring me when I discovered Jack had brought his journal with him from New York. Jack had started maintaining a journal since his sophomore year in high school. I dug up the pre-college journals as a supplement to understand his thought process. True to himself, Jack recapped his first year at college in vivid detail. It was extremely useful for placing people and events. I was shocked at the level of insight Jack had on everyday life and even on me. He concentrated so much on the positive aspects of people and situations; I didn't think he recognized the seedy, ugly side of human nature. Yet Jack saw the complete picture, even with his beloved Papa. Jack wrote in his journal one day early in his freshman year at Yale, "Papa called me today. He's just about fed up with Joe. He never has quite forgiven him for moving out on him. However, I think the chief problem between the two of them is they're too much alike. Each is set in his ways, quick-tempered and dogmatic. If only they could see their similarities, they'd respect their differences."

Jack also had a photo album with numerous pictures, many showing him with an attractive, delicate, and glossy brown woman. That must be Lenora. He spoke of their relationship, though not in much detail. In addition, there were photos of him with his classmates at various occasions. It was an eerie feeling going through his things. He could not have left a better trail of his life though. *Thank you, Jack, for your self-exploration. You're looking out for me, even in Heaven.*

I made decisions about how I would approach the initial semester. One critical item of business was to terminate the relationship with Lenora. There was no way I could carry out being Jack in an 'intimate' relationship. I wouldn't know where to begin. I set in motion the wheels of ending the relationship with Lenora a couple days after I arrived on campus. I planned to tell her I had 'hooked up' with an old girlfriend over the summer. I didn't think it would be difficult, given that I didn't know her. Yet, once more, I had underestimated the situation.

Lenora and I met at the Manhattan Diner, not too far from campus. Arriving somewhat late, I viewed Lenora through the window. She was sitting at one of the booths slurping down a shake. Lenora was an absolute knock out in person. *The photos did not do her justice. Jack had excellent taste in women.* Tempted to continue the relationship on this basis alone, I detailed all the reasons it was necessary to give her up. Lenora came running to greet me halfway as I entered the diner. *You would have thought I was a rock star or something.* "Jack!" she said as she pulled me to her and planted a kiss on my lips. She had a melodic voice that conjured up robins chirping on a sunny spring morning. Her lips tasted of sweet wine. I returned her warmth with energy I couldn't help but feel. *How could you not get caught up in the moment when someone greets you like that?*

Lenora was about 5' 5" tall. She was model thin, yet very shapely. She had cat eyes that were acute and interestingly seductive. Her waist fit neatly in my arms. Her heart-shaped lips made me want to touch them once more. I stopped myself and we walked back to the table with her arm possessively around my waist. Lenora was gorgeous and evidently not fully aware of the effect she had on men. There wasn't a man in the establishment that did not slyly glance at her with yearning as we went back to our booth. I secretly relished the attention Lenora commanded. *It spoke volumes of my own male prowess.* I wore it like a badge of honor.

Lenora was beaming at me as she took her seat in the booth facing east. I was drawn to her magnetic smile and shimmering, velvet skin. "Snap out of it, Joe," I said under my breath. You are here for a reason. You cannot risk your future for a woman you don't even know, no matter how desirable. I reminded myself of this over and over again. I willed my loins to follow suit. *Think with the correct head, Joe.*

"What are you thinking about, Jack?" Lenora gazed at me with a flirtatious bat of her eyes. She twirled her thick silky locks in the process. Her other elbow was propped up on the table with her head resting on her hand. It was extremely provocative. *I was way out of my league with this one.* I wanted her just the same. "Nothing," I responded, "I'm just soaking in the rays of your beauty." Lenora's smile broadened. The hand that once swirled her luscious charcoal threads began nervously circling the water glass. *I still have my touch with women,* I concluded smugly. *Of course, this is not the way to set up a break up,* I reminded myself. However, it was the most stimulating fun I'd had in months.

Lenora began to pout. "Why didn't you return my calls over the summer, Jack? You called me several times in New York, but once you went home to Cleveland I never heard from you. Didn't your dad tell you I called? And why did you leave the job in New York anyway?" These questions were enough to shock me into reality and sober me up. "Lenora, there is something I have to tell you." I took in a deep breath to gather strength for crushing such a beautiful, warm and spirited soul. The old me wouldn't have thought twice about telling a woman goodbye. *What was happening to me?* It was clear that Lenora knew immediatcly from the preface of words what was going to spew from my mouth next. *If you only knew how much I want you,* I thought as I began the descent.

I could see Lenora visibly bracing herself for disappointment and loss. Her lips began to quiver as she spilled out the words, "Jack, just get it over with; I know what you're about to say. I just want to hear it from your own lips." By this time, Lenora's back was erect and her hands were gripping the strawberry shake she had ordered prior to my arrival. She pierced me with expectant eyes. "To answer your earlier question, Lenora, I left New York in haste because of a family emergency. I ended up staying home for the summer." I said with composure, leading up to the main event. I reached for her hands, but she snatched them away. "Lenora, you're a wonderful person. The time we spent together will always mean a lot to me. However, I want to be completely honest with you. I ended up getting back with an old friend of mine." Lenora was whimpering softly, "You mean a former girlfriend, don't you Jack?" It was the kind expression of anguish that you'd expect from someone so well bred. She was incapable of making a 'scene.' For that, I was eternally grateful.

Lenora faced me with the entire extent of my damage. Droplets of salty water streamed down her angelic face. I felt like an absolute horse's ass. I knew I was doing the right thing, but a part of me was compelled to take back every word. I resisted by calling on the strength of each inch of my being. "Jack," she said in a mortally wounded animal snivel, "What was the family emergency? Is everyone okay?" I was caught way off-guard. It only served to magnify my shame. *How can she think of me, when I just kicked her to the curb?* "Lenora, my brother got into some trouble, but everything's okay." We sat in awkward silence. It was obvious Lenora had more questions but was afraid to ask them. *What woman didn't want to know why she was dumped; about the competition; and whether she had any chance of getting back the man she loved.* I patiently waited for her to get up the nerve.

It took a while, but the questions came pouring out like a dam building up too much pressure. We discussed each one. I answered them in what appeared to be a forthright manner. I told her that I met up with my old sweetheart from high school, who was also home from school. She seemed to take it better since I said we had been together since tenth grade. I knew she would. I made sure every answer saved her ego. Before the night was through, we were talking about semester classes and potentially pledging for a Greek club. We hugged for a long time in the parking lot before leaving the restaurant. "Lenora, I wish you all the best," I said. It was the first whole truth I had spoken that night. "With any other man who had just given me the ax, I wouldn't believe him, but somehow it rings sincere coming from you, Jack. I will always love you, you know." I ran my finger down her perky nose. "I know." I kissed her once more in spite of myself. The passion made her pull away in confusion. I was embarrassed. I hurried to my roommate's borrowed car and headed toward the dorm.

Lenora and I spoke when we ran into each other. It was awkward, but manageable. We ended up in the same American History class. However, we shared it with two hundred other students, so it was cool. Sometimes I would conjure up different outcomes with Lenora and me, like when we would float into the sunset holding hands and later make love on the beach. Yet, in the end, I knew I had made the most prudent decision.

• • •

I discovered Jack was as popular with his classmates at Yale as he was in high school. I left intact the remainder of his friends. Many of Jack's comrades were perplexed by my antics, but attributed it to the breakup with Lenora. Eventually, I caught my groove and fell in line with the pack. Jack's roommate, Chuck, was the most distressing for me. Apparently, he and Jack were close. He kept discussing his future as a major black screenwriter with me. It was quite annoying, but I tolerated it. Most things about him were okay. I just was not the 'chum' he thought he had in me. By the end of the semester we were living separate lives, and I had made my own friends. I decided to keep rooming with Chuck because it was easier to do so.

The adjustments of the first semester were challenging, but invigorating. My classes were exceedingly arduous, probably because I was not prepped with the proper prerequisites. I worked extra hard to get through them. Each Saturday, I would call Papa for encouragement.

"Papa, I don't know if I can handle these classes. I got a C on my first exam in Political Science 202." "Son, I know it's tough, but hang in there," he would say with conviction. "You are as smart as anyone at that school. Both of you were equally gifted growing up." Papa was referring to Jack. We talked about him less and less as time went by. It was like I was continuing his life, meaning he never really died. *How do you refer to the deceased when they never passed away?*

"Papa, I want to come home," I moaned one day, after a literary exam I wasn't sure I passed. "Over my dead body you will." I could tell Papa had a snicker in his voice, but I knew he was serious. One thing Papa never tolerated was a quitter. That was instilled in us from the time we could walk. As boys, Jack and I would take turns playing Papa in chess. *For an uneducated man, he sure was astute at the game.* Many times, we wanted to discontinue when we saw no way out of the web we had woven for ourselves in earlier chess moves. Papa would say in a threatening tone, "No boy of mine gives up. When times get tough, that's when you dig your heels into the earth. There's always a back door for escape when the front door gets jammed. Open your mind, son, and think." *Papa was usually right.*

"Hang in there," Papa repeated. "It's going to be rigorous because you're entering school midstream. You have what it takes to deal with it. You're tenacious and extremely gifted. If I were a betting man, I would put all my chips on you." "Thanks, Papa," I said. "What if I give it my best shot and still fail?" "Then you fail, son. There's no crime in giving it your all and falling short. The sin is not staying to the end." Papa paused a moment. "Keep your chin up, Joe. I know you have it in you." That was the first time he'd referred to me as Joe since the day we agreed that he would call me Jack. It was awkward, but it did have the effect of letting me know Papa believed in me, not Jack. I felt a wave of fortitude sweep over me. The words headed straight to my heart. It was just the shot of adrenaline I needed to continue.

I got through the first semester with three A's and two B's. The work I put into those grades made them especially sweet. Papa was beaming from ear-to-ear when I showed them to him. "Didn't I tell you, son; you could do it! I didn't raise no dummies." He proceeded to call up my aunts to tell them the good news. They believed I was Jack, so they were happy for me, but not especially jubilant. As far as they were concerned, I was supposed to do well. However, Aunt Eulie had a Sunday dinner in my honor. It was just like the old days, except all my aunts were now showing their years. Time had even had its way with snazzy, Aunt Sadie. Her gracious legs had lost some of their tone, and her middle showed the first signs of spreading. Yet she was still a head-turner and smartly dressed from head to toe. For all of Papa's taunting, she never did get married.

It was good being home for the holidays. Papa and I spent a lot of time catching up. I walked him through how I dealt with my new start on campus. We talked about the girls I met during the year. Papa filled me in on his life and the latest news in the neighborhood. It seemed like a lifetime had passed when we discussed all the events that had taken place in such a short period of time. I thoroughly enjoyed the camaraderie with Papa. It also felt wonderful being back in my own skin, if only for a moment.

My high mood lowered a bit when Papa revealed some disturbing news. He said Detective Jones continued to pester him while I was gone. There were at least three more visits. Papa stated with a satisfied grin that each visit brought him no closer to the truth. The detective didn't miss a beat though. He stopped over to visit me during the Christmas break as well.

From our conversation, I got the feeling Detective Jones was not 'officially' on the case any longer. It appeared he was doing this on his own time, but it was annoying nonetheless. He made a lot of statements like we 'looked over this and that.' It was always in past tense. Ridder mentioned a few matters that would have unraveled me earlier. Evidently, he had read more about the missing Hispanic woman in Miami, Irma Rodriguez, who was last seen with a black man fitting my description. The newspaper reported, according to Detective Jones, 'the two were last seen leaving a Joe's Bar in a navy blue, black top BMW convertible, with two other men chasing after them.'

I was very relieved to hear him say they couldn't find her body. So, there was no way to match her with me. If they had, it would have substantiated a lot of Ridder's conjectures about my involvement. It would have also given him a timeline to work with. It was apparent from my conversation with him and the fact that he visited Papa so many times that the detective had taken the case on as some kind of personal mission. *Ridder had no 'smoking gun.'* That was for sure. For me, it made going back to school that much easier.

Returning to Yale was measurably smoother the second semester. I had made it through the storm. I actually looked forward to the chance to soak up more knowledge. I was captivated by the larger-than-life figures of our country's past that helped shaped our democracy today. They were colorful, bold and cunning. I was also mesmerized by the intricacies of our political system. In this, I found my calling. Politics seemed like a world of possibilities. I was drawn to its complexity and stimulating thought. I concluded it was the way to wield power and change lives. *I wanted to do both.*

Chapter 10:

Suzanne

I thought about Lenora from time to time over the school year, even with my many female escapades. I yearned for real companionship. Lenora definitely fit the bill. Of course, that was until I laid my eyes upon Suzanne. I was standing in the registry line; feeling quite satisfied with my chosen major and class choices to buttress it, when she came into view. The woman, or should I say, goddess, of my dreams was five people ahead of me in the other registry line. I willed her to turn her head so I could get a full glimpse of her loveliness. It took at least 10 minutes, but finally she turned to focus on the time on the hall clock.

My heart stopped. She exceeded the image her backside conjured up. Our eyes locked, and she quickly looked away. I knew she would glance once more, if only from curiosity to see if I was still staring at her. As predicted, the goddess focused her soft eyes on my countenance. For lack of imagination, I waved hello and smiled. She gave me back a Hollywood smile of all times. I was feeling like a 7th grader with my first schoolboy crush, clammy, heated and out of whack.

"What's your name," I said in more lip synch then vocal. She stated softly, "Suzanne." Suzanne was next in line, so she turned toward the person in the window. This provided me the perfect opportunity to check her out. Suzanne was honey colored with long straight chestnut hair that rested on her shoulders. She had it parted in the middle. I noticed before she turned that it framed her arresting face, making her even more striking. It was plain that she worked out because, though thin, she was very tone and quite shapely. Suzanne was a tall woman. *In fact, she would give me a run for my money,* I thought. She had to be pushing 5' 10". She made other women on campus fade in comparison.

While most were wearing jeans and sweatshirts, Suzanne was adorned with designer attire. She was refined and casually chic. She had on a mini black wool skirt that showed off her long legs and classic black high-heeled boots. She wore a black and cream herringbone wool jacket with a bright red scarf and matching red leather gloves. Suzanne wore simple, but real gold jewelry. She had black sunglasses resting on top of her head, and her makeup was perfectly applied. She seemed more ready for a fashion runway than classes. *Lenora was good-looking, but Suzanne was the total package.* Suzanne had 'blue blood' racing through her veins. Most men would have found her enormously intimidating, but not me. If one thing I learned on the streets, it's that you go for what you want, and let nothing stand in your way. "The rest of the world be damned," I unconsciously murmured licking my lips. I wanted her in the worst kind of way, and I intended to have her. It was that simple.

Suzanne knew I was still checking her out, because when she was finished registering she turned and faced me with a brilliant smile, waving good-bye. I stood there mesmerized as she floated down the hall. "Wait, Suzanne!" I said louder than intended. No woman had ever walked away from me. I was floored. I dared not get out of line because it took me an hour to get to this point. Now the line was around the corner. This was the last day to register for classes. I stood there helpless, without comprehension. *No one passes up the great Jack Baker.*

Once Lenora and I broke up, I became the best-known ladies' man on campus. It didn't matter the race either. I didn't let a little thing like that deny them of my pleasures. Some of my friends, or should I say Jack's buddies, thought I had lost my mind. I think they ridiculed me partly from jealousy. I wasn't even an athlete and was able to get so much 'play.' I didn't really care what they thought. *There was nothing better than sex to relieve class pressures and help with the adjustment to my new environment.* Some things just don't change. *I have always enjoyed good sex,* I thought with a devious grin. And there was lots of it on this campus. Yale was a gold mine. There were so many 'intellectuals' at Yale; most women were deprived of a 'real' man to satisfy them. *I owe it to them,* I decided, laughing to myself about my analysis of the situation.

After registering for class, I went back to the dorm room to call Dirk. Dirk and I talked at least once a month. We also caught up around Christmas. Papa and I even attended his family's Christmas Eve dinner. I knew it meant a lot to Papa. At first, Papa appeared uncomfortable because of his surroundings, but he soon got over it. Dirk had the nicest family. One of his sisters was a bit of an elitist, but we generally ignored her. I warned Papa ahead of time. Dirk's parents were delightful and made us immediately feel at ease.

I got back to the room and found Chuck already hitting the books. I flopped on his bed. "What's up man?" Chuck said in his nerdy, but attempting to be cool voice. "Chuck, I'm in love," I responded in a dreamy voice. "Yeah, right," he said turning back to his books. "Jack, this must be woman number ten in a matter of days. I thought you really had something to discuss," he said with agitation. "I'm telling you, man," I said, slightly irritated myself, "I've found 'the' woman. I plan to marry her." That got his attention. He faced me once more, this time with a bit more inquisitiveness.

"Where did you meet her?"

"At the registrar's office when I was signing up for classes."

"What's her name?"

"Suzanne."

"Suzanne what, Jack?"

"That's just it. I don't know."

"You don't know. I thought you said you met her."

"I did, sort of."

Chuck repeated my words "sort of," rolled his eyes and turned to face the desk once more. It was clear he was exasperated with me. I picked up the phone, ready to call Dirk to tell him about my new love interest when Chuck interrupted me. "Wait a minute, Jack. You're not talking about Suzanne Montgomery?!" "What does she look like?" I asked. Chuck described the exact woman of interest, except with a little less fanfare. "That's her!" I was thrilled to no end that, now, I knew her full name. It meant I could gather further details on her. Most of all, I would be able to locate her on campus. Maybe I could hang outside her dorm until I got the digits.

Chuck looked at me as if I had just been released from an insane asylum. "Jack, have you lost your mind? You are way out of your league with that one. I know you think you're 'The Man' on campus, but Suzanne is on another level. Do you know who her father is? Have you taken a look at that woman?" Chuck was talking incessantly. I waited patiently. He went on, "Plus, from what I hear, she only goes for athletes and people of the same social circle." I listened very intently, not swayed from my earlier position. Indeed, it made me want her more. *All my life, I was a kid living on the outside.* When I was brought into Dirk's world, I realized even more how 'outside' I was to those who were in. *It would be splendid to have a possession of 'their' world so early in my career.* I was determined to one day live like them. Having the mate by my side would complete the picture.

"Chuck, who is her father, and what does he do?" I asked in a sedate voice. Chuck continued to stare at me is if I were nuts. Finally determining I was earnest about pursuing her, he said, "Jack, I know you're sincere here, but my advice to you is to let it go." "Chuck, you didn't answer my question. I want to know everything about her," I said, trying to keep my annoyance in check. I wanted the information requested and anything else he knew about her. Seeing that I was not going to back off, he gave in. "Jack, this is what I know." Chuck sighed heavily before continuing. "Suzanne's father is one of the biggest trial attorneys in the country, black or white. His name is Clayton Montgomery. He is larger than life. Her family is one of the wealthiest in Atlanta.

"They are 'old' Negro money. Montgomery wealth stems from real estate and banking. There was a time when most of Atlanta's black elite got their start from borrowing money from the Montgomery's. Clayton Montgomery is well connected politically and quite ruthless, except, of course, when it comes to his only child, Suzanne. Suzanne is a second-semester freshman. My girlfriend knows her and says she's a snob. I think she is majoring in psychology. That's all I know."

Chuck sat there waiting for my response to his revelations. I gave none. He eventually returned to his books. I decided to call Dirk later. "Thanks, man," I said as I closed the door behind me. I went to grab some food from the cafeteria before it closed. The stroll to the cafeteria gave me ample opportunity to mull over Chuck's bio of Suzanne and strategize my next moves. From the stats on her, this wasn't going to be an ordinary score. As I sat there eating my hamburger and fries, it came to me. *I need to drop one of my classes and pick up a freshman psychology class. I'd better get back to the registrar's office before it closed.* I hurried out the cafeteria toward Keaton Hall.

. . .

As Suzanne left the registrar's office and headed to the bookstore, she said under her breath, "He's cute. School might be getting a little more interesting," though she thought she'd better stay more focused than she did last semester. Daddy would not tolerate a repeat of those grades. Even Mother was surprised to see her do so poorly. Mother didn't come down on Suzanne like Daddy though. Daddy expected and demanded more. That was apparent from past experience. *I used to be a fairly good student,* Suzanne reflected. She had let herself get distracted by all the attention of those college men. College guys were so different from high school boys. They were so mature and exquisitely designed.

Suzanne sat on a bench in the courtyard in front of the dorm, eating a tuna sandwich reflecting on her life. Everyone thought she had a perfect life. If they only knew the real deal... Enormous sadness swept over her, so much so, she couldn't explain its depth. All her life, she had been attempting to be this ideal person, and for what? So that Mother would love her? She thought about her childhood, and the tears began.

Suzanne had spent most of her time growing up in Atlanta's Cobb County elite black society with her mother. Daddy was gone much of the time. He was working late, traveling or helping a local politician strategize his or her campaign. Politics was Daddy's passion. He often did side legal work for local politicians, sometimes as a favor. But the most joyous times were the rare times when he was home. Daddy was her best friend in the whole world. When he would come home, he would squat down and hold out his arms for her to run into them. "Come here, my darling Suzanne," he would say in his soothing strong baritone voice. She would race to his arms, and he would pick her up and swirl her around. Mother would just stand in the backdrop, watching with a solemn expression. Suzanne didn't care. She was happy. Daddy and she delighted in each other, and that was all that mattered.

After long trips, Daddy would bring her back a present. They were expensive gifts too, like expensive porcelain dolls when she was little and gold jewelry as she got older. One day, she noticed that he never bought anything home for Mother. That day, she thought over the years, this may be the reason for their strained and deteriorating relationship. It seemed to be less of a marriage and more of a union of duty that took more effort as the years went by. She remembered sinking into guilt for getting a gift when Mother didn't.

One day, Daddy and she had been sitting in front of the fireplace in his study. He was in a wingback chair reading the newspaper. Suzanne was sitting on the floor at his feet drinking hot chocolate that her nanny, Reba, had prepared. The fire's flames and the heat given off by its glow spellbound Suzanne. She was seven. Mother had gone to a women's conference in North Carolina for the weekend. "Daddy, do you love Mommy?" she asked out of the blue, looking up at him in earnest. He cleared his throat, "Of course I do, darling. Why do you ask?" "Because I saw the Williams kiss in the kitchen the other night when you and Mother had them over for dinner. I never see you two do that. Plus, you don't hug her, Daddy, like you do me," she said with sadness trailing through her voice. Daddy just picked her up off the floor with unusual sobriety. He kissed her on the forehead and left the room.

When Suzanne was fourteen, Mother took her to a school soccer game. Mother was in a rare light mood. "Are you ready, Suzanne? You look awfully pretty – maybe a little too nice for a soccer game though," she joked, but was partially sincere. Suzanne had spent a lot of time curling her hair, and it cascaded down her back. She had also had started wearing makeup. Mother often had something critical to say, even when she complimented her daughter. Suzanne ignored the remarks, just glad to see her mother in a good mood. Instead, she replied, "Mama, you look quite ravishing yourself." Mother was pleased with the compliment. She was a dazzling woman. All of Suzanne's friends would comment on how pretty her mother was. Mother said, still glowing from the remark, "Thank you, Suzanne. I'm just trying to keep up with my daughter's magnetic charms." Suzanne knew she meant it. She ignored her mother's last statement so she wouldn't be affected before the game and waited to get out of the car. Mother usually had a way of changing her mood for the worse, but it wasn't going to be that way today.

As Suzanne opened the front door, Mother reached for her daughter's necklace. Suzanne had meant to take it off. Mother held it in her hands feeling its grooves, "This is exquisite, Suzanne. Is it one of your father's gifts?" Suzanne nodded, looking down. "It must be nice to be loved so and to receive such beautiful things," she said in a willowy tone, a smirk crossing her face. The necklace was one of Suzanne's favorite gifts from her daddy. It was a gold chain, with an open gold heart dangling from the bottom. She didn't comment. No need to fan the fire. Now Suzanne felt bad. They said little on the ride to the soccer field. Mother pulled up next to Suzanne's friend Marsha's car and let Suzanne out. "Have a good game," she said in a flat voice, looking straight ahead. "Thanks for the ride, Mom," Suzanne said, slamming the car door. She ran toward the field to find Marsha and the rest of the soccer team.

The relationship became even more strained, as Suzanne got older. Her mother seemed to want to antagonize her at every possible opportunity. "I love you, Mother, even if you don't feel the same," she remembered thinking on several occasions. It was a solemn existence. It seemed that the more Suzanne matured, the angrier Mother became. For Suzanne, it was a mountain of frustration and rejection. She wanted to ask her mother, "Don't you realize I want more than anything to share these times with you? I need you, Mom!" Instead, she went quietly, painfully from girlhood to womanhood without her mother's assistance. Her mother wanted little to do with her, and Suzanne resigned herself to accepting that. She didn't have much choice. At the time, she didn't – couldn't - realize it was because her beauty was blossoming, while time was starting to take a toll on Mother's beauty. It was all out competition, or at least it was for Mother.

By the time Suzanne turned sixteen, her mother had started competing for her boyfriends' attention. She also didn't want her daughter to have close friends. Suzanne found it harder to respect her mother, given her behavior. *She was more like a rival than a parent. It was ridiculous.* When Suzanne was in the last semester of her senior year of high school, she had her two best friends over. They were having fun figuring out what to wear for the prom. It was only a week away. Suzanne had never had too many friends growing up, so this afternoon was particularly special. Mother made it a point to make Roslyn and Shelby feel ill at ease. She followed the girls from room to room, asking a lot of questions. Suzanne knew her mother was trying to uncover something wrong with her friends so she could justify having Suzanne later break off the relationships. It was as if her mother didn't want her daughter's friendship, but she didn't want anyone else to be close to her either. Luckily, Suzanne had warned her friends at lunch the day before about how her mother might act. They shrugged their shoulders in defiance. "How strange," Roslyn said as she plopped grapes in her mouth.

Both Roslyn and Shelby were new to Cobb County. They transferred into Suzanne's school during the eleventh grade. Roslyn had moved to town from Washington, D. C. Her parents had divorced, and her mom wanted a fresh start. Shelby had transferred from another private school in Athens, Georgia. Shelby's family relocated when her dad accepted the position of Senior Vice President of Marketing with IBM's Global Consulting Group. Both were outsiders like Suzanne. The only difference between them and her was that Suzanne had been going to the school since seventh grade. Roslyn and Shelby were exceptionally attractive and 'en vogue' women. Therefore, there was none of the jealousy Suzanne usually experienced with other girls. Neither taunted her with 'Little Rich Girl' or 'you think you're better than the rest of us' as she walked down the hall. They didn't mock her or survey her outfits either, and Suzanne had many outfits.

In sophomore year, Suzanne had tried to befriend a new girl named Rhonda, but it seemed Rhonda's sole mission at school was to destroy Suzanne. *What Suzanne did to make this girl hate her so, God only knew?* She was accepted to Ursula on an academic scholarship. Suzanne had been elated when her Biology teacher introduced Rhonda to the class. She came into the school mid-year because of a mix up in her paperwork. It was clear the moment she entered the classroom that she would not pass as 'one of them.' Her hair was somewhat unkempt, and her clothes were not very tailored. Suzanne thought to herself, *no worry; I will teach you the ways of Ursula.* Suzanne was just overjoyed that someone 'real' had entered her life. She was so tired of the 'counterfeit' girls of Ursula. *They were cultured, but had spirits of envy and insecurity. They were pretty packages with rocks inside.*

"Hi, my name is Suzanne," Suzanne offered, extending her hand to Rhonda after Biology class. Most people in the class, guys and girls, had walked pass Rhonda without acknowledging her existence. *How totally rude,* Suzanne thought. *So much for cultured politeness.* If anything, a few of the women had made a point to look Rhonda up and down in disdain. Yet Rhonda did the same to Suzanne. She didn't accept her hand either, but said acerbically, "Nice to meet you, Suzanne." She mimicked Suzanne's Southern genteel drawl with a biting edge. Resentment was written all over her face. It was not the kind of begrudging Suzanne was used to getting. Rhonda's stemmed from a total umbrage of what and whom Suzanne represented. It was like she didn't even see Suzanne. All she saw was Suzanne's clothes, her perfectly manicured nails, her cultivated southern dialect and the sprawling house where she grew up. *Was it her fault that those of power and privilege locked out those that were poor?* Suzanne instinctively recoiled from Rhonda for self-protection. They didn't speak again. From that day forward, they were adversaries.

Rhonda ignored Suzanne in class or anywhere else, for that matter. She would look the other way when they passed each other in the hall. Rhonda was the one who coined the phrase 'Little Miss Rich Girl.' She would say it to others in a voice just loud enough for Suzanne to hear as she walked pass. They would all laugh in unison. The phrase spread throughout the school like wildfire. Just about everyone was calling Suzanne that by junior year. Rhonda fed off the envy of other women and the inferior feelings of boys who wanted to date Suzanne, but didn't have the guts to approach. With the addition of Rhonda, Suzanne's life at Ursula had become unbearable. Suzanne honestly believed that Roslyn and Shelby's arrival to

Ursula in her junior year was God's answer to her prayers. *She would not have survived another term with the status quo.*

Suzanne met them both on the first day of class after summer break. Roslyn was in her Calculus class, and Shelby was in her last class of the day, Spanish. Like with Rhonda, Suzanne went up to introduce herself to both of them after class, but with reservation this time. To Suzanne's delight, their reactions were the opposite of Rhonda's. Roslyn welcomed the lunch invitation in the cafeteria the next day. They were sitting there together having lunch when Suzanne spotted Shelby. "Roslyn, do you mind if I invite Shelby over? She's new too." "Not at all," Roslyn responded, "A chance for another new friend." What a difference in attitude, Suzanne thought, recalling Rhonda's behavior. Shelby came over to join them, and from then on they were all best friends. Instead of calling Suzanne 'Little Miss Rich Girl,' schoolmates began calling the three of them 'Charlie's Angels.' Suzanne didn't care. *It was just such a relief to finally have friends.*

Suzanne enjoyed Roslyn and Shelby for different reasons. Roslyn was playful and funny. Suzanne never stopped laughing around her. Roslyn was 5' 3", but she had the posture of someone imposing. She was an absolutely stunning woman with smoldering sensuality. Her ebony skin, voluptuous body and cat hazel-green eyes made her exotic and mysterious. Men fell over backwards just to get near her. She took it all with good humor. Sometimes, she didn't even notice their pursuit. Roslyn was fixated on her studies. Her parents were both doctors. Roslyn's mom was an internist and her father was a cardiologist. She said it was her 'calling' to follow in their footsteps.

Shelby, on the other hand, was the fashion counselor and cosmetologist. School was something to do until she was able to get her M.R.S. degree. Shelby worked hard to obtain acceptance into a good school to substantially enhance her chances of meeting a 'proper' husband. *At least she knew what she wanted. No sense in wasting a lot of time pursuing dreams that don't address your needs,* Suzanne thought in humor. Shelby was Suzanne's guidance counselor through the men process. It was like Shelby was a natural born man magnet and she knew how to easily distinguish from this pool, the real ones from the counterfeits. Unlike Roslyn, whom men often wanted for sex, the men Shelby attracted offered her marriage, the big house and everything that went with it. *And this was while Shelby was in high school!*

Roslyn and Suzanne were determined to learn her secrets. They watched and listened to her in action. *It was amazing.* Suzanne had to admit that Shelby made the most of her toffee colored skin, lithe graceful figure and short, chic mane. She was best described as a natural beauty. Shelby would walk into restaurants and turn men's heads with minimal make up or effort to her appearance. For some reason, all three girls looked and acted way beyond their years. They dated men their age, sometimes older, and sometimes a lot older, unbeknownst to their parents.

It was foreign to Suzanne at first to have two close female friends. It took a little while to trust the situation. These were the only two women she could recall bonding with in her life, except for maybe her grandmothers. *They were too old to count though.* "Thank you, God," Suzanne said lying in bed one night peering out the window at the stars, "I would have been grateful for one friend; instead, you gave me two, Lord." She fell asleep thinking about their planned trip to the mall the next day and the school dance following that night. *Maybe it was better to associate with people who were equal* she contemplated. Roslyn, Shelby and she got along so well because none of them was threatened by the other's good looks, family wealth or smarts. *Each of them had it all, and it worked.*

This principle also seemed to apply to the men she dated. Whenever Suzanne went out with someone outside her socio-economic circle, he was or became intimidated. If it didn't happen right away, it would surely come to a crescendo eventually. His insecurity would come out in various ways. He'd never compliment her afraid she would think she was better than him; act extremely jealous for no justified reason; or date other women to prove his virility. *Obviously Suzanne made them think less of their manhood.* The reason would remain a mystery to her. *It wasn't worth it,* she concluded. She wanted to be treated well like everyone else. In tenth grade, Suzanne resolved to interact only with her 'own kind.' Of course that backfired too. People started labeling her a snob. Yet Suzanne steeled herself to this. Their opinions meant nothing to her. *These were the same people that never spoke to her, wanted her to fail and spread untruths about her to justify their dislike.*

As Suzanne sat on the park bench in front of her dorm, she drifted back to the memory of that dreadful day a week before prom night. There she sat on the warm wooden college bench feeling such emotional pain her body physically shrank in response. It was exactly one week before her prom when her life spiraled out of control. *Nothing had been the same since.* The day began with Roslyn and Shelby coming over so they could all go shopping for prom dresses. They were in a panic because the prom was just a week away and none of them had anything to wear.

Suzanne wanted to make sure she looked especially ravishing, because she had been asked by the biggest 'catch' at school. Bobby Tate, was the school's quarterback and absolutely sumptuous, with bulging muscles and buns to match. Every girl in the school was green-eyed with envy when they heard the news of his selection. She didn't want him to regret having asked her. Plus, Suzanne knew people would be watching them intently that night. *Bobby had been the one that introduced her to the wickedly enticing world of jocks she became so addicted to later in life.* She learned that athletes have egos the size of rich boys' egos, maybe even larger. They also could handle her very well. She was proof of their masculinity and prowess. *Testosterone must do something to the brain,* she thought. Whatever it was, she liked it.

Roslyn and Shelby came over to Suzanne's house. Shelby agreed to drive her new silver Honda Civic to the mall. They decided to splurge for the occasion and go to the exclusive Phipps Plaza in Buckhead where all the major designer shops were housed. It was a distance away, but worth the extra drive.

"Sometimes, you have to make sacrifices to get the right effect," Suzanne said to Shelby and Roslyn, persuading them it was worth the extra effort. They all giggled at her weak argument. They all had credit cards, so none of them were too worried about price. *What could their parents really say? It was the prom, for goodness sake.*

Daddy was supposed to be on an extended business trip with a gentleman named Clyde Harris. Mr. Harris was running for mayor in Macon, Georgia. If elected, he would be their first black mayor. Daddy had made trips down there before to help Mr. Harris get elected. Lately, he seemed to be making quite a few of them. Daddy would sometimes be gone the entire weekend. Suzanne didn't care much. While it was great to spend time with Daddy, to be honest, she was preoccupied with her own life. Between dating guys, hanging out with Roslyn and Shelby and school activities, she had precious little time. That might have helped her relationship with her mother. They were out of each other's way.

It was early evening by the time they left the mall. It was a hard long day of shopping. The day was quite fruitful and they were basking in the results of their efforts. Shelby bought a strapless turquoise-green satin dress that was fitted closely at the waist and showed off her size 4-figure. Suzanne bought a red silk 'number.' It had a daringly low V in the back that was lined with rhinestones. The front was a halter and it sparkled throughout. *Daddy would kill her when he saw it on her.* Seductive didn't begin to describe this evening dress. She probably wouldn't have been daring enough to buy it if the girls hadn't urged her on. Besides, she thought, *I'm not dressing for Daddy. I'm dressing for Bobby Tate and to give all the catty women something worth being green over.* Roslyn's dress was the simplest, but she didn't need much help from a dress with curves like hers. The gown was black with spaghetti straps. The top half was silk and the bottom was made out of folds of chiffon. They were all very pleased. They had even had time to purchase the accessories, including matching shoes.

They were in the east parking lot heading toward Shelby's car, laughing about the reactions they expected from their parents when they saw the outfits, when Suzanne spotted him. At first, she didn't want to believe her eyes. She froze in her tracks. Her bags fell to the ground as her hands went limp. Roslyn and Shelby kept talking and giggling; unaware that Suzanne was not with them any longer. Eventually they stopped and turned to find Suzanne's unmoving frame with her mouth draped open. "Girl, why are you way back there and looking like that?" Roslyn hollered, looking concerned. Shelby also gazed upon Suzanne anxiously. Shelby touched Roslyn's arm and they both went back to Suzanne with perplexed expressions draping their faces. "What's wrong, Suzanne?" Shelby said once they were close. Suzanne was too numb to answer. Almost in unison, their eyes followed her gaze. Suzanne's father was closing the door of a two-door, red Mercedes. The car must have been his companion's because it was unfamiliar. "Why is he driving that car?" Suzanne wondered out loud in a daze of apparent confusion. The convertible top had been lowered, so the woman he had just let into the car was in clear view. *She was definitely not her mother,* Suzanne noted in utter disbelief. She searched wildly for some explanation, other than the obvious.

Suzanne tried her best to assume the unknown woman might be a colleague her father had met for a late dinner. It was a story she was prepared to live with until she saw him passionately kiss the woman on the lips. Their faces lingered a bit before he reached for his seat belt. As their lips unlocked, the woman affectionately held the side of his face with a degree of ownership that couldn't be mistaken. Shelby and Roslyn put their hands on Suzanne's shoulders for support. "That's not my mother," Suzanne said, speaking the obvious. "Maybe there's an explanation we don't know about," Roslyn said lamely, "Don't jump to conclusions Suzanne." Shelby chimed in, hoping to contain a situation no one could control. "It could be a cousin you're unfamiliar with, Suzanne." Neither was convincing, but Suzanne was touched that they were trying their best to spare her of this impossible situation.

Leaving her packages on the ground where they fell, Suzanne almost ran to the car where her father and the woman sat. The ignition of the car was turning over when he looked over at Suzanne rapidly approaching. His face grew stiff and he shut off the car. Daddy was out of the vehicle. He met up with her just before she reached the targeted destination. Daddy grabbed her arms. She was not aware she had raised them as if ready to swing. "Suzanne, what are you doing here?" He was talking low, so no one surrounding the situation would be able to hear him. Suzanne didn't care. *Etiquette be damned.*

She screamed, "Who is she, Daddy?" Her arms were trying to swing at him. He firmly held both wrists in a fierce grip. "Suzanne, calm down. Making a scene in a mall parking lot does no one any good," Daddy said in a voice that was desperately trying to pacify, but falling way short. "Daddy how could you? How could you cheat on Mama like this, in our own town?!" Tears were streaming down her face with no end in sight. She was wailing hysterically. Roslyn and Shelby remained in the background near her packages, alarm written on their pretty faces. They were too astute to interfere in a family matter.

The woman remained in the car observing the scene with fear and regret for being the center of what was transpiring between a father and his daughter. She was a magnificent looking woman. She was a mixture of black and Asian. Her shiny jet-black hair cascaded in curls. Her Asian shaped eyes were like expressionless pieces of glass in her cocoa brown face. The woman could not have been more than five to ten years Suzanne's senior. She was aghast that her father could be dating someone young enough to be her sister. It only served to add fuel to the fire. Once her father released her arms, Suzanne quickly moved to dodge her father and headed straight to the car. "Leave my Daddy alone, you bitch!" she yelled at the top of her lungs to the woman in the car. She didn't know whether her rage was more from the betrayal of her mom, the shattering of their 'Brady Bunch' family picture she had conjured up in her mind, or knowing that she might not be the center of Daddy's world any longer. She was confused and mortally wounded.

Her father stepped in front of Suzanne, blocking her view of the woman she later found out was named Naomi. His voice was now threatening. She had never heard Daddy speak to her in that manner. It made the hairs on the back of her neck stand on edge. "Suzanne," he said with a long drawl, "I want you to stop making a scene in front of your friends and the world. I want you to let them take you home. I promise I will meet you at the house later, so we can talk." He grabbed her shoulders and squeezed them, looking deep into her eyes. Daddy was sterner than any time she could remember. He was a private man, so she knew he must be livid about her actions. *What did he expect?* However, the mention of her friends was sufficient to assemble some sense of self-control. *Who knew where that control came from?*

Suzanne shook Daddy's hands from her shoulders, straightened her posture and wiped her tears. "I hate you. People used to tease me at school, saying you were a womanizer, but I always defended you. I thought they were just jealous of your love for me. Now I know they were telling the truth. Do you know what a fool I feel like right now?" She spat the words at her father with pure venom. She could not see the woman, but Suzanne could hear her moan from her statements. That gave her limited satisfaction. Clayton Montgomery looked like Suzanne had just plunged a knife into his chest. He lowered his eyes to hide the agony. "Go home, Suzanne. You're only making this worse. No matter what has happened or what I have done, I do love you." She strained to hear him, but comprehended his words. Her daddy went to the convertible driver's seat and got into the vehicle. Suzanne stared at the woman, but the woman did not meet her gaze. Her father started the car and sped away.

Suzanne stood there, mortified. Shelby and Roslyn picked up her packages and came to her. Something had died within her that day. The belief in her father, the belief he loved her above everything, the reference point defining who she was in the world. *It was all gone.* Nothing would be the same thereafter. Roslyn looked her squarely in the face, "Are you okay, Suzanne?" She nodded yes. "It will be alright. Suzanne, I'm so sorry you're going through this," Shelby said in the most compassionate voice. Suzanne responded forthrightly, "I know you are, Shelby, but it won't be okay. Can you drop me home? It's been a long day." Her voice was lifeless. She was utterly drained.

It made it that much worse that Suzanne had thrown such a fit in front of her 'girls.' As they headed toward Shelby's car, she said, "I feel bad you two witnessed all that." They hugged Suzanne simultaneously. Roslyn was the first to speak, "Suzanne, believe me, I have seen worse. In fact, I have been the one in the center of the drama. I was dating two guys, and one of them busted me cheating with the other." She stopped and put her hands on her hips for effect, "Honey child, it was UGLY." They laughed in unison. "You will look back on this one day and know that you have become a stronger woman because of it," Shelby said, sobering them up. Suzanne knew she was correct, but she didn't want to hear that now. They drove home in silence. Suzanne got out of the car and climbed the steps of her palatial residence with dread and misery.

As Suzanne was walking up the steps to the front door, she stopped and waved goodbye to her two best friends. After that, Suzanne went into full hibernation, missing her prom and nearly her graduation. It was a very dark time in her life.

Suzanne entered the house still quite unraveled from earlier events. She quickly said hi to Mother and ascended the steps to her room. Suzanne must have been a mess because her mother asked what was wrong. "Nothing," she said, as she continued her hurried climb. Suzanne knew her mother wouldn't follow after her because she hated 'messy' situations. *Mother would avoid anything that didn't match her facade of a 'pristine' life.* True to this, her mother never knocked on her door.

Daddy kept to his word and arrived home approximately an hour after Suzanne. She was up in her room when she heard him pull into the driveway. Shortly after Suzanne heard the house front door open and then close. Daddy's footsteps were soon near her room. There was a tap on Suzanne's bedroom door. She thought, *I used to love those taps on my door growing up. It meant Daddy would be reading me a story or just saying he loved me before I dozed off to sleep. They were the good times.* "Come in," she said unenthusiastically. Her father tentatively poked his head in her room and gingerly entered. Suzanne was curled up against the headboard holding a pillow. The yellow room always gay and bright, now appeared gloomy. Daddy came over and pulled the desk chair by her bed to face her. He plopped down on the seat as if he were going on eighty. "How are you, Suzanne?"

"How do you think I am Daddy?" she responded caustically.

"I regret what I put you through today. I regret so many things," he said, pleading forgiveness with his eyes. Suzanne looked away, "Daddy, it is a little late for apologies, don't you think?"

"I guess that's true," he said with his shoulders slumped in defeat. His face told the story of his little girl dissipating from his grasp right in front of his eyes.

They sat there awkwardly sensing the broken bond. It was like a close partnership that had turned sour. "Suzanne, I would do anything to set things right with you. You are my world." Suzanne interrupted, "Daddy, I certainly wasn't your world today, was I?" She knew she was hurting him. She didn't want to because she loved him more than life itself. Yet Suzanne couldn't resist the need to make him pay for the enormous suffering and burden his actions had brought. She hadn't made up her mind as to whether to tell mother. Just as she was mulling it over, her father yanked that quandary from her.

"Suzanne, to say you are the apple of my eye would be an understatement. I've adored you from the first time I laid eyes on you. Those big, lucid eyes of yours gazed up at me and tugged at my heart and made me captive. There is still nothing I wouldn't do to ensure your happiness, well-being and security." He got up and paced the floor. Her father stopped and put his hands in his pocket, gazing at her with reflective eyes, "Suzanne, a man passes through this world only once and deserves some happiness, too.

"I cannot live for you forever, Suzanne. Indeed, you have your own life now. It's time we both seek happiness. Please forgive me for what I'm about to do. I hope someday you will understand and exonerate me." Without saying another word, her father rose and quietly left the room. Suzanne ran to the door and called after him to no avail. There was a foreboding knot in her stomach that told the story before it ever happened. Suzanne left the door ajar and waited for events to unfold.

Daddy and Mama were screaming at each other in a way she had never witnessed before. Mother must have been throwing things at Daddy because Suzanne heard glass crashing against the walls and loud thumps pounding the floor. Suzanne returned to her bed and curled up. She couldn't stand it any longer. She placed her hands over her ears. *Why, Daddy, why did you have to go and ruin things? Couldn't you have waited until I went off to school?* Instinctively, Suzanne knew the answer to that question. If she had not run into him in the parking lot he probably would have done so.

The arguing stopped. Suzanne heard the front door slam. She ran to her bedroom window to see Daddy getting back into his black Navigator and slamming the door shut. He backed down the driveway and accelerated so rapidly the car screeched before disappearing into the horizon. *If I did not know it was my mother, I would have thought a wild animal was trapped and maimed downstairs*, Suzanne thought. The wailing got louder and louder until it reached a climax. Suzanne raced down the steps and once at the bottom, saw Mother sitting on a foyer chair leaning forward and clutching her chest with both hands. Her mother's hair was unruly and her makeup was a mess. All colors on her face appeared to flow into each other in a wet array. Suzanne had never seen mother so out of order.

"Mother," she whispered, gently touching her shoulder. Suzanne was afraid to speak in a normal tone of voice. She thought it might shatter her mother's fragile frame. Her mother did not acknowledge her. Suzanne repeated her words a little more forcefully this time and shook Mother slightly. Her mother appeared to have slipped into another world. Mother was whimpering now. She dabbed at her eyes with a crumbled piece of tissue. Then she unexpectedly began talking. It was like she was speaking out loud to herself because she never gave evidence that Suzanne had entered the room.

"You know, he only married me because of you." She then peered at Suzanne for the first time through squinted eyes. Suzanne barely recognized her mother with the contorted expression draping her face. "I thought he was going to let me live in disgrace. In those days, an unmarried pregnant woman was no more than a tramp, particularly a woman of my social status. My father would have disowned me. However, in the end, Clayton did the honorable thing and took me as his bride." Suzanne noticed her mother stopped rocking.

"He never loved me. I tried my best to pretend he did, to make him a good wife. I thought, if I achieved that, he would grow to cherish me. Yet nothing I did was good enough." Mother was lost in reflection as she continued, "And then you were born. Clayton and my relationship would have never made it if it weren't for you. I despised you for it. You stole his heart the minute he laid eyes on you, Suzanne." Mother gazed at Suzanne with a familiar iciness that abruptly made sense. "You had achieved in a mere moment, what I tried to for over two years and could not achieve. You favored me, yet he never saw it. He would tell people that you resembled his mother. What was so wrong with me that he couldn't even concede his child at least had his wife's looks?

"Most men greatly admired my beauty. He did during our yearlong courtship. However, that was before I became pregnant. Your father accused me of attempting to trap him. He planned to attend law school up East, either Yale or Harvard. Instead, Clayton had to settle for a judicial degree from Emory.

Was that so bad that he had to resent me for the rest of our married life?" Mother broke down with emotion once more. Suzanne was speechless from the revelations. It was more information than she could handle, yet she couldn't get enough.

After a brief pause, Mother continued reminiscing. Suzanne leaned forward, straining to capture every word. Mother's voice was always mellow. Now it was barely audible. Suzanne was determined to make sense of her words, vowing not to miss anything. She felt like a person eavesdropping into another's conversation, too riveted by the story to do the right thing and walk away. *Mother was surely having a private discussion with herself.* Suzanne was just the topic of interest.

"Clayton's politeness in our marriage only made matters worse. Politeness to me was in stark contrast to the way his eyes lit up when he greeted you coming home. I received a dutiful kiss on the cheek, if he remembered. It was always after he twirled you around in the air and gave you pony rides. It made me rancid inside."

Her mother didn't bother to look at Suzanne this time. She just kept rambling. "Yet, Clayton wasn't totally blind to women. The times we shared activities together, mainly for business or political social appearances, he made little effort to conceal his interest in other women. He flirted with just about every attractive woman in sight. The reactions he'd get from these women were no less inviting. Who could resist the irresistible Clayton Montgomery? I ignored his womanizing for years and for what? I'll tell you what, to now be made a laughing stock of Georgian society!" Mother found some more tissue lying on the coffee table and dabbed her eyes frantically.

"I knew one day he would fall in love with one of those sluts. Actually, I saw the signs months ago. Like most women desperately holding onto her lifeline, I ignored them. He'll never leave me, I told myself. I didn't calculate into the equation that my 'secret weapon' was all grown up." Her mother's back stiffened. She stared at Suzanne with vacant eyes. "Clayton tells me you met her. That probably triggered the chain of events or at least sped up the process. What's she like, Suzanne?" Suzanne stood there pulling on one of the maroon and cream stripe silk pillow tassels earlier lying on the velvet chaise lounge. She tugged at the tassel nervously, unwilling to hurt mother anymore. *How do you reveal that the woman your father was leaving her for was an exotic beauty close to Suzanne's age?* It would be like punching a person in an open, bleeding wound. She couldn't do it. She refused to do it. Suzanne made no visible recognition of her mother's question.

It was clear mother wasn't going to give up that easily. Mother repeated her words, more vocal this time. The pleading was replaced by a command, "Suzanne, tell me about her. I want to know everything, how she looks; her age, what she was doing with my husband when you ran upon them. I need to know." Mother could be unyielding when she wanted to, Suzanne recalled with mixed emotions. She knew if she were in her shoes she'd want to know as well. *I owe it to Mother,* Suzanne surmised. She recapped the day's events and gave Mother a full description of the 'other' woman. Suzanne's worst fears were realized. The depiction of her rival only served to make Mother hysterical again. Her mother reacted most fierce when she disclosed the age of Daddy's mistress.

$$\cdots$$

Daddy moved in with Naomi the very next day. Suzanne's world was turned upside down in a weekend. She avoided all calls from Roslyn and Shelby. As much as she cared for them, Suzanne couldn't handle their inquisitions or even words of comfort. She recoiled to her room, only eating when absolutely necessary. The pretense that Suzanne lived in a tranquil home was forever shattered. The only good that came out of this nightmare was the realization that mother's resentment of her had more to do with Daddy's love for her than who she was as a person. It was consoling, but had minimal effect on their relationship. Mother and she remained on tense terms. However, they did gain a deeper understanding of each other. They also shared the experience of being deserted by Daddy.

Daddy and Suzanne saw each other at least once a week. Yet it was not the same. He would pick her up on Saturday morning and they would go shopping, to a movie and/or dinner. Neither one of them mentioned Naomi. This made it awkward between them because they both knew she was looming in the distance. It was like having an elephant sitting in your living room; you're hosting a tea party and pretending it isn't there. Suzanne still loved her father, but she had lost respect for him. *How could he be so selfish?*

Just before Suzanne went off to Yale orientation, Daddy dropped the bomb on her. They were at a small café called "Breezes" not too far from the house. Suzanne was sipping on a Coke and eating vanilla ice cream when Daddy disclosed the plan. "Honey, there is something I have to tell you," Daddy said with a tone that indicated it was of grave importance. Suzanne put down her spoon and gave him her full attention. "Yes, Daddy," she responded on guard. They were just now at the point of laughing again. Squaring her shoulders, Suzanne urged her father on, "Go ahead and spit it out, Daddy." He placed his hands over hers on the table. "Suzanne, I don't know how to put this, other than to just throw it out there. I plan to marry Naomi. We want to get married on December 20th." Suzanne instinctively pulled her hands away. It felt as if someone had slapped her.

"You have already set the date?" Daddy made no comment. Suzanne continued, "Obviously whether I approve or not means nothing. Daddy, do as you want, you always have anyway." She turned her head away. Suzanne went on, "You know I'll never accept her Daddy. I already have a mother. Plus, she is closer to a sister anyway." The situation was too harrowing to completely digest. Suzanne was being catty and she knew it. She just couldn't resist the temptation. *Maybe I'm being the selfish one*, she pondered for a fleeting moment before brushing the thought aside. *It's my right to be,* she concluded. They sat there, both unwilling to move from their position.

It was clear the good feelings of the day had faded. "Daddy, I'm ready to go home," Suzanne said. Suzanne didn't finish the ice cream she was earlier enjoying so much. Her appetite had evaporated. Her father drove her home with only the music from the radio and their thoughts keeping them company. As Suzanne opened the door, she turned to Daddy unsmiling, "I hope she is worth it Daddy." Suzanne got out of the car and slammed the door behind her. She climbed the house steps without looking back. Daddy took awhile before driving off.

With all the events of late, Suzanne was glad to be going off to school. Yale was as far away from Georgia as she could imagine. She thirsted for a fresh start. *I will miss my 'girls,'* she reflected. Neither one will be close in distance to me once school begins. Shelby was to stay in Georgia and attend Spellman. Roslyn chose to go all the way to California and attend Berkeley. Suzanne teased Shelby, "Are you aiming for a Morehouse man?" "You know it girl," Shelby said, smiling broadly. The three of them burst out laughing. *I will miss them terribly,* she mused once more. *At least we had time to spend together the summer prior to school starting, that is, once I was able to get my 'act' together.* They agreed to stay in close communication. Indeed, they would remain her dearest friends for life.

Suzanne's first time on Yale's campus was the last time Mother and Daddy were together. Mama drove her up to Connecticut. Daddy took a flight a few days later and met them up there. Mother and Suzanne took turns taking over the wheel. It was actually a pleasant ride. Once Daddy had finally left Mother, it was like there was no longer a reason to keep Suzanne at bay. Mother let down her guard and tried to reach out to Suzanne. Her mother also knew she was all she had left and that was short-lived. They stopped at restaurants, went shopping and sightseeing in Washington D. C. and New York before reaching their final destination. It was a costly adventure, but Mother was definitely not one of those soon-to-be divorced women that had to worry about finances. Daddy agreed to give her the house and an alimony most workingwomen couldn't dream of earning. Suzanne determined it was his way to assuage his guilt. Whatever the reason, Suzanne was glad he would take care of her.

At the time when Suzanne said goodbye to Mother, she didn't know it would be one of the last times she would see her in her right mind. Mother slowly disappeared into a world of fantasy no one else could enter. Suzanne said goodbye to the physical being that day, but the mental and emotional beings of Mother were fleeing as well.

• • •

Yale was an adjustment for Suzanne. The change was as much to do with her family life as being so far away and at a new school. Her dorm mate was actually very nice. She was a brunette; average looking white girl from upstate New York named Rebecca. Rebecca was one of those 'deep-thinkers,' planning to save the world. Suzanne had to admit that half the time she didn't know what her roommate was talking about or why she felt so passionately involved. *It was not like she was ever poor, gay or even a minority.* Because of this, they didn't click at first. Eventually they learned to respect each other's views and enjoy their time together. Rebecca was at least a person she trusted. *That means a lot these days,* Suzanne mused. However, neither one of them spent much time in the room, making time spent together sparse.

Suzanne decided to major in psychology and minor in French. She dreamed of going to Paris one day. Mother had offered to let her travel for a year in Europe before going to school, but she was ready to begin rewriting the pages of her life. She declined. Suzanne majored in psychology to figure herself out as much as anything else. She was experiencing mood swings and bouts of depression. She planned to counsel troubled children once she graduated. Suzanne wanted no one else to experience the stress and alienation she felt growing up, *no one*.

Friends in her life were again limited, she noted. Unlike high school, Suzanne didn't reach out to anyone. She was too busy trying to find herself to worry about knowing anyone else. Suzanne had a few friends though. *Why they chose to be apart of my life only God knows,* she first contemplated. She figured out they were more interested in being 'seen' with her than befriending her. She was surprised to learn people knew of her father. They'd ask Suzanne how it felt to have such a powerful dad. Unbeknownst to her, Daddy had several highly publicized murder cases under his belt. He was famous. His wealth was also public knowledge. To her, he was Daddy. She never imagined Daddy could be anything more than that. She also knew the women that 'hung' around her greatly admired her style and the numerous men she attracted. These women reminded Suzanne of paparazzi rather than buddies. Yet she didn't care. *She was glad to be surrounded by persons to ward off the loneliness and feelings of despair.* She became promiscuous on campus to achieve the same.

Suzanne built a reputation around campus that was not for the faint at heart. Like she had done during her last year in high school, she dated rich boys and jocks, lots of them. Suzanne honestly enjoyed sex. However, whenever the relationship got close, she would drop him faster than he could say the word 'commitment.' Suzanne just couldn't handle anyone needing anything from her. She didn't feel strong enough to risk more loss in her life. Nor did she trust men. *Just look at what Daddy did...* Her view of men had changed drastically since learning of Daddy's extramarital relationship. She hadn't totally released her resentment towards him either. Daddy came to the university on several occasions during the first semester. Despite herself, Suzanne was elated to see him. They would walk around campus and talk about what was going on with her. Daddy rarely brought up his own life.

On the second occasion Daddy came up, he asked Suzanne if he could bring Naomi next time. She emphatically rejected the idea. Before he left Suzanne said with total sincerity, "Daddy, I don't hate you anymore for your choices. You're happier than I've ever seen you. This makes me happy. I'm just not ready to get to know Naomi. However, I hope to be soon.

I'm sure she is a very nice lady." Daddy stared at Suzanne like she had just given him the matching ticket to a $100 million lottery. He smiled broadly and his eyes twinkled in his handsome face. "Thank you Suzanne." Daddy pulled Suzanne close and gave her a long hug. He kissed her on the forehead. Suzanne nearly purred in response. "For what, Daddy?" she said, suspecting what he was referring to. "For being the special woman you are and for loving me in spite of what I have put you through," he stated with emotion. "Daddy, then we owe each other thanks." They hugged again for a few minutes and let go. Suzanne was surprised to see his eyes moist. "Daddy, if I've never told you this before, you're a superb father. I love you dearly." *She meant every word.*

Suzanne met Naomi during the holiday break. Naomi was indeed a very warm, giving and likable person. Suzanne was instantly drawn to her. She kept her guard as much as possible because she felt betrayal to Mother. They eventually became friends and later confidantes in spite of her efforts. Suzanne never let Mother know about this relationship. *Some things were better left unsaid.*

Mother was getting on with her life or so she thought. *There was no sense in derailing the process.* She was looking fabulous and had actually started doing volunteer work at an underprivileged middle school! Mother had come a long way and Suzanne was extremely proud of her. Their relationship had also evolved in a manner that neither had expected. Mother met Suzanne when she got off the plane and they never stopped talking on the way home. They conversed at least twice a week during the school year. Suzanne concluded that the family was healing. *Maybe what happened was the best thing for all of them,* she ruminated. *It is strange that some things need to be broken before being properly put together.* Suzanne didn't know at the time, Mother's impressive mend was just a facade for her benefit.

• • •

Suzanne was ready to return to school after the Christmas holiday, but it was difficult leaving home. She played 'catch up' with Shelby and Roslyn during the break. It was like coming home to sisters. They spent a lot of time together during the holidays. It felt like she was putting her feet back into old comfortable slippers. *Everything felt good again.* Both friends noted she looked terrific. They also said it was nice to see her smile once more. Suzanne couldn't help but agree. Shelby and Roslyn looked fabulous as well. Shelby had lightened her hair to a reddish-brown color and Roslyn had put on five pounds, but still had a figure to stop traffic. They were all adjusting to the schools of choice. Roslyn said she met the man of her dreams a month before the break. His name was Ziare. They hung on to her every word as she described him. Shelby and Suzanne both felt a little envious, but was elated for her. "Keep us updated, girl," Suzanne said at the end of Roslyn's monologue. Shelby chimed in.

Being back on the 'greens' of Yale was an eerie feeling, Suzanne reflected. *Maybe it would've been easier if it were a school she had picked for herself,* she surmised. Instead, it was the dream of Daddy's for her to be there. *I'm now ready to get serious about my classes regardless,* she mused. *Daddy was so disappointed with my grades last semester,* Suzanne recalled, while registering for her current classes. *I'm making other changes as well,* she decided. *No more sleeping around, for one. It has been an empty experience, looking back. I'm not ready for a relationship, but 'bed hopping' is not the answer either.*

In spite of herself, Suzanne did thoroughly enjoy men, she noted, with a seductive smile crossing her countenance. Maybe she would just date and practice abstinence. *That will surely help me focus on my grades, if nothing else,* she thought *The old me would never have walked away from such a 'cutie' like the one at the registrar's office, but the new me is going to be strong.* Suzanne deliberated on her recent actions with a degree of confidence. Her mood lifted as she concentrated on her present goals. The darkness that had set over her from thoughts of her past was now history. She sat on the courtyard bench in front of her dormitory, concluding that *she had to move on with her life.* Suzanne wrapped up the remainder of her sandwich and dusted her skirt off. She was ready to head to her room and start 'cracking' the books.

"Hello pretty lady," he said. Suzanne nearly jumped out of her skin as she looked up to see the provocatively handsome, dark chiseled face with the soft brown eyes from the registrar's office. "Hi," she responded back, feeling nervous, but not sure why. "I see you're alone. Can I sit down?" he said with boldness. *He's obviously sure of himself,* she concluded. Suzanne wondered if he were new to campus or had she been restricting her radar screen to too narrow a range. "The last time I checked, this bench was owned by the university, not me," Suzanne replied mockingly. With that, he smiled in kind and laughed. "I like a woman with a sense of humor and spunk." The chocolate Greek God extended his hand to her, "I didn't get to properly introduce myself at the registrar's office, Jack Baker." She met his firm grip with her own. "Suzanne, Suzanne Montgomery," she said in a faint voice. "It's nice to make your acquaintance, Suzanne." His voice was both charming and seductive and it titillated her senses. He affected her in the most definite way. *Goodness he is beautiful!* Suzanne never imagined he would appear even more delectable up close. However, she recommitted herself to her goals and quickly swept her wicked thoughts aside.

Jack sat down beside her. Neither of them said anything for a few moments. "What year are you in, Suzanne?" he asked. She got the strange feeling that he already knew, but answered him anyway. "I'm a second semester freshman," Suzanne replied, finding her manners. *How could I have been so sarcastic with someone I don't even know,* she mused? "What year are you, Jack?" Suzanne countered. "I'm in my sophomore year," he replied. The conversation went on for a while. Suzanne hadn't been this engaged in a conversation in some time. *He's exciting, sexy, funny and intelligent,* she thought. A huge red flag went up. Suzanne popped up from the bench. "I have to go," she said, trying not to appear anxious. Jack rose as well, "So soon. What's the hurry?" Suzanne lied, "I promised to meet a friend for dinner and I didn't realize the time." "Will I see you again?" he inquired. "I'm sure we will run into each other around campus," she answered evasively, and attempted to walk away. She knew she was really running away inside.

Jack blocked Suzanne's path. Before she could escape, he picked up one of her hands and placed it in both of his. Gazing deep into her eyes he said, "Suzanne, I was hoping to be able to call you." In spite of her better judgment, she gave him her number. Jack called Suzanne that night. Suzanne told Rebecca to say she wasn't there. She regretted her impulsive move. Suzanne really wasn't quite sure why she was ducking him. *The truth be told, I'm scared stiff,* she concluded. *At least I can keep my resolution until the first day of classes,* she decided. Suzanne felt vulnerable and bothered. *Why does he affect me so?* She called Shelby and Roslyn for help to figure things out.

Suzanne thought about Jack as she put on her pajamas. She knew he was not an athlete, even with the well-defined body. He also isn't one of the wealthy guys on campus, as she reflected on his slightly 'offbeat' mannerisms. *Most rich boys wouldn't make such a 'scene' over my looks. They're used to drop-dead gorgeous women. Sleek people are a part of the scenery. They also think of themselves as equally good 'catches.' Suzanne liked the attention,* she decided, as a tingling feeling swept through her body. *So who are you Jack?*

Suzanne started her classes the next day and was taken aback to find Jack in her freshman psychology class. He waved at her as Suzanne went to a seat in the first row. She wanted to be as far away from him as possible. He caught up to her after the class anyway, "Suzanne." She turned around with little choice. "I didn't know you were taking this class, Jack," Suzanne stated with a degree of suspicion. *He registered close to the time she did, but would not have known she was taking the course,* she concluded. "Yeah, I decided that every 'politician' should understand the psychology of his constituents. You remember I told you I was pre-law with the intention of running for office someday," Jack said earnestly. "Yes, I remember you saying that," Suzanne replied.

From then on, Jack made every effort to see or call her. They talked for hours on the phone, mainly about what was going on with her. Suzanne noticed that Jack rarely discussed his life, except as it related to classes. He would also discuss school events, like his run for class president. He became the first African-American student body president Yale ever had. One day on the phone, Suzanne asked him, "Jack, how come you don't mention your family more or talk about life back home?" He got quiet and then answered, "Suzanne, there's nothing really to mention. I told you, I grew up poor, didn't have a mother, and Papa is still in Cleveland. What's to add?" Somehow she felt she was putting him on the spot. He wasn't eager to discuss home life. Since hers was no 'Brady Bunch' experience, Suzanne understood. Suzanne eventually left it alone. She partially attributed his reticence to insecurity due to the contrast in their economic status. Suzanne shrugged off the possibility that there was anything more. She rationalized away the fact that she didn't adhere to her own rule of dating only those from her world. "Jack was different," Suzanne told herself. "He has way too much going for him to ever be intimidated by me."

Jack and Suzanne's relationship advanced in spite of her protest. By the end of the semester, she was captive. Jack obtained a summer job at a law firm in Charlotte, North Carolina, so he could be close to Suzanne in Atlanta. He passed over the firm in New York that had given him an opportunity to intern a year ago, even though they were by far the more prestigious firm. Suzanne was moved. Jack won over both Daddy and Naomi; even Mother was smitten with him. Jack conveyed his interest in political life and from that time forward, Daddy and him were the best of friends. They would sit in Daddy's study and discuss politics for hours on end. By the time they went back to school in the fall, Jack and Suzanne were going 'steady.'

They got engaged in Jack's senior year. He went on to Harvard Law School. Suzanne remained at Yale to complete her degree in child psychology. They called each other faithfully throughout their time apart. The two were married the summer after Suzanne's graduation. They had a small wedding ceremony at Jack's insistence. Shelby and Roslyn were her bridesmaids. Rebecca helped to coordinate the day and Daddy gave her away. Jack's father, three aunts and friend Dirk Patterson, along with several classmates from Yale and Harvard attended. Mother could not attend due to illness, at least that's the reason she stated. Suzanne decided Mother could not bare seeing Daddy with his new wife.

Daddy bought the couple a black Mercedes sedan as a wedding present. He said no 'respectable' attorney would drive anything less. Everyone was duly impressed. Jack was thrilled. It was the happiest day of Suzanne's life. She joined him in Cambridge for his second year of law school. Soon after Jack graduated from Harvard law school, he joined the prestigious Boston firm of Tate & O'Reilly. Suzanne became pregnant with their first child shortly thereafter. They named her Gabriella Marie Montgomery. Marie was for her little sister that she never knew. She died at birth.

Jack had taken the unusual step of taking on her last name instead of Suzanne taking his. He said it was his way of forgetting the past and starting a new life with her. Father was honored and saw it as a chance to keep his 'stamp' on her. Mother and Suzanne both thought it was a little odd, but said nothing. *Whatever Jack wanted to do was fine by her.* Their son, Maxwell John Montgomery was born three years after Gabriella. It was two days after Jack won his first political office seat in the Massachusetts state senate. At age 28, Jack was the youngest state senator Massachusetts had ever had. It was even more remarkable because he was African-American. He worked tirelessly to achieve the first steps on his political journey. Suzanne was always there at his side, campaigning fervently. Jack would often say to Suzanne with a cocky smile, "You're looking at the first African-American president of the United States,

Mrs. Montgomery." She would laugh, but knew he was dead serious. With his first big political win, he was definitely on his way.

Suzanne was so in love with Jack that she thought her heart would burst from the pressure of it all. He literally rocked her world. No man had ever made her feel this way. Her feelings for him only grew stronger after they were married. All their friends and family referred to them as the 'perfect' couple. Indeed, she also viewed her life with him as ideal. Sometimes she would stroll along the beach with their two children near their expansive home on the North Shore and wonder why God had smiled on her so.

Suzanne tried not to notice how things had changed between Jack and she. She also chose to ignore all the rumblings of Jack as a 'womanizer.' However, the more Suzanne reflected on their relationship, she noted that little was that different. She was simply seeing their reality now through plain glasses. *Don't be silly,* she'd convince herself, *Jack and I spent lots of time getting to know each other before walking down the aisle. He loves me,* she'd repeat to herself. *We are perfect for one another. True, things are different since Jack's first State Senate win. It's not the same as compared to when there was only Jack, our one-year old Gabriella and I.* Yet with all the effort Suzanne put in maintaining her picturesque facade, she could no longer ignore the loneliness that once again spread over her like a suffocating blanket.

Chapter 11:

Political Seduction

I entered the chambers of the Massachusetts State Senate feeling all the power and privilege that the body held. I began shaking hands of the key members as if I'd known them my entire life. *I did know them,* I mused confidently. I had studied them as if I were studying for the World Chess Championship. I willed myself to recall each data point as I looked upon the elderly, distinguished faces. Every media article detailing my campaign 'upset' mentioned my age. *However, the only 'upset' for me,* I reflected with a degree of cockiness, *was that I didn't win with a wider margin. With all the time, energy and strategy that went into my campaign, I should have won hands down. Yet a win is a win in politics,* I thought, pressing my chest out ever so slightly. I straightened and smoothed my tie as though preparing for battle and headed into the crowd of political elite. First, in my line of fire was Senator Thompson. *Why not start at the top?*

Like a computer calling up information, my mental files on Senator Thompson raced to the forefront. I knew Senator Thompson voted 'for' all bills dealing with the environment and 'against' big business legislation. Senator Thompson never introduced legislative initiatives himself. However, he was the force behind them. It was also strongly rumored Senator Thompson was madly in love with his 35 year old Chief of Staff, Melissa. They say, though pushing 60, he became quite the young buck in the presence of his vivacious and sensually appealing political ally.

It was softly spoken that he would do just about anything for her. That is, everything except give up Chassy, his wife of 37 years. However, Melissa had never asked him to leave her. They both understood that the appearance of stability and 'family values' was extremely important for his career longevity. Senator Thompson was up for re-election next year. I pumped Senator Thompson's hand vigorously, absorbing a bit of the senator's power as I did. I resolved to get to know him well. *He was definitely a power broker worth having on my side.*

Pausing only for a moment more of small talk, I moved on to shake hands with Senator Wilkinson. "Good morning, Senator Wilkinson. I'm Jack Montgomery," I said with enthusiasm and a tone of dutiful respect to the senator. I flashed my pearly whites with a grin that I knew from experience was simply irresistible. Senator Wilkinson responded back warmly and returned my grip energetically. *No one can resist me,* I thought wryly, remembering the cocoa-colored beauty I had seduced at the bar on U Street the night before. "Ah, yes, Senator Montgomery, I was looking forward to meeting you. A very clever campaign you ran." Senator Wilkinson spoke with admiration and a glint of something in his eyes that I could not quite read. *Interesting.* I would have to find out the inscrutability behind the hooded gaze. *There was nothing more energizing than a mystery.*

"Thank you, Senator, and please call me Jack," I feigned a degree of humility. "Let's go for drinks one day this week, Jack," the senator said. It was more of an order than an invitation. "I'd love to, Senator Wilkinson. Is Friday good for you?" "Perfect. I'll see you then. Let's meet at noon in my office, and we can go from there," the senator commanded. I responded with measured grace while searching out my next target, "Great. I'll look forward to getting further acquainted." "Likewise, Jack," the rotund senator, belted out as one hand patted my shoulder and the other hand rested on his hefty waistline.

I spoke to a few more senate members and decided to take a break from the non-stop hours-long hand pumping and positioning. I went for a drink of water and then fresh air to assess my first impressions. *Not too bad for such a short period of time networking,* I surmised with pride. *This freshman reception might pay off indeed. To think I was viewing it as a waste of valuable time. It was evident the senators and representatives were sizing up us newcomers. So far,* I believed *I was making a good impression.* I reflected on the last couple of hours with a sense of approval that only comes from arduous, tireless efforts and an expanded ego.

Heading outside into the cool fall air, I examined my new surroundings with its historic buildings, vast lawns and aged bronze, now greened over with time. A sense of awe and surrealism swept over me. *How did a poor boy from Cleveland get here?* I rubbed the back of my head and leaned against the side of one of the few modern buildings on the legislative campus. I propped one foot up against the concrete structure and slipped into deep contemplation. "I will make a difference," I said under my breath with a determination I had become familiar with since college days. *I'll do it for you, Jack,* I vowed with a sense of contrition. *And Papa, I will do it for you also. Though mostly,* I thought, *I will fight to make things right for 'my' people trapped in the 'hood.' Nothing warrants living in such substandard conditions.* I recalled the rats and roaches crawling over children as they slept, the dreary beige crumbling walls darkening the spirits of its occupants, the cracked mint-colored lead paint kitchen slabs of poison and the leaky ceilings that were almost guaranteed to follow anytime it rained. *We are not animals. We're entitled to better.*

Maybe if there were more to live for, people wouldn't choose to die such fast and hopeless deaths. Thugs like me would lose their appeal. The lure of their power to an illusion of escape would not be so attractive. Waves of anguish flooded my lungs until I could barely breathe. This happened less frequently as time went by. However, there were still many moments like this. Even the nightmares had not completely subsided after all these years. I still had times when I would bolt up from bed drenched in sweat. My heart would be speeding like a racehorse trying to place at the Kentucky Derby. There were variations of the dream or, rather, nightmare, but they had a similar theme. In each case, Jack was taunting and chasing me. Sometimes he would also shove a long, crooked finger in my face and call me a phony, a hypocrite and a murderer. I shuttered as I recalled those damp, chilling nights.

I will play the game and I will win. The resolve made my fingers ball into fists. *The people shut out from a world of civility, graciousness and splendor are depending on me. What other choice do I have? I will be the voice for those passed on the street without their humanity even acknowledged. I will stand up for those who are feared because of the color of their skin.* My face was set as I again focused on my luscious setting. *None of the people from my neighborhood would be welcome here,* I thought with disgust. *Papa, I just hope you live long enough to see me get to where I need to go to really make a difference. This is merely a stepping-stone.* I reflected on Papa's expression of gratification the day I was sworn into office. Aunt Eulie said Papa practically phoned the whole neighborhood about it. "Your ears should be on fire, child, if not burned up by now," Aunt Sadie chimed in. I chuckled. Papa embarrassed me with all the boasting, but I knew it was part of being a proud father.

I still needed Papa's strength and wisdom to keep me centered. With laborious persuasion, I had convinced the old man to join me in Massachusetts. Papa most likely agreed, because many of his friends were fading away anyway. It was good to have him near, whatever the reason. *Here I was almost 30 and still wanted my Papa around. Oh well.* I pondered my boyish longing for a bit. I remembered when getting away from Papa and having my own independence was my number one goal in life. *It's funny how things can change.*

Regressing once again to less noble thoughts, I recalled last night spent with Vanessa. In an instant, I felt my loins stir. *Why did the affairs start,* I wondered? *Why can't I stop? Maybe it's the rush and the thrill of it all. Perhaps it's boredom with my marriage.* I felt a sharp wave of shame. *It isn't fair to Suzanne,* I admitted, chastising myself in the process. Suzanne had been a stellar wife. She was a large part of the reason I was in office. Suzanne has stood by my side at every important political event, placed phone calls for me and even sent mailers on my behalf. She leveraged her father's political connections to raise a level of funds virtually unheard of for a non-incumbent.

No less important was the picture she presented with our two-year-old daughter, Gabriella. Suzanne only grew more beautiful after the birth of Gabriella. *She had the grace and style of a black Audrey Hepburn,* I thought with half reverence. Suzanne was charming and engaging. The media and political world were simply in love with her. On top of this, she was an impeccable mother. *I don't deserve her,* I decided for the thousandth time. *Why does she love me? If she really knew who I was, she wouldn't. Suzanne, do you know you are married to a low-life, drug-dealing murderer?* I thought back on all the times she attempted to console me during the nightmares. I pushed her away. "I'm fine, Suzanne. Stop babying me," I'd say.

I knew I had built a wall between Suzanne and me, but I couldn't help it. I couldn't risk losing her, but I couldn't risk letting her 'in' either. It wasn't just the career. I needed her in so many ways it scared me; with Suzanne I was vulnerable. *I didn't like that,* I concluded with unbridled vulnerability. Suzanne was my lifeline to goodness and purity. It was a world I wanted into desperately, but never felt worthy. My relationship with Suzanne was a paradox to even me.

When she entered a room, I would peruse her shapely silhouette with the deepest yearning and raw desire. Yet I couldn't bring myself to make love to her. Sometimes we would sit at the breakfast table on Saturday morning, conversing once the nanny took Gabriella away. We'd laugh and debate political issues. Suzanne was exceptionally astute at politics. Her analysis and insights on the issues were remarkable. Her synopsis regarding the subject was equally quick. I would often ask her opinions on various topics. She would give me fair, balanced and well thought positions. Yet Suzanne never suggested how I should vote on any given topic. I appreciated this sensitivity. It demonstrated that she believed in my judgment as well as hers. Suzanne often spoke words of wisdom to me. "Use your conscience as your ultimate compass, Jack. Let your heart speak to you." She would say, "Put aside the politics of the moment and do what is right. That will stand the test of time." Suzanne said these words with conviction and passion. This was no dainty, 'fluffy' woman.

Suzanne was an enigma to me. There were aspects of her that I couldn't fathom would exist. *How does such a 'silver spoon' woman have this kind of depth of understanding of human nature?* There are so many layers to my pretty wife that I found myself engrossed in our conversations and just the presence of her. Suddenly, I would catch myself and withdraw. I'd utter a lame excuse to leave the room. I felt enveloped in her being. The closeness I shared with her petrified me. I could not allow myself to feel comfortable with her. *Simply put, my wife made me feel less of a man, not more. With Suzanne, my imperfections were magnified. It was like walking on freshly fallen snow with muddy boots.* I knew Suzanne practically worshiped the ground I walked on, but I couldn't return her love, not in the way any respectable man should. *What was wrong with me?*

Eventually, we shared less and less. Suzanne gradually withdrew into herself. Her voluptuous lips smiled, but her eyes no longer danced. We also didn't spend much time together anymore. When I was not traveling the state of Massachusetts like a man trying to conquer Goliath, I was working long hours at the office. When we were together, it was usually for a political function to keep my face in front of the 'money machines.'

We were two strangers living under the same roof. A part of me was greatly saddened by it. At times, I missed Suzanne and our relationship. I longed for the bubbly glow she had when I entered the room and that special giggle at my dry, English-humored jokes. I longed for the intimate caresses she gave me. Yet part of me had to admit, I was more at ease with the distance. Conversations with Suzanne were now limited to politics and about Gabriella. It was a lot less complicated that way. The countless affairs served to pad the distance between us.

With self-disgust I realized the first affair took place when Suzanne was 5 ½ months pregnant with Gabriella. We had only been married a little over a year when I ran into a sexy paralegal that worked on the floor below me. She had a thick chestnut mane with crystal clear, baby blue eyes that were quite inviting. I had begun experiencing restlessness in my marriage. Suzanne was physically miserable being pregnant, and sex with her was out of the question. Her girlish figure was a contortion of sharp curves going in the wrong direction. On top of it, my hours were brutally long at the international law firm and I needed to release.

Yet, if I were totally honest, I just saw something else I wanted in other women. It had all the exhilaration, danger and risk familiar to my past. The mere idea of conquest made my blood rush. It was also an avenue to alleviate my qualms and dread of becoming a father. I really didn't think I was up to the task. I'd never been around children and surely was not a fine example of bringing someone joys as a little one myself. I thought of Jack as a child and breathed a sigh of relief. *Maybe I would get lucky. However, I deserved a taste of my own medicine,* I thought. *It would be poetic justice to have a little me.*

Conquering Karen, the paralegal, was easier than I anticipated. In fact, finding women to share in my tawdry affairs was not too difficult. I had a string of fleshly relationships after that. Their names and faces were a blur. The liaisons became second nature over time. There was something to be said for sophisticated, independent career women. They enjoyed the challenge of the unavailable. Yet, I must admit I also slept with a few married ones. *Don't get me wrong. I was never proud of my record.* It had become an addiction. The more I tried to stop, the more potent the temptation became. I knew Suzanne probably suspected something was awry in our relationship. She never broached the subject though. It was like termites silently eating our wooden home up from the bottom.

I mustered the strength to halt my behavior when I saw her. She was a ruddy brown bundle of elation. Suzanne insisted I be in the hospital room when she gave birth to Gabriella. I was horrified, but knew I had no choice. I nearly fainted when Suzanne was screaming in pain. The doctor and nurses were yelling "Push, Push. Harder!" I survived the messy spill of the slippery bundle pouring from my wife's 'private place.' *I wouldn't have missed it for life itself.* Gabriella's little bottom was struck firmly, and she let out a wail. Her cries got louder as they cleaned her off. She quieted suddenly when the nurse placed her in Suzanne's arms. Suzanne never looked more magnificent. We were both crying with joy as we gazed down at our little girl. That moment was solidified in my mind forever.

Papa was in the waiting room. He jumped up when I came to tell him the news. Suzanne's parents were also there. Her father was anxiously holding his new wife's hand. Dirk was in town on business and was also present. I was met with a unified sigh of relief when they saw me come down the corridor. What had just taken place was so clear that I didn't need to utter a word. I did anyway. "Suzanne and Gabriella are doing fine," I said with the deepest sense of euphoria. Papa grabbed me and held me tight. He nearly took the wind out of me. "Congratulations, son!" Dirk was only a moment behind him. We embraced each other for quite some time, like only a long deep friendship could merit. "Way to go," Dirk said. As usual, his cryptic statements held enormous meaning. Members of Suzanne's family took turns expressing their congratulations. Clayton Montgomery patted my back at least three times. His eyes were moist and his face was filled with an indescribable expression. *I was lucky as hell to have them all.*

I snapped back to the present, drank some water from the fountain just inside the hall and returned to the reception to meet and greet the remaining members on my mental list. I returned to the event with unspoken sadness and regret for the past.

· · ·

I hardly had time to get settled into the small, unassuming third floor junior senator's office, before Friday was upon me. However, I was very much looking forward to having lunch with the all-imposing Senator Wilkinson. I don't know whether it was the feeling of inclusion, the chance to mingle with the politically elite, or a chance to pick his brain that thrilled me most. Senator Wilkinson was undoubtedly one of the 'best in the business' - *and believe me, politics is a business.* As I crossed the lawn to Senator Wilkinson's building, my pulse quickened.

"Good afternoon, Jack," Senator Wilkinson bellowed, as he vigorously shook my hand. His office was expansive and tastefully arranged. There was lots of mahogany wood, plants and detailed prints. There were also photos of Senator Wilkinson with the Governor of Massachusetts and the Mayor of Boston. One picture showed him with the President of the United States. Wow! The room reeked of 'arrival.' We exchanged small talk as we went into the private dining room of the senior senators. Senator Wilkinson greeted several people as he led me to his favorite table in the back. People were watching me with curiosity. Senator Wilkinson had a reputation of not taking just 'anyone' under his wing. *I was evidently the chosen one. It felt good.* I met each and every gaze with an outward air of confidence I didn't quite feel inside. I was aware that to be groomed by Senator Wilkinson was to be guaranteed political success. He had clout. The senator was a political magician in his own right.

"Sir, I'm honored you asked me here for lunch," I said as we sat down at our table. The senator waved his beefy hand, pushing my comments aside. "Nonsense, the pleasure is all mine, Senator Montgomery." The senator got directly to the point, "You know I don't waste time on just anyone, Jack." I kept silent. He continued, "I think you have something special, Senator Montgomery. I haven't quite determined what that something is, but I will." Senator Wilkinson placed his napkin in his lap and ordered a martini. *This would have never been allowed during working hours at the law firm.* I did my best to contain my surprise.

The senator went on, "You're bright, and Jack, articulate, savvy, and you've got a nice image. However, there's another level to you. I sense a toughness that's not thoroughly explained by your background, thorny as it is." Senator Wilkinson sipped his drink and waited for my response. I gave none. He started once more with a thinly veiled inspection of me, and not missing a beat. "You know, I like you Jack. You're an anomaly. I relish inscrutability. And I greatly admire talent. Your campaign was cunning, masterful," he stated. "Thank you, sir," I replied with deference.

The senator chuckled, "Any other man would have come up with a response to satisfy my curiosity by now, Senator, but you haven't even attempted to explain yourself." I responded respectfully, "There's nothing to explain, Senator Wilkinson. What you see is what you get." The senator belted out a guffaw, amusing himself at my expense, "I like you, Jack," he said, "You've got balls." "Thank you, Senator," I said, uncertain of just how to reply. I didn't know what he expected, but I must have passed the test.

Whatever happened that day bonded us for a long time to come. Senator Wilkinson was my most ardent advocate in the State Senate. He fiercely protected my initiatives and shielded my back from the many knives anxious to pierce the skin. I, in turn, kept his record of protégé success. I was commonly referred to as the 'golden boy' of the State House. Many senior members conferred with me before taking a stand on an issue.

Much of who I am today politically, I gratefully accredit to Senator Wilkinson. 'Willy' as I fondly called him, kept me on track politically. *There ain't no bullshittin' Big Willy. Strange how he never was impressed with my charming anecdotes.* I appreciated that.

During the three years in Massachusetts state government, I grew up. It was a political metamorphosis. Within that time, I learned to control my responses and channel my convictions into constructive action. I learned to discern people's intentions and expectations from what they stated on the surface from what they really wanted. I was also more willing to take risks to push things through the political maze. And I'm sad to say, I became a master at manipulating minds and matter to acquire the desired results. I told myself that the ends justified the means. I honestly believed that. In the span of three years, I had become one of the state senate's power brokers. I was the ripe old age of thirty.

The most important thing that happened to me during this time had nothing to do with politics. I became a daddy once more. Suzanne gave birth to Maxwell. He was six pounds, eleven ounces and nineteen inches long when he entered the world. Unlike Gabriella, who hollered and fussed, Maxwell peacefully transitioned into consciousness. Suzanne stroked his hair, and he quietly stared into her loving eyes with alertness and pleasure. His tiny fingers wrapped themselves around one of hers and he wiggled ever so slightly. With narrowed eyes, he slowly became cognizant of the other looming figure beside his mother. Maxwell peered at me with curiosity. At that super-natural instant, we became one.

Chapter 12:

The Race

The Massachusetts Statehouse was little league compared to the treacherous waters of Washington. Everywhere you looked, alligators were snapping at your toes, parasites were sucking the blood out of you and leeches were attaching themselves to your rising coat tails. *I had been schooled well, but I could never have prepared for what lay before me.* D.C. was the Mecca of privilege, deception, corruption, manipulation and raw power. What once were knives in my back had now become daggers. Cutthroat ambition was faintly cloaked under civility. And those with the power were rarely ever willing to relinquish it.

However, that's what made it so much more intriguing, I mused, as I sat at my desk skimming a bill on landfills. *It had been a bumpy, bloody climb, but worth every step.* Rubbing my chin, I stood up and walked over to the window facing one of the other congressional buildings. The cherry blossoms were in bloom, signaling the arrival of springtime in D. C. I was in deep reflection as I peered out the window, thinking back to the days of the exhausting and bitter campaign.

· · ·

I can't wait until this is over, I thought, placing my arm strategically around my wife's slender waist and smiling as cameras flashed. People clapped with wild enthusiasm. *If I have to give one more damned speech, I'm going to kill someone.* "Thank you, thank you very much," I said with energy and self-assuredness. I threw in a hint of feigned humility, and the crowd ate it up. "I hope that your enthusiasm today will translate into a vote for me tomorrow!" I said. That was a direct unadulterated statement and truth.

Charming the crowd with an ease that was uniquely mine. I waved vigorously and nonstop. I pumped the hands of those standing on the platform with me and stepped down from the stage. I then took Suzanne's hand and helped her down too. We rushed to the waiting limousine to be swept off to the next stop. I heard the crowd chanting as my 'right hand' man egged them on "Jack!" "Jack!" "Jack!" The car door shut, and there was a moment of treasured silence. The driver pulled away. From Boston, Suzanne and I headed to Newton for an indoor speech. After that, we made our way to the North Shore for a fund-raising dinner and an evening of dancing. The schedule was downright grueling. Suzanne and I stared at each other with worn, weary eyes. Yet we both knew we were reveling in the meteoric ride. It was the ultimate experience for thrill seekers. It was the Super Bowl of political life. We were each prepared in our own way for the game.

I looked at my wife with awe. The events brought us back to feelings we hadn't had since first married. "So what did you think, honey?" I said like a child presenting a piece of artwork to a parent "You were brilliant, darling, as always." Suzanne beamed. Her pearly whites glistened in the dusk lighting. Darkness was soon approaching. "I especially liked the way you mentioned the educational decline reflected in the lower test scores in Boston's public schools. It's probably the most clear-cut failure of Rick Copeland's legacy," she said. I leaned over to my wife. My lips were a hair's width away from Suzanne's luscious pair. "You're only saying that because it was your idea." A wicked grin spread across my face and my eyes danced with merriment.

Suzanne couldn't help but respond. Her face flushed golden red and her breathing became weighty. "That's very true, soon-to-be Congressman Montgomery. And don't you forget it." She giggled as our lips brushed. Soon, we were French kissing in the back of the limousine like teenagers. I finally pulled away from her to see the driver peering into his rearview mirror at us. He was plainly amused. I cleared my throat as an apology and glanced out at the spinning landscape. *You've got to control yourself,* I noted, aware of the stirring in my loins.

Feelings of sentiment returned as I turned back to meet the gaze of my splendid, glamorous wife. "Thank you, Suzanne," I said with unguarded emotion. "For what?" she returned with delight, yet puzzlement in her voice. "For supporting me, for always being there, even during the choppy times." We both knew I wasn't an ideal husband or father. "You've always managed to overlook my unfavorable traits." My eyes watered repentantly. "I don't deserve you." *There, I finally said it,* I thought, sighing in relief. *It is out in the open.* I regained control; reminding myself we were not alone.

It's deplorable enough for the driver to see me 'making out' with my wife, but tears would be the final straw, I thought. *Everything you do has a way of seeping out to the press. The glass between the driver and us kept out the sound, not visuals. I couldn't afford to let my private life become public domain,* I realized, *especially with my checkered past.* I attempted to inconspicuously wipe my eyes dry.

The affairs with all those nameless faces came rushing back to me. I looked away from Suzanne for a moment, again in dishonor. *How could I be so selfish and stupid?* I could see from my peripheral vision that Suzanne was staring over at me like a woman with a grade school crush. *What does she see in me?* I asked myself for the hundredth time. Suzanne answered my unspoken thoughts as if she were reading my mind, "Jack, you won me, my love and my devotion. I love you and I always will." She touched my hand affectionately. I unconsciously moved it away in disgrace. We rode the remainder of the trip in silence.

• • •

"Jack, you've got to get more confrontational in this race. Copeland is tearing you apart. He's making a mockery of you on the 'family values' front," Bo said with zeal I wasn't sharing. I sunk further into the plush chair of the hotel lobby couch, feeling like the only thing I needed was a stiff drink and a firm bed. *A warm soft body wouldn't be too bad either,* I mused with hunger and confusion. I couldn't afford for the 'old Joe' to show his ugly head with Suzanne by my side every step. Nor did I want to see him. "Look Bo, I know you have a point, but I think my best defense is to focus on the issues," I said. Bo threw up his hands in frustration.

I felt agitated, even though I knew Bo only meant well. We had built a fierce camaraderie from my state house days. Bo was one of the attorneys lobbying for the Nstar electric utility. The company sought to maintain their polluting practices. The cause was questionable, but I liked his style. I conveyed to him with assurance that one day we would work together. "A man like you is critical to have on his side," I stated. Bo was a 'Bulldog' one couldn't shake. Yet he was packaged in a 'Golden Retriever' veneer. Bo managed to get his way much of the time and you still had to love him. Our connection was instantaneous. *He reminded me of myself.*

Bo set his bottled water down. He ran his fingers repeatedly through his reddish-blonde hair. *I knew I was annoying him. In some twisted way, I took pleasure in it. He was always so well put together.* "Jack, as your campaign manager, I will be the first to tell you issues may be the most important thing in your mind, but image matters a hell of a lot more to the public. It's the public that votes. It's the public that will put you in office." Bo was vexed by what he believed was my lackadaisical attitude. He began pacing the floor.

Bo stopped abruptly and stood in front of me. He said in a low, paranoid voice which was notably uncomfortable in the public setting of the hotel lobby, "Jack, there are rumblings on the street about your extra-marital affairs. It's believed that Copeland is behind the rumors, but of course, no one can prove that." Bo braced himself for my reaction. I gave none. I sat hauntingly still in the green velour wingback chair, not saying a word. Bo continued. "Jack, we may soon need to do damage control. If you don't go on the offensive, I'm afraid the bridge to Congress may just collapse under the weight of your personal debris."

The silence between us was deafening. It took me a while to gather enough composure to speak. I was sweating profusely. I wiped my brow with one sleeve to conceal the total impact of his words. Bo stood there anxiously awaiting my response. He had an expectant look on his narrow, yet pleasant features. Patience was never one of Bo's strongest points, but now I needed him to have some. Bo was moving too fast, and I required time to process the potentially enormous consequences of my actions. I felt like someone had just thrown a bucket of ice in my face. A chill raced down my spine. I imagined Suzanne's reaction to such news. Visions floated in my mind of my children being taunted at school with taunts such as, "Your daddy is a whore and a cheat," and worse. I felt like balling up and reentering my mother's womb - forever. I'd never experienced these feelings before. It was not a wonderful feeling either. I straightened up in the chair and cocked my head up to meet Bo's eyes. Bo gave me his undivided attention as I accessed the situation and my options. My words were weighted carefully to ensure I retained Bo's full support. Even though Bo and I had a solid friendship, matters such as this could strain any relationship.

Matching Bo's unrelenting glare, I confessed, "Bo, I've had a few indiscretions in the past. However, they shouldn't be anyone's business, except maybe my family." Bo began to walk the floor once more, only faster this time. He stopped and faced me with disbelief written on his now beet red Irish face.

"Jack, how totally naive can you be?! It's everyone's concern because, unfortunately, it speaks volumes about your character. This is especially so given that your wife is so adored by the public. She's a major part of your success." Bo had a high degree of irritation in his voice that was rising with every word he spoke. I knew he uttered the truth. I also knew he was very fond of Suzanne and the public mirrored Bo's reverence of her.

How could I explain to Bo, to the public, to my family, why I cheated on such a gracious and remarkable woman? What do I say to her family? They have taken me in as their son. Suzanne's father, Clayton, had poured tens of thousands into my campaign. I recapped this with a sinking feeling. *More significantly, he entrusted me with his daughter's well being. I've failed so many people.* I felt the enormous penalty of my actions. I sat there without defense. Whatever I said would fall short. *People might understand one affair, but countless ones.*

I found something deep within me to face my demons. "Bo, I don't know what to say," I stuttered, feeling self-conscious. Bo stood there with his body tense. He began frantically running his fingers through his tussled hair once more. Finally, both of his palms rested on his temple as if he felt the onset of a very bad headache. I hated letting my friend down like this. *The irony was that none of the women meant anything to me. They were a moment of passion; a shot into my never satiated ego; relief from my demons; and the ability to feel like a man again, if only for a little while. I couldn't even remember many of their names,* I realized with dread. I stood up, hoping this would help me better explain my actions.

"Let's find a bar and have a drink," Bo said, guiding my right arm and leading me out of the classically designed New England hotel. Everywhere you glanced in the lobby were crystal chandeliers, luscious floral arrangements, golden drapes and antiques made of the finest wood. *It was odd how quickly I became accustomed to such surroundings. How long had it been since I was removed from the deterioration and rot of the ghetto - ten years?* I distractedly pondered this as Bo and I stepped out into the crisp night air.

The 'hawk' greeted us the minute we left the toasty building. Winter in New England was one level up from Cleveland. Suddenly, nostalgia for my hometown hit me like I was smashing into a wall going 100 miles per hour. *It's probably my current circumstances,* I deduced. *I felt alienated and needed something familiar to immerse myself in.* "How about Nicky's Pub?" Bo suggested, abruptly snapping me out of my thoughts. "Sounds good," I stated without fanfare. *It didn't matter where we went.*

We found a table away from the crowd. There weren't many people to avoid. It was a Tuesday night in the dead of winter. Not many people ventured out at this time, unless they were desperate for a 'good time.' Nevertheless, we wanted as much privacy as possible. We ordered a couple of drinks and sat there until they came. It was a sobering moment for both of us. I peered over at Bo with unadulterated desperation for his assistance. I was drowning, and I needed rescuing. *Bo was my savior.* "Bo, tell me man, how should I handle this?" I was eager to take any advice that he gave me. Bo had years of training in 'dodging bullets.' There probably wasn't a lawyer around who didn't, but he was one of the best by far. Bo sighed heavily before answering, as if to summon the courage to verbalize it. He cleared his throat and took the plunge.

"The first thing you'll need to do is to come clean with Suzanne," he stated matter-of-factly. Bo waited for my reaction. I nearly spit out the double scotch on the rocks I was drinking. A part of me knew this was coming. Yet, when it came, I was no more prepared for it. Bo went on decisively mapping out the steps necessary to keeping my campaign on track. I listened intently to every word as if my life depended on it, at least my political life. "Jack, if you're to survive these scandals, you and Suzanne will have to show a unified front. How do you think she'll deal with the news?" Bo paused and looked me squarely in the eyes. "To tell you the truth Bo, I don't know. She is a very good woman. Suzanne has supported me through some rough times, but it's hard to say," I said resolutely. I wanted to get away. Anywhere would do.

180

"Jack, you'll also need to admit your doings to your remaining family and campaign staffers. Nothing is worse than hearing news like this from an outside source," Bo said, trying to prepare me for every possibility. I realized what a loyal friend he was and was grateful for his 'we can get through this' attitude. *A lesser person would surely have jumped ship.* "Is there anything in particular that you should tell me regarding your liaisons, Jack?" Bo braced for the other shoe to drop. I didn't give it to him. "No, Bo, nothing I can think of." "Good," he said with relief, relaxing every muscle in his face. "Let's start damage control as soon as possible, Jack. The rumor mill can be vicious. It's said that Copeland's got a couple of women willing to come forward. One is white, and the other is African-American. The white woman could alienate your black voters, but there's not a thing we can do about it.

"My suggestion to you, Jack, is not to deny the affairs at this point. State that you've done things in your past you deeply regret, mostly because of how adamantly you feel about maintaining a strong family structure. Have Suzanne and your children physically standing beside whenever possible." I could tell Bo's analytical mind was well at work. Now that Bo was in full swing, he appeared to be enjoying the challenge. "By the way, Jack, how far back do these affairs go? I need to know what we are dealing with here," Bo said, looking into his drink, obviously ill at ease for asking me the question. *I didn't want to confess, but knew I'd better be honest. Bo was the only man that could deliver me. He was my lifeline.* I admitted emotionally, "The first affair started when Suzanne was five months pregnant with Gabriella." "Jesus, Jack! What the hell were you thinking? We can only pray that this type of information doesn't get out. No amount of damage control in the world could patch that gaping hole." I didn't, I couldn't, utter a comeback.

Bo and I spent an additional hour drinking to take the 'edge' off. As we left the bar, icy rain began to fall. Bo pulled his jacket up to his chin and ducked his head close to his chest to protect himself as best he could from the heavy, chilled droplets. He patted my back to reinforce his enduring support for me. *I knew I owed him big time.* "Let me know how it goes," Bo said with barely cloaked anxiety in his voice. "I will," I mumbled, turning to face his troubled eyes.

I hailed a cab to take me back to the hotel where Suzanne, Gabriella and Maxwell were waiting. I knew Gabriella and Maxwell would be in the next room with our nanny, Norrine. They were almost certainly asleep by now. It would give Suzanne and me ample time to talk. It was a conversation I would do anything to avoid. Yet, I knew my political future rested on the next few hours to come. As I got into the warm, dry taxicab and shut the door behind me, I couldn't help but feel like a prisoner in his final hour, heading for the guillotine.

. . .

"Thank you, sir," I uttered, getting out of the cab in front of Newberry Square Hotel. A handsomely uniformed doorman greeted me. "Evening, Mr. Montgomery. How are you this brisk night?" "Just fine. And you?" I said. *I was always able to turn it on when required,* I thought with a degree of satisfaction. The doorman stepped in front of me to assist me inside. *'Fine' was actually the emotion furthest from what I was feeling.* I had the acute sensation to bolt for it as I strode into the open brass door with the appearance that I didn't have a care in the world. This time, I didn't even glance at my surroundings but headed straight to the elevator. Once the doors closed behind me, I pushed the 14th floor button. I noticed my fingers were trembling ever so slightly. "Suck it up, and just get it over with," I mumbled as I put the plastic card into the door slot. The light went green. My throat closed. It was show time.

"Honey, is that you?" Suzanne said, her melodic voice calling from the bedroom. "Yeah, it's me," I said, with minimal joy in my voice. Suzanne came out of the bedroom into the suite's richly decorated living room. She was wearing sky blue silk lingerie. *She's the best imitation of a Victoria Secret model I've ever seen,* I thought offhand. *Maybe I should have one more drink;* I considered as I caught the sight of her. "Hi baby," I said with as much normality as I could muster. Suzanne was not buying it. "Jack, is something wrong? You have a strange expression on your face." Suzanne stood squarely in front of me and placed her hand on my shoulder. Her big, lustrous eyes fell on me, longing for inclusion. "Honey, you want to talk about it?" she whispered in the most intimate way. It was clear she assumed my uneasiness had to do with the campaign. *She was right in one way.* I sucked in air for extra strength and directed, "Sit down, Suzanne. I have something to tell you." I knew I sounded brusque, but it was all I could do to get the words out.

Perplexed, Suzanne sat down on the heavy silk, green and salmon embroidered French sofa. *She became one with the furniture,* I oddly noted. *They were a blend of loveliness.* I sat beside her on the couch and faced her with a sense of foreboding. "God be with me," I murmured. I realized that this was the third time I'd prayed to the Lord. The first was to get me out of Miami alive. The second prayer, I recalled, was when I was given another chance by taking over Jack's life. I recalled praying to God to allow me to make a life that would honor Jack's memory. *I haven't kept those promises too well. However, I still want that, Lord,* I thought silently. I picked up Suzanne's slender hand and began softly stroking it.

"Suzanne, I love you," I said, barely audible. It was true. *Why did I do this to her? She deserves so much better than this, than me.* I rested my eyes on her fretful face. "Jack, what is it?" she repeated. "You're scaring me. Did Bo say something to stress you out? I know you two were a lot longer than originally planned." Suzanne was growing more frantic by the minute. I finally answered, "No, Suzanne, Bo didn't reveal anything more than I already knew." "Then what is it, baby? Why are you acting so bizarre and mysterious?" Suzanne was undoubtedly frustrated.

She pulled her hand away from mine as if to protect it and her heart, as if she knew something very unpleasant was on the horizon. I could tell by her stiff back she was preparing for the worst. Tears pooled in her eyes even before I uttered a word. "Suzanne, I don't know where to begin, so I will start at the end. The reason I was so long with Bo is that he was preparing me for what is about to be revealed publicly regarding my past." Before I could continue, Suzanne frenetically interjected. "What about your past, Jack? Does it have to do with the women you've been seeing during our marriage?" Droplets were now gushing down her cheeks. She tried unsuccessfully to wipe them away before more arrived. I offered Suzanne my handkerchief, but she savagely shoved my arm away. I was speechless on so many accounts. It was hard to say what surprised me the most, her actions or my feelings of helplessness.

I was most astonished that Suzanne had been aware of my affairs. And that she never confronted me about them. The anguish I had caused with my 'escapades' stunned even me. My destruction was echoed in her crumbling personage. Suzanne's perfectly arranged face lay now in pure devastation. She was the epitome of poise and grace, but she appeared on the verge of hysteria. I'd never seen her like this. It unnerved me.

Suzanne popped off the sofa in a fury. She started pounding my chest. "You didn't think I knew, huh, Jack?" she screamed, violently pushing me with all her strength. I fell back on the sofa completely unprepared for physical retaliation. I quickly recomposed and stood up to protect myself as much as to calm her down. *There's no fury like the fury of a woman.* Suzanne came at me again with both fists flying. She was again hammering as hard as she could into my chest. I did little to stop her. I knew it was necessary for her to vent all the built up resentment she must feel toward me. I also had it coming. I took the beating as long as I could and then grabbed her tiny wrists. However, Suzanne was stronger than I expected. She struggled free like an animal recently captured from the wild. She was wailing over and over again, "How could you, Jack? How could you disgrace me like this publicly? Wasn't your private humiliation enough? Why don't you love me? Why?"

Suzanne finally regained control and then went limp. Her hands fell to her side. Unexpectedly, Suzanne hurled her left hand back and slapped me across the face. The impact was so severe, for a moment I saw stars. I stood there attempting to contain myself. I allowed the stinging to subside before I further broached the matter at hand. I wanted us to discuss this as two adults.

Suzanne's vocal cries slowly became whimpers. Her body folded onto the sofa. Her head was lowered and her hair was violently tussled. A wave of incredulity came over me like a typhoon crashing onto shore. "Suzanne," I said attempting to pull her chin up to face me, "I do love you. I'm profoundly sorry that I've hurt you like this. If I could take back my actions, I would." Venom sprung from her lips. Her striking features were contorted as she exploded once more, "Liar! You lying son-of-a-bitch! I've given you everything, Jack, and somehow I'm never enough! And now the whole world will know how much of a fool I am for loving you. Our children will know Daddy as the lying, cheating, skulking bastard he is." With that, Suzanne stood and slowly walked to the bedroom. She turned, and for the first time, I saw contempt for me on her lovely face. "You'll have to find another place to sleep tonight, Mr. Montgomery," she said with marked sarcasm. "Maybe one of your many women friends can put you up for the night." Suzanne went into the bedroom with all the dignity she could muster, and slammed the door. That night I heard her through the bedroom walls, crying profusely. I fitfully slept on the sofa in the living room. It was the longest night of my life.

Sunshine came flooding through the windows forming silhouettes on the olive-gray walls. It gave the room a golden hue. I faintly heard the sound of traffic in the streets below. The light and humming drums of people moving about their daily lives was sufficient to motivate me from my shallow sleep. Memories of the gruesome scene with Suzanne the night before came rushing back. It was my reality. I lay on the sofa a few minutes more, too frightened to face her. Finally I managed to gather adequate grit to 'face the music.'

I got up and softly tapped on the bedroom door. I suspected Suzanne was probably still sleeping. *I was the only morning person in the family.* I recalled how, on Saturday morning, I would be the only person up. I'd go into the kitchen to eat cereal and read the newspaper. Many times, after a couple of hours, I would hear the pitter patter of Maxwell strolling in to join me. It was usually around 9:00 A.M. At three years of age, he was slightly off-keel with his gate. Maxwell's bare feet would make a slapping sound on the hardwood floor as he headed to the breakfast table. "Daddy," he'd say in his child-like, curious voice,

"What ya eatin'?"

"Cereal, son. You want some?"

"Sure, Daddy."

It was our Saturday ritual. I always had cereal on Saturday morning, and Maxwell usually wanted me to share it with him. We would munch down the cereal, and Maxwell would drink his remaining milk from the bowl. I'd usually click on cartoons once he showed up. We'd laugh about something silly on the tube. Of course, Maxwell's laughs were more boisterous and longer than mine. It was our time to bond. *I treasured those mornings.* Gabriella, not to be outdone by her younger brother, would wake up maybe a half hour later and come into the kitchen as well. She'd look like she just fell out of bed, eyes puffy and hair resembling a bird's nest. That was a trait she inherited from her mother. *Suzanne left a lot to be desired when just getting up.* "Morning, Daddy," Gabriella would say in her sleepy, private school voice. She'd kiss me on the cheek with unbridled affection and much fanfare. Already, at five, I could tell she was going to be a heartbreaker like her mother.

Gabriella would go over and plop in front of the TV next to her brother. She rarely ate breakfast, but opted for drinking orange juice. *This was another trait of Suzanne's,* I reflected, as I snapped back to the present. *God, I love those kids. I cannot lose them. I cannot lose Suzanne. They're all that really matter to me. The campaign be damned! I will drop out tomorrow to preserve my family,* I realized as I headed to our bedroom door. My pounding on the door got louder each moment Suzanne did not respond. It served to further embolden by my decision.

Suzanne eventually came to the door. Her eyes were red and swollen. My heart wrenched at the sight of her. It sickened me to see her in this condition. To know I had caused it made matters worse.

"Good morning, honey," I said in a feigned, lighthearted tone. Suzanne was no fool. She looked me over despondently and dropped her arm from the door. She left the door open and lethargically went back to the bed to once again get under the covers. I followed her to the bed feeling lost. Suzanne curled up on her side in a fetal position with her back to me. "What do you want, Jack?" Suzanne mumbled. I could barely decipher her words since her head was lowered under the linens. I was encouraged that she was at least speaking to me. "Suzanne, I want to talk." She rolled over and pulled the covers from her face and glared at me. I was faced with the extent of her fury, resentment and humiliation. It was an unsettling moment. I reminded myself that I created this situation with my own actions.

"Suzanne, honey," I said, undaunted by her glare, "We both had a turbulent night, but I think we're more level-headed now, and it would be a good time to discuss this." Suzanne didn't reply. She lay there with little to no movement. She lay staring up at the ceiling, not acknowledging my presence. I placed my hand on her shoulder. After an awkward minute, Suzanne stated matter-of-factly, "Say what you have to say, Jack, and get out." The lack of passion in her voice was the most off-putting. *She was always so full of life.* I ignored her tone and began anyway, "Suzanne, can you at least sit up and pretend to be engaged in this conversation?" I was agitated, in spite of my resolve to keep cool.

Suzanne moved the covers to her waist and sat up. Her back was against the headboard. She still refused to look at me. "Have you checked in on Gabriella and Maxwell?" she inquired. Suzanne never took her responsibility as a mother lightly. I admired and appreciated this. Usually by now, I would have spent time with the children. Norrine would update me on the children's schedule for the day. Not today though.

"No honey, I haven't. I will check in on the kids when we're done." "Okay." I waited for her to say more, but she followed with nothing, so I broached my 'prepared' speech. *This was the address in which all the practicing of speech delivery, style and tone had prepared me for.* I sat down on the bed beside her.

"Suzanne, darling, I know I've royally screwed up," I uttered in my most apologetic and downtrodden voice. "If I could absorb your hurt, I would do it in an instant. We both know I can't. It's destroying me to see you like this. My actions have been despicable. My disregard for our family cannot be explained away or even justified. You're the best thing that's ever happened to me. I adore you Suzanne." I noticed Suzanne's back stiffen ever so slightly when I spoke my last words.

Soft quiet tears were tumbling down her cheeks. She continued to focus on the wall in front of her. I waited with all the patience I could assemble. Still, she did not respond. Needing to fill the silent air, I went on. "Suzanne, I will do anything to keep you. I need you, so incredibly much. I'm nothing without you and the children. I'm willing to drop out of the race and spare all of us the dishonor if it will keep us together." Now my eyes were moist. Though trying my best not to, my shoulders started to heave and I released my pent up yearning for forgiveness. I broke down and wept. Suzanne turned to me. For the first time in 24 hours, I saw compassion in her eyes. Her exquisite facial lines softened, and she even attempted to smile, though unsuccessfully.

I didn't realize it, but I had dropped to my knees on the floor by the bed. Suzanne started stroking the top of my head as if I were her child and not her husband. "Jack, do you really mean it?" she asked in a far away voice. "You couldn't possibly give up something you've worked so hard for, Jack. I wouldn't want you to." She continued in a broken voice struggling for self-possession. "You deserve to be Congressman Montgomery. The people deserve to have you as their voice in Washington." She paused. "And I want to be the powerful congressman from Massachusetts' wife," Suzanne stated with a determined tone and a slightly wicked expression creeping onto her face.

Her countenance quickly returned to stone. "Jack, I do believe you love me in your own messed up way, but your love is toxic. With every new woman, and I knew about them all, another part of me died. I questioned why I was not good enough to hold you here at home. My self-esteem eroded with every affair. I try to pour all my energies into Gabriella and Maxwell to validate my value, but it never suffices." This time, Suzanne was the one who waited for a reaction, but like her, I had none. Only Suzanne could tell me how the story would end. She literally held my life in the palm of her hand. I sub-consciously held my breath in anticipation for the tale to unfold. Suzanne went on.

"Jack, I've been thinking and not just last night. Many women can look the other way during their entire marriage while their husbands 'play the field.' My mother did this for 20 years. I can't." Suzanne continued. "I use to wonder how growing up Mama could put up with all Daddy's womanizing. She never uttered a word regarding it. We both knew I was also aware of it. Over time, I lost respect for my mother for tolerating his behavior. It made our naturally strained relationship, even more tattered. And now, here I sit in the same position. Its funny how life has a way of repeating itself." Suzanne's facial expression was wistful as she traveled back in time. Suzanne gradually became again cognizant of the present and went on, reinforcing her earlier edict. "Anyway, Jack, I refuse to live a life like my mother. She became bitter and resentful. It ate her up inside. In the end, she was nothing more than a shell."

My heart sank into my shoes. I nearly tuned out the remainder of her monologue after her forceful words. *I've lost her,* I concluded. *I lost her, and I had no one to blame, but myself.* I started making a mental list of matters to be addressed to back out of the race, much less where I would temporarily live. I had difficulty paying attention to the remaining words spilling forth from her mouth. However, just as I was standing up in defeat, I heard the tail end of Suzanne's final sentence. It sounded like "I will stand by you through this." I wasn't quite sure I heard her accurately, so I asked her to repeat the words. "Obviously, to be such an important issue Jack, you aren't listening to me," Suzanne said indignantly.

Suzanne folded her arms. She met my eyes with unfamiliar directness. "Jack, like I was saying, I will outwardly support you as the dutiful, loyal wife during this campaign and even afterwards. I want to see you or rather us rise to the highest political ranks. I believe in your talents, convictions and motivations of public service. I also believe the children need their father." I tried to contain myself, but a schoolboy grin rapidly spread across my face like wildfire. My heart jumped a beat and my palms got clammy. At least, that was until I heard the rest of what she had to say.

Suzanne was speaking faster than usual, almost tripping over words as she released them. "Publicly, we will be one, Jack. Privately, we will live separate lives. Jack, if you want to screw every bimbo from Maine to Massachusetts that is totally up to you. I wash my hands of that area of your life." I wasn't used to hearing Suzanne speak in such vulgar terms. Both that and her message threw me off guard. Suzanne was only gaining steam. "Jack, from now on, when we travel, I want to sleep in a separate bed. We will be a couple in public and name only. Of course, we'll share matters regarding the children. Despite your 'extracurricular activities,' you're a very good father. Gabriella and Maxwell adore you. I'd never do anything to harm your relationship with your children. However Jack, I will no longer be your doormat." With that, she arose from the bed, put on her matching blue silk robe and glided into the bathroom, slamming the door behind her. I stood there speechless.

Not knowing what to do with myself, and unable to absorb the entire conversation at once, I decided to go check in on the kids with Norrine. I walked into the adjoining hotel room to hear Norrine and the kids in the bathroom. Maxwell was in the tub giving Norrine a very hard time. Gabriella had just finished bathing. She had an oversized towel wrapped around her petite frame. Her legs and feet were dripping wet. I entered the bathroom to Maxwell's whining. He was arguing that he'd been in the tub too long and he wanted out! "Hi, kids," I said, picking up Gabriella high into the air. Her damp hair splattered water on Norrine and me. *The conversation with Suzanne made me acutely aware that there would come a time in which this 'play' time would no longer be possible.* I realized that I'd better enjoy every moment with my children. Maxwell, no longer whining, began splashing in the murky water in which he sat, setting his water toys into frenzy. "Daddy, are we going to the movies today?"

I'd forgotten I had promised the kids a matinee movie. It was the middle of the week, but I felt I owed them for pulling them out of school early and taking them on the road with us. I was gone so much on this trip. I knew the kids weren't having much fun. However, I would have to break this particular promise today. *There is so much to do in terms of damage control.* I thought about the need to call a staff meeting, and phone Papa, and of course face Suzanne's dad and step mom. I wanted everyone prepared for when the news broke. *This was a nightmare. However, it was better than the alternative,* I reminded myself.

"Max, would you mind if I broke this promise for just today? Daddy has a lot to do today. Things have come up that I was not expecting." I could see the disappointment on his miniature face. I hated letting him down. Gabriella was also standing there; sober, in the spot where I had placed her back down. "How about," I said in an artificially excited voice, "This Saturday we catch the movie and go for ice cream afterwards. Would that make it up to you?" "Yeah!" they screamed in unison. "Can I have chocolate, Daddy?" Gabriella asked as if the decision was one of great importance. "Of course, darling, you can have whatever flavor your heart desires," I said jokingly, pulling at one of her ear lobes. She bellied over with laughter.

I straightened up, thinking about what lay ahead of me. *I'd better get started as soon as possible* I ruminated. "Norrine, are you okay with having the children today? Suzanne should be available much of the time. You'll have to check with her about her exact schedule." Norrine nodded her head in affirmation and smiled. I kissed the children goodbye and headed out. I couldn't help thinking how little I'd know regarding Suzanne's schedule from henceforth. *She made that perfectly clear this morning,* I thought sourly.

As I returned to our side of the hotel suite, I could hear Suzanne crying into the phone. "Daddy, I feel so betrayed. How could he do this to me?" She sobbed some more and then got quiet as if listening. "Daddy, did you ever love, Mama?" I heard her ask into the phone. Suzanne looked up as I stood in the bedroom doorway examining her.

Suzanne was back on the bed, but now fully dressed. She had on a combed cotton black turtleneck and taupe wool pants. She was wearing black suede boots to complete the outfit. Her hair was pulled back in a ponytail. There was none of the makeup and glimmering jewelry that usually went with the attire. Instead, she wore only a watch. *Even still, she was breathtaking.* A wave of lust came over me. I quickly squelched it out. *If there were ever the wrong time,* I thought. *Just at the time our sex had been better than ever, this had to happen. In fact, our marriage had been moving to another pinnacle.*

Suzanne glanced at me with not a trace of twinkle in her eyes remaining. She quickly stated into the phone, "Daddy, I've got to go. He's back." She quietly placed the phone on the receiver. "Jack, how are the children doing?" "Fine," I said, disturbed she had already told her father about matters. *There were so many issues still to be discussed.* Trying to bring things closer to a natural state, I made small talk about the kids. I conveyed Maxwell's hating his bath and the fact that I changed the date for taking them to the movie. There was silence on Suzanne's end.

Suzanne stood up and gathered her purse and the rental car keys. "Jack, I'll go check on the children and then I'll be out a good part of the day." I noted that she did not volunteer her proposed whereabouts. I dared not ask. "What if something comes up and I need to contact you?" I asked awkwardly. "Call me on my cell, Jack. Isn't that what you usually do?" she answered flippantly. Suzanne walked to the front door of the suite. I followed anxiously behind her, knowing I no longer had any say in her activities. It was a difficult pill to swallow. My ego and my spirit were bruised. Suzanne turned and said unenthusiastically, "Bye, Jack. I hope your day goes well." We both knew what she meant. "Thanks." It was all I could say. As Suzanne made her way down the hallway toward the elevator, I knew our relationship would never be the same.

Shortly after Suzanne left, I placed a call of my own. "Dirk, here," Dirk said in his textured, collected voice. "Hey Dirk, this is Joe." "Joe! Hey, it's been a while, man. I've been thinking about you, wondering how the campaign is going. Every now and then, I'll watch cable news and hear blurbs on the race. How's Suzanne?" Dirk, as usual, was dominating the conversation. I couldn't squeeze a word in. That was Dirk. Part of it was his natural enthusiasm. The other was his privileged background, where you were 'entitled' to the majority of the conversation. Dirk was my dearest friend. *Some things you just overlook,* I conceded with amusement. *I probably wouldn't have even noticed this, if I hadn't needed to talk so badly.*

"Whoa… Dirk, too many questions at once," I laughed. "Why don't we start with you? It would be a whole lot simpler. How's life treating you, man? Do you still like San Francisco?" Dirk responded in his natural, warm, inviting way, "Loving it. And life right now is pretty good. You remember that paralegal I told you I met about a year ago?" I did remember her. "Yeah, Dirk, Marlene was her name, wasn't it?" I answered. Dirk responded like a man hopelessly in love, "That's her. Well, we've been dating seriously since then. I'm thinking about asking her to marry me. I've never felt this way about a woman, and you know, I've been through a lot of them." "Really? That's great, man. She sounds like she's very good to you. I hope it works out, man. Then I'll get a chance to meet her." As much as I tried, I knew I sounded a little flat. It wasn't that I wasn't happy for Dirk. It was more that it reminded me how bad my relationship was going with Suzanne. In spite of myself, I felt envy.

Dirk was too astute to let my reaction to his news slip by. "J., that was the most lackluster response I've ever heard. I detect something in your voice." *Leave it to Dirk to be so blunt.* "What's up, man? I know you can't be 'sweating' me with that knock out wife of yours. And, now that I'm thinking of it, what's with the phone call in the middle of the day? You're too much of a workaholic to call me at this time." Dirk was teasing, but earnest at the same time. He knew something was wrong. "Dirk, you got me, man. I'm happy for you; you know that. I've just been having some marital problems of late. You know I can never let life go too well before screwing it up. I think I've done irrevocable damage this time," I said with tremendous remorse. I could hear alarm in Dirk's response. "J., what's going on?"

Without pause, I recapped events for about fifteen minutes. I discussed the affairs, the pending announcement of my transgressions by my competitor, my confession to Suzanne and her reaction. I left nothing out. *One thing about Dirk is he allowed me to be comfortable being me.* I desperately needed to unload, and who better to do it with. Dirk let out a long sigh after I finished. "Joe, you really have messed up this time. How could you risk something so good? What the hell is wrong with you?" Dirk asked in disbelief. "Dirk, is this suppose to make me feel better, because it isn't. I know I messed up." I was highly agitated. I should have suspected this would be his response. "Sorry, J. I just mean you've done so well for yourself. To think you would jeopardize all of it is mind-boggling. You know I want it to work out. I always desire the best for you, man. If there's something I can do to help, just ask." I knew his offer was genuine. *Dirk had proven himself time and time again.*

"I know you do, Dirk. Thanks. Just letting me release has been incredible. Suzanne said she would support my run, though nothing else. I have no one to blame but myself. I'll work it out. I need to win the primaries, so I can make it to the general election. I am the favorite. I hope I can maintain the lead once the news breaks. Wish me luck, man." Dirk said in his sincerest voice, "You know I've got you on that. Let me know how it turns out. Maybe I can come see you in January for the inauguration. I may be going to a bar association lecture in New York around that time anyway. I'm thinking about inviting Marlene."

"That would be great, Dirk. It's been a while and it's always good seeing you. I would love to meet the woman that managed to steal the great Dirk's heart. She's got to be quite a woman. Take care, man. Let me know if you make it over this way." "Will do, J. You take care of yourself." After hanging up with Dirk, I felt better. At least I knew I had one person in the world that would support me no matter what. I placed a quick call to Papa prior to heading to my staff meeting. That also went surprisingly well. *Maybe I could get through this better than I expected.* I closed the hotel suite door and headed down the hall.

This was the hard part. In fact, it was hell. I brought the staff together and broke the news to them. It was horrendous facing all the disheartened, yet fiercely loyal souls staring back at me. I knew I was letting them down. *What could I do? It's impossible to change the past. They have been working so hard for me. They believe in my mission and me. How could I restore their trust? We would need to start with open dialogue, that much was certain.* These were my key supporters and my friends. The respect had been mutual. The six of us sat around a conference table in one of the hotel meeting rooms. I spoke with candor; "I want to discuss a serious matter with you this morning. The situation could be the end of my campaign."

Faces were intensely staring back at me. I continued, "After what I have to say, some of you may change your opinion of me. If, afterwards, you no longer wish to back me, I will certainly understand." I met each pair of eyes around the table before plunging in. Expressions ranged from bewilderment to intense caution. I kept my tone professional as I conveyed the details of the pending scandal. You could hear a leaf falling from a tree. The silence was deafening. At the end of my confession, I repeated, this time to a more apprehensive audience. "I know I've screwed up. I have no defense. However, I do value your support and your camaraderie." I once more met the various eyes staring back at me. "Let's talk about it and get everything out in the open. We will need to present a unified front when the story breaks. I'd like to keep all of you on board if possible. You're critical to my success. You've been a jolt of energy to my campaign. I need you. Your organizational skills and enthusiasm have been second to none."

We talked for several hours about the situation, what to do about it, and how best to counter my opponent Some persons were visibly outraged with me. Others were more understanding than I expected. Emotions ran high during this time. It was almost liberating to come clean. I phoned Suzanne about having dinner with the staff that evening and she agreed.

We all went to an Indian restaurant that night. Suzanne's relaxed, engaging posture did wonders to restore the group's morale and momentum. *I figured they felt that if my wife could find forgiveness in her heart, they could do no differently.* All of them stayed in the end. Little did they know an Oscar was waiting for Suzanne back at the hotel. *She had definitely missed her calling as an actress.* I was truly indebted to her. "Thank you honey," I said with my eyes as I looked at her across the table. I knew she 'got' my visual communication. Our eyes locked for what seemed a minute, and then she looked away.

The last item on my 'to do' list was to meet with Suzanne's father face-to-face. I had to have his support to pull the campaign off. Clayton was the political powerhouse, and everybody knew it. He might live in Atlanta, but his political network was felt from the West to the East coast and in between. *Suzanne's father made things happen in an almost mysterious way.* Plus, the campaign money raised by the mere mention of his name was phenomenal. It so happened that Clayton was in Boston for a conference on tax law. He never missed a chance to see his daughter when possible. The conference was merely an excuse. I suspected that Suzanne had gone to spend the day with him.

After leaving Suzanne back in the hotel room, I went to meet up with Bo to report my progress and also to phone Clayton in Bo's presence. Bo was excellent for bouncing off ideas on my approach to Suzanne's dad. He was familiar with Clayton from business and political interactions in the past. They weren't exactly friends, but they respected each other's capabilities in their profession and each other's style.

Bo and I met at Pigall's, a trendy restaurant in Boston that attracted a lot of politicos. Bo wanted to make sure I didn't appear as though I was in hiding, with something to suppress. We assumed most of the political 'talking heads' already knew the news by now. Bo concluded out loud, "You might as well get this over with sooner rather than later, Jack." True to word, I entered the restaurant, and a pause fell over the room. Then there was a hum of low voices shortly after I passed each table. I greeted as many people as I could, like nothing was different. I could tell some were expecting the opposite reaction. *I liked that I kept them off guard. It showed I was still on top of my game.*

Bo and I had immediately got a table, even though Pigall's had a line of patrons waiting. *Boston knew how to treat its politically elite. After all, the state was home of the Kennedys'.* We were seated at a table for two. Bo slipped a $20 bill into the host's hand. "Thank you, Sal," Bo stated. Sal nodded his head. Smiling warmly in acknowledgement of Bo's appreciation, he left us. Bo turned to me once we were seated, "You handled yourself well, Jack," he stated with a sense of satisfaction as he looked around the dimly lit restaurant. It was home of the 'Who's Who' of politics. "I thought so too, but thank you for your concurrence," I said with a grin. I knew I bordered on cockiness at times. This was one of those moments. Bo chuckled under his breath and shook his head.

Bo got pensive, "So it appears you've been busy since I gave you the 'talk on the street.' That's good. Time is of the essence. I'm particularly pleased Suzanne is going to stand behind you." I didn't say a word. It was as if Bo didn't listen to the remainder of the story regarding Suzanne and me. Once I said I had her political wife's dutiful support that was all he needed to hear. Bo was off running. *The rest was incidental.* Bo went on, "I figured your staff would come around. They practically worship the ground you walk on, Jack. Anything short of mass murder, and they'd defend you. Now, all we have left to contain is Clayton Montgomery's reaction. Though, Jack, we both know, outside of Suzanne, he's the most critical player. Clayton is the heartbeat of your political life. You know that, don't you, Jack?" *I'd have to be stupid not to know that, Bo*, I wanted to shout at him. *Bo could be so theatrical at times.* Instead, I replied, "Yes, I'm aware of that, Bo."

The waiter came to our table, and Bo ordered a rib eye steak with mixed vegetables and a potato with lots of sour cream. *I could see his arteries cringing at his choices.* I ordered salmon and vegetables. *Maintaining the physical image required discipline.* We ordered a bottle Merlot. I followed up on Bo's earlier remarks, "Bo, how do you think I should approach Montgomery?" I sincerely wanted his opinion. I knew what he'd said earlier regarding Clayton's influence on my campaign was right on target. Gingerly, Bo put down his glass of wine. "Jack, Clayton has been one of your biggest fans, but you have betrayed his most precious treasure, his daughter. Suzanne is his world, despite the pretty young woman he married."

He went on, "If I were you, Jack, I would be straightforward with Clayton. I would admit I messed up. I'd tell him I'll keep my pants zipped up from now on. I would reiterate how much I love Suzanne. You do love her, don't you Jack?" Bo asked, watching me carefully. Now it was time for me to put down my glass. "Of course I do, Bo. What hell kind of question is that? I never meant to hurt Suzanne. I was reckless," I stated with a fervor and irritation I absolutely felt. "Good. I'm glad to hear that. There was a time I wondered, but hell, it is none of my business anyway," Bo stated in an odd tone I couldn't place. I was furious. "You're damn right, Bo. It's none of your damn business." Bo was overstepping his boundaries, and he knew it. Yet I couldn't shake the feeling that I thought it strange Bo would even question my love for Suzanne. *What kind of image was I portraying to the world?*

We spent another hour at Pigall's and departed. Of course, I was to call Bo after the meeting with my father-in-law. "Here goes nothing," I said as I dialed Clayton's cell phone. I wanted to confirm our meeting before heading over. I was to meet him in the bar of the Ritz-Carlton Hotel. I had thirty minutes to make my way to the other side of town. "Clayton Montgomery," Clayton answered in a distinguished, established voice. *You could tell he was a mover and shaker; just by the way he answered the phone.* "Dad, it's, Jack. Are we still on for 8:00 P.M.?" I asked, trying to keep the trepidation out of my voice. *Confidence was always the best posture when dealing with those in a position to crush you. Never let them see you squirm.* Clayton hesitated for a moment before responding. "Yes, Jack. In fact, I'm looking forward to our meeting." His tone was casual, but I noted the undercurrent. "Great. I'll meet you in the bar as we discussed earlier," I replied without indicating any recognition something was out of place.

Traffic was heavy for a Wednesday evening, but I managed to get there just at 8:00 P.M. Clayton was already at the bar with a vodka and tonic in hand. He saw me in his peripheral vision, because he swirled around on his seat upon my approach. "Good evening, Jack," Clayton said as he inspected me with a critical eye. *He always did this,* I recalled. It used to make me uncomfortable. What was really unusual, however, was his calling me Jack instead of 'son.' *The night was getting longer by the minute.* I was not playing by his tactics. "Hi, Dad," I said, emphasizing the latter. I knew by the way he tilted his head to one side he caught my meaning. "Let's grab a table," Clayton responded in kind. Clayton addressed the bartender, "Bring him a scotch on the rocks. Thanks." Clayton never asked, but rather commanded.

I sat across from my father-in-law feeling like I had been caught with my pants down in the midst of a brothel police raid. His disapproval was plain before he ever uttered a word. I thought it best to let Clayton speak first. I sat there patiently. I was reluctant to meet his gaze and focused instead on a napkin on the table while he spoke. "You know, I think of you as a son, Jack," Clayton said with a sense of imminent dread, "but no one messes over my daughter, Jack. Suzanne is my reason for waking up in the morning. She is the last thing I envision before I close my eyes at night. Her well-being is paramount." He went on in a controlled manner, "I've never seen my baby girl like this. When she came to me this morning, and I saw the heart wrenching you had caused, I was ready to rip your no-good heart out. Nobody messes with my girl and gets away with it." Clayton's speech was measured and very balanced, as if a volcano lay just beneath the surface. *I'm glad we're in a public place.*

I thought it wise not to let Clayton continue. He was working himself up. *I need to cool things down.* "Dad, I know I deeply hurt Suzanne, but you must believe me when I say I love your daughter, very much." Clayton penetrated my eyes with intent to uncover the truth. What he saw must have sufficed because his stiff posture relaxed slightly and his expression of stone mitigated. I decided the best tactic to handle my father-in-law was like Bo concluded, frankness. Clayton was too shrewd for anything else. "Dad, I would like to say that I'm the perfect husband and father, but we both know it isn't true. However, I am genuine in saying I cherish your daughter and my children. I'm nothing without them."

"I've done a lot of soul searching these past few days. I had to ask myself why I would cheat on a woman with everything going for her, looks, brains and the warmest spirit I've ever encountered. Honestly, she has it all." Clayton was hanging on my every word, measuring each one with precision. I needed his support, but I also greatly respected him. What Clayton Montgomery thought of me mattered. I took a few sips of my scotch and dove in feet first. "Dad, the answer to this question may startle you. It's not that I don't think highly of Suzanne. Maybe it's that I think too much of her. Most times, I don't feel like I measure up when I'm around her. Her beauty, her sparkle, her wealthy upbringing and legendary father... Where do I fit into this perfect picture? What do I have to offer her? I'm a poor boy from Cleveland that made good. I am nothing special."

"Other women make me feel whole again, if just for a moment. Their eyes gaze into mine with pure admiration and wonder. Their bodies yield to my command. These women demand little and give all of themselves to me. It's heady. I feel a power I don't have with Suzanne. I can't wholly articulate it." I instinctively knew Clayton understood. Suzanne had shared with me his tainted past. His female escapades almost lost him his daughter at one point. If nothing else, I knew Clayton could relate. *However, this was his daughter,* I reminded myself. I shifted uncomfortably in my seat.

Our conversation lasted for two hours. I bonded more with him during that time than all the years I'd been married to Suzanne. Clayton was a huge supporter, but now he was also a confidant. I made many promises to my father-in-law. I told him I would take much better care of his baby girl's heart. I vowed I would not cheat on her again. In addition, I pledged I would win back her trust. I meant every covenant I made. Later that night, I conveyed much of the same sentiments to Suzanne. She listened with evident reservation and did not verbally respond.

It was a tough time for us. The campaign was grueling. The scandal took a heavy toll on the family and supporters. Yet, we all survived it, growing stronger and more committed in the process. Suzanne and I were never the same though. There was an unspoken distance between us. Her eyes lost their passion when she looked upon me. And true to her word, we slept in separate beds. Yet through it all, I admired her fortitude. Suzanne stood by me in the midst of a hurricane. She continued to guide my campaign from behind. She remained the devoted mother to my children. *What more could I ask for under the circumstances?* I kept my word as well. I never cheated on her again, at least until I met Nicola. That was many years later.

I won the primary by a surprisingly wide margin. There were eleven percentage points between my closest opponent, Rick Copeland and me. It was a margin greater than anyone expected. The final election with my republican counterpart was a walk in the park. He was dull, out of touch and uninspiring. We beat Steve Bantry, hands down. The victory was a time of grand celebration. It was a time of profound reflection. Most of all, it was the road to redemption.

Chapter 13:

Congressman Montgomery

Moving to Washington D. C. was like coming home. *D.C. is a sexy city, if you can call a city that. You can smell the power in the air.* Suzanne and I found a lovely townhouse in George-town that was sufficient to accommodate our two children. The townhouse's charm and character more than made up for its lack of space and steep price tag. I instinctively knew we would like it there. We felt like Cinderella sliding into our glass slipper. The city pumped life back into our family that was desperately needed. For the first time in months, I saw Suzanne light up over something.

Suzanne and I relished discovering Georgetown. We took strolls down its streets. Suzanne would peer into the windows of the quaint shops displaying their eclectic wares. We'd stop to have coffee at a café or hang out in one of the bookstores, perusing magazines or digging through the discount book bins. Sometimes we would simply partake of tea in the bookstore's coffee shop. It was both relaxing and energizing to our spirits. The children often accompanied us on these outings. Other times, they would stay with Norrine. We convinced Norrine it was in her best interest and ours if she would move with us to the political Mecca of D.C. Our case was most effective because Norrine was as enthralled with the children, as they were with her.

The townhouse gave Suzanne a project to focus on other than me. This, I believe, was also good for her state of mind. *Creativity has a way of boosting one's sense of self.* Suzanne was an exceptional decorator and she had an open canvass. I took it upon myself to introduce Suzanne to one of the other Junior Congressional wives. I knew she would hit it off with Maxine. I had met Carlton and his wife, Maxine, at a welcoming reception on Capitol Hill earlier in the week. Suzanne was exhausted and had decided not to attend. Maxine was one of those lively, 'tell it like it is' women. She was warm, earthy and grew up not too far from D. C., in Northern Virginia. She knew the culture, and she didn't mind telling you about it. Carlton came from a congressional district in North Carolina, in the state capital of Raleigh.

We invited the couple over for dinner that Saturday. Suzanne and Maxine bonded instantaneously. In fact, over time, Suzanne talked of Maxine as fondly as she did her high school girlfriends, Roslyn and Shelby. It was marvelous witnessing their friendship flourish. Suzanne never had many close female friends. Maxine was such a self-confident woman she appeared to take Suzanne's striking appearance in stride. They discussed design ideas, went shopping for the new home and talked incessantly on the phone. I suspected I was the subject of their 'low voice' conversations. I must admit I found it annoying as hell. However, I put up with it to see Suzanne connect to the human race again. *I would have tolerated just about anything for that.*

It was difficult having a marriage in name only, especially when it came to my physical needs. I was insatiable in this area and always had been. In the old days, Suzanne didn't mind fulfilling my healthy sexual appetite. *My, have things changed,* I reflected with disenchantment. The lack of a sex life really tested me at times, but I kept my word to my wife and father-in-law. I didn't mess around. I did, every now and again, pay a 'hooker' to 'take the edge off.' That wasn't cheating in my mind though. *It was totally different. A 'brother' has to take care of his needs. I don't know their names so they can't count. Plus, prostitutes provide a professional service. I didn't have to worry about them flaring up in a possessive rage and calling my wife or talking to the press for fame.*

Feeling a bit uncomfortable with my thoughts, I returned to the matter at hand. I looked down at the pile of papers on my expansive mahogany office desk with an exasperated expression. *This 'crap' never ends,* I concluded with frustration. *However, even with all the nonsense measures, I had to admit my work still gave me the excitement of a six-year old on Christmas morning.* A grin slowly spread across my face as I energetically tackled the items in front of me.

I read the proposed house rule summarized crisply by my Legislative Aid, Erin Rody. Once again, I noted with veneration the handiwork of my young, gifted staffer. *This guy did flawless work!* I perused the documents with hawk-like focus and a desire to read between the lines. *The latter was a talent worth gold in politics.* I jotted down questions for Erin regarding the landfill bill. I could skim a document with ease, capturing only what was important. It never failed to amaze my staffers.

Flipping through the remaining stack of documents on my desk, a bill caught my attention. The proposed house rule sought to redirect funds from urban economic development programs to a general community service budget to be used at the discretion of the state. Hence, the dollars could, but would not necessarily have to be, geared to urban concerns such as after school programs, AIDS education and teenage pregnancy. The pending house rule on the surface appeared innocuous, but the net effect would be to allow money to be moved away from urban issues to politicians' pet projects under the umbrella of 'community service.' I searched for the name of the congressman introducing the H.R. It was Stuggart. *I should have known,* I thought, rubbing my head with a sense of aggravation. *The bastard. He even gives republicans a bad name,* I reflected with disgust. *This proposed measure would pass over my dead body.*

I might not be 'the Man' at home anymore, but I do hold clout on Capitol Hill, I mused. I scribbled another note. Though Erin's summary was thorough, I wanted him to provide me with the full proposal. I planned to be well equipped for the inevitable 'showdown.' My blood was surging faster in anticipation of what lay ahead. "This is why I became a congressman," I mumbled, "to protect the less fortunate. Jack would have done nothing less."

I remembered Jack's return from his first year at Yale. He was passionate and full of conviction. Jack was sure that he would change the world. Many of his views were borderline militant. I used to roll my eyes at his edicts regarding the world and the inhabitants thereof. I viewed his sentiments as 'soft.' Real men fought battles, not for hearts and minds. Jack would talk of fighting racial injustice, eradicating poverty and providing educational parity. I would only half listen to him, thinking he was so out of touch with reality. *Now that I look back, I realize that Jack was fully aware and completely plugged in.*

"Jack, have you looked out your window lately?" I'd say to him with a patronizing twist to my voice. "What we need to eradicate is black on black crime, drugs, and women selling themselves for a hit on a pipe. The white man needs only to sit back and let us destroy ourselves." Jack would get this grave look on his face, "Joe," he'd respond with despondency, "Those are the symptoms of a broken people. We've got to solve the roots of our decay." I'd shoot back, "Jack, ain't nobody care about what happens to our race. In this country, a black man will always be one level above an indentured servant. The 'man' keeps his foot on us. That is a fact and it will always be that way." Jack would stare me square in the face, "I care, Joe. I care and that matters." Even during Jack's holidays and summer breaks from school, he was always devising ways to improve the plight of the 'little guy.'

He used to amaze me. If anyone should have been passionate about eliminating the 'meanness' on the urban streets, it should've been me. I was making my way through its harsh waters. I saw my 'homies' fall one by one over rampant and uncontrolled anger. I saw women giving themselves away to anyone who would show them the slightest resemblance of love. I experienced the unceasing tension of watching my back and trusting no one. Jack went to schools where the topic of the day was 'who was sleeping with whom' and 'who was not fashionably acceptable.' What did Jack know about the ghetto? He only had a temporary address there. I meditated disdainfully *it was my home.*

Yet every passing year, I recognized the enormous wisdom of my twin brother. He was so advanced for his years. The more time passed, the more I admired his insight. *Why did it take me so long to get what you understood as a teenager, Jack?* For a flash moment, I felt admiration intertwined with the resentment as I so often felt for him growing up. *I'm still catching up to you, Jack. Even now, I'm enormously aware of my inadequacy. No wonder you were Papa's favorite.* I got up, stretched, and walked over to the window. I had to shake off the demons of my youth. "I loved you, Jack, in my own way. I hope you realized that," I said under my breath. "You were and are my better half."

I paced the maroon carpet, creating a path in the process. I had so much to sort through it was overwhelming. I was lost in the past with thoughts of Jack. I was engrossed in the implications of the potential house rule. I was also dreading the evening planned with my estranged wife, Suzanne.

I thought I would have won her back by now. Boy, had our marriage gone awry. To Washington, we were the perfect couple. A society column once wrote, "They are glamorous, attractive, bright and completely devoted to one another." However this facade ended though once the door was closed. Suzanne went to her bedroom and I went to mine. Every time she shut her door, I felt a shiver run down my spine. *How long will this go on? Haven't I paid the price of my sins?* It's been two and a half years since that fateful night. *I cannot handle her aloof 'pleasantries' any longer. I want my wife back! Tonight we're going to have to talk.*

The knock on the door jolted me back to my surroundings. "Come in," I said offhandedly. Erin cracked the door and tentatively poked his head around. "Hello, boss," he said in his usual upbeat baritone voice. "I figured you'd still be here. You're the only congressman I know that sticks around after 8:00 P.M." *There's nothing to go home to,* I wanted to say. Erin studied my demeanor. "What crocodile got up your ass?" he said, apparently enjoying himself at my expense. We often joshed with each other. It was part of the camaraderie. Erin became sober, studying me once more. "Jack, is everything alright? Do you want to talk about it?" I knew I needed to pull it together by the reflection in Erin's hazel-green eyes. His curly sandy blond hair that framed his dark complexion was falling to one side as he examined me. I came around from my desk and guided Erin to the round table.

As much as I valued Erin as a colleague and relished our friendship, I wasn't about to discuss my personal life with a subordinate. *Things have a way of leaking out in Washington. No one was airtight. At least when you confided in other members of Congress, you knew they had their own skeletons to defend. They had something to lose if word got back to you they were the source. Staffers had everything to gain.* "Erin, nice work, as always," I said with the utmost sincerity and respect. Erin beamed. I wasn't known for giving praise easily. "I want to talk with you about several of the initiatives being put forth in the House Appropriations Committee."

I had worked hard to make a name for myself. *The reward was being invited to the right committees.* The House Appropriations Committee was one of the most powerful Congressional committees. It was unheard of for a junior congressman to be a member. Yet, after only one year in Congress, members of the committee invited me to lunch. I was first approached by Congressman Grueger to join him on the golf course one Sunday. I knew it was just a matter of time then. A few months later, Congressman Mann announced that he would retire and not seek re-election. I got the offer to be his replacement on the House Appropriations Committee.

It was the official beginning of a flourishing congressional career. Nothing got to the floor that didn't pass the committee. We ultimately controlled the 'purse strings' of every piece of legislation. *Funding implications and support were critical to a bill being given a chance at survival. Without the money, there was no viable measure;* I ruminated, feeling every bit of the magnitude my membership held. *Talk about affecting people's lives,* I thought as my ego expanded ever so slightly.

"Sit down, Erin," I commanded. Erin sat at the table with his cup of coffee in hand. He leaned forward in his seat, ready for a lively debate. I regularly questioned him on his analysis and chosen positions. Other less secure folks might have been intimidated by my challenges, but Erin appeared to actually be invigorated. You could see his mind churning behind the hazel-green mirrors. *For all the kid's good looks you would think he'd be on a date every night of the week.* However, by the long nights and weekends he spent in here, he must not have had a life. *I wonder what he is running from or to,* I thought sheepishly. *Everyone has a story. I wouldn't dare ask him; in case I built an expectation that I would reveal my history in turn.* I forced myself back to our conversation. I joined Erin at the table carrying my own cup of java. It was 8:10 P.M., but neither one of us was ready to retire for the night. I crossed my legs and leaned back in the chair.

"Erin, there were several initiatives that caught my eye. These include the landfill proposal for states running out of space and the pollution controls initiative designed to put tighter controls on power plant waste allowances. However, I suspect you know the proposed bill gaining my utmost attention." I waited for Erin and me to meet mentally. We usually did. "Well, if I were a guessing man," Erin grinned knowingly, "I'd say it was the proposal put forth by Stuggart. After all, urban issues are your trademark, Sir." We both laughed. I thought *if I can manage it, Erin would be a part of my staff forever. Erin belongs in a leadership role though. Our country needs young political talent like his.* I made a mental note of it. I kept that mental note, too, as I helped him take on ever-growing responsibility in key positions.

"Erin, tell me all you know about this proposed House Rule on urban economic development redirection. I don't just want you to repeat your summary of the initiative either. I want your reasoning behind your conclusions. I want you to give me background on Stuggart's motivation for the proposal. I have my thoughts on the bastard, but I'm sure there are more objective opinions. And, of course, by tomorrow morning, I want a copy of the full document on my desk."

Erin recanted what he knew, providing editorials along the way. We were there until almost 10:00 P.M. We discussed the potential effects of the proposal from different angles. We speculated about who would support the measure. In the end, we discussed ways to defeat it in committee. The bill would never see the light of day. By the time I turned over my car engine, I was ready for battle. I would read the full document to make sure I accurately presented the facts. It only took one or two misrepresentations to totally lose credibility. I knew this by watching others falter. *It was never a pretty picture. Once credibility dissipated, so did your support. You were 'toast.'* I had never made that mistake.

After my meeting with Erin, I glided my BMW into the late night traffic for home. I still planned to talk with Suzanne regarding our facade of a marriage. It had been a long day, and I felt my eyes getting heavy, but this didn't dissuade me. Pulling into the townhouse, I deliberated on what I needed to do to balance my personal and political life. By the time I entered the house, it was near 11:00 P.M. The house was eerily quiet. I knew, in part, I worked the long hours to avoid the emptiness of my home life. *That would stop!*

I rose around 5:00 A.M. the next morning, with an air of determination. I crawled out of my unfulfilled bed with my heart pulsating. This time, I was out of the bed without the usual race across the room to turn off the alarm. I grabbed my robe and headed to Suzanne's room without delay. I pounded on the door feeling all the mounting embitterment of three years. I knew Suzanne would be still asleep, but I didn't give a damn. I pounded harder. My only concern was waking up Gabriella and Max, though they would be getting up in about an hour anyway for school.

A groggy, tussled Suzanne suddenly stood in front of me at the door. *God, she looks sexy,* I thought. I despised that my 'manhood' began to rise in response to her. I looked down at it. *How could you betray me at a time like this?* I stared back at my estranged wife in defiance. "Jack, what are you doing? It's five something in the morning," Suzanne moaned, while pulling her cinnamon velvet robe tighter. "Suzanne, we have to talk." I brushed passed her into the delicately decorated bedroom that should have belonged to both of us. I shut the door behind me. Suzanne had a curious, irritated expression draping her face. "Jack, what could be so important that it has to be discussed at this hour of the morning?" Her voice was rising as she followed me back into the room. She went to the plush, welcoming sofa near the bed and slowly sunk into it. She looked up at me with a tense, nervous posture. "Jack, are you leaving me?" I could tell Suzanne was bracing herself for the worst. The question caught me off guard because it was the furthest thing from my mind. *How I would love to not disappoint her*, I thought with accumulated rage over her physical rejection of me. I remembered my children, the image I needed for my career and the lifestyle. I also reflected on her overall support and knew I couldn't succumb to the temptation, even if I had the inkling to do so. *Plus, I love her.*

However, I decided to 'play' with her a bit. *That was the least I could do.* I peered down at Suzanne with an unrevealing countenance. "Why do you believe I'd be leaving you, Suzanne?" I was anxious to see what she had to say. I've always wondered whether I was even close to being forgiven for my past transgressions. I'd paid dearly for them. Suzanne never gave me one indication. *If I knew she was close to calling a truce, perhaps I'd be more patient.* Suzanne took a while to respond. She wrung her hands and looked at the floor. She said in an almost timid voice, "We haven't exactly been spending a lot of time together." *Was that an understatement!* I decided not to let her off the hook so soon. I continued to dissect her, daring her to go on. She took the bait. "Jack, I know I haven't been there for you sexually for quite a long time," Suzanne said with incredible effort.

"For the first two years, I wanted to pay you back. I wanted to make you feel the rejection and hurt you caused me for the first ten years of our marriage. But, in this last year, it's been more pride then anything else. I've actually wanted you back in my life in that way, but I didn't know how to let you know. I'm also petrified of getting close to you again. The heartache you caused me was almost more than I could bear." Suzanne was outwardly shivering now. Tears were streaming down her enchanting face as she wiped them away in hopes of regaining composure. My heart thawed as the words flowed from her lips.

I gently pulled her from the sofa and wrapped my arms around her lithe frame. *What have I done to this woman,* I thought with a deep sense of remorse. *She's such an inviting soul.* Though Suzanne was a tall woman, I still stood over her. She tilted her head up to me and then buried it back into my shoulder. She appeared so vulnerable. *Had she always been this way, or was I the reason?* "I love you, Jack," Suzanne whispered as she nestled herself further into my body. I pulled her to me, "I love you, too, Suzanne." We lost all sense of time and argument. I lifted her chin and gave her a long, passionate deep-throat kiss. Her lips tasted of honey. *I had forgotten.*

Suzanne groaned with pleasure as I guided her backward to the bed. Memories of her heated body pressing to mine came flashing back and I was further stirred. I hastily ripped her velvet cinnamon robe and satin burgundy pajamas off her shoulders, popping two top buttons in the process. I felt the warm soft heaviness of her breasts and willed myself not to release prematurely. I gingerly leaned down to suck each one. Suzanne exhaled in surrender. *Three years of pent up tension was hard to tame,* I reflected. *I was acting like a caged animal just re-*

leased into the wild. "Get a hold of yourself," I said mentally. It was a futile effort.

I grabbed Suzanne's lovely legs from under her and we fell into the bed. I snatched off her matching bottoms and lace panties and buried my head in her softness. Suzanne arched her body up so tensely I could barely breathe. It only served to heighten the sensation. Slowly I moved up her body, kissing and caressing each part tenderly. Finally, I made it once again to her mouth and we kissed so long I was heady afterward. I parted Suzanne's long legs and plunged deep within her. Suzanne gasped in pleasure and we rocked back and forth until we both came in ecstasy. For a long time, we held each other until we heard the patter of little feet making their way down the hall. "We better get up, Suzanne," I said wistfully. *I could have stayed in her embrace forever.* "Mmmm, I know; you're right," Suzanne responded dreamily. Yet we both remained suspended in the glow of passion moments more, unable to move.

There was a quick knock at the door. We made sure the kids learned to do that as soon as they could walk. We wanted no 'surprises' during the early days of child rearing. You could tell the knock was just a formality, because the door quickly swung open. Max's eyes got wide and his left hand snapped over his gaping mouth. He stared in disbelief at Suzanne and me in each other's arms under the covers. Maxwell began giggling and bending over with laughter. Once he regained control, he came galloping across the room to the bed. "Mommy, what is Papa doing in your bed?" he asked, completely unaware of the implications behind the question.

Suzanne smiled sheepishly, totally avoiding the question. Instead, she affectionately rubbed his head and said matter-of-factly, "You little one, need to get ready for school. What do you want for breakfast?" Before Max had a chance to answer, Suzanne responded with, "How about blueberry pancakes and eggs?" Maxwell beamed. He started jumping up and down exuberantly while clapping his hands. Suzanne crawled out of bed, turned Maxwell around toward the door and patted him lightly on the butt. "Max, go get washed up and I'll see you downstairs in 15 minutes, okay?" "Okay, Mommy," he said while running excitedly out of the room. He stopped and turned around. "Are you going to have breakfast with us, Daddy?" Maxwell asked with a wanton expression. It tugged at my heart.

Usually I didn't have time to eat breakfast at home, except on weekends. "Sure, son," I said, thinking how I'd better call Clare to move my appointments. *First sex, and now breakfast. What a bizarre, delightful morning. I could get used to this.* I smiled broadly at my gleeful son. *It was hard to believe he was six years old. Where did the time go?*

Suzanne crawled out of bed once Maxwell left the room. She gazed dreamily at me, "You were magnificent. I'd forgotten what I was missing." Suzanne's lips curled seductively. I pulled her back onto the bed. "So were you, madam," I murmured, nuzzling her neck. Suzanne playfully struggled to release herself from my grip. "Congressman, you had better get up as well. Your civic duties await you." With that, Suzanne gently touched my face and headed downstairs to prepare breakfast. Gabriella was sitting at the table, along with Maxwell. Both were dressed in their Catholic school uniforms. *Wow, do I have beautiful kids,* I noted with pride as I joined them at the table.

Suzanne was at the stove flipping pancakes. She glanced up briefly to acknowledge me. "Hon, do you want a cup of coffee?" she asked, already reaching for a mug from the cabinet before I could affirm. She placed the mug of rich, perfectly brewed coffee on the table in front of me, poured the cream in and stirred. She didn't miss a beat. Suzanne then returned to the stove in time to flip a flawless pancake. I watched her in amazement. "You're incredible, you know that," I said flirtatiously. I could tell the kids were observing the new behavior between their parents. The table was absolutely quiet. There was no frivolous chatter from Gabriella or whining from Max. There was not senseless bickering between the two of them.

I got up and grabbed Suzanne's waist from behind. She giggled. "Jack, stop it. The kids are watching," she whispered in a low voice. "Let them watch," I said without a care. "If it's wrong to hold your wife, then we're teaching our kids the wrong lessons." Suzanne wiggled from me grinning ear-to-ear. She brought the eggs and pancakes to the table and went to get the milk for Max and Gabriella. As soon as she sat down, the children's playful chatter started up again. I noticed the kids' laughter was more vibrant, and that I received an unusually generous helping of food. *Now this was the kind of morning that energized you to spend the day fighting on Capitol Hill.* I wiped my mouth in total gratification and got up from the table. I was ready to start the day. I leaned over to Suzanne and affectionately kissed her on the brow. "Suzanne, the meal was excellent. I'll call you from the office." I planted a peck on the cheeks of Gabriella and Maxwell and left for the office. Suzanne said as I was departing, "Drive safely honey." I closed the door behind.

I normally listen to jazz music to keep my nerves at bay in the midst of rush hour traffic. *D.C. rush hour traffic is an animal unto itself. However, today was one of those days where the music is coming from inside.* I didn't even bother to click on the radio. *Damn, that sex was good.* I reflected on my earlier liaison with Suzanne with renewed longing. *What a fool I've been to jeopardize my marriage with meaningless indiscretions.* I somehow willed my mind back to matters concerning the nation. I phoned Clare to obtain my revised schedule. *Good, my meeting with Congressmen Lee Stuggart had been pushed back a couple of hours. That would give me more time to prepare.* I rode the remainder of the way mentally making notes for the critical face off.

The day went fast. *Of course, I missed an hour or so,* I reflected with a smile. *It was well worth the lost time.* However, it gave me only lunch to skim through the entire urban economic redirection proposal. Our meeting was at 2:00 P.M. *If I focus solely on it during the time allotted I should be fine,* I concluded. *I'll use the hour before the meeting to strategize, make a few phone calls to get backing for my position and clarify areas of the proposal's content.* I had a brief meeting to assure other matters of importance were on track with my Chief of Staff, Matthew Culmers. After that, I was ready to peruse the document. The further I got into it, the more exasperated I became. *How dare the son-of-bitch try to bring such a shallowly cloaked bill to our committee and think I wouldn't stop him!* My street fighting instincts began to resurface. *I'll not only defeat this proposal,* I determined, *I will humiliate him in the process. He deserves nothing less.*

This proposed House Rule was a direct challenge to me. It was known that Lee Stuggart 'had it out' for me. He resented my rapid rise in Congress and my high public approval numbers that in a matter of eight years in office he couldn't come close to matching. This time around, Stuggart barely got re-elected by his district's constituency in Oklahoma. He'd poured millions of his own money into the campaign and still nearly lost to an unknown! Stuggart was well aware I was the one who spearheaded the current legislation for urban economic development. It was my 'baby.' I didn't get everything I wanted, but most of what I proposed appeared in the bill. "You want a showdown, Stuggart, you'll get one," I remarked under my breath. *There is no love lost between us.*

Reenergized, I replaced the phone receiver with the last backing assured. The phone calls to sure up support for my position took longer than expected, but they were successful. It was now five minutes before 2:00 P.M. I had asked that Stuggart meet me at my office to discuss the proposal. *We would play in my back yard.* I subconsciously rubbed my hands together in anticipation of my prey. At exactly 2:00 P.M., Clare knocked gently on the door and poked her head through. "Congressman Lee Stuggart is here to see you," she stated. "Send him in, Clare. Thanks," I responded, feeling my pulse quicken.

"Good to see you, Lee. Have a seat," I offered my handshake and gesture toward the chair with thinly veiled insincerity. *We both knew where we stood.* "It's nice seeing you again, Jack," Stuggart formally countered and shook my hand. He sat in one of the chairs directly across from my paper-filled desk. "Can I get you a cup of coffee?" I knew he never touched the stuff, but thought it only polite to ask. "No thanks, Jack." We then made the traditional small talk about the wife and kids before getting down to business. *This always seemed like such a waste of time to me. I don't even like the man, much less care about his family, but I knew it was important to play by the political rules.*

The conversation thinned, signaling time to get to the matter at hand. I cleared my throat, ready for battle. "Lee, we both know why I invited you here," I said with an intensity I could not disguise. Stuggart sat back as to provide confirmation. He said nothing. "I've had a chance to look over your proposal on urban economic development and wanted to clarify a few issues." Stuggart listened intently. His steel blue eyes matched mine in defiance. It was apparent this would be no lame duck. Stuggart was equally used to getting his way on the Hill.

Stuggart had none of my charm or political savvy, but he did have an arsenal of his own. He was the kind of politician that you were terrified to cross. He shoved his agenda down people's throats with few standing up to him. Stuggart could be ruthless. On top of that, he had a memory matching some computers. Members had paid a dear price for going against him. Stuggart made it his business to know all the 'dead bones in everyone's closet.' He also knew the right people to disclose them to, should it be necessary. Hence, if you wanted to challenge Stuggart, you needed to be squeaky clean. *Politicians are rarely immaculate beings.* The other option was to be well connected, making him think twice about his own political price. *I was the latter.* I stayed tuned in to my congressional network for exactly that reason. I decided some time ago that my best protection from political parasites, like Stuggart, was to have my own parasites. *The bones in my backyard weren't buried too deep and were easy to find.*

I crossed my legs, leaned to one side and began stroking my chin as if in deep thought. *I didn't want to appear too aggressive.* "Lee, frankly I have some concerns about the bill." Stuggart waited a moment before he addressed me, I suspected it was to cool down his own internal thermostat. I studied

Stuggart's face to gauge how thorny the battle would be. Unfortunately, he had a poker face. It disclosed absolutely nothing. I discreetly inspected Stuggart further. *He might be handsome, with a full head of chestnut hair and translucent blue eyes, but underneath the surface, Stuggart was as cold as a Siberian winter. Those magnetic eyes were a reflection of poorly cloaked malice.*

Stuggart suddenly leaned forward without warning, with one hand lifted in the air, as if to calm my objections. "Now wait a minute, Jack. Before you start ripping apart my proposal, let me explain my position." This told me Stuggart recognized my clout on the committee. *I give him a few points for having that much sense.* Stuggart was normally too arrogant to believe he needed to explain his position to anyone. He began by repeating pretty much what was already in the document. He followed by indicating the fallacies in the current House Rule. This served to further infuriate me. *How dare he?* Finally, Stuggart rambled on about the lack of results most urban economic programs have shown in the past and the unfairness of most of them. *I was at my limit.*

I interjected with little patience remaining and showing minimal civility, "Lee, I think you're way off track." I then took each of his arguments outlined in the proposal and demonstrated my reasoning for why they didn't hold up. I refuted his positions that the urban economic development programs have shown little results. I backed this up with facts, citing cities like Philadelphia and Chicago that have run test urban programs for the past five years. In those cities alone, new urban businesses have sprung up at a rate that surprised most, increasing by 38 and 41 percent, respectively in this relatively short span of time. In addition, I gave Stuggart figures regarding reduced unemployment in those same urban communities, as well as diminished crime rates. I then carefully dissected the proposed urban economic development program practices and its potential flaws. And I showed the loopholes set to appease the Republican Party. *If this passes through committee and was placed on the floor for an up or down vote, it might just pass with the way it was cleverly worded,* I thought. *This cannot happen.*

Stuggart was speechless. He was clearly taken aback that I had done such thorough homework on the topic. He was probably also caught off guard by my passion. The blunt way I countered with facts his thinly veiled racist remarks regarding urban conditions served to make him uncomfortable. *I don't give a damn if he is discomfited,* I ruminated. *If you're bold enough to try to slip this past me, then you've got to be willing to take the heat.*

After Stuggart's feeble attempts to reply to what I had stated, I stood up. I extended my hand to him, "Thanks for coming by. I think we're both clear on each other's position." Stuggart closed his portfolio in a huff and stood up as well. He matched my grip. "Jack, it's been a pleasure," he said dryly. Stuggart headed toward the door. I intentionally put him off balance. "I hope you know, Stuggart, I plan to do all I can to defeat this proposal in the committee. I don't believe it merits going to the floor." Stuggart's back stiffened, and he turned to me with frigid eyes. His face was beet red. It took him a moment to recoup. His controlled voice lashed out at me, "Jack, you can do whatever you damn well want to, but I intend to see that this bill gets through the committee and passed on the floor." A shiver of excitement went racing down my spine. "Do as you wish, Lee. I just thought I would put you on notice," I said.

I continued, "Lee, I hate to inform you, but I've already got the wheels rolling. The support is there to defeat this bill in committee. More than anything, I wanted to meet with you to tell you not to waste any more energy on it." I was enjoying the battle of wit and might. I did all I could not to show it. "It won't be as easy as you think," Stuggart said, seething through clinched teeth. However, he appeared worried. Stuggart's words and body language were incongruent.

I stood there with one hand in my pocket. I knew I was living up to my cocky, son-of-bitch reputation. "Yes, it will. And you know why?" I said, waiting for him to take the bait. Stuggart couldn't resist. "Why?" he asked, resentful for falling for a method used since the times of Moses. "Because, Lee, we both know why you want to give the funding to the states to use under a 'community services' umbrella. You really want to give the money to the lily-white suburbanites to beautify their parks and increase their soccer fields for prep school children to play on. Well, it's not going to happen. This government has an obligation to help those less fortunate and perhaps of another color sometimes. I, for one, intend to see that we meet our obligations."

Fumes shot from Stuggart's ears. His one free hand was balled in a fist. The other hand was clenching the portfolio as if for life itself. "Jack, you know everyone says you are a presumptuous asshole. Now I know firsthand. Contrary to what you may believe, you don't own the Congress. You don't even own the committee. You may have the ear and sympathies of some powerful members of the House, but that doesn't make you invincible." I laughed. "Is that a threat, Lee?" Our eyes locked like two rams' horns clashing. Lee gave no follow-up response. I continued. "Because if it is, Lee, then be forewarned that not only did I do my homework on your proposal, but I also did my homework on you."

I could see Stuggart flinch ever so slightly. I moved over to my desk, sat down and began sifting through my papers to dismiss him. "Thanks again for stopping by, Lee," I said without looking up from my papers. Stuggart did not respond, but slammed the door behind him. Once Stuggart was gone, I looked up from the work on my desk and smiled. "Now that was an effective meeting," I said with a broad smile. I leaned back, pushing out the chair and crossing my legs on the desk. I placed my arms behind my head to recap our conversation.

I effortlessly maneuvered through the political maze to defeat the newly proposed economic development bill. Apparently, Stuggart had more enemies than he knew. *Was that easy, or am I not finding the House stimulating any more,* I wondered. I concluded *I was finding the 'game' a bit too unrewarding of late. It was getting stale.* More and more, I found myself not wanting to get up in the morning. *Simply put, the thrill was gone. The battle with Stuggart was a prime example.* I would normally be on a high for days after that. *Not any more. I need a new challenge,* I thought.

Suzanne must have also sensed my waning Congressional enthusiasm. One day, out of the blue, she came up with the 'magic pill' when she suggested that I run for Minority Whip. "It will definitely give you a fresh mountain to conquer. The Democratic Party is in dire need of new leadership in the House. You'd be the first African-American to secure the position, but then, what else is new?" *Suzanne was such a big fan of mine.* I was touched. I pulled her close, "As usual Suzanne, I like your idea. Maybe you should be running for office." She beamed.

The position of Minority Whip was being vacated by Senator James Braggs. I recalled Braggs' reason for stepping aside. On a televised "Meet the Press" interview he recanted a rehearsed speech regarding time commitments of the position and conflicting personal requirements of his family life. On the Hill, it was rumored he was asked to step aside after the 'blood bath' the Democratic House took in the recent mid-term election. Democrats went from the majority party to the minority party during the time I was elected. *Luckily, we still had the Senate.* If he didn't step aside, the rumor was that those in leadership positions were planning to expose to his wife his illicit affair with a young male staff member named Edward. *The world of politics is a complex animal,* I thought, as I pulled up into the driveway of my Georgetown home.

I successfully met the challenge. I used my political reserves to become the first African-American to become Minority Whip. I spent two years in this role. By the time the next election rolled around, the Democrats were the majority party once more. I moved the Democratic Party to triumphant wins in the House. We were now two hundred and twenty-six to two hundred and six in favor of our party to the Republican Party, with two Independents in place. However, the Independents most times sympathized with the democratic position. It was quite a feat, and I was proud of the accomplishment. The day after the elections, the phone didn't stop ringing with congratulations on my leadership. The strategy of capitalizing on difficult economic times under a Republican president was always a solid one. *It was a shame I had to convince my own political party to push something so obvious.* They wanted to narrow in on the healthcare crisis and social security trust fund depletion. *Imagine that.*

I knew the visibility of being appointed Speaker of the House and eight years of congressional service would serve me well, but for what? One year later, I was again returning to my original unsettled question. I was elated by the Democratic Party's increased influence in shaping legislation. Yet, I felt a familiar longing for higher challenges and a new frontier. I sat at my desk staring out the window. It was nightfall, and the skies were black. I stood up and placed my hands in my pockets and continued to peer out the window. *Why am I so edgy,* I pondered? *I have an unmatched political career; a good family life, and I'm in a solid financial position. Yet I feel something missing inside.* I decided to give Clayton a call. Over the years, Suzanne's father had been instrumental in shaping my political career. *Clayton was a second father in every sense of the word.* He also had political muscle and knew how to use it. *It's hard to believe Clayton Montgomery had been in my life for eighteen years now and my father-in-law for sixteen. Where did the time go?*

I picked up the phone and dialed his number. "Hi, Dad," I said in a drained voice. Clayton detected my mood instantly. "Hello, Jack. What's going on, son? You don't sound yourself," Clayton said with a sense of apprehension. "I don't know, Dad. That's just it; nothing is out of the ordinary. Everything is moving along smoothly. It's going almost too well." Clayton paused for a moment before speaking. I knew he was deciphering between the lines. *He was very good at that.* There were times I would call him to help me figure out the 'true' political issue I was confronting. He was always on target. *No wonder the man moves in the circles he does,* I surmised with admiration.

"Jack, I've heard this in your voice before. It was when you were in the state senate. You're restless, aren't you?" I mulled over Clayton's words, finding the truth in them. *Maybe I was.* I further meditated on my father-in-law's analysis. "Dad, I think you're right. I could never quite articulate it. I've been feeling this way for a while. I believed that being Speaker of the House would be enough. I mean, how could it not be enough?" I knew my dissatisfaction was coming through. I felt extremely guilty for it. I didn't want to seem ungrateful for a magnificent career and life, especially to Clayton who had a hand in creating it. *Most people would trade places with me in a nanosecond. Here I was complaining.* "Son, it's no need to explain. We both know you're appreciative. There is nothing wrong with wanting more. You remind me of myself when I was younger. I guess I've said that to you a few times now." We laughed. And I sighed in relief.

"Well you can always run for President," Clayton said in a light tone. I knew Clayton never made statements half-heartedly. Clayton sobered. "Jack, you will be a compelling contender for the presidency one day. That is definitely the destination your career is racing toward. If you weren't thirty-eight years old, I'd say it would be now. However, no matter how good you are and how much you have to offer the country, you won't be taken seriously at that age. Credibility is paramount." My back stiffened. *'Mr. President' had an invigorating ring to it.* Yet, I knew Clayton was correct. Age does matter in politics. It was astounding that I had reached the pinnacles I had in such a short period of time. The media had mentioned it on numerous occasions, along with my ethnicity, of course.

Clayton continued, "You know Jack, you could run for the Senate. You would make an exceptional senator. It would further your visibility and influence in Washington. Let's not forget, the top of the House is still lower than the bottom rung of the Senate." I didn't quickly respond. I thought it over. *The idea was appealing.* "Dad, I think you may have something here. Let me talk it over with Suzanne." I said that more for Clayton's benefit than anything else. I wanted to reiterate the fact that I was keeping my word to him regarding Suzanne. I knew Suzanne would support whatever career decision I made. Again, she was just that type of woman.

It pleased Clayton immensely that our marriage was doing well once more. He had pulled me aside one Thanksgiving holiday and thanked me for returning the glow back to his daughter. Now on the phone, Clayton commented on my intention to confer with Suzanne with clear pleasure in his voice, "Yeah, son, that's a good idea." I thanked Clayton for his enduring support and advice and hung up. I had practically made my decision before placing the phone on the receiver. However, there was one final approval I did need.

"Hello, Papa," I said, feeling more confident and directed after my conversation with my father-in-law. "Hello, son. How are you?" Papa sounded elated to hear from me. I warmed under my father's welcome. *What was wrong with me? Why was I still seeking Papa's approval? How old and accomplished did I have to be?* Papa was, of course, more nurturing than Clayton during our conversation. He also had a way of keeping me from being 'too big for my britches' as he liked to say. I smiled. I recalled the struggle I had convincing Papa to move to Maryland after just having him follow me to Massachusetts. "I like roots, son, even if you might be a gypsy," he said with half-hearted indignation.

Papa and I talked about my running for the Senate when Edison Halbrat from Massachusetts retiring in a year. Papa was enthralled with the idea, more so than I would have imagined. It was enough to confirm to me I was heading in the right direction. Halbrat was stepping aside for health reasons. I had been dismayed and disappointed after hearing the news that Edison was diagnosed with prostate cancer. *First, Senator, then President of the United States... I liked the ring of that. However, today I need to focus on my duties as Speaker of the House.* I began sifting through the papers on my desk.

$\backsim\!\!\!\circ\!\!\!\frown$

Chapter 14:

Nicola

Nicola Patricks sat in the press conference room anticipating the arrival of the newly elected senator. *This was big news.* He was the first African-American to be elected to the Senate in at least eight years. She recalled Carol Mosley Braun's Senate acceptance speech. *So many promises unfulfilled. What a disappointment to see her go down like that,* Nicola thought, visibly shaking her head. She had a feeling this one was different. *For one, he was a man. That should hold off some of the target practice on his back. We've still only come so far with this equality thing. Yet there was even more to him.* Nicola squinted her eyes to get a better view of the senator as he made his way into the Press Room. She tossed her chestnut-colored mane, as she usually did when she was excited. *My, my, my, he was a strapping buck. Senator Montgomery was even better looking in person than on television.*

Nicola jotted down a few additional questions to ask the dapper senator. Totally unaware of the admiring glances she was getting from others in the room, she frantically scribbled down even more thought-provoking questions. *You have to take advantage of the opportunity when it presents itself. I might never get a chance to evaluate the senator firsthand again. I'm here on business,* she reminded herself, not to be caught up in a schoolgirl crush. She chastised herself for her earlier thoughts. Journalism was the pulse of her life.

As the first African-American Editor-in-Chief of Washingtonian Magazine, Nicola had a lot to prove. She was going on three years in the role and, still, she felt the pressure. *It's not fair that we have to carry the weight of our race* she meditated. *Some things you just accept and move on.* If she could snag an interview with the highly visible Senator Montgomery, he just might provide her signature piece. First, she would need to get his attention and let him know she was worth talking to.

Nicola had dressed carefully for the occasion. She had worn a tailored burgundy wool skirt suit, silk cream camisole and high heel black pumps as part of her arsenal. She was aware that image was more than half the game in the world of journalism. She twisted her gold watch to determine when the session would start. Patience was never her strong suit. "I hope this press meeting starts on time and ends promptly," she remarked under her breath. *Many of these meetings were late. Half of them weren't even worth the time.*

Just then, she heard rumbling in the crowd and saw flashing cameras and knew the show had begun. Nicola looked up from her notes to see Senator Jack Montgomery coming out of the sidelines and striding across the podium with his lackeys lagging behind him. His usual co-conspirator, Bo Elison, was by his side. *Boy, was he a loyal ally,* she thought, remembering the scandals and political controversies surrounding Senator Montgomery during his campaign. Bo had defended him against them all. *It must be wonderful to have someone like that in your corner,* Nicola thought. Loneliness was her constant shadow. She spent so much of her time working she had little time for girlfriends. Most men found her intimidating.

Nicola couldn't help noticing another man by Montgomery's side she'd not seen before. He was obviously well bred and very distinguished looking. *He was quite handsome in his own right, if in a 'pretty-boy' way.* Hmm. Nicola wrote down a note to find out more about him. She later learned his name was Dirk Patterson, a childhood friend who had recently joined Senator Montgomery's team as a legal advisor. They were said to be extremely close.

Nicola watched with fascination as Senator Montgomery presented himself to the press. He slowly drew them into his magnetic web. *He reminded her more of a movie star than a politician. For one thing, it was difficult to get past his Holly-wood looks.* Senator Montgomery was every bit of 'tall, dark and handsome.' She couldn't remember being so aroused by a person's physical being in years. *When did she get so shallow?* She was there to focus on the politics of the man, not his looks she reprimanded herself. Senator Montgomery stood erect at the podium. His 6' 2" muscular frame stood confident, commanding attention. The press was in a trance. Montgomery smiled and his countenance lit up like Las Vegas at dusk. *It was just amazing.* Like the rest of the press, Nicola was at the edge of her seat. She leaned forward in anticipation, crossed her legs and began writing on her pad once more. *I'm going to recall as much of this as possible for my editorial in Washingtonian Magazine,* she resolved. *She might just be seeing a future President here.*

"Good afternoon, ladies and gentlemen," he said with poise. Thank you for coming. I hope I will have time to address as many questions as you have for me. However, it is no secret the real reason I'm here is to allow you to get to know me better. That includes my goals as a Senator representing the great state of Massachusetts." *Senator Montgomery was gloss personified.* He made a few conciliatory comments about his opponent, State Attorney Bill Prachett, and then turned the focus back to himself.

In a matter of 15 minutes, Senator Montgomery had laid out a political agenda very close to that of his track record as Representative Montgomery. It was a socially 'liberal' view of government that yet emphasized fiscal responsibility. In addition, his agenda encompassed environmental concerns and capitalized on the strength of the nation's diverse population and the campaign finance reform debate. He also stressed the desire for bipartisan cooperation. Montgomery's track record in all these areas was impeccable, including reaching out to the Republican Party. However, there was nothing new in his speech. *The only surprise was that he was sticking so closely to it.*

The nation, by most indications, had remained in conservative mode. And as the economy continued to shrink, that would probably continue. Yet, Senator Montgomery ran on 'liberal' views and won. He even won by a significant margin. The senator apparently paid little attention to the sentiments of many of his constituents and the nation at large, for that matter. His agenda, as he bluntly put it, was founded on doing what is morally right. His reasoning persuaded Nicola. *Somehow, when he spoke of poor children, giving back to the community and saving our national treasures, it all seemed practical.*

The minute Senator Montgomery agreed to take questions; Nicola shot her hand into the air. To her surprise, in the sea of hands, Senator Montgomery chose her. "Yes," he asked, looking directly into her eyes. She stood, still barely taller than those remaining seated. She articulated her question flawlessly. Her eloquent style of probing had become her trademark. She was very proud of that. "Senator Montgomery, we've heard this agenda from you before. It is, basically, what some might term the 'liberal' position you had in the House. What's different?"

Senator Montgomery replied with an expression of amusement, "Thank you for the question. While I don't quite see you, I did hear your question clearly." The press core broke out into rancorous laughter. *If she had been white*, Nicola thought with annoyance, *her face would have been beet-red right now. How dare he make fun of her stature in front of her colleagues? Two can play this game, Senator,* she thought. She was indignant. Embarrassed, she smiled back at him and waited for his response.

"To answer your question, there is absolutely nothing new. The positions I have taken in the past were positions I took because they were the right things to do. I believed in them then, and I do now. I will fight for the people of this great nation, the common man. There are many people still locked out of the 'land of opportunity.' I'm hoping that bringing matters to a higher level of awareness in the Senate will allow me to further impact the direction of this nation." *Well put,* I acknowledged with begrudging admiration.

He's a little too smooth for me, Nicola decided. *Men like him think they own the world. They also believe they're entitled to whatever they want.* She recollected with distaste the constant stream of powerful men hitting on her. Many were married. *What gave them the right to assume that their married status was nullified in her mind based on their station in life? D.C. was so devoid of morality it sickens me,* she thought. Nicola scribbled down notes from Montgomery's response to her question and other questions. Despite herself, she found Senator Montgomery engaging.

The press conference lasted exactly the 45 minutes slated. A stream of hands was still in mid-air when Bo Elison stepped up to the podium, "Ladies and gentlemen, I'm afraid we are out of time," he said respectfully. "The senator will be happy to meet with you at a later date to further answer your questions. However, we do appreciate your time and attentiveness. He looks forward to getting to know all of you better as time goes on. Again, thank you for coming." Nicola reluctantly gave the senator another high mark for ending on time. She liked a man of his word.

Nicola was gathering her papers when she felt the presence of someone behind her. To her astonishment, she turned to see Senator Montgomery. It was highly unusual for a senator to single out anyone in the press. They traditionally kept their distance to give the appearance of unbiased coverage. The only exception was if you were a member of the presidential press team. Nicola did her best to conceal her shock. "Sorry, Senator, I didn't know you were behind me," she said in a composed voice. *Why was he making her heart race?* She contemplated this while attempting to pull herself together. Flashbacks of photos of his spectacular wife and elegant children came to mind. Nicola had even seen the family in person once. It was from a distance during one of Senator Montgomery's campaign speeches. She subtly glanced at his wedding ring to remind her to behave. *Why are all the interesting ones taken?*

Before the senator had a chance to respond, Nicola extended her hand to greet him. "Hello, Senator, I'm Nicola Patricks." She scolded herself for not following protocol and letting him introduce himself first. He was definitely unnerving her. Senator Montgomery met her hand and smiled flirtatiously. His handshake lingered a moment too long. She recoiled in an attempt to limit its effectiveness. Unfortunately, it was too late. Remembering the senator's womanizing reputation from the past was enough to snap her out of it though. *She would not be his prey,* she decided forcefully.

"I know who you are," the senator stated with ease. His confidence bordered on cockiness. "You do?" Nicola said, unable to contain her shock. "Yes, I inquired about you the second the press conference ended. By the way, excellent question. I was hoping someone would ask me that. You played right into my hands." He chuckled at his remarks. She could not help but smile in return. She could see why he was where he was. "You gave an excellent response to my excellent question, Senator," she said with a hint of acerbity. He ignored the edgy tone.

"Anyway, Nicola, it is a pleasure meeting you. I'd better hurry to my next engagement. It's nice to be in such demand." He grinned at his comments. "Thanks again for the question. Maybe I'll see you around." The senator waited for Nicola to respond. His eyes perused her body, lingering on certain parts. He didn't bother to conceal the desire in his eyes. Nicola felt flush, yet embarrassed. He continued with the conversation, "I'm perplexed that I haven't seen you at other media events." "I try to avoid these things as much as possible, Senator," she said, "However, there was such a buzz about you that I decided to attend. Normally I send someone in my place." She regretted her comments as soon as they left her mouth. That was all she needed, pumping up an already enormous ego! Senator Montgomery beamed, obviously pleased by Nicola's comments.

It was apparent those remaining in the conference room were staring at the two of them with immense interest. Washington liked nothing more than a scandal. Two attractive African-American 'heavy weights' would be too much temptation for Washington to pass up. Both of them were aware of it. Montgomery turned to leave, "Take care." "Thanks," Nicola said, attempting to lend some professionalism to the situation. She had the sensation she had been caressed. One of her colleagues walked up to her after the senator left the room.

"Nicola, what was that all about? You two almost looked intimate over there." Walter waited for a response with hawk eyes examining her reaction. She gave none. She was used to 'busy bodies' like him. All her life, she had dealt with them. *Walter was the eye of the hurricane of every rumor in the office,* she recalled with annoyance. She certainly didn't intend to be his next victim. "Walter, the senator was just introducing himself. He thanked me for my astute question, joking that he could not have staged it better." Nicola added for authenticity, "The senator also wanted to apologize for making fun of my height." Walter seemed to accept her explanation and questioned no further. With that, she walked off, leaving Walter to make what he chose of the situation.

• • •

Bo and Dirk flanked me in the back seat of the black Mercedes sedan. The driver glided us to our next event, a luncheon on Capitol Hill. My thoughts were still back with the vivacious Nicola. *That is one sexy woman,* I reflected. Her body invited you at every angle. What a treat for my first press conference as Senator. I smiled recalling our conversation. *She was a feisty one. You wouldn't believe she'd have that kind of spunk when she practically had to crank her neck just to speak with me.* I chuckled under my breath at the thought of the petite Nicola trying to 'take me on.' Bo turned to me. He had an odd expression on his face, one of preparing for danger just around the corner. "What's so amusing, Jack?" Bo asked in a dry voice. It was plain he really didn't want the answer, because he had a good idea where my thoughts were. It had been six years since we became a team, but Bo read me as if he'd known me my entire life.

"Nothing really, Bo. I was thinking back on my conversation with that luscious Nicola. She is a knock out." I was attempting to sound casual. I could see from peripheral vision Dirk was inspecting me as well. OK, so they were both troubled. "So we're on a first name basis with her, are we? Look, Jack," Bo said with uncontained agitation, "I know she's a tantalizing woman, but you need to leave that alone." "What do you mean by that, Bo?" I asked innocuously, knowing damn well what he meant. "I mean, Jack, remember the days of old. We went through a lot of trouble to clean up your image. Thus far, you've lived up to your promise. Don't blow a stellar career for a piece of ass. I don't care how dramatic the curves and pretty the face." Bo's voice was gaining volume. He was a man with an explosive temper, I reminded myself.

"Bo, I don't deserve that. All I said was a few words to her after the press conference." Bo barely kept his cool. He took a deep breath and loosened his tie. "Jack, don't give me that bullshit. I know you. You had a 'bone in your pocket' before you reached your destination. All I'm saying is, think about how far you've come and what you have to lose before making another move in that department. You also have a pretty sensational family, Jack. I thought things were going well."

I couldn't respond. I knew Bo was absolutely on target. What the hell was I doing? I lowered my head in self-defense, "Bo, you're right. I give you my word it won't happen again. I just haven't met someone that stirred me so in a long time. She's the embodiment of sex appeal, and I lost my head. The irony is that I don't even think she's aware of her effect on men. It draws you into her more because of it, you know." I turned to Dirk for empathy. Instead, I found him staring at me with a blank face. Dirk said nothing, but his look said it all. He evidently concurred with Bo. *How could anyone not concur with Bo,* I thought.

I knew Dirk would have little to say in this area anyway. He had his own skeletons to bury. Dirk was found in bed with another woman in his vacation home in Napa Valley. His then wife had followed him there, suspecting him of infidelity. Marlene waited until nightfall to confront the two of them. I guess she wanted to make sure they were caught in the act. Dirk conveyed that Marlene had cornered him once before regarding an affair, but he had fervently denied it. According to Dirk, it was close to 10:00 P.M. when Marlene must have let herself into the back door. She found them in the middle of intercourse. He was in the guest room pouncing on a blonde with big boobs. Her name was Rhoda.

Marlene lost her mind. She started screaming hysterically over and over again, "How could you betray me with this white bitch!" She ran into the kitchen and grabbed a butcher knife, threatening to cut off his balls. Marlene then grabbed Rhoda's long tussled mane, attempting to cut it off. They started swinging at each other like two deranged animals. According to Dirk, it was downright ugly. "I tried unsuccessfully to stop them. That's when I finally called the police. I was scared shitless, man," Dirk said in a well-bred trembling voice. "I thought Marlene was going to kill us both. I think Rhoda's being white made it worse. All I could think of was whether Marlene had a gun."

Dirk admitted he wanted out of the relationship a long time ago, but didn't have the nerve to do it. In his mind, Marlene was too possessive and clingy. He felt suffocated. *At least there were no children,* I thought. They had tried unsuccessfully to have kids the first five years of marriage. It turned out Marlene was infertile. That only served to make her more insecure. Life could be a bitch. However, Dirk's failed relationship had worked out well for me. Dirk wanted to get away from it all - the marriage, the stress of a very lucrative international banking legal practice, everything. I told him that if I won the Senate seat, I would need a legal and political advisor.

I really just wanted to get him back East. Dirk belonged on the East coast, and I needed him. There were so many sharks at your back in politics. Dirk was one of the few men I trusted. The night of Senate confirmation, I called him and told him to make his way to D. C. He easily agreed. It was a Dirk I was unfamiliar with, fatigued, despondent and tentative. A week later, Bo and I met him at Dulles Airport. He appeared drawn, but still possessed those patrician good looks. I introduced Bo to Dirk and we took him to the Ambassador Hotel to get settled. Bo and Dirk instantly hit it off. For that I was grateful. Both meant the world to me, and I was in a rare sentimental mood.

The three of us rode the remainder of the trip to Capitol Hill in silence. It gave me more than a little time to realize the extent of my foolishness. *These days Suzanne and I had a good relationship. The marriage had improved drastically since that fiery morning, two years ago. Our love life was simply unbelievable.* The friendship and zealous political backing had also resumed. I discussed most issues with Suzanne. She had sound advice and a transparent way of viewing matters I'd never discovered in anyone else. *Suzanne was just amazing.* I was only partially able to dismiss feeling something remained seriously awry in our marriage. It never occurred to me that I was the root cause.

· · ·

Nicola headed back to the Washingtonian Magazine building ready to start her piece on Senator Jack Montgomery. She could think of nothing else. She could think of no one else. She desperately attempted to steer her mind away from the dapper senator but found it an arduous task. She recollected the lingering touch of his hand and soft liquid brown eyes perusing her contours. "What has gotten into you, girl?" Nicola asked herself with self-loathing. "Have you lost your mind? The man is married and has two children! God forgive me," she murmured, "because I'm going to fry in Hell if I keep going down this path."

Nicola parked her silver Audi sports car in the garage dedicated to Washingtonian Magazine employees and headed into the building. She would do the piece on Senator Montgomery and that was all. After that, she would avoid him like one does going to the dentist, she decided with absolute resolve. *He was trouble, and she was weak.* She smiled to herself. *Senator Jack Montgomery might as well be the Devil himself. It was hard enough to be a Christian in this town without bringing temptation to your front door. I might be a career girl, but I have needs,* she acknowledged. She reflected on the longing she rarely satisfied. *It wasn't easy being a black professional woman in Washington.* The female to male ratio was also greatly stacked against her. She tried hard not to feel pity for herself. Instead, she headed to her office with the intent of diving into the project.

She labored on the article profiling the hottest new senator in town for the remainder of the day. She left for home shortly after 6:00 P.M. "It's been a long day," she pronounced, rubbing her neck and acknowledging the dull throb in her head, "It's been a long year in fact." As Nicola headed toward Northwest D. C., she realized just how starved she was for male companionship. *I could do with a man,* she thought. *My cat Buddy doesn't count.* Again, she pulled into her brick townhouse with the determination to not feel sorry for herself. She would focus on changing her circumstances. *Maybe she was too picky like Mama told her. Perhaps she should lower her standards. If only she knew how.* It had been over five months since Lemont and she broke up. Nicola recalled the countless men she'd dated prior to Lemont, and her mood sank. *Why couldn't she find someone to love her? Why couldn't she hold on to a man longer than two months?*

She picked up the New York Times in front of her door and unlocked the mahogany wood entrance to her townhouse. Buddy was sitting there patiently waiting. Nicola's mood began to rise. "Hello little fellow," she cooed, while bending down to greet him. Buddy started rubbing his body against her legs and purred loudly. "You love me, don't you, fellow? I can always count on you," she said, picking him up. She carried Buddy to the kitchen for both of their dinners. She clicked on the kitchen television to listen to the news. 'NBC Nightly News' was recapping Senator Montgomery's earlier press conference. The senator was smiling broadly into the cameras while summarizing his future plans in the Senate. *He was quite striking,* Nicola noted, once more feeling aroused. She nibbled on her salmon Caesar salad, clicked off the TV and headed into the bedroom. She read some more of a Mary Higgins Clark mystery novel for two hours and decided to call it a night. *Her last thoughts before sliding into unconsciousness were of the dashing senator from Massachusetts.*

• • •

It had been a couple of weeks since Senator Montgomery's press conference. Nicola was back to her old self. *Thank God,* she thought, with a sense of immense relief. *How could she have let herself be so disturbed by someone so unavailable? She must have experienced temporary insanity.* She remembered her promise to herself of not getting involved with married men. "You're not that stupid or fraught, girl," she stated under her breath. Plus, it was just plain wrong. She asked herself how she would feel, knowing her husband was cheating around on her. *There are good and free men out there,* she reminded herself. She just needed to get out more. *Nicola reflected on the number of times various girlfriends had invited her out with them.* Each time, she had either needed to work late, travel out of town or was just plain exhausted from all the activity surrounding her job. "I need to get a life!" she said to herself, "and I will start by taking up Delia's invitation for that ambassador's party this very weekend."

Nicola was deliberating about which article to use on the 'Pulse of the Nation' editorial when the phone startled her back to her surroundings. "Hello, Nicola Patricks here," she said in a professional tone. "Hello, Ms. Patricks. This is Jack Montgomery." Her hand went limp, and she nearly dropped the phone. She paused to gather herself. "Hi, Senator Montgomery," she responded, trying to sound as normal as possible. "Call me Jack, Nicola."

"So Jack, what can I do for you?"

"I just wanted to thank you for the incredible spread you did on me last Friday."

"You're quite welcome. Everything I said was true."

"You're most flattering, Nicola. However, there's another reason I called." The senator cleared his throat.

"Oh."

"I wanted to see if you were available to do lunch with me this Thursday."

Nicola paused once more, "I don't think that's a good idea, Senator." Nicola made a point not to call him Jack. It was too familiar. She had no intention of crossing the line.

"Why not?" the senator asked in a feigned fatally wounded voice.

"I'm an objective voice to the public, Senator. It doesn't look good fraternizing with the very persons I'm evaluating. I just wrote some very flattering things regarding you. It may be misconstrued if I'm seen doing lunch with you several weeks later. You do understand?" she said. In her mind she said, "And because you are married…"

"Yes, Nicola. I see your point. As disappointing as it is, I agree with your assessment. I guess I will have to seek someone else's opinion on this matter."

Nicola knew what Senator Montgomery was doing. He was throwing out a hook in hopes she would fall for it. Unfortunately, her journalistic curiosity kicked in despite her attempts at restraint. "What matter is that?" The senator stated in a dismissive voice, "It's not that important, Nicola. I should get to this meeting. I know you're exceptionally busy. It was good talking to you though. Take care." He hung up. She slowly put down the receiver. *Now that was a strange conversation, she reflected. Where was this man coming from?*

Nicola forced herself to concentrate on her work the remainder of the morning. She decided for lunch to go to the nearby park, despite the November chill in the air. She needed fresh air to clear her head. The conversation with the enigmatic senator resonated on her mind. *It's better than eating at my desk like I normally do,* she decided. *What better setting to dust away cobwebs than the park?*

The air was brisk, but she found a bench near the brick fence to partially block the fierce intermittent breeze. She sat on one of the benches and unpacked her tuna sandwich and apple. Nicola had planned to use this time to map out her future goals, both professionally and personally. *She planned to stay at Washingtonian Magazine for another two years. After that, she would leave, but to where?* Nicola had always been a long-range planner, so in her mind, time was of the essence. Plus, she felt restless. A total of five years was enough on one job. Yet, instead of planning for the future, she found herself alone in the park on a cold, blustery day, reflecting on the past. She was once again the little dark girl growing up in rural South Carolina.

• • •

"Mama, do you think I will be an actress someday?" Nicola asked her mom with anticipation of affirmation a six year old seeks from the woman bigger than life itself. She had put on her mom's high heel pumps and her Sunday dress and touched the whole outfit off with Mama's red lipstick. She smiled brightly at Mama who was in the midst of ironing clothes for Papa and her older brother Randall. Mama smiled at her in return, "Darling Nicola, you can be an actress or anything else you want to be." She then went sober, "However, more than anything right now, I want you to take off that dress. You know you only have two good dresses to wear to church, and we can't afford to buy you another one." Mama continued, increasing somewhat in volume. "Also, put back those shoes of mine. I told you about going in my closet and putting on my things. And wipe that lipstick from your mouth. There'll be a lot of years passing before you can wear that stuff." Mama moved around from the ironing board and lightly whacked Nicola on her bottom. "Now get, child." Nicola ran giggling out the room. She could see Mama smiling, despite herself.

At twelve, just after watching a Perry Mason rerun, Nicola came to Mama again. "Mama, I think I want to grow up to be a private detective and uncover crimes that no one else can solve." Mama gazed into her daughter's sparkling eyes as she did when she was six and said in her warm, rich, melodic voice, "Child, you can be whatever you want to be with a little hard work and faith in God." She pulled Nicola to her and held her for a long time. Nicola felt so special then. *She felt the same way when she was with Mama today,* she reflected.

It was sophomore year in high school when Nicola discovered she had a gift for writing. Her English teacher had the class do an essay on 'What it would take to achieve world peace.' It was one of those assignments that you had to read out loud. Nicola worked on it for a week. She spent the entire Saturday at the library studying philosophers and becoming abreast of what conflicts were in the world. Yet, the light bulb went off when she was in Sunday school. Her Sunday school teacher, Mr. Henderson, talked about Jesus and his ability to give one peace. He talked about the need to treat others like you want to be treated. Nicola titled her paper, "World Peace is Not Given; it's Won." In her paper, she outlined the various philosophers' beliefs on peace and conflict and talked about the teachings of Christ. Nicola was the last person that day to read her essay. Four of her classmates and she gave their presentations out loud that day. There was utter silence during Nicola's talk. At the end, she stared back at her fellow classmates with nerves so raw she could have jumped two feet if someone had tapped her. Henderson had an expression of astonishment on his face.

He got up from one of the back student desks and walked to the front of the classroom, "Miss Patricks, that was simply splendid! It was superb." Mr. Henderson beamed with an air of introducing a protégé to the world. He turned to the class, "Does anyone have comments?" Nicola waited anxiously and prayed they did not. She didn't have the confidence for criticism or to answer unrehearsed questions. The lapse of time was unbearable. Finally, a boy named William, whom Nicola knew had a crush on her since ninth grade, raised his hand. "Yes William," Mr. Henderson said in his proper English diction. William stood up and held his heart with both hands, "I thought the essay was beautiful. I think the author of it is even more beautiful." The class burst out in laughter. Nicola found herself even smiling. It served to relax her just a little. "Thank you, William, for that constructive criticism," Mr. Henderson said sarcastically. He looked at Nicola, "Nicola, you can sit down now. Thank you."

Mr. Henderson came up to her at the end of the class period, "Nicola, if you have a moment, I'd like a word with you." She didn't know what to think. Nicola was petrified Mr. Henderson was mad at her for bringing up religion in his class. Instead, it was quite the opposite. "Nicola, while I agreed with everything you said, I was most impressed with the way you said it. I think you have a gift for words. I do not come to this conclusion very often; so don't take what I'm saying lightly. I would suggest you pursue a career in communications. Your writing and delivery are superb." Mr. Henderson paused for Nicola's reaction. It was obvious he sought to guide a young gifted mind. From day one, he lectured on pursuing one's dreams. He also constantly had the class reading books dealing with overcoming human struggle. He was a wonderful teacher, Nicola thought, recalling the days when her dreams were planted. She remembered how she had run excitedly into the house after school, seeking Mama. Mama was in the kitchen whipping up Nicola's favorite dish, meatloaf with mashed potatoes, gravy and green beans. Nicola could smell the food when she opened the front door.

"Mama, guess what?" Nicola said rhetorically. She was unable to keep the exhilaration from her voice. "What baby?" Mama said with dancing eyes. She stopped her onion cutting in anticipation. Nicola was bursting with energy as she conveyed her story. "You know the essay on world peace I worked on? Well, I read it in front of the class today. After class Mr. Henderson came up to me and said I would get an A+ on it, but, more importantly, Mama, he said my writing is so good I ought to pursue a career in writing or communications." She waited for Mama to say something, anything. Nicola was afraid her mother would think it was a terrible career path to follow. Not that she ever did tear down any of her daughter's ever-changing dreams, but this one somehow was more important than the others. Mama was true to herself though, "Nicola, that's a wonderful career. I can see you on the evening news now." She resumed chopping the onions. "I'd love to hear the essay honey. Did you bring it home?"

Nicola popped from the kitchen table chair and sprinted across the room to grab the essay from her book bag. "You ready, Mama?" "Go ahead child, I'm listening." Nicola began reading the essay. After a while Mama slowly put down the cutting knife, wiped her hands on her apron and turned around to listen more intently. She was mesmerized. Once Nicola finished, Mama came up to her and squeezed her so hard it nearly took the breath out of her. Tears were rolling down Mama's face, "Nicola, that was the most exquisite essay I've ever heard. I would say that, even if you weren't my daughter. However, you being my daughter makes it even more divine. I'm so very proud of you. I've always been, but never more so than today. I want you to read it to your father when he gets home. Your teacher is right, you have found your calling, child."

Mama had always been Nicola's rock of inspiration. Daddy on the other hand, made her feel like a princess. He would repeat to her over and over again, "Nicola, you're a beautiful girl you know, both inside and out. Don't let anyone tell you otherwise. Don't let anyone take that away from you." Even through her college years, Daddy would say that. She remembered when her boyfriend in freshman year at Vanderbilt University broke up with her. He started seeing another girl in her dorm. Nicola came home from school the following weekend to heal her wounds. Daddy saw her in the living room crying into one of the sofa pillows. "What's wrong baby doll? Is school going okay? I know it's going to be tough your first year, but you just have to hang in there." Nicola looked up to see his concerned compassionate eyes staring down at her. She started sniffling, "No, Daddy, it's Kenneth. He dumped me for a girl down the hall." She began to sob uncontrollably. Daddy sat down on the sofa beside her and put his arm around her. He repeated his magical words. She loved him so. He was much of the reason she worked so hard in college. The day she graduated summa cum laude, Daddy's eyes lit up like a Christmas tree. "Baby, I'm the proudest father there ever was," Daddy said as he and Mama embraced her.

Nicola's family was poor, but they had dignity, she noted with fierce protectiveness. Maybe her parents didn't give her brother and her everything they wanted, but Mama and Daddy provided them with all the essentials. Education, hard work, service to others, and most importantly, spiritual development was emphasized above all else. Those were the ingredients for greatness, she reflected. They didn't have a choice but to succeed. She thought back on her childhood, and her body tingled with pleasure. Neither Mama nor Daddy had any more than a high school diploma, but they thought the sky was the limit for their children. Mama worked in the cafeteria of a local community college. Daddy was a mechanic in General Motors' service department. He also did odd jobs for people in the neighborhood.

Nicola's parents were resolute their children would have a better life. Daddy used to say, "Brains over brawn always wins out. Don't end up like your Daddy, darling." Nicola never forgot those words. Papa died eight years ago when she was only twenty-six years of age. He died of a severe hemorrhage to the brain. Mama cried like a lost child at his funeral. We all did.

I wish I could find someone like you, Daddy, Nicola thought as she rose from the park bench to head back to work. She wondered whether she was asking too much. Back when she was twenty-seven, she did meet a wonderful guy. His name was Richard. She met him while covering a story in Nashville on reducing crime in the city. He was a public defender. They dated for a little over a year, but, eventually, Richard got tired of the 'status quo' in their relationship and wanted something more serious. The timing had been all wrong for Nicola though. It was a period in her life where she was extremely engrossed in her career and wanted to make a name for herself. She just couldn't give Richard what he wanted at the time, and, now, she regretted her lost love. Richard was married with three children and living in Los Angeles.

Today, Nicola was more than ready, and there was no one. She thought of her brother, Randall, who was having his own difficulties at love. He was a handsome neurological surgeon unable to find happiness. *Go figure,* she thought despairingly. With that, she decided she should officially give up, at least for now, on her chances to uncover true love ever again.

· · ·

The Kenyan Ambassador party was Saturday. Nicola had promised Delia she would not back out of it. In fact, she found herself actually looking forward to the event with mounting anticipation. "It's been too long," she murmured, as she arose from her bed. She stepped into her slippers and headed toward the kitchen for a hazelnut cinnamon coffee. It was the earliest she'd awakened on a Saturday morning in quite some time. She knew she had a packed schedule. Normally, Saturday was the day she allowed herself to sleep in and enjoy something fun, like watching movies or sitting by a fire with hot chocolate. It was a day for also catching up on errands and general cleaning. However, today was different. Nicola had set this day aside to beautify!

The Kenyan Ambassador party was one of the hottest parties in D. C. It was said the Ambassador of Kenya loved to entertain and speared no expense in doing so. An invitation was extremely difficult to come by. Delia was a known D. C. socialite who stayed tapped into the rich and powerful. Her husband, Dale, was one of the top political consultants in the country. He helped strategize the most successful democratic campaigns in Washington's history, including President Bill Clinton's re-election and Senator Bernstein's nomination to the Senate. Luckily for Nicola, Dale was out of town with a client the weekend of the party. So, Delia asked her if she was interested in accompanying her.

"Nicola, now I know you're probably going to turn me down, girl, but I've got one of the most sought after invitations in town. Do you want to go with me to the Kenyan Ambassador party? I'm giving you exactly five minutes to give me a yes or no. There are way too many people vying for an invite. I know you're always so busy, but at least think about..." "Yes. I'll go," Nicola said with a thrill that was detectable in the pitch of her voice. Delia stopped in mid sentence, "What did you say?" Nicola repeated her acceptance, enjoying Delia's surprise. I will teach you to put me in a box, Nicola thought with sadistic pleasure. "Delia, when is it?" Nicola never kept up on these types of things. It was apparent from the silence on the other end of the phone 'Ms. Motor Mouth' was still recovering. Nicola laughed, imagining the expression on Delia's face.

Delia finally began squealing with elation, "Nicola, I don't know what has gotten into you, but I am thrilled that you're joining me! I thought I was going to have to ask my boring friend, Patty. I owe her an invite. She's extended me invitations to I don't know how many affairs. By the way, the party is this Saturday. I know it's short notice, but Dale wasn't absolutely sure he would have to make the trip and was trying to attend. However, this still gives you three days to prepare." "How should I dress?" Nicola interjected. Nothing was worse than when Delia got on a roll. "Nicola, you're definitely out of the loop. Of course, it's formal attire. I know you have something in that closet of yours besides business suits." Nicola said nothing, not wanting to incriminate herself further. Even though they were close, Delia sometimes intimidated Nicola with her sophistication and 'femme fatale' act. Delia agreed to pick her up at 8:00 P.M. on Saturday for the party held at the Ambassador of Kenya's home in downtown D. C. Nicola felt herself stiffen in a panic. I guess I haven't been out in a while, Nicola thought. I hope I still have my mingling skills.

She sat at her kitchen table sifting through the Saturday newspaper to see which stores currently had sales. She decided to just head to Tyson's Corner Mall in Falls Church. She should be able to find something there. She knew she needed to get out early, because her hair appointment was at 1:00 P.M., and they also needed time to give her a manicure and pedicure. *If I'm going to go for it; I might as well go all the way,* she concluded, feeling suddenly frisky and frivolous. Nicola headed for the mall like a woman on a mission.

The mall had its usual Saturday crowd, but Nicola promised herself she would not be defeated. It wasn't long before she spotted an exquisite velvet chocolate gown at the Rubin boutique. The gown was a lot more then she had originally planned to pay. But how often do I buy something so useless, she reflected with a sinful smile. She decided to try it on. Once she put it on, it became obvious she had to take it home. The dress took her breath away. It was form fitting and figure flattering. The top portion was brown velvet lace with floral chocolate sequin flowers covering the arms and shoulders. The floral patterns seductively covered forbidden areas. The bodice was cocoa-colored velvet. It draped snugly to the floor. The back plunged daringly low and had a satin tail that spread its wings when you walked. She knew she looked wonderful. The store clerk came in to see if Nicola needed any further assistance. She caught her breath as she stared at Nicola viewing herself in the tri-mirror. "You look fabulous!" the clerk said admiringly. Nicola blushed. The sales woman continued, "Girl, if I had your figure, I'd buy that dress myself." "Thank you, you are most kind. I think I'll take it." The sales assistant rang up the dress, and Nicola left the boutique. She softly sang to herself as she strutted to the car. "So far, so good," she murmured. She was exceptionally pleased with her purchase.

The salon was crowded when Nicola arrived. She was concerned her appointment time would not be kept. Yet, true to its reputation, Coiffures took her on schedule. Bernita, the beautician, helped her to decide on a simple, yet chic haircut. By the time Bernita was done, Nicola's hair was parted just slightly off center with one side crowning her face and the hair on the other side tucked behind her opposing ear. She kept the length so it hit at her shoulders. It was quite seductive. Bernita had added subtle burgundy highlights to bring out Nicola's chestnut colored strands. During the time her hair was being treated with a deep conditioner, Nicola had a manicure and pedicure. The final result when she viewed herself in the full-length mirror was, WOW! "Girl, you know you have it going on, don't you?" Bernita said, laughing as she belted out the words. "You've done a wonderful job, Bernita. Thanks, girl. Maybe I'll meet the man of my dreams tonight. If that happens, I will have to come back and give you a bigger tip." They both laughed. "If that happens, Ms. Nicola, you will owe me your next paycheck! Have fun tonight, girl. I'll see you in a couple of weeks," Bernita said as she went to work miracles on her next client.

Nicola was ready exactly at eight o'clock. She barely recognized the woman in the mirror. She was so, so alluring. Nicola giggled at the thought of the vamp appeal she would have tonight. Women were going to hate her this evening, she deduced. The thought initially made her uncomfortable, but she shook off the feeling. She intimidated women anyhow. No matter how nice she was to them and how moral she came off, they always stared her down with a threatened look in their eyes. She realized they were afraid to have their boyfriends or husbands around her, as if she planned to steal their mates. *Why would she want their significant others, if she could attract any man she desired?* It made no sense. *Screw them,* she thought disdainfully. *Thank goodness she had a few dear friends like Delia.*

Nicola swirled around once more in the mirror to get a better view of her creation. Just then, the doorbell rang. She saw Delia was prompt as always. Nicola swung the door open to see Delia exquisitely clad. Her honey blonde tresses were piled high on her head with a few strands gracing each side of her countenance. Only Delia could pull off that hair color and still look totally sophisticated. It had an almost unnatural look on most African-American women. Delia had on a black velvet wrap that cloaked much of her gown, but Nicola did see it was haltered and black silk.

Delia's eyes bulged when she stared at Nicola. "Girl!" She followed Nicola into her townhouse. Delia circled her like she was studying an expensive piece of art. "Nicola, you look sensational! I didn't know you could clean up so good," she said, laughing at her own wit. "Thanks Delia, even if that is a left-handed compliment." Nicola was beaming. She took a deep breath. "Delia, don't leave my side at this party. I know what a social butterfly you are. It's been a while since I've attended one of these affairs. I'm feeling anxious. I almost want to back out." "Girl, the way you look tonight, I should be the one backing out. I didn't know I was going to have to vie for attention with 'Miss Thang.' However, I promise to stick close to you. Now, let's go. It's one thing to be fashionably late; it's another to be rude."

Ambassador Nikaya's home was superbly done. There were fine antiques and impressionist oil paintings throughout. African art was interwoven to add dimension and connection to his heritage. Undoubtedly, the African art was primarily Kenyan. The party was underway when they arrived. It was standing room only. In the front room people were talking, drinking and laughing while contemporary jazz played in the background. The melodic tones of a live singer emanated from the next room. The artist was singing jazz with a touch of blues. Food was overflowing. Desserts were on decorative table displays, and servers were crisscrossing the rooms offering shrimp, stuffed mushrooms and other scrumptious morsels. Champagne was bubbling at maximum velocity. Nicola saw what Delia meant about Ambassador Nikaya's knowing how to throw a party. The ambiance was exhilarating. It had been too long.

Delia and Nicola certainly caused a disturbance when they entered the affair. A number of heads turned and conversations paused at their entry. Nicola wasn't sure whether it was seeing two black women unescorted to such an event or the way they looked. It was probably more the latter. She again scanned the room. Nicola recognized a few faces from the media world and decided to say hello. Nicola smiled, realizing Delia had left her side five minutes after arrival. She couldn't help herself. Delia knew half the town. Delia was probably meeting the other half tonight, Nicola thought sardonically.

"Hello, Steinar," Nicola said to one of the newscasters on NBC's WLKW local station. "Hello, Nicola. It's wonderful to see you again. Great party, isn't it?" "Yes, it is," she responded. "Wow, do you look terrific," he said. Steinar moved to one side for Nicola to get a better glimpse of the woman beside him. "Nicola, I'd like you to meet my wife, Kate." Nicola extended her hand to his lovely auburn-haired wife. She smiled brightly, "I love your dress. It's simply smashing." "Thanks," Nicola said self-consciously. Steinar inquired as to whom Nicola came with, and she told him she accompanied Delia Strafford. He instantly knew the name. *Does everyone know her,* Nicola wondered in amazement? She lingered a couple minutes longer and then made an excuse to mingle. Feeling a bit more self-assured, she decided to wander through the endless rooms to see if she would spot others she knew.

Each room had more food, music and people. The place was filled to capacity. Everyone appeared to be having a grand time. Nicola was having an amazing time herself. She remained in one of the rooms where people were dancing. The music was a mixture of up-tempo swing, Motown and Latin beats. It was an eclectic array of tunes, but the songs worked well together. Best proof was that this room was one of the most crowded. She found a spot against one of the walls and stood watching people move in ways they wouldn't remember the next day. She grabbed a glass of red wine from one of the waiters making his way through the crowd. "Nicola, this is your last glass," she said to herself under her breath.

She sipped the wine and tapped her feet to the beat of the rhythmic music. Soon, she was swaying without a care. After a while, she leaned one shoulder against the wall as she faced the crowd dancing in the center of the floor. "Hello, Nicola," someone said in a familiar low sultry voice from behind. An arm circled the small of her waist. She turned to peer up at Senator Jack Montgomery. He was grinning ear-to-ear. "Nicola, I've seen some fine sights in my life, but surely tonight you have made the top ten list. Seriously Nicola, you look delectable." She was flattered, but tried her best to conceal his effect on her. Senator Montgomery was being extremely flirtatious. He devoured her with his eyes. "Thank you, Senator Montgomery. I didn't expect to see you here tonight. In hindsight, I'm not sure why not," Nicola, said in a girlish voice she didn't recognize. "I told you to call me Jack," the senator responded with feigned indignation. She giggled in turn. *My behavior is scandalous,* she thought, as if she were an objective observer.

They talked for several minutes. The chemistry between them was insurmountable. Her nerve-endings were on edge. She needed to save herself, so she made a pretext to leave the senator. She told him she needed to find Delia. She explained Delia was most likely searching for her by now. As she passed by him to find Delia, the senator gripped her arm, "Can't she wait a few minutes longer? I'd like to dance with you." "I don't know if that is a good idea, Jack. Where's your wife?" "Suzanne couldn't make it tonight. Our daughter Gabriella came down with the flu," he said. "Suzanne wanted to be home for her." "And you?" Nicola asked with curiosity, "Why didn't you stay home as well?" "I planned to," he stated, "but Suzanne insisted that I come. She felt when a Senator is trying to make a name for himself, he needs to be seen at one of the most important social events of the year. I agreed with her." He had an answer for everything. That was such a perfect response. "Well then, Senator, Jack, I guess the answer is yes. I would love to dance.

They stepped onto the dance floor to a Latin beat. The song had a throbbing, hypnotic rhythm. They danced the Mamba flawlessly in synch. Senator Montgomery was a remarkable partner. Their bodies melted into one as they lost themselves in a series of tunes. Nicola looked over to see Delia heading straight towards her. "Excuse me, Senator," Delia said in a polite tone, "I need to steal Nicola away from you for a moment." "No problem," Jack stated unperturbed. Delia practically yanked Nicola off the floor. "Nicola, have you lost your mind! You and the senator were making a spectacle of yourselves out there on the floor. Everyone was staring and whispering about the two of you. I wanted you to meet a man here. But, next time, make sure he's available!" "I know, Delia; you're right." Nicola was absolutely mortified by her own behavior. She and Delia talked for a few minutes more before someone wanting to say hello to Nicola's ever-popular friend interrupted them. Nicola stood there a minute before excusing herself. She just wanted to get out of the room.

Everywhere Nicola turned she was getting appreciative stares, from both men and women, but she realized that the men had something in their eyes that invited her further. After wandering through several rooms of entertainment, she found herself back in the dancing room. *This room is by far the most invigorating,* she thought. Besides, Senator Montgomery should be gone by now. No sooner did she enter the room than someone asked her to dance. He was a distinguished Caucasian gentleman with silver hair and dark sideburns. *He is quite handsome,* she thought as he swept her onto the dance floor. From that point on, she didn't stand still. Men were actually vying for her attention. There were a number of men that wanted to take their interaction beyond dancing, but none of them piqued her interest.

She did give her number to one middle-aged gentleman. He was a Senior Partner at Booz Allen & Hamilton consulting firm. His name was Rod Peters. Rod had lived around the world and was quite intriguing. He was definitely worth getting to know better, even if only for a friend. *She would get out more often though,* she concluded. *If nothing else, the flattery was good for her ego. There was a 'sea' of men out there. Working all the time could make a girl forget what she had to offer.* She would start making more social rounds.

Exhausted and hot from all the bopping, Nicola went out-side to the terrace. The air was brisk, but served to cool her body back to normal temperature. The slight breeze actually was refreshing. It was just what she needed to revive her. "Are you having a good time, Nicola?" She turned to see Senator Montgomery once more. She turned back to face the pitch-dark gardens. It was a message to the senator that she prayed he would respect. "Yes," she said in a flat and uninviting voice. She kept her back to him. The senator did not take the hint. "I watched you dancing with your endless suitors," he said in a possessive voice. The nerve of him! Nicola turned to meet his gaze. How dare he be jealous? Doesn't he realize he has a wife and children at home? Her anger got the better of her. "Senator Montgomery, if I didn't know better, I'd say you appear slighted. However, I know that is not the case since you have a family waiting for you at home," she responded, trying to sound removed.

Senator Montgomery moved closer to her and gazed down at her seductively. He didn't respond to her statements, but rather said, "Nicola, you're completely unaware of how mag-nificently unique you are, aren't you?" He raised his finger and rested it on her lips. She knew she should move away, but found herself planted by the warmth of his manliness. Her breathing got heavy. "Nicola, I found myself disturbed by the sway of your body." *The brazen arrogance of this man,* she thought, but he mesmerized her and she was unable to respond with the indignation he merited.

The senator inspected his setting to make sure they were alone. *So, he was not entirely immune from how others per-ceived him,* Nicola noted. He must have concluded they were by themselves. No one else would be crazy enough to be out here in the dead of winter, Nicola concluded. Feeling valiant, he went for the kill. The senator lifted Nicola's face up to his with the same finger that had traced her lips, "Nicola, I've wanted you since the moment you asked me that question at my press conference. I've thought of you for months since." In a desperate move to rescue herself once more, Nicola skirted past him. She put one hand up with her palm facing him, "Jack, please don't go any further. I think you're very appealing, but I don't want to be involved with a married man."

Nicola rushed past the senator to return indoors, but he blocked her path. "Nicola, wait. I know I've had a reputation of being a womanizer, but that part of me is in my past. I've changed. I haven't been with another woman for over ten years." He stood there like a college boy anxiously waiting for her to respond. At first, she wasn't sure what to say. She felt a mountain of emotions ranging from guilt, indignation, and desire. However, mostly she felt disloyalty to God. *Why was this man making her life so difficult? God, why haven't you stepped in by now? You said you would give me no greater temptation than I could bear,* Nicola recited in a frantic silent prayer. *This is one time she needed His help.*

There were a thousand women who would leap at the chance to be with the senator, married or not. *Why would he choose her?* "Then why ruin a good record, Jack?" Nicola replied. "Because of you," he said instinctively. "I've never met a woman like you. Besides being stunning, you're intelligent, warm and enormously articulate. You excite me. You're full of life and determination. I've haven't met a woman as sure of herself as I am." Nicola was flabbergasted. Nicola replied guardedly, "How do you know all this about me, Senator? We've only had a few encounters." She was still off balance from conflicting sentiments. "I may not have consistently approached you, but I've been actively observing you for a long time. I've read all your editorials. I run in many of your professional circles due to my need to stay tapped into the media. I inquire about you frequently. I have my ways," the senator said with a boyish grin. "Plus, I read people very well. That's a huge part of why I've gotten as far as I have." Her heart melted. She knew she needed to remove herself from the situation, fast. Red flags were dropping all over the place. "I better go, Senator," she said, stepping around him in haste for the building. The senator held her arm. He swung her around and passionately kissed her on the lips. After a while, she mustered the conviction to pull away. *She could have stayed in his arms forever.* It was the most intoxicating kiss she'd ever experienced.

Nicola peered up into the senator's eyes, unable to speak. Somehow she managed to find her voice, "Jack, that should never have happened." Her voice was faint, and she knew her body had betrayed her. "Nicola," the senator said in a strange, weighty voice, "I know it shouldn't have happened, but I'm glad it did." "I must go, Senator. Let's pretend this never took place." She picked up the bottom of her velvet gown and ran back to the festivities. She felt his eyes on her with every step she took. She was no longer feeling very festive.

Once inside, Nicola found Delia, "Delia, I'm ready to go," she stated in an impatient manner. Delia stared hard at her. "That's fine. It's getting late anyhow. Are you okay? You look like you just saw a dead uncle or something." Nicola lied. "Yeah, I'm fine. I'm getting tired; that's all. It's been an incredible night, but exhausting. If I forget before you drop me home, thanks again for inviting me." Nicola added flattery to divert Delia from any suspicions. The tactic worked. "Nicola, you know you're so welcome, girl," she said in a light, charmed tone. "It was a great party. The ambassador lived up to his reputation once again," Delia said wistfully. They were both worn out and said little on the way home. For that, Nicola was eternally grateful.

Life after that party was never the same. *Why couldn't she stop thinking about him,* Nicola despaired. She chastised herself to no avail. It had been five days since the Kenyan Ambassador's party and the feel of the senator's lips on hers was as strong as if it happened yesterday. Nicola was so lost in thought she didn't realize her secretary, Lori, had walked into her office. Lori had an inquisitive expression, but she said only, "Nicola, there is someone here to see you." Feeling agitated that someone would just drop in on her when she had so much piled up on her desk, Nicola responded brusquely, "Lori, who is it? I really don't have time to take visitors." Lori stated tentatively, "I think its Senator Jack Montgomery. At least, it looks like him. I didn't want to ask his name, because I didn't want to seem like I don't recognize him." "Tell him I'll be right out." Nicola's heart was racing faster than an Olympic sprinter crossing the finish line. She took out her compact and checked her appearance. *She was glad she had taken extra care to look good that morning.* She had an interview for BET highlighting successful black businesswomen. She had worn a form-fitting evergreen pants suit with a gold satin camisole underneath and a floral pendant on the lapel. She patted my hair as she walked into the lobby in high-heeled cinnamon-colored pumps.

The senator was impeccably dressed as usual in a charcoal gray pinstriped suit, white shirt and burgundy tie. The white shirt highlighted his luscious dark complexion. *Lord, why would you allow this beautiful specimen of a man into my life?* Nicola struggled to control herself while greeting him. "Good afternoon, Senator Montgomery. This is a nice surprise." she said in a professional voice. She labored to sound conversational. She was well aware of the curious glances she was getting from her secretary. Jack understood and matched her tone. "Nicola, you said stop by anytime I was in the area. So, I was in the area and wondered if you were up to grabbing a bite to eat."

She couldn't come up with a reasonable excuse to refuse, and the truth was she didn't want to. "Sure Senator, I'd enjoy having lunch with you. Normally I eat at my desk, but it may do me some good to get out of the office for a change. Let me grab my purse." Nicola went to her office and got her purse out of the desk. She gathered her coat from the back of the door and returned to the reception area. Jack was standing there with hands in his pockets. He looked like a schoolboy waiting to walk his girl home from school. *And what am I doing with the butterflies in my stomach,* Nicola wondered. She concluded *they were both outrageous.*

It was the beginning of an affair that would last five years, *Nicola often recalled with sadness.* Strangely enough, the only person she confided in regarding her tawdry affair was Jack's right hand man, Dirk Patterson. So many times she would meet Jack at the end of a meeting with Dirk or Bo. They all grew to know each other quite well. The three of them shared a history together. At the center of it all was Jack. Nicola knew Bo's loyalties were strained in his friendship with her because of his fondness for Suzanne. Both Bo and Dirk knew there was more to the story regarding Jack and Nicola than Jack was letting on. Each had indicated that to Nicola in their own way. They would have had to be extremely naïve not to pick up on the vibes between them. Unlike Bo, Dirk probably understood the situation better, due to his past marital troubles. Jack told Nicola all about Dirk's history. Dirk also tended to stay out of other peoples' personal lives.

One day, Nicola just had to release. She called Dirk at his office. He had extended the invitation to call him if she ever needed anything. She did after Jack failed to meet her as planned one evening. They were supposed to meet at Marcello's Restaurant. Jack's meeting with Dirk was due to be over at 6:00 P.M. She and Jack were going to meet for drinks afterward. Nicola arrived at the restaurant to see Dirk sitting at a table alone, stirring an obviously long-sitting drink. "Where's Jack?" she asked, approaching the table. "That's a very good question," he said. "I don't know. Jack was supposed to meet me here at 5:00 P.M. to discuss legal matters. I tried him on his cell phone and still couldn't reach him." Nicola was about to go when Dirk asked if she wanted to sit down and have a drink with him. "You're already here, Nicola," he said. It had been a long day, she thought. *Why not?* They ended up staying a couple hours chatting. It turned out; Dirk was more than a handsome face.

Nicola tentatively dialed Dirk's phone but secretly hoped Dirk would not pick up. "Dirk, I'm sorry to bother you, but you said at Marcello's that if I ever need anything to give you a call." "Hey, Nicola. It's good to hear from you. What can I do for you?" He actually sounded elated to hear her voice. She was emboldened. "Dirk, I need to talk. Can we meet somewhere?" She again was unsure of herself, but she was desperate. *Who else could she talk to? Surely, Mama would not understand.* Mama had been bugging her to settle down for years. She would be furious to find out Nicola had been wasting her life on a married man, much less disgraced. Nicola was her 'good Christian' daughter after all. She would make her a grandmother someday. *Mama would need to pray for her day and night if she knew.*

Dirk responded easily, "Nicola, why don't you come over here. I work out of my home. I live near Capitol Hill off of 7th Street. It's a quiet brownstone on a secluded street with total privacy." It was as if Dirk knew what she wanted to talk to him about. Dirk answered the door in a gray turtleneck shirt, jeans and tan leather moccasins. "Come on in, Nicola. Have a seat. Can I get you something to eat or drink?" Dirk was the gracious host. "No thanks Dirk. I just need to talk." Nicola had come over to his brownstone expecting a bachelor's pad. Instead, it was decorated in high style contemporary. There was glass, marble, chrome and leather everywhere. Colorful contemporary paintings and black and white prints adorned the walls.

At her first chance, Nicola bared her soul. To sum it up, Dirk's reaction to her revelations was uneventful. He undoubtedly suspected the romantic relationship a long time ago. The only reaction she did get out of him was when she confessed to how long it had been going on. Nicola was sobbing by the end of her confession. "Am I a bad person, Dirk? Good people don't cheat around with other people's husbands," she said, moaning. Dirk held her and stroked her hair. He tried his best to mitigate her guilt. "Nicola, don't be so hard on yourself. We all fall short. You didn't intend for it to happen. You're a wonderful person; one of the best I've ever known. Besides, Jack has as much responsibility in this as you." The words were comforting, but not enough. However, it did feel like he had taken an elephant off her back after she left him.

The guilt was ever-present. "Lord, forgive me," Nicola said under her breath, driving home one Saturday from grocery shopping. She knew her affair with Jack was immoral, but she hadn't sufficient strength to end it. *She told herself to stop being such a 'goody two shoes,' to loosen up.* She thought *she would dip her feet into the water only and just go out to lunch.* That had been a grave mistake. Like all sins, the initial enticement was better than the grand finale. She had discovered that, by the time you figure that out, you're sucked into the vortex of despondency and lost forever. It was as strong as any addiction. She had tried to break it off to no avail, at least three times. Each time, Jack would talk her out of it. *That wasn't difficult to do.*

Nicola looked to the heavens for any answer at all. She knew she should do the right thing, but Jack defined so much of her at this point. She didn't want to be a home wrecker, but she loved him. Jack was the person she'd been praying for all her life. *Should she have stipulated that he be available?* Nicola knew it did no good to blame God for her own frailty. *Would she ever be free of him?* She stopped at an intersection and wept into the steering wheel while she waited for the light to change.

Chapter 15:

The Senator

Congressional life was starting to take its toll. I sat in the cigar-smoked room with three other members of the Senate. I pretended to be engrossed in the conversation. I was really thinking about the last few evenings with Nicola. My spine tingled with the thought of our time together. I quietly sipped the pricey cognac with my head tilted to one side, offering the appearance of total engagement. In just one term in the Senate, I had built a reputation as a mover and shaker. *Proof was the invitation tonight.*

There was already 'buzz' about my running on the Democratic ticket for the next presidential election. Most assumed I'd be the vice presidential candidate, but a few political heavyweights had even connected the words presidency with my name. My political clout had snagged me an invitation to the Senate's Harvard Alumni Club by a senior Senate member. When I walked into the club, I noticed there wasn't a single woman in the room where we sat, except to serve. I was one of only two African-Americans admitted. *So much for democracy*, I thought dryly.

Senate life took politics to the next level. There would be no boredom setting in with this position. Every decision held gravity. *Only the presidency had a greater impact,* I thought. The House had been easier to maneuver through. Not that I couldn't handle it. It was just that the degree of stress, at times, seemed insurmountable. *What did people expect out of their senator anyway?*

The intensity of everything I did also went up a notch. Everything I said or did was analyzed and interpreted. Much of the interpretation was distorted and taken out of context. My voting record and stance on issues were scrutinized under a microscope. It was downright annoying; yet, I conceded that, even with all its down sides, the Senate was where I wanted to be. This was the big league. I forced myself back to the present. It was crucial to be fully involved in the conversation at hand. This invitation was too vital not to capitalize on it. I was sitting there with three of the most powerful men in the Senate, Democrat or Republican. *I'm having drinks with three of the most influential men in the world,* I thought.

Rick Talbot gripped the cigar hanging out of his mouth and inhaled deeply the disgusting cancerous smoke. Hensel Whitaker and Thorton Maddock sat in adjacent chairs and completed the trio. Rick stated in a resounding voice, "Jack, I'm glad you could join us." His words seemed to come from nowhere, because we had been sitting there for over an hour. Rick intently scrutinized me. "Jack, there's a reason we wanted you to meet with us tonight," he said. My curiosity was immediately piqued. All three gentlemen were observing me with a forethought you would give your first airplane flying lesson. *I didn't know this was a 'meeting,'* I mused with caution. *Should I be worried?* Unconsciously, I sat up in my chair.

I peered at the three of them and carefully weighed my words, "Gentlemen, it's my pleasure to be here tonight. It is quite an honor to be invited." I was being sincere. I didn't take the invitation lightly. Rick cleared his throat, "Jack, we have been tracking your political career since you joined Congress as a House member more than ten years ago. To put it bluntly, we've been duly impressed. You conduct yourself like a man born for political life. And the loyalty of your following is phenomenal. That includes here in Washington and in your home state. Quite frankly, we also see that pretty wife of yours as an enormous asset to you." I was unable to respond. I had a strong sense as to where this conversation was going, but dared not 'jump the gun.' I couldn't bear the disappointment if I were wrong. However, it seemed to be going where I thought it was.

It was plain all three had discussed the subject prior to our meeting. They seemed of one mind. I waited patiently as Rick continued, "Jack, we believe you have leadership quality. The way you took the House back into Democratic control; your command of the House thereafter; and your brilliantly executed Senate race, tells us we have our man." My heart missed a beat. I couldn't stomach letting this play out any longer. "Your man for what?" I inquired, painstakingly attempting to keep expectation out of my voice. Hensel interjected before Rick could respond, "Our man for President of these United States - that is, when our recently elected Republican one has completed his four years." He went on, "We want to ensure John Stokes does not have a second term. We have faith that you will be the one to stop him. Of course, if the economy keeps eroding the way it is, it will take care of him for us." They laughed in unison. Again, it seemed as if I was talking to one individual with three heads. After finding my voice, I replied, "Gentlemen, I don't know what to say." Actually, I had a thousand things to say, but didn't want to appear self-serving. *No one likes a cocky son-of-a-bitch, least of all other egomaniacal senators.*

I decided humility was the best approach. "I'm extremely flattered, gentlemen. Yet, my concern is that, even in three years, I will still be short on experience. I would have served one full term, plus a few extra years in the Senate. Most candidates for President have 20 years under their belt. I'd be coming up against a tough pack. I'd also be just forty-six years old. That's quite young for President, much less the other strike against me." Rick and Thorton's eyes dropped to the floor. Only Hensel continued to look me in the eye.

They knew I was referring to my race. *The nation has come a long way,* I reflected, but racism is still 'alive and kicking.' I felt it was best to get all the issues on the table early in the game. Let's see if they really want me. Rick now burrowed into my eyes. He leaned forward, placed his cigar in the ashtray and rubbed his hands together before diving in, "Jack, your points are well taken. Actually, every one of them we have discussed extensively amongst ourselves. We'll be delighted to share our views with you if we can gauge your level of interest. It's quite a commitment you'd be undertaking." *Now that is an understatement,* I thought.

I continued in a relaxed mode, "Gentlemen, let me have a few days to mull over the idea. I would need to talk with Suzanne. It's as much of a commitment for my family as it would be for me." The three of them shook their heads in affirmation. Rick resumed puffing his cigar as he stared at me. He leaned forward once more, "Jack, we do have to ask you one question." He cleared his throat uncomfortably. "As you know, image is everything in politics. We're aware of your past affairs. Considering the situation, we believe you handled matters as well as possible in your last campaigns. So, we're not particularly concerned about them at this juncture, plus they were 'moons' ago. They are hardly relevant in this era of quick minutes and yesterday's news."

Thorton interjected, "Jack, what Rick is getting at is whether you have any fresh 'dead bones in your backyard' that would hold you back. We don't want to prime you for office, only to find out we have the wrong guy. After all, we have our own credibility to uphold." It was an exceedingly bumpy moment. The air was thick with cigar smoke and anticipation. I wanted to sink into my chair as I recalled last night's 'heat' with Nicola. When did life get so complicated? If I confessed, I would have undoubtedly washed away all dreams of the ultimate prize. If I departed from the truth, I ran the risk of discovery. I decided to throw the die.

"Gentlemen, I can assure you there are no fresh 'bones' as you put it, Thorton." With years of politics and street life behind me, I knew how to deceive without breaking a sweat. *Deception was a skill that served me extraordinarily well in pub-*

lic life. I was remorseful for my deception, but I felt I had no choice. *When would it ever end?*

Rick, Thorton and Hensel were apparently satisfied with my answer. Shortly afterward, they enthusiastically laid out their plans for taking back the White House. I was to be the 'White Horse' galloping to save the day. *However, I was not that naive.* John Stokes would be a formidable opponent. No one gives up that much power and prestige without going for the jugular. My bet was John Stokes would be no different. I mentally geared up for the task. Stokes' style was to attack with charm and finesse. *You wouldn't realize you were being devoured alive, until you disintegrated into political dust. That type of rival was the most treacherous*; I thought, recalling a similar situation in my last race. I had won only by a narrow margin. The Republicans were a vicious bunch. They'd put a spin on anything to make themselves look good. If the economy were slow, they'd blame it on the Democrats' not letting a certain tax-cut bill through Congress. If the economy rebounded, they'd say they did it single-handedly. Republicans were also renowned for their 'deep pockets.' *Money was face time, and face time translated into votes.*

The distaste was mutual. From a Democrat's point of view, Republicans were mean-spirited, selfish, greedy individuals trying to build and protect their wealth at the expense of others' freedoms and well-being. However, the flip side of it was Republicans felt that Democrats were attempting to steal their purses and their way of life. *Well, if I had the chance to do anything about it, those son-of-a-bitch Republicans would pay for stealing food out of the mouths of babes in my old neighborhood and similar places across the land.* I smiled inwardly, thinking of how Nicola often got on me for using foul language. "Jack, clean up your language," she'd say not too sweetly, "Or one of these days the Lord may do it for you!" I solved her complaint by simply not swearing around her. *How did I manage to have an extramarital relationship with a God-fearing Bible girl,* I pondered? Of all the gorgeous sexy women in the world, I fell for a certified religious fanatic. Half the time we're making love, the other time she's preaching at me about changing my ways. *Go figure.*

Fear began running through my veins. *What was I going to do about my relationship with Nicola?* I had never felt this way about a woman. I cared deeply for Suzanne, but it was different. A wave of guilt drenched me. Suzanne had been there for me. She warranted so much more than I could give her. She deserved my undivided devotion. "I'm sorry, Suzanne," I murmured. What was wrong with me that I couldn't give her that? I never could. With Nicola, I felt at home. I was accepted, and more importantly, understood.

Maybe it was that Nicola and I both grew up poor and could relate to the streets. Perhaps it was Nicola's toughness. She didn't take any crap from me. I respect her. I saw myself in her without my tainted debris. Nicola and I had an instantaneous bond. I wished it were just a casual affair. It would have made my life so much simpler. I'd been remarkably faithful to Suzanne before I met Nicola. However, when I fell, I fell like a rock. Facing facts, I loved Nicola. She made me feel alive. Nicola ignited my spirit and balanced me. I had never thought I was capable of really loving someone. Nicola also made me think in ways I never imagined, like whether there was more to life than what I saw. Again, I sought relief from my thoughts by concentrating on the matter at hand. If only my home life had been half as smooth as my political persona. Then again, it was a situation of my own making.

The meeting with Rick, Thorton and Hensel continued for another two hours. Discussions ran from stances on issues, such as healthcare, stem cell research, the environment, the economy, the Middle East and terrorism, to football picks. I ended the night liking those guys. They were old and out of touch but sharper than porcupine needles. *It was refreshing to match intellect to intellect,* I thought. So much of my time was spent in negotiation and compromise, hand holding with other Senate members to get an agenda passed and directing staff to get things done. Rick, Hensel and Thorton might have been from another generation, but they had wisdom that came from experience and from awareness of today's dynamics. The three had been in the 'game' before I hit puberty. *They would be extremely useful to me. Plus, they were the most energetic, shrewd political heads I had ever met.* I left the Harvard Club feeling like I'd been handed a golden wand.

I raced home like a kid wanting to show off his A+ on a math exam to his mom. I burst into the house. Suzanne was in the kitchen making chicken stir-fry. *She really was a delightful cook,* I thought offhand. I came up behind her and rested my hands on her tiny waist, whispering in her ear in a low sexy voice, "Put down that knife before you hurt someone." Suzanne turned around to see a beaming husband greet her. "Jack, what has got you so excited? I cannot remember when I last saw you like this." Suzanne returned my smile with one of her own. "Baby, have a seat." I grabbed her hand and dragged her over to the kitchen table. "Okay, Jack, what can be so electrifying?" Suzanne was obviously tense with anticipation. I told her every little detail of the meeting, and tears rolled down Suzanne's cheeks. She stood and rested her head in my chest, "Jack, I'm so happy for you. Words cannot begin to explain what I'm feeling right now."

"You mean you're happy for us, Suzanne. I would be nowhere if it weren't for you." I meant every word. "Even the senators mentioned that you've been an enormous asset to my career." I pulled Suzanne away from me to peer down into her eyes. "Thank you for always standing by me. Are you sure you're up to this?" Suzanne wiped her face with the hand towel she'd been cooking with, "Jack, I wouldn't miss this trip for anything." We hugged for a long time, taking in the moment. I wondered how Nicola would take the news, knowing that each moment with her from henceforth took on a whole new level of risk.

• • •

Accepting the offer by the three gentlemen was like signing a contract with the Devil, I thought, pulling up my schedule of meetings, events and guest appearances. The agenda was downright exhausting. Somehow the trio, as I fondly referred to them, had bypassed the seniority system of the Senate and got me nominated as Chair of the Finance Committee. They also had me on at least five subcommittees, including Energy, Agriculture and Defense. *How do they expect me to keep at this pace for two more years,* I thought? I stretched my legs to re-energize them.

My head was throbbing. I was on my third cup of coffee preparing for a debate scheduled in two days. I begrudgingly admitted their strategy – which was killing me - was working. The momentum of requests for my guest appearances on the various news shows had sharply escalated since the start. I found myself as the informal spokesman for the Democratic Party. I reached the pinnacle when the democratic Senate body approached me to be their new Leader. Rick, Thorton and Hensel made a point to emphasize they had no impact on the body's decision. "We had nothing to do with this one, Jack," Hensel said, as they laughed in unison over a celebratory dinner with Suzanne and me.

I felt uneasiness regarding my rapid rise to power and over-all position in life. Life was going too smoothly. *When things ran this well, there were usually consequences to pay.* There always had been in my life. My golden touch had become my trademark in the Senate. One newscaster even remarked that 'Senator Jack Montgomery's articulate, charismatic approach, quick intellect, unwavering positions and good looks have made him the hottest political ticket in town. He's the man with it all,' he stated. One Sunday while out on the road campaigning, Suzanne called me on my cell to tell me about the reviews of my appearance on 'Meet the Press.' "Really," I said with amusement, "They obviously don't see me looking for my keys every morning running out of our home half-dressed with a bagel in my mouth." Suzanne and I laughed. It felt good to share some light moments with her again. So much of our time together was focused on the children, preparation for my campaign, juggling schedules and maintaining household matters, we hardly knew each other anymore.

My thoughts moved immediately to my evenings with Nicola again. I knew it was not fair to either woman. Both warranted more. It was only a matter of time before I would be with Nicola I daydreamed. I vowed that, *as soon as I won the election, I would leave Suzanne and join her.* It was a selfish thought, and I tried not to think of the consequences of my actions. *Everyone deserves happiness, right?* I wasn't exactly unhappy with Suzanne, but rather bored and unfulfilled. I also refused to contemplate the degree of courage it was going to take for such a bold step. *No President had left his wife while active in the White House. Maybe they did it before or afterward, but never during. It would be uncharted territory.*

I was going over yet another summary of a bill proposed for review by the Agriculture Committee. I had persuaded Erin from my representative days to follow me to the Senate. It was an easy sale - greater prestige and more money. As before, Erin was more than up for the job. I thought about promoting Erin to be my new Chief of Staff once in the Senate, but I depended on his cunning mind and sharp decision-making capabilities as a Legislative Aid. I did let him know that if I got elected President, Erin would be first in line for the Chief of Staff position. *How had I met such good people? Better yet, how had I earned their loyalty and trust?* If only they knew who I really was. I rubbed my temples in an attempt to soothe another grueling headache and to wipe out the images of the past. In twenty-five years, you would have thought I'd have been over my youthful indiscretions by now. *It was strange how the past could grip your spirit and not release it.*

I looked over at the office clock in wonderment. *How did it get to be 9:30 P.M.?* I stood and walked to the massive window facing the courtyard. It was pitch black outside. Sparkles of light lined the D. C. streets while highlighting the various white granite buildings. I stared into the darkness feeling it penetrate my spirit. If I were half the man everyone thought I was, I'd be walking on water. I reminded myself of the battles I'd fought on Capitol Hill in behalf of the poor and downtrodden. I reminded myself of my successful lobbying of fellow members in the Senate to pass laws to limit the sale of assault weapons, increase community policing and finance after school programs, along with educational reform. Yet, in the end, it wasn't enough.

Every time I read about another young African-American male getting shot over drugs, my insides tightened with guilt. *There was no excuse for the path I had chosen. There was no excuse for the many lives I had destroyed in the name of power and glory. It was all so useless. If Jack hadn't died, I'd probably still be out there running a game on society. However, more than likely, I would have ended up at the bottom of one of the Great Lakes or in a penitentiary with my fellow drug lords. I was unable to shake the demons of my past.* I put my hands in my pants pockets and lowered my head. *Why, Lord, did you give me a second chance?* "I don't deserve your grace," I said under my breath. Feeling the weight of my forty-four years, I shut down the computer, clicked off the desk lamp and shut the office door behind me.

Once in the car, I dialed Nicola, "Hello honey." "Jack, where are you? I thought you were coming by to see me after your meeting on the Hill." Nicola said in a whining voice. I felt in the last year or so, Nicola was losing her patience with our situation. Our first argument about it had been about eleven months ago, but I saw it in her eyes way before then. After a passionate night making love, Nicola rolled her back to me and said in a barely audible voice, "Jack, what are we doing?" I knew what she meant, but decided to not play along, "What do you mean, what are we doing? What kind of question is that? I thought I just made love to the woman I adore most in this world." Nicola turned to face me with a resolved expression. Her head was propped on one elbow as she peered down at me. "Jack, you know what I mean. God, I love you, but I can't take this any longer. The clandestine meetings, the pretenses in public, the spiritual decay... It's devouring me. Jack, I didn't ask for this."

Nicola popped out of bed. She was butt naked. All of a sudden she started wailing hysterically. Her hair was all over her head like a wild cat. Her boobs were bouncing around as she grabbed her forehead. "Jack, we need to end this or make it right!" Nicola was talking very loud now. I was petrified the neighbors would hear her. "Calm down, Nicola," I said in my most comforting voice. "Jack, don't tell me to calm down," she responded waving her hands frantically, "I am tired of sneaking around. I'm not like this. I hate who I've become." Nicola dropped onto the bed. She put her head into her lap and began to moan.

My chest tightened. I was afraid I was losing her forever. It was something I was not prepared for. Nicola had been a part of my life 'on and off again' for five years now. Nicola once broke it off with me two years into the relationship. She said her conscience couldn't handle it any longer. That lasted for six months. The longing to be in each other's presence was simply unbearable. Nicola phoned me one day to say that we could be 'friends.' She said she really missed not having me in her life. However, within the week, we were back in each other's arms, making passionate love. *It's hard to give up something so comfortable with someone that truly knows you and accepts you in every way.*

Nicola had replaced Suzanne as the woman I confided in and sought counsel from. Nicola, not Suzanne, was the woman I went to when I needed the world to be softer on me and when I wanted to believe in humanity once more. Nicola understood me like no one else. I was free to be myself. I didn't feel on defense like I did with Suzanne. I even, one day, alluded to Nicola that I was not all I was 'cracked' up to be, and that I had a very checkered past. Her response was to murmur in my ear, "Jack, we all have made serious mistakes in our lives. No one is perfect. Your past is in the past. I think the nature of growing up poor lends itself to doing things you normally wouldn't do to just survive. I was one of the lucky ones." She then cradled her head on my shoulder and moved closer to me.

Fear of losing Nicola marched through my veins like light-ning racing through a metal pole. I pulled the covers off and went around the bed to console the woman I depended on like breath itself. "Nicola, look at me." I pulled her face toward me and her ebony eyes stared back. "You know I love you, Nicola, with all my heart."

Nicola interrupted, "Jack, sometimes love is not sufficient." I put my hand up to quiet her. "Shhh, let me finish. I know this relationship has been difficult on you. It's been arduous on both of us. You deserve so much more. I want to give you that." Ni-cola started to speak again, and I raised my finger to her lips. "Nicola, I want to make you an honest woman. I want you in my life forever, as my wife." Nicola's eyes got big, but she didn't say a word. "I've been wanting the same thing you have for a while now, but I currently have such a public persona I've tried not to let my mind even go in that direction." Nicola's face was awash with a sea of emotions. I could tell she wanted to believe me but was suspicious. "Really, Jack?" Nicola re-sponded, seeking affirmation. "Really, Nicola, I would love to grow old with you." The room lit up as a bright smile spread across her face.

Nicola nestled her head into my shoulder and soon we were making love once more. It was different this time though. Ni-cola gave herself completely to me in a way I had never ex-perienced. I lay beside Nicola after we were spent. I stared up at the dark ceiling, mentally constructing the best way to tell Suzanne I wanted out of our marriage. *How do you tear apart someone's world that has been only kind to you?* I had no an-swers.

Suzanne was a fine woman. Even though we had grown apart over the years, it was as much my fault as hers. I was stricken with angst. Plus, there were no real flaws in the rela-tionship to justify my betrayal. There never had been. I lay there next to Nicola, feeling the weight of my selfishness and reviewing the extent of the consequences that lay before me. Gabriella and Max would take it hard, even though they were practically grown. Gabriella would be attending my alma mater, Harvard, that Fall. Max was just two years behind her. Both of them adored their mom. *How would the split affect my relationship with them?* My insides were churning once more. *What about my run for the presidency? Could the public forgive my transgressions this close to the election?* My mind was racing. All roads led to defeat. I abruptly realized how impulsive my promises were to Nicola.

I got up and went to the bathroom. I took a Tylenol PM to get some sleep before another strenuous day. I stared into the reflection on the medicine cabinet door. I looked surprisingly run down. "Another long evening at work with a sleep over at Nicola's," I stated under my breath. Guilt flooded in once more. How many times over the years had I given Suzanne various reasons for my absence? The life I lived on the road often made it easy. "Joe, you deserve a sliver of happiness too," I justified while swallowing the pills. "The world be damned." I slid back into bed and draped my arm around the woman I cherished, melding my body with her silhouette. Little did I know that my world was about to drastically change, and not for the better.

. . .

"Mr. President, today is your lucky day, sir," Augustus Marcello said in a gravel voice from too many years of heavy smoking. His chapped hand gripped the cell phone tight and held it close to his ear so he wouldn't miss a word John Stokes uttered. It wasn't every day you had a client this powerful. President Stokes could make business boom in ways Marcello never dreamed of. Imagine, the President of the United States as a reference. Of course, he'd need to be extremely careful when 'dropping' the President's name. No one ever wanted to admit using a private eye, unless it was for catching a cheating husband. Marcello recalled his waning bank account and licked his lips in anticipation of pending business. Of course, getting the pay-off from this one job would keep him going for some time. Marcello drew another puff on his cigarette with his free hand.

The President was obviously paranoid. He was speaking on his private line, but practically whispering on the phone. Marcello strained to hear him.

"Mr. Marcello, what do you have?" John Stokes said hungrily. This town of D.C. would always keep detectives employed, Marcello thought, laughing to himself. For two weeks straight, the President had called twice daily for news on the guy. However, Senator Jack Montgomery was either squeaky clean or he was very careful. Being that Jack Montgomery was a politician, Marcello had cast his vote on the latter. He had urged the President to be patient. "Well sir, your patience was worth it. I think you hit the jackpot," Marcello said smugly. John Stokes interrupted, "Get to the point, Augustus. I don't have a lot of time for bullshit." The President was noticeably agitated. Marcello was offended, but kept his cool. Too much was riding on this partnership, he reminded himself. These powerful types were all the same. They think the world revolves around them and that they control everything within it. He would shove his irritation deep within his belly. John Stokes must believe the senator is a real threat, Marcello decided. The level of impatience went up with these types when they had something to lose. The President of the United States was reputed for keeping an ear to the corridors of Washington. Knowing whom to squash and when was half the battle in maintaining the throne.

"Yes sir. Sorry for not getting right to the point," Marcello said respectfully. "Well, tonight, I followed Senator Jack Montgomery to a residential location in Northwest D.C. He went off the beaten path before he circled back to the rear of a townhouse. Anyway, to make a long story short, the senator was visiting a woman. Undoubtedly, the woman is his mistress, or at least they're having a 'fling.' I took clear view snapshots of the senator's face in her kitchen. They later went to her bedroom. I have a photo of him closing the blinds. The senator was in such haste he didn't shut them completely. I have a snapshot of him and the woman embracing and participating in a deep throat kiss. It's not a great photo, but you can make him out enough to incriminate him. Not that I'm implying anything," he quickly added.

Marcello went on with fervor, relishing in his coup. "The two clicked off the lights, so I wasn't able to get any love scenes. I waited another hour or so behind the townhouse to take a snapshot of the senator coming from the place. His facial expression was, at best, cautious. I took a close up of him, so that you could see what I mean." Marcello thought the line had gone dead because there was complete silence on the other end. "Are you still there, Mr. President?" he asked in a worried tone. He didn't want to lose the momentum or the payoff. *Negotiations were best when the skillet was hot!*

"Yes, I'm here, Mr. Marcello. I'm just soaking in the information. You've done an excellent job," he said, "Nice work." Marcello beamed from the compliment. It's not everyday a 'hot shot' talks highly of your work, he thought. "Thanks," Marcello said with renewed enthusiasm. "However, there is more, Sir. The real story is who the woman is." He paused for effect. "I thought her faced looked familiar. She's a stunning black woman, I might add. Anyway, once I verified the townhouse number, I called my guy back at the office to confirm who owned it. Are you ready for this?" Marcello went on without waiting for a reply. "The owner is Nicola Patricks, the Editor-in-Chief of the Washingtonian." He heard the President suck in air on the other end. "Augustus, I cannot say this enough, you have done outstanding work. I'm going to throw in a sizable bonus for your efforts." "Thank you, Sir, for the words and, of course, the additional funds. It's nice doing business with you," he replied. Before Marcello could say goodbye, the line went dead.

Marcello had parked on another residential street not too far from the scene. He sat in the vehicle a moment longer to take in his good fortune. He reached for the bottle of Jack Daniels, took two large swigs and wiped his mouth with the arm of his already soiled jacket. He had given up concerning himself with how he looked so long ago he couldn't remember. He figured his line of work was the root cause. Seeing the armpits of life did something to the psyche. Yet this night made him feel proud of what he did. *There was nobility in exposing those living double lives.* He took a moment longer before turning over the engine of his Ford Taurus. He decided to celebrate his hard-earned victory and drove off in search of his favorite prostitute, Cookie.

ॐ

Chapter 16:

Catchin' Up with the Past

Ridder rinsed his face; accidentally splashing water onto his adoring golden retriever, Lily, in the process. Lily wagged her tail in delight and sat at attention. He peered down at her. "Sorry, Miss Lily, I didn't see you down there. I'm just trying to wake up, girl," he said, with affection only a master could understand. Ridder dried his hands and petted her on the head. He squatted to meet her eye to eye, "Let's get some breakfast, shall we?" He went to the kitchen of the small two-bedroom apartment and pulled eggs and bacon out of the refrigerator. He retrieved the coffee and dog food from the cabinet. After filling Lily's bowl with dog food and getting the coffee brewing, he headed to the front door to pick up the Sunday paper. He did love the New York Times. He bent down to grab the paper but felt a sharp pain in his back as he rose. "Damn!" he yelped in anguish, "A sure sign you're getting old. Nothing works according to the instruction book," he griped under his breath limping back into the tiny apartment.

He slowly made his way across the sparsely decorated living room and headed back into the kitchen. "Nothing like a warm breakfast, a fresh cup of brew and the Sunday newspaper, is it Lily?" Lily moaned in response. Once the eggs were scrambled, bacon fully cooked and the coffee was made, Ridder settled into one of the chairs at the small kitchen table. He took a couple slices of bread from the bag and spattered them with butter. Two more years to retirement and he would have this luxury every day. He smiled. It was hard to believe he'd served thirty-three years on the Cleveland police force. *Maybe career stress was why his body felt so banged up.* He supposed he could have taken early retirement at fifty-five like a lot of the guys, but he had wanted to wait it out to get the full retirement package at sixty-two. *After years of alimony and child support, I need everything I can get,* Ridder thought to himself and chuckled. He could've done a lot worse than retiring as a Lieutenant Detective at the unit. Life had been fairly good to him. He remembered aspiring to be Police Chief. *That seemed so long ago. It was amazing how life's dreams faded into life's reality at some intersecting point. It was hard to say exactly when that happened.*

Ridder dug into his breakfast with a ferociousness of a man stuck on a deserted island with nothing to eat but berries. He flipped open the newspaper with a zeal that had endured over the years. As he used to tell his daughter, Adelle, an informed man was an equipped man. He loved to irritate her by saying that to her too many times over the years, even when she was in college. *You're never too old to hear words of wisdom,* he thought with a grin. Ridder was eternally grateful that Samone let him maintain a solid relationship with their daughter over the years. Their split was bitter, but Samone didn't want Adelle to pay the price for it. In the long run, it was beneficial to both of them to see Adelle as healthy and whole as possible. Even when Samone remarried six years later, she kept her word.

Adelle turned out to be more than Ridder ever could have imagined in a child. *It was just amazing something that good could spring forth from his doing.* A glow spread over him as he reflected back to the summer when he gave his daughter away in marriage. *It was the proudest and saddest day of his life.* He washed down the remainder of his food with orange juice. "You're someone else's responsibility now, baby girl," he murmured. He immediately felt extremely lonely. *Maybe he should have remarried.* Yet, he knew Samone had been right when she accused him of being married to his work. He glanced down at Lily, lying by his feet, to remind himself there was still companionship in his life, even if it was four-footed and furry. He knew he was being silly. Ridder comforted himself with the knowledge that Adelle would always be his little girl.

Ridder read the headlines of the New York Times, 'New Terrorism Alert.' *How many times can we hear these alerts before we become numb,* he pondered cynically? He continued to peruse the various article titles. Each article was more depressing then the previous one. 'Economy on the Slide,' 'Six Killed in Multiple Car Crash in L. A.,' 'New Evidence Linking Smoking to Down's Syndrome Births.' *Why do I read this stuff?* He wondered as he continued skimming the various articles. He flipped page after page to drink in world events. Finally, he made his way to the back of the newspaper where headlines from throughout the nation were highlighted. His eyes caught the attention of an article titled, 'Can Police Solve a Crime Committed 25 Years Ago?' He began reading with mild professional curiosity.

You could always learn new techniques, even after years in the business, Ridder concluded. He reflected on his words of wisdom to Adelle and smiled. The article went on to say that a car had been recovered from a Florida swamp. The car and body were discovered on one of the swamp banks. First estimates were that it was a female in her early twenties. The body was completely decomposed. Only skeletal remains were uncovered. The woman had a gunshot through her skull and was strapped in to the driver's side seat. It was further estimated that the car had been pushed into the swamp some 25 years ago. The discovery of the vehicle was made due to Florida's efforts to control the state's mosquito population. Evidently, the automobile had been buried in shallow waters and surfaced shortly after massive flooding in the area caused the vehicle to dislodge.

The article went on to say the Florida police suspected the event was related to a drug deal gone wrong down in Miami, but didn't give reasons for the connection. Early indications of DNA matches were that of a Hispanic woman by the name of Irma Rodriguez. Interesting stuff, Ridder thought as he moved on to the next article. Half way through reading the next story about a woman, whose child was kidnapped as a baby in Nevada, he paused. His mind was racing.

He dusted the cobwebs off his rusty brain to recall the events of the time. He remembered trying to nail a young punk named Joe Baker with Puto's death, but couldn't because the timelines didn't match up. *Twenty-five years ago would have been right around the time of Joe Baker's and Puto Sanchez's deaths.* Ridder unconsciously moved closer to the edge of his chair. What would the chances be that the woman's body found in Florida was related to those events so long ago? He remembered speaking to a kid from the 'hood' during his investigation of the deaths of Joe Baker and Puto Sanchez. The youngster had recited a conversation he overheard with one of Puto's 'assassins' regarding Joe Baker's body being disposed of down in Miami. There was supposed to have been a Latino woman with Baker at the time.

It probably couldn't be connected, Ridder thought, shaking off that odd sensation he got when he smelled something awry. He attempted to finish the article on the woman in Nevada, but found the distraction too great. The description of the recently discovered car was an exact description of the one witnesses said the woman and Baker drove off in. "Too many coincidences are no coincidence," Ridder said out loud. He decided to 'surf' the Internet and see what he could uncover.

Ridder began his investigative work by entering "Puto Sanchez" into his favorite search engine. The last article on Sanchez was from the Cleveland Herald at the time of his death. There were several earlier clips on Puto as well that described his links to various crimes in Miami. Most were related to convictions on drug trafficking and racketeering.

He was just about to give up, convincing himself that he was merely obsessed with a past failure, when Ridder decided to pull up Dyke Johnson's 'rap' sheet. Dyke Johnson was supposedly one of Puto's main henchmen killed in the drug deal gone wrong in Miami. Ridder learned of him during his investigation twenty-five years ago. Dyke had a record approximately two pages long. *It was nice that they had finally linked up the states, giving police access to the criminal history of a person throughout the nation. This man was no saint,* Ridder deduced as he scanned the charges against him.

The entire effort appeared fruitless, until Ridder noticed some notes included in Dyke's record. The notes read, 'It is believed that Dyke Johnson has ties to the 'Black Angels' gang in Cleveland, Ohio. It is suspected that he supplies much of the gang's cocaine through his Miami, Florida channels.' Ridder's heart raced. *What did it mean?* He knew there was a link between the morning's New York Times story and the case twenty-five years ago, but he didn't know exactly what it was. *There was nothing more thrilling than an unsolved case. He was old now, but not washed up. If he could solve this puzzle, he might be promoted to Chief of Police after all. At the very least, he would surely leave the force with honor. That was worth something.* Ridder wanted most to witness the pride in his daughter's eyes as her father was honored for his tenacity. He imagined himself accepting an award at a ceremony with his daughter present.

Ridder got up and paced the floor of his undersized space. He then went back into the kitchen and poured another cup of coffee. Lily followed. "What do you think, old girl?" Ridder said to Lily as he petted her soft head. Lily panted and wagged her tail in response to his strokes. He went back to the computer and put in Irma Rodriguez's name. The story in the New York Times came up again. There was a photo of Ms. Rodriguez and the possible defendant outlined in the article. "That's one fine dame," he murmured. There was not much else of substance on her.

Ridder entered Irma's name into the national police database, but there was no rap sheet on her. It appeared that Ms. Rodriguez was squeaky clean. What the hell would a high-powered attorney be doing associating with a thug like Joe Baker? Ridder knew it wouldn't be a first for an upstanding woman to get involved with a man of questionable repute. He felt defeated. He continued to sip on his coffee, hoping it would kick-start his mind. "Think, Ridder," he said out loud. The word 'high class' suddenly shot into his mind. *Those were the words the kid used to describe Joe Baker's girlfriend.* He remembered, because it struck him as odd that a low-life could attract such a woman.

Ridder went into his storage closet and pulled out notes he had drafted on the case some twenty-five years ago. It took a while to search through all the boxes of files, but he finally located them. Luckily, he saved everything. He pulled out the file on Joe Baker. He could barely decipher his own scribble, but he eventually found the notes on the conversation he had had with the kid, Fernando Romero. *Right, that was the kid's name,* he recalled. Ridder scratched his head in satisfaction. He dissected the statements by Fernando with mental tweezers. It was like a firecracker went off in his head. "I've got it," he said, "Irma Rodriguez had to have been Joe Baker's girlfriend."

Puto must have been made to believe that Joe Baker and his girlfriend died and were dumped in the swamp. His men were probably too afraid to tell Puto the truth. They had never killed Joe Baker. They couldn't have killed him, because Irma Rodriguez would not have made it to that location with a bullet in her head. It would make no sense for Joe to kill her himself. How the hell did Joe Baker survive? Ridder stared out his high-rise window deep in thought. *Maybe he had been right all along. Joe Baker never died that fatal night in Cleveland, because he would have been still making his way back up from Miami. Instead, the person that perished that rainy night had to be his identical twin brother, Jack.*

Ridder knew he had no concrete evidence to back up his theory. His hunches were just theories once again. That's why he'd had to drop the case in the end twenty-five years ago. Ridder needed proof of, at the very least, an undisputable timeline. He was convinced of his conclusions. He had the tenacity of a Pitt Bull going after its prey, and it was time justice was served. His irritation with Jack Baker during the investigation resurfaced as he marched back to the computer with determination. He typed in the name of Jack Baker and pushed "enter."

Something very odd occurred. There was coverage on Jack Baker through his graduation from law school. There was even information on Jack Baker marrying a woman by the name of Suzanne Montgomery, but his life went no further. Suzanne Montgomery apparently came from an esteemed family because there was an article on their marriage in the society section of the 'Atlanta Journal Constitution' newspaper. Ridder studied the picture of the couple. That was Joe Baker alright.

Ridder had kept the case open for five whole years after his department dropped it. He finally decided it was useless and told himself to just get over it. The task of releasing it from his mind had been arduous though. He was not one to give up, and the failure made him feel defeated. The thought of a guilty man roaming the streets also did not sit well with him. Yet there were daily crises at the precinct to tackle, which helped him, move on. Ridder examined the picture of Suzanne. *My, she was a knockout. Joe has good taste in women,* he thought begrudgingly. Ridder was still perplexed by the lack of information on Baker after the wedding.

What if Joe took on his wife's last name, instead of the other way around, he thought. It was outside tradition, but not unheard of. "It's worth a shot," Ridder said out loud raising his eyebrows. He entered the name "Jack Montgomery." There were so many articles on Jack Montgomery that Ridder would have needed the remainder of the day and evening to read through them all. He decided to skim the most recent articles. There was one just two weeks prior titled 'Senator Jack Montgomery Takes on the Establishment.' The article outlined Senator Jack Montgomery's 'pet' programs in the Senate to help inner city children excel in school. With the article was a picture of Jack Montgomery.

Ridder's heart skipped a beat when he stared back at Joe Baker. It was as if he were hurled back into time. He rubbed his chin uncontrollably and stared at the photo for a few minutes more, just to make sure. *He was unmistakably examining a much older, more sophisticated Joe Baker. The droopy large brown eyes were the hallmark of the 'one and only.'* "Well, well, well," Ridder whistled. "The hometown boy makes good." Ridder continued under his breath, "However, won't the world be surprised that the hometown boy, is really a murdering thug. And now I can prove it, Joe. Mr. Senator, I will show you were down in Miami at the time of the murders of Dyke Johnson and Irma Rodriguez."

Ridder jumped up from his desk chair in exhilaration. He paced the floor to get his mental 'juices' flowing. He stopped and cocked his head to one side. "I have myself a timeline," he said in glee. His nerve endings were standing at attention. "There is no way you could be in two places at once, Jack Montgomery," Ridder said, continuing to talk to himself, "unless you took that return flight from Miami, which I don't believe you did. You are 'toast,' Sir." Ridder smiled and clapped his hands together as if he were trapping a bug. However, he forced himself to reason with a level head. He didn't want to be tripped up later by some fancy high-powered attorney. Yet, the same conclusion kept coming back to him. *There would be no other means of transportation that could get Joe Baker back to Cleveland at the time of his supposed death, than by plane.*

Ridder sat back down and stared at the computer screen as if in a trance. *What should I do with this information;* he contemplated, realizing he was sitting on a time bomb. He couldn't put the cart before the horse. *He would need an airtight case to confront someone so powerful. Maybe I should take a little trip to Miami,* Ridder surmised. He pulled up travel sites on the web to book the cheapest flight.

. . .

The restaurant was warm and elegant, but Suzanne hardly noticed her surroundings as tears blurred her view. Maxine tried to console her, to little avail. She put her hand on Suzanne's shoulder and squeezed it slightly. Suzanne just needed a chance to release her anguish. Maxine's very presence served its purpose. Just the opportunity to express betrayal helped tremendously. Suzanne had only known Maxine since Jack had become a Congressman, but it felt like they had been friends all her life.

How could Jack do this? Suzanne's shoulders heaved up and down in silence. Finally she mustered the strength to speak. "She is beautiful, and young. I can see why Jack was drawn to her spark and energy. I've been nothing more than a housewife. What impact do I have on the world?" Suzanne said in defeat. Her cries gained volume. She tried to restrain herself in the public setting as best she could. She felt sadder than a woman experiencing the miscarriage of her first child. It was like losing something from deep inside. She continued, "I knew he was seeing someone a long time ago. There was no concrete evidence, but I just knew. A woman knows these things, you know." Suzanne's eyes came back into focus and stared at Maxine. Maxine's expression was a reflection of the devastation Suzanne felt.

"I probably should have fought for him, Maxine. Instead, I reasoned if I just ignored it, he'd eventually tire of her and return to me. After a year or so, I knew that wouldn't happen, but I still didn't confront him. My answer was to turn away and run. We haven't made love in fifteen months. I remember him asking me, 'Suzanne, why do you withdraw from me every time I touch you?' I gave him no response except to go upstairs, shut the door and fall on the bed in tears. Maybe I just don't have what it takes to hold the interest of someone like Jack."

Maxine interrupted, "Suzanne, now you're talking crazy. That woman has nothing on you!" Maxine cradled Suzanne like a child who had just fallen and was badly scraped. She rocked her back and forth. Maxine continued, "Suzanne, I appreciate your baring your soul to me, but I'll be damned if I'll see you go out like this. You have to pull yourself together. Jack is the one losing out here, and if he is too obtuse to see it, that's his problem, not yours."

Suzanne was grateful that the hostess had kept her word to find them a table in the back of the establishment. She was a mess. Maxine pulled away from her and looked her in the eye. Suzanne felt immobilized; shoulders slumped while continuously wiping the ever-flowing tears from her face. It was a futile effort. "Suzanne," Maxine said, "I have a confession to make. When I met you some ten plus years ago, I was enormously intimidated. Very few people threaten me. To say you were gorgeous would have been a gross understatement. You were so much more than that. Suzanne, you still are the most gracious, stylish, classiest woman I know."

Maxine hesitated, "To tell the truth, I wasn't even sure I wanted to be your friend. I felt flat in your presence. I even had the unimaginable fear that Carlton would forget me when he laid eyes on you. However, you were so warm, friendly, funny and fun, I couldn't resist your inviting, open heart. I guess I shouldn't be divulging all this. What a witch, huh?" They hugged once more, longer this time. Suzanne pulled away. "Thanks, girl," she said, smiling faintly even though her eyes were dead. "Let's get out of here," Maxine said gathering her purse and mink. "Call me after you've talked with the bastard." They embraced once more and said goodbye with camaraderie rarely shared. "Maxine, go ahead," Suzanne softly stated, " I think I'll stay a little longer."

After Maxine left, Suzanne sat there for a while longer soaking in the magnitude of the deterioration of her life. In a matter of days, her world had shattered into pieces so small it was impossible to put them back together. *All of Jack's previous affairs were dress rehearsals compared to this one. This was the real deal. It was bound to happen sooner or later. However, she would rather not have been the last to know.* She felt like she was shrinking in her seat.

Suzanne recalled being in the middle of picking wallpaper at 'Designs by Ralston' in Northern Virginia for the face-lift she was planning for their new home, when Maxine called her cell. "Hey, Maxine," she said, flipping through the wallpaper book. There was something dreadfully wrong in Maxine's voice. "Suzanne, where are you?" Maxine said in a distressed tone. "I'm at 'Designs by Ralston' in Falls Church. I thought I'd get a head start on selecting wallpaper for the dining room. I know you were planning to assist me on Saturday, but I couldn't wait." "So you haven't watched television lately?" Maxine asked. Her voice had an uncomfortable edge to it. "No. Why?" Suzanne asked as an inexplicable panic rose in the pit of her stomach. "Maxine, what's going on? Why are you asking me so many questions?" "Suzanne, it's Jack. He is all over the news."

Suzanne immediately stopped flipping through the book and moved the cell phone closer to her ear. Maxine's statement was too much for her to respond to. She knew the bomb had dropped. Maxine waited a moment before continuing. Her voice was hushed as if someone could overhear her, even though Suzanne knew Maxine was calling from home. This frightened Suzanne further. "Suzanne, you don't know how much I hate to be the one to tell you this, but Jack has been caught with another woman. It's not just any woman either. The woman is Nicola Patricks. You know - the black Editor-in-Chief of the Washingtonian Magazine.

"No one knows for sure how it got out. The rumor mill is saying someone hired a private investigator on Jack. They took photos of the two of them in the window of her home in D.C.'s upper Northwest. They also bugged her residence and have some extremely damaging conversations. Many people believe the Republican Party is heavily involved. An 'anonymous source' sent the photos and copies of the phone conversations to Channel 5 news. The information is probably hitting the national airwaves as we speak. Suzanne, I am so sorry."

Suzanne leaned against the display counter; feeling like the room had taken off into a spin. She nearly fainted before finding her footing. Something within her willed her to stand firm. It was all too much to absorb though. Finally, she said, "Maxine, thanks for letting me know. It's at least better than hearing it on the evening news." Suzanne's voice was hollow. She knew if she said much more she would become hysterical. *How could Jack humiliate her like this in front of the entire world? He promised after his first confession of unfaithfulness that if she took him back, he would be devoted to her.*

Maxine and Suzanne both remained on the phone, not saying a word, then Maxine spoke up. "Suzanne, meet me at Remington's restaurant in Arlington, say about 4:00 P.M. I know you're in shock, and that's understandable, but I want to be there for you, okay? You shouldn't be alone now." Suzanne barely managed the fortitude to respond, "Okay, Maxine. I'll see you then." Suzanne drove the entire trip in terror. She thought people were staring at her as she went to her car. She refused to put on the car radio, in case they discussed the matter. She headed directly to Arlington. Half way there, she pulled over to the side of the road and wept uncontrollably. "This can't be happening," she cried in despair.

• • •

Nicola looked like a wounded puppy when Dirk arrived to meet her at the National Art Gallery. He thought it was an odd place to get together, but he could see why she chose the place. It was least likely to draw attention. The media was in frenzy once the story broke regarding her affair with Jack. It was all D.C., much less the nation, could talk about. Her picture was flashed on every morning news show, evening news, and late night news and entertainment programs. It was a nightmare come to life.

Dirk perused Nicola's frame as he brought her into his arms for a long and comforting hug. Her eyelids were puffy. The whites of her eyes were pink, most likely from crying and little sleep. For the first time ever, Nicola desperately needed makeup. "Nicola, how are you holding up?" Dirk asked, continuing to visibly inspect her. He was troubled, to say the least. Nicola was the kind of woman that treasured her privacy. She had allowed only two interviews regarding her appointment as the first African-American Editor-in-Chief of the Washingtonian Magazine. She only gave the interviews to provide inspiration to young African-Americans striving to reach their dreams.

Now, Nicola was unable to walk out of her own home without a hundred cameras flashing. Reporters breathed down her neck at every turn, shoving microphones in her face. Nicola peered up at Dirk with such heartbroken eyes his throat closed. "Dirk, I wish I could say I'm handling this well, but I'm not. My life has been turned inside out. I'm afraid to even go to work. I'm petrified to stay at home. I can't go to the grocery store for goodness sake."

Nicola went on, "My mother called me and told me I disgraced the family. She said she was glad my father was in his grave, so he wasn't there to witness the sins of his beloved daughter. She called me again three times after that. Each time, the conversation was much the same. The last time, Mama broke down on the phone. I feel horrible for putting my family through this. I can't remember a time when Mama lost control like that. Not even at Daddy's funeral did she shed such tears. Worst of all, Dirk, I'm worried about Jack. I haven't spoken to him since the story leaked." All Dirk could do was rub Nicola's shoulder in support.

"Dirk, people I don't even know are yelling out of their cars 'home wrecker,' 'bitch' and other Godforsaken names I'd rather not repeat." Tears began to stream down Nicola's lovely face. Dirk pulled her to him once more. "Nicola, why don't you stay with me for a while? I'd love to have your company." He meant every word. He adored her. Over the years, they had become more than acquaintances through Jack. They had become friends.

There were times when Jack could not find time for either one of them. They would soothe each other's sense of neglect. Nicola gazed up at Dirk through murky eyes, "Dirk, you're sure you want me? I don't want to be a burden. You know I'm carrying a lot of baggage these days. I don't want to suck you into my tornado." "Nicola, don't be silly," he said, pretending offense, "I'm a big boy. I can handle myself, thank you." She smiled weakly. "Okay, in that case, I'd love to stay with you." "Wonderful," Dirk said, experiencing an excitement he refused to acknowledge. They stayed at the museum for an hour longer and went through the various galleries. The magnificence of the artwork had a healing effect on both of them.

Nicola and Dirk slipped out into the night. Nicola tied a scarf over her head to hide her face. She was unnoticed as they made their way to Dirk's car. "Nicola, we can pick your car up in the morning. It's probably better to ride with me in case someone followed you here." Nicola shook her head in affirmation. They walked to his vehicle in silence. Once on the road, he glanced over to her, "I have an idea. What do you say to take a few days off to go to Maryland's Eastern Shore with me? We could make it a long weekend. You know I have that beach home in Ocean City. I rarely ever use it." Nicola did not respond at first. He could tell she was mulling over the idea as she did most things in her life. "Dirk, I think it's a splendid idea. I really need to get away." She smiled at him with her lips and eyes for the first time that evening.

Nicola faced a pack of wolves waiting for her at her townhouse. She stayed at her home just long enough to gather her personal items and pack for the trip to Ocean City. Dirk waited for her in the car. He didn't want his presence to add to the feeding frenzy and speculation. Once she came back, he quickly drove up and swooped Nicola and her luggage. They took off. Camera lights flashed as they sped away. Once safely away from the mania, Nicola called her administrative assistant, Charlane. She conveyed that she would be taking several vacation days and wouldn't be back until Monday. Charlane could understand why. Charlene responded on the speakerphone, "Have a restful trip, Nicola." Her voice was compassionate, "Don't forget to have fun for me. I'll hold down the fort until you return." Charlane did a girly laugh and they said goodbye. Dirk was grateful for her loyalty to Nicola. At least someone else was there for her.

. . .

Nicola's face softened as she thought of Dirk while packing for the trip. Instantly her mood lifted. She was ready to have some fun for a change. Even her relationship with Jack had been nothing but work lately. She was constantly trying to move it out of the quicksand it kept sinking into. It was transparent to Nicola now that Jack was never going to leave Suzanne. He had too much invested in their lives together. She also knew that there was a part of Jack that loved his wife, whether he knew it or not. In a strange sense, she found herself relieved once she had accepted it. It gave her the wherewithal to finally make the decision to end the relationship. She despised being the other woman.

When Nicola was with Jack, the 'high' was surreal. However, when he would go, she was on an emotional roller coaster spiraling downward. She found herself moody and despondent. She obsessed about where he was and what he was doing. She would wonder whether he was spending time with his wife Suzanne and then felt bad for being jealous. Nicola was so incredibly lonely when Jack wasn't around. She was unwilling to share these feelings with anyone, afraid they would uncover her dark, seedy secret of adultery, but her emotional world was built around Jack. His schedule became her schedule. His troubles became her anxieties. She was in disarray.

As Dirk drove silently, Nicola reflected that making the decision to get on with her life made her feel like she was a recovering alcoholic. *The irony of the story breaking at this point*, she thought, *was that Jack and she were ending the affair*. They both realized it was going nowhere. They wanted to preserve the deep affection they had for one another. Eventually, both or one of them was bound to resent the other if they continued down the current path. Nicola felt a fury rising inside of her. The media played only the parts of their phone conversations that suited the media's purposes. *It was so utterly unfair.* She put on her sunglasses and a hat to hide her face. She had said an out loud prayer before getting into Dirk's car, "God, help me to deal with anything and everything that comes my way." She gathered her bags and entered Dirk's chambers of tranquility.

Nicola rode to Dirk's home in Reston, VA, with an inner peace she could not explain. Maybe it was because everything was out in the open at last. All the clandestine meetings, the surreptitious rendezvous were wearing her down. "It's only right that the payment for my transgressions should be steep. Lord, forgive me for betraying you and myself" she said under her breath. Nicola felt almost giddy by the time they pulled into the driveway of Dirk's massive home.

She remembered looking at homes on the market with him. She had helped him select the divine structure. It was a spectacular house, with hardwood floors and a gigantic stainless steel and wood kitchen. The foyer had a sparkling yellow hued crystal chandelier dangling from its ceiling, and the living room had an oversized marble fireplace. Nicola had also helped Dirk choose colors for the various rooms and new pieces of furniture to fill the massive space. The end result was superlative.

Before she had a chance to get out of the car, Dirk was around to Nicola's side of the car. "Welcome to my humble abode," he said with a grin. They both laughed. "Dirk, I wouldn't exactly call this humble," she remarked. Nicola continued to make fun of him. "Dirk," she said, "What are you going to do by yourself in this enormous house? You should settle down with a wife and kids. I'm ready to set you up with any a number of friends. You just need to say the word." Dirk smiled broadly, but made no comment. Nicola was quite serious underneath the humor. She had girlfriends that would leap at a chance to snag him. By the time they crossed the home's threshold, they were both in a good mood.

Dirk was most likely overdue for a vacation as well. Besides continuing to handle Jack's legal concerns, he had built up a very lucrative law practice in D.C. His clients consisted of members on the 'A' list, from politicians to business powerhouses. He even had a few athletes as clients. Dirk had the reputation of being shrewd, having high integrity and looking out for the best interests of his clients. The latter two attributes were rare commodities in Washington, even outside of politics. The fact that he was likeable and handsome didn't hurt his career either.

Dirk and Nicola crammed the trunk of Dirk's slate gray Lexus E430 with luggage and beach gear and headed for the road. However, the first stop was to pick up Nicola's car near the museum. She found a nearby garage to park it in while away. They were finally on our way to a moment of freedom.

Dirk had packed a picnic basket with wine and champagne for the trip. When Nicola looked at him inquisitively, he remarked with a twinkle in his eyes, "This here champagne is for a toast to new beginnings." "I can't wait to drink to that, Mr. Patterson," she said with utmost sincerity. Nicola felt lighter. Getaways were always cathartic to her soul. Nicola stared out the window at the scenery as it whizzed by.

They arrived at Dirk's beach home by nightfall. The small bungalow was quaint and cozy. It consisted of two bedrooms, a living room, a kitchen and a dining room area. Every room had an ocean view, except the spare bedroom and bathroom. The architecture was open and bright. "This is such a nice place, Dirk," Nicola said, examining the home admiringly. "Thanks, Nicola. Let me show you to your room."

In the morning they got up at sunrise and had breakfast on the deck. Dirk whipped up blueberry pancakes, steak and poached eggs. The meal was divine. "Dirk," Nicola said jokingly, "I've never seen this side of you before. You're a fabulous cook. The meal was scrumptious. You can cook for me anytime." "Thanks for the offer," Dirk responded mockingly. They laughed in unison. "Seriously though, Dirk, why have you never remarried? I know it's none of my business, but still." She knew she was prying, but she couldn't restrain herself. The question had crossed her mind more than once. Dirk stopped eating and stared at her with his head slightly cocked. His eyes were piercing. "Maybe, Nicola, I've never found the right woman. Marriage is a very serious matter. I will never, ever lightly enter into it again. It seems the really good women are never available." He stared at her. She wasn't sure whether Dirk had a double meaning behind his statements. She decided not to pursue his statements and looked away from the intensity of his stare. She felt herself blushing.

After breakfast Dirk and she went for a walk on the beach. They lingered in the shops on the boardwalk. That afternoon, they went back to the beach and rolled up their pants legs, gingerly putting their feet into the ocean. The water was surprisingly tepid. The ocean had already started to warm for the long summer ahead.

It was a balmy, breezy day, the perfect picture of spring. The couple laughed and talked and laughed some more. Nicola had never seen Dirk so mellow. Her disposition soon matched his. She felt wonderful to be joyful again, if only for the moment. Dirk paused and looked down at her with pensive eyes, "Do you love him, Nicola?" he asked out of the blue. At first, Nicola did not respond. She didn't know how to answer him. She had actually been asking herself that very question lately. Plus, she was caught totally off guard. Their prior conversation was about their favorite movies of all time. "Dirk, do you want my honest answer?" Dirk shook his head in affirmation. "The truth is I'm not sure. If you'd have asked me that a year or two ago, I would have screamed yes at the top of my lungs. Now, with all that has happened and the amount of time that has passed without a commitment on his part, I feel numb inside. I think I want more than Jack can give. In addition, our entire relationship was founded on deception. That's no way to ensure a lasting relationship. I will never forgive myself for it."

From that moment on, Nicola's relationship with Dirk altered in a subtle and yet powerful manner. They talked for hours on end. They explored each other's views on world events, love, family and most of all, commitment. They went to the movies, shopping, and to the various attractions known only to Ocean City, Maryland. Dirk and she had a blast! Nicola hadn't had this much fun since she was a child going on family vacations.

Dirk did his part to keep the atmosphere light. He kidded with her incessantly. After their earlier conversations about Jack and the scandal, they made an agreement not to bring up the subject for the remainder of the trip, and they didn't. Nicola was almost able to keep the rest of her life at bay as well - almost. At nighttime she would toss and turn, to find herself in the morning drenched in sweat. *Would the nightmare ever end?*

The day before they were due to return to D.C., Dirk and Nicola decided to go to the Charter House Restaurant on the bay. It was a pricey place known for its delectable steaks and American cuisine. Nicola put on a slinky black spaghetti strapped dress and high-heeled sandals to match. She made a special effort with her makeup and hair. She wasn't sure why she was making such a fuss over her appearance. It's just Dirk, she told herself. Why did she care? "Wow, you look breathtaking," Dirk said whistling, while checking out every inch of Nicola's body. She glowed at his reaction. "Dirk, I wanted to look nice for our last night out," she said in an unfamiliar girly voice.

Nicola knew her voice and demeanor were purely flirtatious, but she couldn't help herself. Dirk came up behind her and draped her in her evening wrap. He whispered in her ear, "Nicola, nice is not exactly the word I had in mind to describe you." She giggled. *What are we doing acting this way,* she thought to herself as Dirk opened the car door for her. They were behaving like two teenagers going on their first date rather than a last night out with an old friend.

They were seated right away, because Dirk had made reservations earlier. Saturday night was one of the restaurant's busiest nights, and this was no exception. The ambience was unmatched by any fine restaurant Nicola had ever been in before. There were elegant crystal light fixtures that graced the walls and emitted soft lighting. The walls themselves were covered in maroon and gold silk wallpaper. The one wall facing the bay was completely made of glass. It offered an unparalleled view of the yachts parked in the marina. Restaurant tables were exquisitely draped in white linen, with candles and floral arrangements as centerpieces. The chairs were made of overstuffed burgundy velour and medieval tapestry. The restaurant spoke of unadulterated elegance, sophistication and expense. The host brought them to their table next to the magnificent window with an unrestricted view of the bay. He pulled Nicola's chair and placed the linen napkin on her lap. "Someone will be with you shortly," he said with a subdued smile. He bowed slightly and walked away.

Nicola turned to Dirk. "Dirk, this place is dazzling! You have really outdone yourself." Dirk smiled broadly, "Nicola, I want our last night together to be special." She felt a wave of heat float through her being as he spoke. They penetrated each other's eyes for what seemed a minute or more until the waiter interrupted them. "Good evening. My name is Layne, and I will be your server this evening." They were barely able to tear their eyes away from each other to acknowledge Layne's presence. "Can I start you off with a bottle of wine?" he asked in a discriminating tone. "Actually, I'd like to start with your best bottle of champagne. We are celebrating new beginnings tonight," Dirk responded. "Certainly, Sir," Layne said with a knowing grin. "May I suggest Aspante 1956. It was a very good year." Dirk nodded his head in affirmation, and the waiter went to retrieve it.

Dirk turned to Nicola, his dapper, aristocratic face showing signs of anxiousness. "Nicola, you don't mind my selecting for us do you?" "Not at all Dirk. I love a man who takes charge." she replied genuinely. That trait was a huge turn on for her. It made her feel safe and protected. "Then should I choose from the menu for you as well? I've been here on several occasions and there is one dish I believe you would enjoy." "Certainly, Sir," she said with a wicked smile. "I'm at your disposal." Dirk chuckled. The waiter returned with the most delightful champagne Nicola had ever experienced. Dirk made their selections, and the waiter went away once more. They stared out the window, both feeling a moment of uneasiness. There was so much underneath the surface that was not being said. So much had changed between them.

Dirk took the first jump into untried waters. "Nicola, I have a confession. I haven't been totally honest in my reasons for bringing you here tonight. There is so much I want to say to you, but I don't know where to start. Maybe a part of me is actually afraid to begin." Nicola listened intently. There was something inside of her that knew what was coming next. The strangest thing is that she couldn't wait to hear his revelations. She wanted to savor every word Dirk was about to utter. "Dirk, why don't you just dive in," she offered, hoping to give him encouragement. Dirk's eyes dropped, and then he raised them to meet hers. It was clear he was fearful of rejection. She was struck by his vulnerability. Here was this strikingly handsome, highly successful attorney from one of the most established families in Ohio, afraid that he would be turned down by little ole Nicola. *I'm just a southern girl from a working class family,* she thought.

Dirk continued, "Nicola, for years I've admired you from afar. Yet you were the woman of my closest friend, so I had to respect that. However, with recent events and your statements the other day, I believe things have changed. I don't want to seem like the wolf waiting in the shadows for a chance to pounce on his prey. However, right now I'm not as worried about my image as having a chance with the woman I adore." Dirk waited for Nicola's reaction before continuing. She was too moved to speak. He must have read her eyes, because he continued. "Nicola, I love you. I knew you were special from the minute I met you. You've only reinforced this over the years." Her eyes began to brim with saltwater. For the first time in her life, she felt truly loved. There were no split loyalties, no fragmented feelings and no mixed messages. She placed her hand on Dirk's to let him know his words were accepted in the warmest manner. "Dirk," she finally said, "I love you too. The time spent here has shown me that in so many ways. I was so focused on getting what I wanted from Jack, I didn't realize the person I needed the most was already there for me. Thank you for making me aware of what I had been blinded to for so long." Dirk rubbed her hand affectionately and looked at her starry-eyed.

They ate their dinner in the warm glow of silence that couples have when words don't measure up. At the end of dinner, Dirk said tentatively, yet hopefully, "Nicola, this is probably not the right time, but I want you to know when the right time is here, I want to spend the rest of my life with you." Nicola didn't know what to say. Everything seemed so off kilter and sudden. There were so many loose ends to tie up. There was so much to make right. It just felt too selfish to think of her own happiness at a time like this, but it was fundamentally comforting to know the man of her true dreams was there waiting for her.

Dirk and Nicola rode back to the beach home as one. They were barely able to close the door behind them before her wrap was tossed to the floor and they were in a passionate embrace. They kissed for a long while, and then he took her hand and guided her to his bedroom. Dirk stepped behind her and unzipped the little black dress. "You don't know how many times I've dreamed of this," he said, as he caressed her body and guided her to his down filled linens. They dropped on the bed in a white-hot moment of love and lust and something neither one of them expected, ecstasy.

Chapter 17:

Entrapment

The paradise I'd built so carefully was crumbling around me like glaciers in the Artic after years of global warming. I sat in the 'Big Easy' bar not too far from Capitol Hill drinking my troubles away. It was the only recourse offering even temporary relief. *I was suddenly confronting my demons head on,* I reflected, as I swallowed my fourth martini. They're mocking me, taunting me, daring me to defeat them. "I'm losing the battle," I murmured solemnly. Yet, oddly enough, I had a sense of vindication. There should be a price to pay for the many lives I had shattered. The walls were closing in on me fast. In fact, they were just plain tumbling down.

I swayed slightly as I stood. I paid the bartender and made my way to the door. He asked me whether I was driving. "No, I'm not driving, Mister Bartender," I slurred contemptuously as I lifted the last of my drink into the air. "I happen to work right down the street." I exited the bar to the smell of spring rain. I stepped onto the pavement without a purpose, and a soft breeze rushed passes me. *Even the wind had more direction than me*, I thought cynically. I hadn't shaved in several days and my suit was creased from wear. I knew I should at least go shopping, but I couldn't muster the will. Suzanne had kicked me out with only the clothes on my back.

"I don't want to see your face again, you no good bastard! How could you do this to me, to our family? How could you do this, after I took you back the first time? You promised me, Jack," she railed. Suzanne didn't cry this time. I assumed there were no tears left to be shed. Her eyes were green-gray pools of venom. She didn't raise her voice until the end." Do you know what your actions are doing to our kids, Jack? Gabriella called me from school traumatized. She said she's the laughing stock of the campus. Max is afraid to attend his senior prom. Get out! Just get the hell out of here, Jack! Seeing your face sickens me," she shrieked as she tossed me my keys. Suzanne slammed the door behind me with such force I could feel the whoosh of wind.

Walking away from the house, I pulled the collar of my charcoal gray suit together to protect myself from the damp air. I gathered my dignity, got into my silver 'Beamer' and backed down the driveway with no particular destination in mind. The sting of Suzanne's words still rang in my ears. The exchange with Suzanne was strike one. As I sped down Interstate 395, headed away from my home, my cell phone rang. "Hello," I said into the speakerphone, hoping it was Suzanne. There was so much remaining to be said. It was difficult to break through her hysteria.

"Hello, Senator Montgomery, or should I say Joe Baker," the unfamiliar voice sprang forth from the cell phone. My hands shook so violently I nearly dropped the phone. I switched the phone from speaker mode. "Who is this?" I asked in a strained voice. I felt panic rising out of the pit of my stomach. Flashes of my past flew before my eyes. I was suddenly thrown back into time. I pulled off the highway and turned into the parking lot of a McDonald's restaurant to calm my nerves. I nearly hit a kid crossing the street in the process. "Hey, watch where you're going!" the kid shouted from a safe distance.

I sat in the parking lot, again holding the phone to my ear and trembling uncontrollably. I waited for the voice on the other end to respond to my question. There was no reply. I assumed he was African-American from his tone. The familiar stranger finally spoke up. "Senator," he stated sardonically, "Does the name Ridder Jones ring a bell?" I sifted through the archives of my mind to no avail. It was a futile effort. Then, like a light bulb turning on, the name and the detective's somber, asymmetrical face appeared mentally before me. I had been so intimidated by him, I remembered with renewed apprehension. I was a kid then, I reminded myself. However, I was still unable to shake off my earlier gut reaction of alarm. *How could this be happening? Why now? God, am I not dealing with enough right now?* It was strike two. Searching for answers, I sank in my seat and peered up to the sky out of the front window of the car.

I responded back to Ridder in a calm and collected voice, "Yes, Mr. Jones, I remember you." Two could play this cat and mouse game, I determined irately. Ridder was back in my life for a reason. I knew it couldn't be good. I'd wait for him to show his hand. Ridder obviously was prepared for battle. "Senator Montgomery, I believe we have a lot to discuss." Ridder's voice was as frigid as Nebraska in the dead of winter. A jolt of electricity sprinted down my spine. "Sir," I interjected before he could continue with his manipulative tactics, "I think we said all we needed to those many years ago. Now I've got a lot of pressing concerns to attend to at the moment, if you will excuse my curtness." My voice no longer cloaked the contempt I felt towards this man. *How dare he intrude in my life at a time like this?*

The detective didn't appear deterred by my statements. "Oh, I've read and heard about your troubles, Senator, but I think this matter is worth further discussion. You see, I had suspicions regarding you at the time of your supposed brother Joe's death. Yet, try as I might, I couldn't substantiate that Jack Baker was the one who died that fatal night. Call it a gift from the gods, but I now have proof you cannot be the man you claim to be. In fact, I would go as far as to say you're really Jack's low-life, dope dealing, thug brother, Joe Baker. Your secret activities that have recently come to light simply demonstrate your character has not altered, I might add."

Heat welled up in me to the level I thought I'd explode into a volcanic eruption. *How dare this son-of-a-bitch judge me.* I haven't seen him since my youth. He knows nothing about my life. I quickly reminded myself of the times I failed to lasso my temper and the consequences I paid as a result. "Get ahold of yourself," I murmured. Ridder was evidently seeking a reaction from me. Maybe he was bluffing. Whatever the case, I wouldn't play into his hands. I'd be damned if I'd hang myself!

Politics had trained me well at this game. I felt gratitude for the many years of service in the public arena. Ridder was testing me. That was sure. Yet he must have something of merit to raise his hideous head from the ashes of time. I put off the temptation to brush him aside. *Burying rot has a way of later biting you in the ass,* I reflected. My current situation was a case in point.

I took a deep breath before responding. "Ridder, you undoubtedly have something on your mind. I'd rather not have this conversation over open air. Do you want to meet?" Ridder hastily replied, "That is a splendid idea," he said caustically. He appeared to be having fun taunting me. Ridder continued, "How about Sunday? I can meet you at Burnett Park near the playground. We can find a more private spot from there." I responded, "Fine, Ridder. Let's say 2:00 P.M.? You apparently have my number if you need to change the time." It was my turn to be sarcastic. Ridder readily agreed and we hung up. He obviously had mapped out the location ahead of time. *So, he's got this all planned,* I recognized with increased caution. At least a meeting Sunday should give me another couple of days to gather my thoughts. Maybe I could sniff around to find out what he's got on me.

That had been my morning before I started drinking. I hailed a taxi to take me from the bar back to the hotel where I was staying. I had purposely chosen a hotel not circulated by the 'political club' of Washington. The Chancy Hotel was modest, yet comfortable. Seclusion over luxury was a good trade off. I went to my room and fell on the bed exhausted. I located the remote on the end table and clicked on the television. I was careful to avoid any news. I didn't need to watch the world recount my shortcomings. Let them harass someone else. Instead, I watched a rerun of the 'Frazier Show.' I found myself unable to laugh at the show's rich humor. I turned the television off in disgust and rolled over to take a nap.

The remainder of Friday whizzed by in a foggy daze. I immediately sank into a deep sleep after days of not resting at all. Saturday was just as unproductive. Instead of finding more information on my situation with Ridder, I went to a nearby liquor store and purchased vodka. I then ordered room service the entire day. The remainder of the day was spent eating, drinking and watching TV. I knew I was withdrawing from the world.

Sunlight streamed through the never closed curtains to wake me. As I opened my eyes, my cell phone rang. I leaned over to retrieve it from the end table and flipped open the top. My eyes were still groggy. It took me a few seconds to focus on the numbers displayed on the phone's face. "Hello, Nicola," I said in a half sleeping voice. I had ambiguous feelings about hearing from her. I knew I should have tried to reach her by now. The story had broken Tuesday evening and went national Wednesday morning. It was now Sunday, and we hadn't spoken. I felt so responsible for corroding her life, I couldn't face her. The burden of her demise was on my shoulders.

The other part of me still longed for her caress and conversation, even after she told me she wanted to end our affair. "Jack, how are you?" Nicola asked in a sincere voice. Always the considerate one, in spite of everything. That was the part of her I loved most. I realized I'd experience less guilt if Nicola would curse me out.

"Nicola, I'd like to say I'm handling things, but why bother lying to you. You always see right through me anyway." I needed to unload. "Suzanne kicked me out the morning the news went national. I've been in a hotel ever since. I'm afraid of showing my face on Capitol Hill, but I know I can't avoid it much longer. However, I get the feeling, Nicola, you didn't call me to hear all this." I stopped in mid-stride. I knew Nicola was dealing with so much herself; I didn't want to burden her down with my shit. I reflected that I had often been accused of being self-involved. "Jack, you know I always want to hear what's on your mind," she said, "Even though we're no longer in a relationship, I always want to be your friend." I was moved by Nicola's words in spite of the situation. All I could think of was, *I do love you, Nicola, in my own way. I wish you were still a part of my life. I only agreed to let you go, because you requested it.*

"Jack, we've both been through a lot this week, but the reason I'm calling is to say I'll be back in Washington this evening, and I want to talk with you. It might be best to meet somewhere in a Baltimore suburb to avoid the press. Neither one of us needs any more trouble." I sensed something had altered with Nicola but couldn't quite identify what. The tone of her voice was friendly, but distant. She seemed guarded. She was usually an open book. *And what is this about being out of town?* "Nicola, sounds good. Let's shoot for Monday evening. I will get back to you with a time and location." Nicola hesitated, "Jack, there is so much to tell you. I'm not sure how you will take much of it, but I need to be honest with you." With that statement, I knew it was strike three. "Okay, Nicola. You know I always want to hear what's on your mind too." "Take care, Jack," she said in a faraway voice again. The line went dead.

First things first, I thought while showering off the residue of two days without bathing. As I scrubbed my body a second time, I devised a plan of action. "You can't wallow in your troubles forever, Joe Baker," I stated out loud, "You're a survivor and always have been." I decided to deal with Ridder first, then Suzanne and Nicola thereafter. After all, there probably wouldn't be a Suzanne and Nicola around to deal with if Ridder wasn't handled. I knew there were other people I subconsciously avoided as well, namely Papa, Dirk, Bo and Clayton. I knew I also needed to contain the situation with my sponsors in the Senate. They were most likely murderous just about now. I would deal with them when I'd had a little more time.

I'll call Papa when I'm done showering, I decided. He's left numerous messages on my cell phone, and I felt shameful for avoiding my own 'blood.' Undoubtedly, by now, like everyone else, Papa had been barraged with all of the media publicity surrounding my affair. I just hadn't been up to talking to Papa about my mess earlier. "It took what seemed forever to witness the pride in your eyes for me Papa. You naturally had them for Jack," I said solemnly out loud. "Now I've gone and shattered it." I needed Papa more than ever. I longed for his comfort. Over the years, we'd grown closer than I ever thought possible. We traveled together on my campaign trail. At least Papa did as much as his health would allow. Papa had been diagnosed with diabetes and high blood pressure eight years ago. His health continued to deteriorate.

I knew it was partially because Papa was not doing the things his doctor had prescribed, with the exception of taking his medication. Papa still ate fried foods and did no exercise. When I'd get after him, he'd respond cantankerously, "Son, don't bother me with that nonsense. A man has got to have some pleasures in life. Otherwise, what's the point of living?" I'd try to persuade him that his views lack sensibility. *Papa was so stubborn though,* I reflected with a weak grin. That new woman in his life was not helping matters either.

Urtha was a wonderful person and good to Papa. However, her taking care of Papa included fixing good old southern style food. Her meals often consisted of high fat, fried and highly caloric dishes. Urtha could stand to shed a few pounds as well. One time, I mentioned this to Papa. Papa got defensive. "I happen to like a hefty woman," he said in a huff. "There's more to hold and love." Papa laughed heartily at his own remarks. I couldn't help but chuckle.

I exited the shower with my mind mulling over all that lay before me. For the first time since the scandal broke, I felt ready to tackle my challenges. I dried myself off and shaved. *I was like a new man,* I thought as I brushed my still damp 'crop.' It was amazing what simple grooming could do for the spirits. I went back into the bedroom and put on a black turtle-

neck and blue jeans. I had purchased them the day after Suzanne kicked me out without a care. I tried my best not to think
of my last encounter with her. I knew my mood would sour.

After putting on my watch and wedding ring, I flipped open
the cell phone and dialed Papa. He answered on the first ring.
"Hello," Papa said in a tired voice. I started to lose my courage
and hang up, but I stopped myself. "Papa, it's me," I said. I was
returned to a place in time when I called Papa to bail me out of
jail for drug trafficking. The feeling of letting him down was
familiar. "Son," Papa sounded so concerned, "How are you?
You've been all over the news. I've called you numerous
times." I wanted to crawl under a rock for shelter. The strange
thing was that I wanted to take Papa under there with me. I
truly needed him and wanted to protect him at the same time.
You don't know how it hurts me to hurt you like this Papa.
"Sorry not to get back with you, Papa. I just needed some time
alone." Papa seemed more worried than angry or hurt.

There was an edge of disappointment in his voice when he
next spoke. "Son, are things as dire as they portray on TV?" I
didn't know how to respond. Should I pretend to be doing fine
to make it easier on him? Should I be real with Papa and get
the guidance I seek? I decided on the latter. "Papa, I don't
know what they're saying on TV, because I have purposely not
listened to it, but if I were a guessing man, I'd say my career is
currently hemorrhaging and in desperate need of mending."
Papa responded gingerly, apprehensive of my answer, "How
are you and Suzanne doing?' Papa loved Suzanne like his
daughter. He had said so on many occasions. I don't know
which he was prouder of, my stellar career or my ability to capture Suzanne as my wife. I realized that both were teetering on
the edge of catastrophe. "Papa, Suzanne threw me out of the
house. I'm calling you from a hotel room." There was nothing
else needing to be said. "Oh," was Papa's response.

We were quiet for a moment on the phone. It was uncharacteristic for us both. We usually bantered back and forth about
the children, politics, home life and any other events happening
in our lives. Papa had become my best friend over the years.

When I was a teen, I tried everything I could to escape him and then to gain his approval. Here again, life had come full circle. I was once more in quest of his approval despite my shortcomings. Papa didn't disappointment me.

"Papa," I said shortly after my cryptic comment, "I wish I could say the stories were untrue, but unfortunately I cannot. I've messed up pretty bad." Papa kept silent, so I continued. "I've done a lot of terrible things, and undeserving people have gotten hurt as a result. That includes my children, Suzanne and Nicola. As much as I don't want to admit it, I manipulated Nicola into our affair and into maintaining it. I've destroyed my marriage and I may just have lost my relationship with my children. In the end, it wasn't worth it."

Papa cleared his throat like he usually did when he was about to say something important. "Son," he said with an emotionally filled tone, "I regret this had to happen, but you were headed for a wall at 100 miles per hour. The only way out was for you to acknowledge and take account for your actions." It was as if he knew what I needed to hear in order to survive. "You know what Joe," Papa continued, "I've never been more proud of you than I am at this moment." I was stunned. I wasn't sure how to react. I hadn't realized it, but when I thought about it, Papa, as usual, was correct. "Papa, I never know what's going to come out of your mouth." We both laughed. "Even though you're right, I wish I had come to this realization without all the destruction." Papa said with wisdom only found after sixty-seven years on this earth, "Joe, storms mold us into men."

Papa and I talked a few minutes more. He gave me advice on how to deal with the Senate and the public uproar. It was solid counsel. Papa might not have attended a university, but his 'street smarts' were unmatched. The man was as shrewd as the best in Congress. Before I hung up, I promised Papa I would do all I could to save my marriage. "Papa," I said, "It took this to comprehend how much I do actually love my wife. I know I pushed Suzanne away over the years. I felt inadequate in her presence. I put her on a pedestal and could not relate to her. We naturally grew apart as a result.

"To make it easier, I convinced myself I didn't love her and sought the embrace of other women. It took a lot of self-introspection to come to these conclusions." I continued, "I don't know if it's too late for us, but, I'm going to give it my all to keep her. I'll need to be honest with her about everything, if I stand a chance. Even about my past." Papa and I both knew what I was talking about. Papa interjected, "Joe, it's definitely long overdue. I thought you should have been forthright with her from the beginning. Suzanne may be a well-bred woman, but she's one of heart and compassion. To this day, I believe you wouldn't have lost her with your revelations. In the end, son, you had to do what was comfortable for you." I felt wiped out. "You're probably right, Papa," I said in a low, weary voice. "Back then I felt incapable of taking the risk."

"Papa," I said with the earlier fear of disapproval creeping into my voice, "Since I'm being open here, there's more on the subject." Papa waited for me to continue without uttering a word. "I know I have to make it right with Nicola as well. You probably don't want to hear this, but I think you would like her. Nicola is a decent woman who got caught up with a dishonorable man." Papa responded easily, "I believe she is, son. I couldn't see you risking so much for just anyone." I could no more stop the words that followed, than I could hold back a moving locomotive. I was compelled to unload what had been bottled up for years now. "Papa, I have feelings for Nicola. Right now I'm not exactly sure what they are.

"What you heard on television and saw in the papers was probably mostly true, but what the media didn't reveal was we were ending the affair. I'd like to say I was the noble one, but I wasn't. Nicola needed me to commit to her and make her a honest woman. I kept promising her I would, but I made every excuse possible to delay matters. I was still teetering on the fence, trying to delicately balance dual lives. She had finally had enough." "Joe, I don't know what to tell you," Papa said in a sympathetic tone, "The only advice I can give is to search your heart, and go with what it tells you. You know I love Suzanne. She's like a daughter to me, but life is too short for you not to grasp a chance at happiness."

I was about to get off the phone and then remembered I had not updated Papa on Ridder's reappearance. I filled him in on Ridder and our conversation. When Papa spoke, he sounded strained. "Be careful, Joe. Find out as much as you can from Ridder while revealing as little as possible. I remember his tenacity back in the day. Keep me posted, son. You know I'll do anything you ask of me." Papa handed me back the gift of life with those last words. If my world turned completely topsy-turvy, I still had his love. "Thanks, Papa, but I'll be okay. I'm a grown man now." I attempted to make light of the situation, but neither one of us was buying it. We said our goodbyes with the intention of talking after I met with Ridder.

I made a few other calls to start the damage control process. I called Dirk at home and didn't get an answer. I left a message for him to call me when he got a chance. I then phoned Bo. He picked up the phone on the second ring. "Hello, Bo," I said cautiously. Bo's friendship over the years had been invaluable to me. I didn't know whether my latest escapades had sent it 'over the top.' I knew how fond he was of Suzanne. "Jack," Bo hesitated awkwardly before uttering his next words, "I've been worried about you, man. We need to talk. As your public relations person, this has been a catastrophe. Not knowing where you are and what you want to convey, I've been 'winging' it – unsuccessfully, I might add. When can we meet?" I could see Bo getting into his high energy, 'get down to business' mode. I wasn't ready for that yet. "Bo, I can appreciate where you're coming from. Let's meet mid-week. Until that point, avoid answering direct questions from the press. I need to do some damage control on a personal level right now." Bo said he understood.

We talked a little longer about general 'stuff' regarding the political scene and his family's welfare. Before hanging up I said, "Bo, thanks man." "For what?" he responded, "For sticking by me during the good and tough times. I've always been able to count on you, and you know my failings more than most." Bo laughed to lighten the air, "Jack, don't go getting sentimental on me. You know Washington rips people like you alive and then eats their remains while they're still warm." I couldn't help, but laugh at the mental picture. "I'll be in touch, Bo." We said goodbye and hung up.

The last of my calls were the toughest. They were to Suzanne and Gabriella. Neither accepted my phone call. Suzanne let her cell phone and home voice mail pick up. I left a message for her to call me. I added that I wanted a chance to speak with Max. When I phoned Gabriella, I heard Gabriella whisper to her roommate to tell me she wasn't there. To think my little girl wouldn't even accept my phone call shattered me. I hung up feeling emotionally bankrupt and deflated. Gabriella used to idolize me. I relished in her approbation. In the past, her daddy could do no wrong. I was bigger than life. Now she doesn't even want to speak to me. I rubbed my hand across my forehead. I decided to clear my mind by taking a stroll. In this part of downtown D.C. no one knew or cared who you were. I closed the hotel room door softly behind me.

• • •

Wandering through the streets was soothing to my spirit. I tried my best to avoid thinking about my daughter's rejection of me. I wrapped my jacket tighter to blunt the chilly air. *What a difference a day makes,* I thought, feeling the coolness penetrate my clothes. Springtime was unpredictable, and so was I. In one moment, I couldn't wait until it turned warm for good, and the next, I was barely cognizant of my environment. I aimlessly glided through the city deep in thought. I looked up at one point to find a historic brick church facing me.

I examined the stained glass windows, intricate carvings of stone and mortar and the steeple, reaching as far heavenward as the eye could see. The church was unmistakably a monument to God. I felt compelled to enter the building. Morning service was taking place in the Baptist church. I looked at my watch to discover it was after 11:00 A.M. I'd been walking for almost two hours. I found a seat in the back of the sanctuary. What was I doing here? The last time I had entered a church was when Suzanne and I got married twenty-five years ago. Even then, I only acquiesced to marrying in a church to appease Suzanne and Papa. I inspected the foreign surroundings with suspicion and a strange sense of longing.

The gospel choir sang songs of praise. An offering was collected during the last song. I didn't place any money in the basket. Instead, I sat there thinking, cynically, churches were no different than politics. Everything ultimately was based on money and greed. The preacher stepped to the podium once the choir and ushers were done. "Good afternoon. Let us say a prayer of thanks to the Lord before I present to you the message today," he said in a hearty, baritone voice. I didn't bow my head, nor did I close my eyes to pray. I continued to observe.

The preacher began the sermon in an unexpected way. "We all have sinned and come short of the glory of God," he said, "No one is without blame or shame." I found myself leaning forward on the bench. For so long, I had felt I was the only flawed person out there. I listened with renewed curiosity. The minister spoke of starting from a place of sin, but allowing God to heal the spirit to achieve greatness. He spoke of the apostle Paul who persecuted Christians and then later led the crusade for Christ. The minister discussed Peter's denial of Jesus and his later fervent efforts to redeem himself through passionate ministry.

The pastor continued, "None of us would make it through the 'pearly gates' if it weren't for the grace of God. Yet, though God has forgiven us, we must also forgive ourselves," he added. "Depend on the Lord to right your wrongs and move your life forward with assurance that you are forgiven. Then you will be empowered to act on your beliefs." My body felt aglow. The sermon was poignant. Tears rolled down my face. I dropped my head to hide from the world. I was uncomfortable with my emotions, but for the first time, my soul was at rest. I was finally home.

The minister gave a call for salvation, but I couldn't bring myself to go to the platform. "That's just too much to ask of me right now, Lord," I said under my breath. "But now, right at this moment, I believe in you." For the first time, I understood what Nicola was talking about. I felt His spirit. Where had He been all these years? I lingered in the back of the church, in a corner, attempting to avoid having others notice my presence. As the church emptied, I saw the tall, imposing dark figure make his way toward me. The black and white robe flowed weightlessly in the air as the minister's gait was one of confidence and 'blessed assurance.' "Senator," he said, extending his hand to me. "Hello, Reverend," I responded back.

The pastor was more intimidating up close. His eyes were closely set and penetrating. His frame was larger than it appeared at a distance, and his hands practically swallowed mine as I shook his hand. "I'm so glad you could join us. I'm Pastor Wilkins," the minister said with genuine warmth. I wondered why he didn't appear to judge me like so many had since the scandal was unleashed. "To tell you the truth, Pastor Wilkins, I don't know why I'm here. I'm not even sure how I got here. I was aimlessly wandering the streets of D.C., and I looked up in front of this church."

The minister regarded me. His index finger rested on his cheek and his head was cocked to one side. After a moment he said, "Senator, maybe the Lord called you here." I shifted my feet. Why are his words disturbing? The preacher continued, "Senator, I feel heaviness in your heart. I'd relish an opportunity to speak with you further. Do you have time during the week to stop in and see me?" Before I had really mulled it over I said, "Yes." We set a time for Wednesday afternoon. Why did I agree to that, I wondered as I left the church and headed for Burnett Park. It was 1:30 P.M. by the time I left the place of worship. I knew I needed to hurry to make it there by 2:00 P.M. for my meeting with Ridder. I entered the blustery spring air in stride.

. . .

I made it to the park with ten minutes to spare. I located the park bench near the playground and took a seat. I played out every possible scenario in my mind as I waited for Ridder. My mental images went from confrontational to pleading with him to forget the entire matter. Deep in thought, I failed to notice Ridder's approach. His voice jolted me back to consciousness. "Have you been waiting long?" Ridder asked, standing over me. I looked up to see a man past his prime. An expression of sobriety and caution draped his chocolate face. His lanky frame stood tall. His hands were shoved into the pockets of his gray trench coat. It was apparent Ridder was in control of this meeting. He knew he had the upper hand. I told him I had not been waiting long and suggested we go to Winston's Café for greater privacy. We strode together in silence.

Once we were situated at Winston's, Ridder conveyed in painful detail what he had on me. If I had been an objective party I would have had to admit it was an impressive list by any standard. Ridder had made a trip down to Miami after noticing an article in the paper regarding a car that had been recovered in a swamp near where my Uncle Ray Turner lived. "At first I didn't think anything of the story, Senator," Ridder smoothly stated, "until I read further that the woman's skeletal frame had a hole in her forehead and the car was a BMW convertible."

Senator, you see, I recalled interviewing a kid on the streets during my investigation of the deaths of Joe Baker and Puto Sanchez. The boy told me the word on the street was Puto set Joe up in Miami in a drug deal, and the deal went south. Puto was furious when he learned one of his partners got 'toasted' in Miami by his archrival. The kid said Puto got even more explosive when he found out Joe's body was never located. According to the kid, the only justice Puto felt was in Joe's woman getting caught in the crossfire.

"Senator, with a little further exploration on my part, I found witnesses who confirmed that Joe Baker was in Miami.

Others even saw Joe leaving in a BMW convertible from a Joe's Bar with a Spanish-looking woman. The newspaper said the woman retrieved from the swamp was Hispanic. She was later identified as Irma Rodriguez. You see, I don't believe in multiple coincidences, Senator."

Ridder stared intently into my eyes, attempting to penetrate my thoughts. I gave him nothing. If he had x-ray vision, he would have seen my liver down in my knees. For a second, I thought I would lose control of my bladder. *Damn, I figured this part was buried forever.* The memories flooded back to me like it happened yesterday. The ghosts of my past transgressions greeted me with a vengeance. Irma's beautiful sunlit face swirled into my vision. She seemed so real I wanted to reach out and touch her. The vision quickly dissipated. I was left with only Ridder's sharp glare. His expression was one of disappointment. He evidently hadn't achieved the reaction he'd hoped for.

Ridder continued, "So you see, Senator, the puzzle put itself together right before me." Ridder was about to say more when the waitress appeared to refill our coffees. "Let me know if you need anything else," the waitress said with a southern drawl. She lingered at our table for a moment, smiled sweetly and moved over to the couple adjacent to us after we both briefly glanced at her. Ridder greedily finished the Danish from earlier and washed it down with more coffee. He started speaking again before he had fully swallowed his food, *the uncivilized bastard.* "Anyway, to make a long story very short, the recent trip to Miami was quite fruitful," he said.

He continued after swallowing the last of his food and pushing his plate aside. "Normally each jurisdiction is very tight lipped about their cases, but I know someone on the force down there that owed me a favor." I was as still as night air after a major storm. What the hell did this joker want me to say? I found him distasteful. Lord, forgive me for that slip, I quickly followed. The irritation with Ridder grew as he spoke to me in a casual, familiar manner. Ridder might know my past, but he didn't know me.

Ridder repositioned himself in his seat and continued, "When I sniffed around down there in Miami, it turned up you had an affair with this woman, Irma Rodriguez, behind her fiancé's back. That would lead me to believe this was the woman seen in your get away car. I had an arduous time finding the same witnesses to the scene some twenty-five years later, but I finally located two of them." Before he could continue, I interjected, "Ridder, this is all very interesting, but you need to come up with more than this 'cow manure' if you want a reaction from me." Surprised by my blunt remarks, Ridder paused in mid-sip of the remainder of his coffee and peered over the mug's brim at me. I didn't flinch. I had regained my bearings. *You do not intimidate me, asshole,* I thought.

I could tell Ridder was 'hot under the collar' after my brusque remarks. That pleased me to no end. Ridder put down his coffee. "Maybe this will hold your interest more, Senator?" he said with acerbity. He leaned forward like a jaguar poised to pounce on his prey. "The police unit in Miami stated that they pulled a gun out of the glove compartment of the car. The bullets in the gun matched the one found lodged in Dyke Johnson's chest bone. However, because of its markings, it couldn't have been the same bullet that went through the skull of Irma Rodriguez." My body froze, but I was also losing patience. "So what, Ridder? It's a fascinating story, but I have quite a bit on my plate that needs to be addressed, as you so eloquently alluded to earlier. If there's nothing else, I have to excuse myself." I rose from the table. Ridder put up his hand to stop me, "Not so fast, Senator. There's more."

Ridder dropped the bomb. "Based on the bullets and gun, I had the Cleveland police force trace any crimes that had been committed in Cleveland back during that period twenty-five to thirty-five years ago and guess what?" Ridder stated rhetorically. "Your name and face came up in the database. Some twenty-seven years ago you shot a guy in the leg and were brought in on charges. Though the case was clear-cut, you got off on a technicality. The markings of the bullets were the same. It proves the bullets were fired from the same gun.

"So, there's your evidence you were at the crime scene in Miami. It also indicates that unless you caught your original return flight back up from Miami to Cleveland, there is no way you could have been the person killed that night in the 'hit and run' accident. It would have had to be your twin brother, Jack, who had arrived in town from New York earlier that evening. Joe, I checked the plane records and you were not on your flight or on any other flight that day. No train or bus, or even car for that matter, could put you in Cleveland in time for your fatal accident." I sank to my chair like a cornered wounded animal. My hands began trembling. I struggled to control them to no avail. I stared at them as if they were not a part of my body. Fear gripped me as I met Ridder's gaze.

"What do you want, Ridder?"

"What every man wants, I suppose," he stated sardonically, "A piece of the American Dream."

"What the hell does that mean?" I said with raw agitation.

"Let me explain," he said folding the napkin on the table that had once been on his lap, "That is, if you have a moment."

Chapter 18:

Choices

Everyone chooses the path he takes at each fork in the road. I had simply made a lot of bad choices. I was back in the hotel room lying on the bed with my head spinning. My mind was reeling from the meeting with Ridder. Just when I was getting back on my feet, life knocked me to my knees. I was in total despair. Where do I go from here? My prior problems seemed immaterial in comparison. I went from career and personal ruin to potential jail time or worse. For the first time in my life, I dropped to my knees and prayed.

"Dear Lord, I know that I'm not exactly what you're looking for in a Christian, but I desperately need you. For so long I've tried to make it on my own. However, I've made a wreck of my life. Have mercy on me, Lord." I murmured the words with my face cradled in my arms and my fingers interlocked into a single fist. I moaned out loud, feeling the weight of my troubles.

A sudden and unexplainable sense of peace swept over me. I knew in my being, no matter what happened, I would be all right. I looked up as I untangled my body and sat on the edge of the bed. "Thank you, God. I don't know why you're willing to take in someone like me, especially after all I've done, but

I'm eternally grateful. I don't understand you, God. Yet I never understood Papa's love for me either." I began to weep uncontrollably, as if purging my soul. My muscles relaxed and my clenched jaw loosened. I wasn't even aware of my tense body up until that point. "Thank you, Lord," I repeated, "for loving me in spite of me."

Keeping my word, I dialed the familiar numbers. "Hey, Papa," I said, fighting to leave the wretchedness out of my voice. Papa picked it up anyway, "How did it go with the detective?" The anxiety in Papa's voice only made matters worse. "Not good, Papa. It's worse than I could have imagined." There was a pause in our conversation to give Papa an opportunity to absorb what I'd just conveyed. "What did Detective Jones say?" Papa finally asked. I repeated the conversation with Ridder to Papa. I could hear him suck in air from time to time. Otherwise, Papa said very little. At the end of my monologue, he said, "Now that the bastard has you on the ropes, what does he want?" It was the first time I had heard Papa curse since the time I had Jack pretend he was me when we were twelve years old.

I responded, "Papa, he basically said I have two choices. He could expose me and bring charges against me for the murder of Dyke Johnson, or I could pay him five hundred thousand dollars to go away. That's his 'American Dream' option." "Shit... Son, if this wasn't so serious, I'd think you were joking," Papa said dryly. "Papa, I wish to God I was." There was another moment of silence between us. The gravity of the situation merited it. "Where in the world does he think you're going to get that kind of cash? I know you're comfortable Joe, but five hundred thousand dollars is quite a chunk of change."

"Papa, I said those very words to Ridder. His position is that there are avenues for me to get my hands on that kind of cash. He said, for example, I could ask my father-in-law for it. According to Ridder, Clayton Montgomery is worth at least $50 million. He said the money would be pocket change to him. I got the feeling Ridder was asking for only five hundred grand because he thought it would be easy for me to produce.

Hence my chances would be high for getting the funds." Papa whistled out loud, "Clayton Montgomery is that loaded. My, that's a nice bank account. Are you going to go to him? It doesn't sound like you have a lot of choices." Papa continued, "Detective Jones is right, you know, if he's worth that much; $500,000 is play money."

With Papa's comments, dread welled up inside me once more. Maybe there weren't any other options. Then I quieted these turbulent feelings. "Papa, as strange as it seems, I believe there are a lot of choices for me to make. This time, I hope to make the right ones. However, there was one monumental choice I made today. I probably should have made it a long time ago." "What's that, son?" Papa said sounding exhausted. "Papa, I gave myself to the Lord today.

"I'm not quite sure how I ended up in front of the Metropolitan Church. I was simply wandering through the streets of D.C., trying to make sense of my life and to figure out a way to deal with Ridder. Yet, something drew me inside the historical red brick building. Pastor Wilkins preached about God's forgiveness and the ability to be redeemed through Christ's grace. The sermon was so moving, Papa. It was as if he was directly speaking to me. I talked with him after the service. We have another meeting set for Wednesday.

"Later in the hotel room, I asked God for forgiveness of my sins and for Christ to lead my life. Giving up complete control over matters, in many ways made me uncomfortable. But let's face it, Papa; I've made a mess of things.

"Anyhow, I started reflecting on events in my life, and I realized that God had always been there for me. He delivered me from the arms of death in Miami. He offered me a second chance through Jack. I believe He has been instrumental in shaping my political career and keeping Suzanne in my life. Papa, Jesus has been with me all along. I've just been too bull-headed to see it. Yet, in many ways, I've always felt his presence, even during the times when I refused to consciously acknowledge his existence. Papa, I'm going to put my trust in

316

God that he will see me through this thing with Ridder. I have
to."

Papa audibly wept into the phone. "Joe, you don't know
how long and hard I've prayed for this day. Whatever happens
next is inconsequential to this. I have a strong feeling it's going
to work out though, son. I don't know how, but I know who's
in charge of all outcomes." "I do too, Papa. I do too," I responded. We hung up after Papa said a prayer to the Lord to
watch over me and for his will to be done.

· · ·

I had a fitful sleep that night. I must have tossed and turned for
hours before falling asleep. I woke in the middle of the night,
my entire body drenched in sweat. Visions of Dyke slowly
slumping to the ground with blood spewing from every hole
haunted me. By the time I arose on Monday morning, terror
had set into every cell of my body. My head throbbed, and my
muscles were in knots. I looked into the bathroom mirror to
find a reflection of bloodshot eyes and panda bear rings under
them. It was not a pretty sight. I threw water on my face and
shaved in preparation for a long day on Capitol Hill. The
shower was long, hot and steamy to calm my spirit. I was no
longer able to avoid the inevitable fate of my career. Anxious
to get it over with, I retrieved my one and only suit from the
closet and put it on like political armor. I looked into my reflection in the dresser mirror and said out loud, "Alright, Joe,
you can handle anything coming at you. Be strong."

Just before leaving the room, I decided to pull out the Bible
in the end table and read. Flipping through the pages, Psalm
137 caught my eye. It had an extremely quieting effect. I was
entering a pack of wolves after a harsh and scarce winter. What
choice did I have, but to confront them? I knew they were
probably sniffing my scent already. I waved down a taxi to the
Hart Senate Building. Visions of wild animals gnashing my
flesh with blood dripping down the sides of their mouths came
to mind as I closed the door and leaned back into the taxi. It

was only a few minutes before we came to a complete stop. I paid the driver and made my way to the building.

There were a few media types who had anticipated my return and had waited by the building to quickly pounce on me. "Senator Montgomery, what do you have to say regarding your relationship with Nicola Patricks?" the tall brunette said with a microphone shoved in my face. I ignored her and kept moving forward. I didn't owe them anything. My personal life was my own business. Reporters are one step above buzzards picking over dead carcasses. I would not be their next dinner. *Why should I open up my life for them,* I thought, pushing past the ever-growing crowd of media. As I neared the door, I heard a male reporter hollering, "Will Suzanne and you stay together, now that she has kicked you out of the house?" I let the glass pane doors close behind me without a response.

I signed in and went directly to the elevator. People were shamelessly staring at me at every turn. Let them stare, I told myself defiantly as I pressed the elevator button a second time. Once on the third floor, I headed directly to my office in the southwest corner. I could hear the trail of whispers as I made my way down the corridors of power. *Let them all talk, and see if I give a damn.* I said under my breath, "Lord, forgive me for my 'sailor' language again. Old habits are hard to break. Help me to get through this day though." Again, an unfamiliar wave of serenity swept through me. I entered my office with my shoulders squared and my back straight.

Joan was on the phone when I entered the reception area of my office suite. She appeared taken aback, but elated to see me. That pleased me immensely. I was quite fond of her. Joan practically managed my life, not just my schedule. I viewed her as one of my closest allies. I could tell she was attempting to reschedule yet another one of my appointments. I was flushed with guilt as I envisioned the juggling act she had experienced since my abrupt departure. I silently mouthed to her to meet with me in my office in approximately half an hour. She shook her head in affirmation.

A few staffers came out of their offices to welcome me back. Their faces were both apprehensive and relieved to see me. I retrieved a cup of coffee from the freshly brewed pot and exchanged small talk with a few of them, including my now Chief of Staff, Erin. I had promoted Erin from Legislative Aide just two months prior. I told myself Erin's career ambitions had to be equally weighed against my analytical requirements. That gave me the courage to do the right thing.

No one from my staff was willing to discuss the elephant sitting in the center of the room. It was just as well though. What could really be said? 'I'm sorry, Senator, to hear that your life has been destroyed in the past week.' I didn't quite realize how distressed I was to return to the political 'Mecca' until I lifted the coffee mug to my mouth and realized my hand was shaking. Shortly thereafter, I headed to my office to run for cover. I quickly shut the door behind me. I ran my other hand over my short 'crop' and gazed at the massive pile of documents lying on my desk. *And this is just the hard copy mail,* I thought, feeling overwhelmed. I booted up the computer and braced myself for a flood of e-mails. I had an acute impulse to bolt from the office, out the building to find a taxi to the nearest airport for a destination of anywhere. "You can do this," I solemnly said out loud and planted myself into my desk chair.

With great resolve, I began to systematically attack the humongous stack of legislation requiring approval. There were also briefings on committee activities and white papers from various lobbyists and civil action groups attempting to sway my opinion. Somehow, the focus on work relaxed my nerves and built my wherewithal to deal with whatever came.

I could hear Joan in the distance, filtering through the incessant phone calls. It seemed that only five minutes had passed, but evidently it was a half hour, because Joan was tapping on my door. She poked her fire engine red hair in my office, "Is this still a good time, Senator?" she asked. I smiled and waved her in, "Is there ever a good time, Joan?" I spread my hands out to the swell of papers remaining in need of attention. We laughed, and she slid her slim frame into the room and placed herself at the small round table in the corner.

Joan placed a notepad and pen on the table with a miniature tape recorder. I also found a notepad and pen, grabbed my coffee, and joined her at the table. We sat across from each other in silence. I knew Joan was still uncomfortable. Lord only knew how much I hated putting her in this position. It never ceased to amaze me how many other people had suffered from my actions. I cleared my throat, "Joan, I need to know what's been happening in my absence." I didn't bother to mince words. I needed the facts to devise a solid game plan.

Joan looked away, unable to meet my gaze. I continued to emphasize the point, "Joan, I know the question is probably making you uneasy. I'm fully aware my reputation has been severely tarnished. However, I need to know exactly what is being said in the political hallways, formal and informal. It's alright if you hurt my feelings." I smiled at my last statement, more so to mitigate the tension than at my own humor. It had the effect I was seeking. Joan met my eyes and provided a faint smile of her own.

Joan was still noticeably unsettled, because she shifted slightly in her seat. She also nervously fingered her pearl necklace. "Senator, I hope you mean what you're saying. The word on the street is that you're finished here in Washington. I don't believe it though," Joan quickly added. I expected to be disturbed by her words, instead I felt motivated to prove the jerks wrong. "I'm washed up, huh," I stated. By the expression on Joan's face, I knew this was the tip of the iceberg. I encouraged her to proceed. "Joan, I know there's a lot more being said. Don't hold back. The only way I can defend myself is to know what I'm facing."

"Okay, boss, if you want the truth, I'll let you have it," Joan said in surrender. I got up and faced the window to brace myself for the worst. I didn't want to lose too much 'face' in front of my subordinate, no matter how endeared I was to the person. "Let me have it, Joan," I said with my back to her. Joan subconsciously lowered her voice, "Senator, the democratic leadership is furious with you. Hensel Whitaker has been phoning here every hour on the hour since the story broke. He said it is urgent he and the others meet with you. According to the 'rumor mill,' the democratic leadership is crowning a new 'golden boy' as we speak. Many say your chances for the White House no longer look promising." Joan paused. "Do you really want me to continue, Senator?" I turned around to see a fretful expression on her usually poised, professional countenance. I shook my head yes, and waited.

I was glad I thought to put my phone calls directly into voice mail. This was going to be a long meeting. Joan suddenly looked sad, "Senator, people are saying that, without Suzanne, much of your 'magic' is gone. She's the real force between the two of you. You're nothing more than a figurehead." This got to me. After all the time, energy and effort I had put into my career. I sat very still, attempting to suppress my ever-flaring temper. *The sons-of-bitches had always resented my success.* They tolerated me only because they thought, someday, they'd ride on my coat tails. This time, I didn't apologize to God for swearing.

Senator, are you okay? You look drained. Joan inspected me with concern. I didn't want to alarm her, so I willed myself to compose. *What did I expect anyway?* It was not anything worse than what political analysts were saying to the media. It felt harsher coming from my peers. "Joan, I'm fine," I said, "It's been a very long week, and it's just started." She shook her head in agreement.

"Thanks for putting up with all this nonsense, Joan. I appreciate your loyalty. I'm also eternally grateful for your candor. Why don't you fill me in on my schedule for today and take the rest of the day off." Joan's eyes brightened, "Thanks, boss. However, there's one other thing you should probably know. It appears that evidence is growing that President John Stokes' camp is responsible for leaking the story. Evidently, he sees you as a significant threat to his re-election." I didn't know why this had not occurred to me before she stated the obvious. John Stokes was known to be ruthless. It all began to make a lot more sense. I had been so careful. *John Stokes must have hired the best investigator in town*, I reflected bitterly.

"Senator, no matter what happens, you know I will support you," Joan added, "I haven't forgotten how you gave me the position when my husband and I first split. I'd still be looking for a job, having been out of the market for ten years. You even gave me time to come up to speed. And there have been so many other incidents where you've shown this sensitivity and support to my family and me. You will always be on my 'A' list, Senator." I was moved beyond words. I searched for my voice. "Joan, your words mean a lot to me. Thank you." We switched gears, and Joan and I reviewed my agenda for the day. She had scheduled a meeting with Rick, Hensel and Thorton today just in case I showed up. I could always count on Joan's adroitness. I had the utmost admiration for her.

After we reviewed the agenda, we went over my schedule for the week. I added a meeting with Bo and Dirk and one with Clayton Montgomery. Last, I incorporated my meeting with the minister. Joan looked at me with unveiled astonishment. I smiled with a Cheshire cat grin. "Joan, the Lord has been knocking on my door for a long time. I just had to have him break it down before I would invite him in." Joan didn't respond, but instead came around the table and gave me an uncharacteristic hug. "I want you to know, Senator, you've been in a lot of people's prayers, including mine. There are many who still admire and believe in you." "Joan, as always, thanks for holding down the fort. Now, please go home and enjoy the rest of the day on me."

When Joan left my office, my mood became somber again. I wasn't looking forward to meeting with Hensel, Rick and Thorton. Yet, I knew I owed them as much of an apology as I did my staffers and constituents, if not more of one. Those guys had put their reputations on the line for me. They had taken a risk when they selected me as the 'heir apparent.' Up until this point, they were congratulated for their foresight. Now they were, in all probability, sharing my disgrace on top of dealing with my deception. I stared at my watch. One and a half hours before the guillotine time; am I ready? Maybe I should devise a strategy to get us all out of this calamity. At least they would know I realized the extent of the damage I'd caused. That should count for something, shouldn't it? I didn't even manage to convince myself. Afraid to face more ridicule, I ordered delivery Chinese food and continued to erode the mountain of documents on my desk.

After finishing my lunch, I left my door open in anticipation of their arrival. Since Joan had gone for the day, Rick, Hensel and Thorton would come directly to my office. I heard them charging down the hall at exactly one o'clock. I stood up behind my desk as they entered my office. There was none of the congeniality I was used to from them. Hensel appeared more enraged than the other two, but none of them looked pleased. Hensel had had his reservations about me from the start. I wasn't at all proud of my dishonesty to these three, yet I thought *they should understand. I have the 'skinny' on each one of you as well,* I thought defiantly. I do my homework too.

Hensel's past business dealings had been exceedingly questionable. At one point, his investment firm had accused him of embezzlement before entering politics. The firm eventually dropped the charges against him. Many people believed it was dropped to spare the firm the embarrassment and tainted credibility. Rick was known to frequent gambling tables in Atlantic City. He was also 'pickled' with alcohol much of the time. And Thorton, it was rumored, liked to visit S&M spots to meet women that were willing to tie him up and 'dominate' him. I recanted this information in my mind to maintain my composure. *How dare they be so judgmental?* The only difference between them and me was that I got caught. I realized that in the game of politics that was everything though. Truth in Washington was defined by evidence, publicly shared.

"Good afternoon gentlemen," I said, hoping to ease the tension. None of them responded, but rather brushed past me and found a seat on the burgundy leather couch against the wall opposite the small circular conference table. I did not comment on their lack of response. "Gentlemen, can I get you some coffee?" I inquired politely. Rick spoke first. "Cut the bullshit, Jack. You've pulled enough wool over our eyes, don't you think? We're not in the mood for more of your bullshit." Hensel chimed in, "Jack, you've had us here like terrified five day old carcasses with buzzards flying over our heads. We want some answers. You can start by telling us the entire truth, that is, if you know it, Jack." Hensel continued, "Sometimes when a person is a pathological liar like you, they have difficulty distinguishing between what's real and what isn't." Hensel's face was flushed. You could almost see steam blowing out of his nostrils.

For a moment, I thought he was going to lunge across the coffee table at me. Instead, he leaned back in his seat in an obvious attempt to gain control. I was relieved, in spite of the fact that I was fifteen years younger than him and in much better shape. Thorton did not speak, but rather sat there coldly, staring at me. He and Rick were undoubtedly waiting for me to reply to Hensel's questions. The directness coming from the three of them initially threw me off guard. It showed the extent of their frustration.

I tried to collect my thoughts. I wasn't sure whether to attempt to diffuse the situation or get right to the point. I chose the latter. "You know, Hensel, I deserve that. What I did was unacceptable. I should have been honest with you all from the start. Yet, I'm sure you can appreciate that a man is entitled to keeping his personal life private," I said, penetrating each set of eyes separately. It was my way of letting them know I was aware of their dark sides. I could tell by the recognition in their dilated pupils that they received the meaning behind my words. The words were like pouring truckloads of ice into a towering inferno. The effect was immediate.

It was Rick's turn to talk. "Jack, we understand your predicament. We really do." Rick's face had softened considerably since he'd entered the door. "However, you must understand our position as well. We've been made to look like fools. It is well known in Congress that we are your backers. We've poured an enormous amount of time, effort and money into you, Jack. That's why we asked you up front if there was anything you needed to put on the table." With the reference to that specific question and my previous response, Rick's countenance went dark and smoky again. I shuddered as I thought back on it myself. *Why didn't I confess then? At least, they would have made a conscious decision to move forward or not.* I responded to Rick, "In those days, I thought I was invincible. Truth be told, gentlemen, I was downright arrogant. It never occurred to me that my affair would be exposed. Plus, at the time, I was planning to leave Suzanne and marry Nicola. I was betting on constituents having short memories. I thought that, as long as they saw a family image, it usually sufficed. Take Ronald Reagan and his checkered past, for example."

The three gentlemen listened intently to my response. Nobody interrupted. When I was done, Thorton spoke up, "Jack, I think we need to provide you the same honesty we would have expected from you. The three of us have discussed the matter and have decided to throw our hats in the ring to support another candidate. While we still admire your skills as a politician, we don't think you'll recover from this blow, at least not in time for the presidential election." After his statement, Thorton stood up. The others rose shortly thereafter. I remained seated to catch my wind. Thorton's words were like a boxer punching me in the gut at 30 miles per hour. The fact that they were expected did nothing to diminish the blow.

My dignity finally forced me to my feet. "Well, gentlemen, if that's your position, I guess there is little left to be said. Thanks for coming." I turned to Thorton, "I do appreciate your candor. Of course, I differ in the belief my political life is short-lived, but it's clear from the curt nature of our meeting, you all have made up your minds." The three of them headed to the door. "Oh, one last thing, just to satisfy my curiosity, who is your new golden boy?" They stopped in their tracks and turned to peer at me. Hensel looked down quickly before he spoke. His eyes boldly met mine, "Our new man is Virgil Manex."

I must have appeared dumbfounded, because Rick put up his hand, "Jack, now I know he isn't the strongest of candidates, but he is a two-term governor of North Carolina. We'll work to polish him to the level that we need him." Thorton interjected cynically, "We didn't have a lot of time to search around, Jack." I stood there a moment with my head cocked to one side. It was plain they wanted to get my opinion of their choice. I wouldn't disappoint them. My ego wasn't entirely gone. "All I can say is if I wasn't insulted before, I surely am now. It's going to take serious medical attention to help that patient. If you can pull this off, I believe you three should be magicians, not politicians." I chuckled at my remarks. They didn't join in. Rick stated coldly, "Good day, Jack. I wish you much success." They walked down the hall in silence.

I didn't get much work done the remainder of the day, in spite of the enormous backlog. The meeting with Rick, Hensel and Thorton weighed heavily on my mind. Maybe if I didn't have so much respect for the guys, I would not have taken it so severely. If they thought I was finished, what chance did I have at survival? I paced the floor to relieve my tension. I was determined to prove them wrong. I would prove them all wrong, if it took my last breath to do so. I gathered my suit coat and briefcase and left the office for the hotel. It was 5:00 P.M. sharp. *So much for burning the midnight oil,* I reflected, recalling the days of old. As I turned the corner three blocks from the hotel, I saw a restaurant offering 'down home cooking." I happily realized I was famished. It's always a good sign to get your appetite back.

After dinner back at the hotel room, I called Bo and Dirk rather than having a face-to-face meeting. In-person meetings were too draining. The conversation was short with Bo, but productive. He suggested that I lay low for a while longer and let more times pass. Bo seemed to think time would take care of matters for me. At the end of our conversation, he asked about Suzanne.

The conversation with Bo became tense. However, I assured him I would make things right as best as I could with her, whatever that meant. He took the statement at face value, for which I was immensely grateful. I hung up with him with his support still intact. "Jack, I know you're going through a difficult time right now, but hang in there, man. You're a survivor remember that. You've got what it takes to beat this," he offered. "Thanks, Bo. I appreciate it. We've been through too many rough spots together." We laughed wearily and said our goodbyes. The conversation with Dirk was similar, but different. There was an unspoken strain that neither one of us openly acknowledged. I assumed it had to do with my situation. Little did I know it had to do with so much more. I was soon to be enlightened.

I rose early the next day to plan. Once I was able to get through the many documents requiring my signature, the day would be relatively light. It was clear from the cold shoulder I received from my peers. I was no longer a part of the unofficial 'good ole boys' club. Hence, there were no invites to lunch or impromptu meetings. I was nearly quarantined by the scandal. It was as if I were invisible. I tied my wingtip shoes and gathered my coat and keys for another day at battle. *Good thing I'm leaving early today,* I thought. The rejection was brutal. My ego was too large to handle constant alienation.

I had phoned Suzanne during the week, both at home and on her cell. She was obviously still unwilling to talk to me. I couldn't blame her. I decided the only way to get through to her was to go by the house and bang on the door until she let me in. Suzanne went to aerobics in the evenings, but I knew I could catch her right around the time Max got home from school. It didn't matter that Max was now a senior in high school. Suzanne still made every effort to be there when he got home. However, unbeknownst to me, Max had soccer practice after school that day.

"Suzanne, you will hear me out," I said under my breath as I left the office late that afternoon. The irony was I wasn't quite sure what to say to her. I knew I loved her, but my feelings were still quite strong for Nicola as well, despite all that had happened. However, I did know one thing. I wanted to come clean about who I really was. I could never have a light spirit until I faced the past and made it right. Plus, Suzanne deserved to know the real me. The deception was like having a golf course built on a decaying landfill. It appeared serene, but underneath was rot, stench and filth. "I'm tired of living a lie," I murmured as I maneuvered through greater D.C. traffic toward our house.

My mind told me that I should crawl back to Suzanne, that she'd be able to save me. I knew Clayton Montgomery would do anything for his beloved daughter. Clayton would never consider helping me with my marriage in the current condition. I recalled Ridder's last words that I should ask my father-in-law for the money. Was it my pride, or finally, my sense of decency, why I didn't want to involve Suzanne or her father? Until I knew what I wanted, I could not and would not use my wife any longer. No more, Suzanne, will I carelessly play with your heart, no more, I resolved.

I drove the familiar streets adrift on a sea of emotions. They ranged from trepidation to longing to regret to relief that my 'Mr. Nice Guy' image was finally shattered. The stress and pressure of keeping the facade was becoming insurmountable. After a while I knew subconsciously I wanted to be caught. Somehow, it wasn't fair that I should get away with so much wrongdoing. I pulled up to our two-story red brick home with twisted nerves and sweaty palms. Suzanne's Lexus sport utility vehicle was parked out front. The conversation I had rehearsed evaporated into thin air.

Why did we buy this massive house for the two of us anyway? Max would soon be off to college, and Gabriella was already there. I surveyed the house and grounds in wonderment, then turned around and rang the bell. There was no response. I waited a moment and rang once more. Again, there was nothing. I knocked on the door gently at first. Then I knocked louder, until I was at a frantic pace. Finally the door swung open. It wasn't the Suzanne I had envisioned. Her face was gaunt and drawn. There were dark circles under her eyes. Her garb was drab, and she was poorly groomed. Suzanne's frame appeared to have shrunk, and her eyes were like icy hollow marbles. I nearly gasped at the sight of her. I knew I was to blame.

"What do you want, Jack?" Suzanne said. Her voice was flat and lifeless. Her arms were folded, and she was blocking the door. I was conspicuously not welcome. "Suzanne, I want to talk with you. I've been trying to reach you, but you're avoiding my calls. I came over as a last resort." Suzanne stood firm. She twisted her features, and her mouth opened, spewing forth venom, "Jack, we have nothing to discuss. I have had all I can take from you. I actually contacted a lawyer several days ago to start drawing up the divorce papers. You win." The earth shifted underneath me, and my eyes lost focus. Even with all that had happened, it never occurred to me Suzanne would file for divorce. I was not the least bit prepared for it. Suzanne had stuck with me through so many storms.

She began to shut the door. I regrouped and pressed my way inside. "Jack, if you don't get out right now I am calling the police!" She screamed at the top of her lungs. I attempted to grab her shoulders to calm her down, but she cunningly bypassed me. "Suzanne, calm down. Just hear me out." "I don't want to hear you out Jack! I want you to leave." She marched back to the door and opened it. "All right," I said, "But you can at least call me by my real name which is Joe." I knew that would get her attention. Suzanne's complexion went pale. She mechanically closed the front door. She looked like she'd seen a ghost. "What did you say?" Suzanne almost ended the sentence with Jack, but caught herself. Her face was muddled in confusion.

"Suzanne, I desperately want to discuss this with you. There's so much I need to divulge. I've been living a lie most of my life. It's been unfair to you, the children and everyone I care about. And I'm not talking about my affairs either. Can we sit down like two civilized adults and discuss this?" I led her into the massive living room and sat her on the gold taffeta sofa. I sat in one of the French embroidered chairs across from her. I held one of her hands. It was cold and clammy. Suzanne was still in shock.

I leaned into Suzanne. I looked her squarely in the face. "Suzanne, for so long I've wanted to be truthful with you, but I was terrified you would leave me or, worse yet, not love me anymore." Suzanne was about to interject when I squeezed her hand to stop her. "Suzanne, let me finish. It has taken so much for me to rip down my protective wall. It might be easier now, since I have nothing to lose." Suzanne respected my wishes and patiently waited for me to continue.

"Suzanne, I've been living a lie since I first met you. You see, Jack Baker was my identical twin brother. We looked so much alike, only Papa could tell us apart. When I gazed upon Jack, I would have eerie feelings that I was staring into a human mirror. Only Jack was the good image of me. I loved him, and yet I resented the hell out of him. I wanted to be like him more than anything in the world. I always fell short. Sometimes I didn't think Papa realized I existed when Jack was in our midst. I was the rebel. Jack was the 'Chosen One.' Not that he didn't deserve this esteem. He was the most decent man I've ever known, past or present."

I paused to catch my breath. I was caught up in a whirlwind of emotions. Suzanne sat motionless. Her eyes were wide open now. She was a blur of unreadable thoughts and expressions. I thought for a moment she might faint. Yet, after some time, the color reappeared in her face. I went on, "Suzanne, I lived a troubled, rebellious and precarious life for my first nineteen years. I dealt dope on the streets. I ripped lives to shreds with my 'enchantment.' I didn't care. I sold it to mothers, children, anybody who would take the bait. It was easy to find buyers in the hopeless section of East Cleveland where I grew up. It wasn't my concern who bought my product, as long as I dominated the streets. Papa and Jack tried their best to lead me away from the streets, but I thought, *what do they know?* Jack is a 'goody-two-shoes' and a 'Daddy's boy,' and Papa was old and out of touch. In the end, Suzanne, I got caught in my own game.

"The streets got meaner and there was no way out. It was all I knew. Papa and Jack were my only connection to the other side. Jack moved further into the mainstream of life with a full academic scholarship to an Ivy League school. I moved out of Papa's house. Eventually, the connection with the two of them dimmed. Fast money, loose women and cronies living my life became my closest confidants. Suzanne, at seventeen I was the kingpin of my neighborhood, at least, until a kid by the name of Puto Sanchez entered the scene.

"Puto had relocated from a gang in Florida. They were heavy drug traffickers. Puto invaded my turf, and we became brutal rivals. I started getting my 'supply' directly from Miami to compete with him. I went down to Miami to seal the biggest drug deal of my tainted career. I didn't realize Puto had set me up. The transaction went terribly wrong. As a result, I killed a man. It was in self-defense, but nevertheless, it was murder. The woman I was dating at the time got shot in the head by one of Puto's guys and died. Irma Rodriguez was a very decent woman, and I loved her. She should have never been involved in the situation. To this day, I cannot forgive myself for her death. So many people died directly or indirectly from their association with me, Suzanne, including my brother, Jack."

Suzanne's hands were covering her mouth. Her eyes were maximized, and she shook her head in disbelief. She stood and backed away from me. "No, no, no," she repeated. I wanted to wash away the agony in her eyes, but I needed to continue like a fish needs water to survive. I forced myself to be immune to her reaction. The burden of my shame and unworthiness pro-pelled me forward. I yearned for Suzanne to know the actual me.

"Suzanne, Jack died in a hit and run accident. He had come home from school. Papa asked him to come home to help me deal with my situation, and before I could get there, he went out to ride his bike in a terrible storm, because he needed to clear his head from the distress I had caused him. Papa told the police that I died that night. The detective on the case at the time smelled a 'rat.' He had no evidence to prove his case. Having thugs as friends allowed me to have the birth records and fingerprints for me and Jack switched. Suzanne, I took over Jack's identity. I did it for survival. In the end, it was my redemption. I was indebted to Jack for giving me a second chance at life. I also desperately wanted to honor the man he was when he was alive. I was beholden to Papa for supporting and loving me through it all. Jack was Papa's heart. My actions snatched him from his bosom.

"I'm not going to lie, Suzanne - fitting into Jack's life was a colossal challenge. However, I really didn't have a choice. The academics were comparatively easy because we both had a gift for learning. I used to be an avid 'closet' reader of any and every subject, while Jack publicly embraced his love of knowledge. The real task was fitting into a mainstream and 'upscale' world I had no concept of or relationship to.

"Suzanne, I met you a year into the transition. You were the real thing. Knowing all this is why I never felt good enough for you, Suzanne. My experiences are also why I'm so fiercely passionate about assisting the downtrodden and forgotten. I guess even out of the ashes of despair, charity can spring forth." I now had my own set of tears.

Suzanne came over to face me. She pulled me up from the chair and draped her arms across my shoulders. She then drew me to her. I wept like a baby. "Jack, Joe, whatever your name is, I love you. I have always loved you, from the day we met. I'm still not sure whether it's a healthy thing, but my feelings are consistent. I do know that it pains me to see you this way. I'm probably more wounded that you've kept this from me for all these years than anything. You really don't know me, do you?" Her eyes were pools of tenderness and suffering. "Why didn't you trust me enough to lift this burden before now?" "Suzanne, maybe because I wasn't sure how you would take being married to a man so unworthy of you," I responded. I was speaking from the heart.

My head was bowed. I couldn't bear to look at her. Suzanne gently placed her hand under my chin and lifted my face until we were staring into the depths of each other's eyes.

"Jack, has this been the wedge between us all these years? When I fell for you, it wasn't because of the person you were, but rather the person I encountered at the time. Knowing where you came from would have made it all the more special. Do you know how special you must be to overcome those circumstances? To come from those experiences and achieve what you have takes a phenomenal spirit. Yes, what you did was deplorable, but you've paid for those sins many times over. You've certainly made up for them with all the good you've done." Suzanne continued, "Jack, we all make mistakes. It's what we do about them that matters most.

"I know you have me on some kind of pedestal, but that's not letting me be a real person. I don't want to minimize what you've done, but we've all done things in our lives that we're not proud of. My life has not been spotless, Jack. I'm not the 'Virgin Mary.' I've always wondered whether you saw me through the years or rather a pampered, rich girl, whose father dotes on her." Suzanne sank into the couch and continued, "My life, in many ways, has been thorny, Jack. This includes my childhood. My mother didn't show me love. Daddy was gone much of the time, and I spent most of my childhood alone. People resented me because of an image and never got to know the scared, vulnerable person inside."

Now it was my turn to hold Suzanne. I sat on the couch beside her and drew her near. "Suzanne, I apologize. I never knew. I regret shutting you out and failing to share with you." Suzanne stared at me in thought, "Jack, was this the reason you so often turned away from me? Your rejection of me stung more than the day I discovered my father in the parking lot with another woman. My coldness over the years was the only way I knew to protect myself. I was defenseless and too in love with you to leave you." Her words bit into the core of my being. To think I had pushed away the very person that held the gift of love and key to self-acceptance.

"Suzanne, I've always loved you. I just wasn't sure how to relate to you. You're flawless in my eyes. In hindsight, I probably did us a disservice. I did have you on a pedestal. In

my mind you're untouchable. How does such an imperfect being like me keep company with perfection? To deal with my
own irrationality, I convinced myself that other women had
qualities that allowed me to feel more of a man. In reality, I felt
insecure and was too much of a coward to face it. With you
kicking me out, I've found the Lord, Suzanne, or rather I acknowledged his ceaseless tugging on my spirit. Accepting
God's forgiveness has permitted me to finally forgive myself."

I watched Suzanne's reaction intently to gauge her reaction.
I knew she believed in God, but we had never discussed religion in our home. I couldn't recall the last time we attended
church outside of Christmas and Easter, and those times
seemed more like a tradition than a concerted decision. I was
afraid she would think I had gone mad.

Suzanne's eyes shined brightly even through her sadness.
"Jack," she said, "This is the best news I've heard in quite a
while. I know I don't practice my beliefs like I should, but God
is who has carried me through our relationship all these years. I
rarely discussed my faith with you, because, as with most
things I had to offer, I felt you really weren't interested." Now
it was my turn. I stood up and pulled her body back erect to
meet my own. I kissed her intensely on the mouth. I was finally
lucid. This was the woman with whom I belonged. "Suzanne,
you're one amazing woman," I said provocatively. I held her
tightly to my chest and to my heart.

"I do have one question though," Suzanne smiled tentatively up at me. "What is it?" I said with an openness I hadn't
expressed with her before. "What should I call you? I mean,
I'm used to Jack, but I can adapt to calling you Joe." We both
laughed. It was a wonderful experience to laugh with the most
important person to me on the planet. I was touched by her
sensitivity. For the first time in so many years, I felt no conflicting loyalties. Nicola was a wonderful person, but I knew
my love for her was shallow compared to that of the woman I
had spent a lifetime with, whose womb brought forth my children and who had stood by me no matter the circumstances.

"Suzanne," I responded with ease, "You can call me whatever your heart desires. However, it may be simpler to call me Jack. It's what you've been calling me for twenty-seven years now. Plus, answering to the name of my brother is an honor." "Well, Jack it is then," Suzanne said pulling me close. There was one last question I had regarding us and it loomed over me like a treacherous black cloud.

"Suzanne, can we sit again?" I moved her to the couch. She sat facing me with a fretful expression written on her face. "Suzanne, I know I want nothing more than to live my life out with you. However, you should be aware of all the risks associated with me these days. The word is that I'm washed up in Washington. So much political damage has been done. I'm not sure I can recover. To be honest, I'm not even sure I want to recover. I'm not complaining, Suzanne. As strange as it sounds, I needed to be brought to my knees to recognize what's important to me. Yet, to ask you to stay with someone heading south, particularly after I've 'dragged you through the mud' is too much."

Before I could finish, Suzanne quieted me by placing a finger to my mouth, "Shhh, Jack, I'm capable of making my own decisions about who I want to be with. D.C. be damned. It's a town full of phonies and parasites anyway. If you want me, really want me Jack, I'm yours." Suzanne stood up once more and crossed her arms. She stared hard and long into my eyes. "Though Jack, I do deserve better than you have given me during our marriage. I cannot and will not let you treat me like that ever again. It took me a while to realize my worth, but I do now."

I was actually pleased to hear those words from her. Bizarre as it seems, I hated the fact Suzanne didn't stand up for herself. Each time I abused my husbandly privileges and she allowed me to, I loss respect for her. "Suzanne, I am elated to hear that. It's about time you stood up for yourself." I got down on one knee. "Suzanne, I promise to honor and cherish you, in sickness and in health, 'till death do us part." Suzanne burst out in tears and we hugged again for a long time.

We talked a bit longer about our next steps. I debated about whether to tell Suzanne about the situation with Ridder. I didn't want to bring her into any more of my 'mess.' Yet, I knew if I wasn't candid, it would chip away at the credibility I was attempting to rebuild. I couldn't afford the gamble. I decided to come clean. I gazed upon Suzanne's exquisite countenance, "Suzanne, there's more to tell you. I'm informing you not to ask your assistance, but to keep nothing from you."

Suzanne appeared perturbed. "Jack, you're scaring me," she said in a low, almost inaudible voice. I rubbed her shoulder for comfort from the impending blow. I then told her everything - Ridder's reappearance, his blackmail, all of it. Suzanne was mortified. She kept shaking her head in disbelief. At the end of my synopsis, Suzanne started pacing the floor. Her back was erect. She stopped to peer out the window. "You know, Daddy could pay this Ridder fellow off, Jack. I think we should pay him and be done with it." She turned to me for my reaction. It came fierce. "No, Suzanne; I can handle this on my own," I said in a harsher tone than intended.

I knew Suzanne was trying help, but I didn't want her assistance. I swung her around forcefully. I shook her gently to emphasize my point. "Suzanne, stay out of this. I don't need your father to fight my battles. This is my problem. You understand!" Suzanne stared at me like an injured animal. Her worry reflected back at me. I released her. Suzanne rubbed her sore arms and I was instantly ashamed for grabbing her so abruptly. "All right Jack, if that's what you want. You don't have to get violent." Her lips were pouting as she spoke in an agitated tone.

"I'm really sorry, Suzanne. I didn't mean to come at you like that. I do appreciate your help, but I have to handle this myself. Thanks for honoring my wishes," I said, gathering my jacket. "I better get going. I need to wrap up a few more matters to sleep well tonight." I affectionately pecked Suzanne on the forehead goodbye. *One of those outstanding matters is to officially say goodbye to Nicola*, I thought, closing the door.

This time the goodbye to our relationship would come from me. I needed the closure.

After he left, Suzanne walked into the kitchen and picked up the phone. She dialed the forbidden seven digits to Daddy's with resolve she never knew she had. "Hi Naomi, is Daddy there? Thanks." Suzanne patiently waited as her father came to the phone. "Buttercup, how are you doing?" Clayton Montgomery said in a worried tone. "I'm fine, Daddy. I actually called you regarding Jack." "Oh," Clayton responded in a cool, not so pleasing manner. Suzanne hurriedly interjected, "Daddy, it's not what you think. Jack and I have finally come to an understanding. There's so much to tell you, but right now I urgently need your help."

$$\approx\ll$$

Chapter 19:

The Journey Back

Nicola had agreed to meet me at 8:00 P.M. in a small cafe in the Baltimore suburb of Glen Burnie. It was a rather inconspicuous, unassuming restaurant that we used to sneak away to during the beginning of our lurid affair. As I pulled up to the place, a flood of memories came pouring back. All the thrill and novelty had worn off now. What remained were mounds of regret for what I had done to Suzanne and Nicola.

I entered the slightly rundown eatery to find Nicola already sitting at our table. As usual, Nicola was on time, and I was running late. I strode over to Nicola without the fear of recognition. Even if the employees recognized us, we had little fear they would blow our cover to the press. With our frequent visits over the years, we had become friends with practically the entire staff. Everyone pretty much kept to himself or herself anyway. It was an unspoken code of the diner.

"Hello, Nicola," I said, coming up behind her. She turned around and got up from her seat. We gave each other a big hug hello. I took off my jacket and sat down across from her. "That's quite a welcome, Nicola. It either means something very good or very bad is up with you," I said as I perused her face, noting that something was definitely different. I couldn't

338

pinpoint what it was though. Nicola laughed nervously and an unveiling grin crept across her sensual lips. *She is one sexy woman,* I thought for the thousandth time. The difference now, though, was that I no longer felt controlled by her luscious spell. I looked down at my ring to remind myself of my commitment to Suzanne and what I had almost lost.

"Jack, how are you doing?" Nicola reached across the table and placed her hand over mine with a fretful expression on her face. I responded, "Nicola, if you had asked me that three days ago, I would have been ready to take my life, but, now, even with all my troubles, I feel like I've been given a new lease on life."" Nicola's cat eyes glistened with curiosity and she tilted her head to one side. "And why is that, Jack?" she asked. I avoided her question, because I didn't think the timing was right. I had it all planned as to what I wanted to say to Nicola and when I would say it. I wanted to let her down as easily as possible. In my mind, even though she had broken it off with me, we were still an 'unofficial item.' I responded evasively, "For a lot of reasons, Nicola."

The waitress came over to our table. "How ya'll doin' tonight?" she said with a country twang. Fran had often served us over the years. She was a good waitress, and I usually gave her a substantial tip. That only helped to enhance the service. "Fran, we'll take two coffees with cream. I'll have an apple pie. Nicola, anything else for you?" Nicola shook her head no, and Fran took off to fulfill our request. Nicola looked down at her hands as she spoke, "Jack, I have news of my own." I stared at her intensely. If I wasn't mistaken, Nicola was blushing. It had been a long time since I had seen her face flushed. Her demeanor was almost demure. Now it was my turn to be curious. "Nicola, there's something different about you." She did not look at me. Instead, she set her sights on the booth across the room. "Why don't you go first with your news," I said. I wasn't sure what to expect, but I was bracing for the worst.

Nicola smiled sheepishly, "Okay, Jack." She leaned back against the booth with her cup of coffee in both hands. "Well, the fact that we were splitting even before the news broke was extremely traumatic for me. After the story hit, my life became unbearable. There were reporters everywhere I turned. I was afraid to show up on the job for fear of ridicule. People on the streets were calling me 'home wrecker' and worse. I wanted to call you, Jack, but I knew you would be living your own hell. Plus, I had just told you I didn't want to see you anymore. On top of that, I was frightened to be in contact with you, figuring it would make matters worse."

I couldn't help but to interrupt. "Nicola, I regret I've put you through this. I wish more than anything that you were not part of this nightmare. I should've known this was bound to happen sooner or later." "Jack, there was no way to have foreseen these events. And I'm a big girl, able to make decisions for myself. I could have stopped our affair long ago. Better yet, Jack, I should never have allowed it to start. There's absolutely no need to apologize." Nicola paused to regroup.

"Anyway, Jack, my life was in shambles. I desperately needed a shoulder to cry on. The only person I thought to call was Dirk." Nicola paused for my reaction. I tried my best not to show the surprise I felt. I could tell from Nicola's face that it was a battle I was losing. Nicola feebly attempted to explain herself further. "Jack, I know this may surprise you to hear, but Dirk and I have been friends for quite some time. Strangely enough, I got to know him from the times he would take your place with your last minute cancellations. He's been one of the few people fully aware of our relationship. His non-judgmental style made him easy to talk to about us." "I bet," I said under my breath. An unfamiliar jealousy swept over me. I reminded myself Nicola was never mine to begin with. There is no commitment in infidelity. The words of Minister Wilkins, whom I had met with the day before, flooded my conscience. The meeting with him was so helpful that we had agreed to have regular weekly sessions. Dirk's an honorable man, I begrudgingly admitted.

Nicola fidgeted with her silverware. She glanced at me nervously before blurting out, "Jack, in the last week and a half, Dirk has become more than just a shoulder to cry on." Nicola's breathing became heavy. I could tell she laboriously continued, "Anyway, I called Dirk during the crisis, and he invited me down to the shore for a long weekend. We had a chance to get to know each other better, and we realized that our bond is deeper than either of us thought." *I bet*, I thought again, sourly.

I had so many mixed emotions with Nicola's confession. Part of me was happy for Nicola. The other part was pissed as hell she could find any other man of interest besides me. *There goes my ego again* I meditated. Nicola deserved someone to love her, truly love her the right way. I knew Dirk was a good man, one of the best. He would treat her well. There was no question in my mind that Dirk would make her happy. Yet, in all honesty, I still felt betrayed. I knew none of it made sense, since I was the person that had planned this meeting to say goodbye to Nicola.

I guess the selfish monster in me was showing its ugly head once more. I had just always thought of Nicola as mine. Now she was sitting across the table going on about another man, no less my dearest friend. I had for some time suspected Dirk was attracted to Nicola. It was nothing that he said or did when he was around her. It was probably more of what he didn't do. Dirk painstakingly avoided looking at Nicola when we were all together. There wasn't a man alive that could resist gazing upon her sensuous body. His actions just weren't natural. I had suspected just the opposite was going on. However, I respected Dirk's loyalty to me. At least he knew his limits. Nicola didn't pick up on any of it. Women can be so naive, especially when they're modest like Nicola.

Nicola was sparkling as she declared her love for Dirk. Her eyes glazed over, like women get when they're 'mad' about someone. I was envious of Dirk, if only for a moment. I couldn't recall witnessing Nicola ever so spellbound with me. She must have read my mind, because she caught herself. Nicola placed her hand once more on mine, "Jack, I'm sorry. I'm being insensitive. It's not that I don't care about you. I will always have a special place for you in my heart. The problem with us never did have to do with how we related to each other. It was the circumstances surrounding our relationship." Nicola looked away, unable or unwilling to show me the depth of her pain.

Apparently, she was not totally over our failed liaison. I was torn in different directions over her hurt. Part of me was made bigger by it. The other part felt immense sorrow for toying with her heart while I decided what I wanted. She was too magnificent of a person to be treated that way. I wanted to make her feel better about finding joy. It was the least I could do. "Nicola, you don't need to justify your feelings to me. You also don't need to explain why you've found comfort and love with Dirk. I've known Dirk much of my life, and he is a stellar and rare individual. I admit that hearing you say you love him is very awkward for me, but I can't but feel elated that two incredible people have found each other." Nicola's eyes moistened. "Jack, thank you. I mean that in so many ways, you cannot imagine. Dirk and I were very concerned how you would take the news." Our eyes locked and we both knew this chapter of our lives had closed.

I leaned back in my seat. "Nicola, I'll be the first to admit that if you had told me this two weeks ago, I'd have gone on an emotional rampage. I might have destroyed half of this restaurant. However, I'm a different man now," I said. Nicola intently stared at me. "Jack, I've noticed a change in you from the moment you entered the cafe. There's a peace about you. How is that possible, given the current circumstances?"

"Nicola, remember all your preaching about the Lord and the need for him to be the center of my life? Well, it finally sank in." Nicola's eyes practically popped out of their sockets. She bubbled over with joy and laughter. "Jack, to say I'm overjoyed to hear this would be a vast understatement! I am so happy for you! If I'd known it would take both of us to sink this low for you to find God, I would have been the one to break the news to the public some time ago." Nicola started giggling, "I wouldn't say I was preaching at you though, Jack." She came around the table and gave me a bear hug. For a moment I thought I was going to suffocate. "Jack, this calls for a celebration. The coffee is officially on me." I had expected her to be happy for me, but the level and intensity of her reaction surprised even me.

I got serious once more. "Nicola, I have more. For years you said that you suspected there was a part of me I concealed from the world. You were right. You're so perceptive sometimes I find it eerie. Anyway, I've done a lot of soul searching. I've decided I need to be completely forthright with those I care about. Nicola, you mean a lot to me, though my actions have not shown it. I'd like to share something about me that's very difficult."

Nicola was too taken aback to respond with words but shook her head in affirmation. I decided to focus solely on my true identity and current situation with Ridder. The fact that I was getting back with Suzanne and had realized the depth of my love for her was immaterial. It would probably only serve to heighten Nicola's sense of rejection. I didn't want to bruise Nicola's ego any more. She had already suffered enough humiliation because of me.

My voice got low as I started detailing my childhood and identity as Joe Baker. Nicola leaned into the table to hear me better. Nicola struck her face and her mouth hung open as I told the story of murder and blackmail. As I furthered my account of events, tears began tumbling down Nicola's face. When I was done, Nicola stated in an unsteady voice, "Jack, I'm mortified at what you've been through. Thank you for sharing it with me. I feel honored that you thought enough of me to show such vulnerability.

"Let me know if you need me to assist you with this Ridder character. I don't have $500 thousand, but I do have a few dollars put aside, and there's always Dirk. I believe his father left him a lot of money when he passed two years ago. He doesn't talk about it, but just from a few statements he's made, I believe he could help you. I know he would want to." As with Suzanne, I was struck by Nicola's depth of compassion and support. I was most greatly moved. "Nicola, thanks. Your sentiments mean a lot to me, but I'm going to try to handle things on my own."

I felt like a broken record, having just said these same words to Suzanne. "By the way, Nicola, Dirk knows everything. He's known since childhood. He helped me cross the bridge. Dirk's been there for me despite my shortcomings. You've got yourself an amazing fellow, Ms. Patricks." Nicola beamed at the comments. She also seemed relieved she didn't have to hide anything from Dirk. Abruptly, Nicola became anxious. "Jack, do you think it's wise to do this on your own? I mean, this guy sounds like he's ruthless. At least think about my offer." "I will," I said half-heartedly to wipe the fret off her face. I glanced at my watch. "It's getting late, Nicola. I appreciate your taking a chance to meet with me. We'd better get out of here if either of us is planning to get any sleep tonight." I walked Nicola to the door, and we departed from the restaurant at separate times as not to be conspicuous.

I got back in my sedan and spun down the road toward downtown D.C. and my hotel. I didn't think it was appropriate to ask Suzanne to move back in yet. It was too early. We both needed to adjust to the idea of a new way of relating to each other. Plus, I really wanted to be invited back rather than to ask for the opportunity to come home. I was deep in thought when my cell phone interrupted.

"Hello, Joe," the voice on the other end said in a foreboding tone. "Why haven't you gotten back with me by now? Better yet, Joe, why don't I have my money?" Ridder's voice was threatening and full of malice. "Ridder, I told you before, I need time. I don't have that kind of money lying around," I responded, trying to keep the panic out of my voice. "And I told your ass to ask that rich daddy-in-law of yours, didn't I." Ridder's voice was losing patience. I swiftly replied, "Ridder, I plan to do that, but I want to exhaust all other avenues first."

Ridder was quiet. When he spoke again, his words were sharp enough to gnash flesh. He spoke in a steely tone, "Joe, I'm in a charitable mood, so I will give you another 48 hours to do whatever it takes to deliver 'the goods.' However, if you don't produce the 'Benjamins' by then, you're finished. Not only will you go to jail, Senator, your reputation will be carried through the mud after I get through. You'll think of the current media coverage of you like a walk in the park. Do you understand me, Senator Jack Montgomery?" The sarcasm in his voice could not be missed. *What did I ever do to this son-of-a-bitch to cause this hatred,* I wondered? I hardly know the man. "I understand you loud and clear, Mr. Jones. Thanks for the extension." It took all my years as a politician to be able to thank this scum of the Earth. "Very well, Senator. I will be back in touch to talk details about where to leave the money. Have a good day." The phone went dead. My heart was pounding and my knees were so weak I could barely accelerate the car. I pulled to the side of the road to regain my composure. This was no time for an accident.

• • •

My timing is incredible, Suzanne thought to herself. She'd get the chance to talk with Daddy face-to-face about Jack's situation. Daddy was back in Washington, lobbying for one of his many causes. She waited for him to arrive at her house with one thing on her mind - Jack. She greeted Daddy at the door warmly. They hugged, and Suzanne immediately dragged him into the kitchen. She started in on the subject of Jack before he could even sit down. Daddy's response was completely negative on the subject. Could she blame him? She'd just called him several days prior, crying her eyes out and calling Jack unmentionable names.

"Suzanne, are you sure you want to let that snake back in your life? You know I was fond of him for years, but he's gone too far this time. I've practically watched him destroy you. How do you think it makes a father feel to see his child crumbling before his eyes?" "Daddy, I'm more than sure I want Jack back. We have talked more in the last day than we did our entire marriage. I still love him, Daddy. Plus, I really do believe this time he is a changed man." Clayton Montgomery said nothing. "Do you know he even accepted Christ as his Lord and Savior in the past week?"

She was pleading with her eyes for Daddy to give Jack a second chance. If she could forgive Jack, why couldn't he? She reminded herself that being in love with a person makes it easier to forgive them. She knew Daddy was only trying to protect her. His eyebrows shot up regarding Jack's being saved. She could tell he was skeptical. "Suzanne, all I can say is be careful. A man will say whatever it takes to get back something he believes belongs to him. Plus, Jack isn't stupid. He knows that to half way save his career, he will need your support."

The last statement cut like a dagger. Suzanne was bleeding internally. *How could her dad think like that? Didn't he believe she had sense enough to detect when she was being used. Did he think that little of Jack?* With all Jack's faults, he had never leveraged her for his own gain. "Daddy, you don't really believe that about Jack, do you?" Her face was twisted in torment. Daddy pulled his daughter to him and gave her a hug, "My beautiful butterfly, Suzanne, no I don't. However, I do want you to be careful. You're so vulnerable when it comes to him. Nothing would please me more than if you're right this time about Jack. I just can't bear to see you hurt again, honey." Daddy patted her face across the kitchen table. She was glad he was in town. She needed him badly.

Suzanne pulled away and gazed at the father she had adored since she was able to utter his name. "Daddy, can you keep a secret? I called you out of your dinner on Capitol Hill for a reason. It was divine providence that you happened to be in town at this moment in time." Daddy's face was one of curiosity, caution and concern. "Suzanne, are you pregnant with another one of Jack's children?" he blurted out. She laughed a little at first and then couldn't stop for about a minute. "No Daddy, don't be silly," she said, attempting to regroup. She sobered when she thought about the conversation that lay before her.

"Daddy, what I have to tell you is much graver than that. It's about Jack, though it affects both our lives. I'll make us a pot of coffee." She sat across from Daddy at the kitchen table with the coffee brewing, and took the plunge. She told him the entire, gory tale about Jack's childhood, identity, trouble with the law and now the blackmail. She only paused when she went to get the richly aromatic java. Clayton Montgomery was dumbfounded. "My God, Suzanne! This changes everything, darling," he said in a mellow, faraway voice, "Everything."

"What do you mean, Daddy?" She was perplexed by his remarks. "Suzanne, my suspicions of Jack may be unfounded. He must really love you to reveal that. He's literally put his life in your hands. It also shows the amount of trust he has in you. The two of you haven't exactly been on the best of terms." She let her father's words sink in. She hadn't thought of it like that, but she was grateful she had won Daddy over. Now all she needed was his pledge of assistance.

"Daddy, thanks for helping me to see that, but, partly, I told you this story to ask for your aid." Daddy paused, "Suzanne, did Jack put you up to this?" She responded emphatically, "Absolutely not, Daddy. He made me promise not to even tell you. He said he was going to handle it himself. I gave him my word. The only thing is, when I asked him what he planned to do, he couldn't say. He finally mumbled something about him figuring it out when the time came. Daddy, that's just not good enough."

Suzanne went over to her father and got on her knees before him. "Daddy," she said through tears, "Please save Jack. I promise you, we'll find a way to pay you back." He petted her head like he would a favorite pet. "Suzanne, I will do my best to get Jack out of this mess. That is, if he's willing to take my assistance. I'm not so sure paying this guy off is the answer. Slugs like him usually keep coming back for more. When they do, the stakes are normally raised. Let me think of a better way. I've had experience with this sort of thing before. However, if it doesn't work, I guarantee you I will get you the funds. Five hundred thousand is no problem, honey, and don't you dream of paying me back. You would think the low-life would have grander dreams than that." Burying her head on her father's lap, Suzanne whispered gently, "Thank you, Daddy, for rescuing me and Jack."

• • •

I was back in the hotel room when my cell phone rang. Fear raced through every nerve ending. Beads of sweat formed on my forehead. I picked up the phone to examine the phone number. I didn't recognize it. Immediately I assumed Ridder was calling me from a pay phone to keep his anonymity instead it was Clayton calling from his hotel room. I brashly responded to the call, "Jack, here." "Hello, Jack," Clayton replied.

I wasn't sure what I felt about his call. Part of me was glad to hear from him, because I knew I should've called him by now to apologize. I didn't come close to keeping my word of taking care of his daughter. The other part of me, the dominant part, wished he would go away. "I can't handle another situation," I said under my breath. I genuinely liked and respected Clayton Montgomery, but I had nothing left. I was in a pressure cooker and steam was boiling from both ears.

"Hello, Clayton," I said, too fearful to call him Dad. Nothing got past Clayton Montgomery, "Jack, you can still call me Dad, son. You and Suzanne are still together, aren't you?" He caught me totally off guard. Why is he being so friendly when I've practically demolished his daughter's heart? I knew the answer almost before asking the question. Suzanne must have talked to him, even though she promised me she wouldn't. Clayton continued, "I'm hoping you can get through this 'rough patch' and the two of you can work it out. I've talked with Suzanne and she wants nothing less, Jack."

I was without words, and on guard. My instincts told me there was more to come. I rapidly recouped, "Alright Dad, I also want to desperately work it out. My family means more to me than anything else in my life. However, to be honest, there is a critical matter I need to take care of before I'm worthy of coming back to your daughter." When Clayton Montgomery spoke again I could tell my statements pleased him. "Jack, that's exactly why I'm calling. I want to help you, son. Suzanne has told me everything, and I do mean everything. I told her like I'm telling you. I will see you through this." I interrupted,

"Dad, I assume by the word 'everything,' you mean the blackmail by Detective Jones," I said, to make sure we were on the 'same page.' I continued, "Dad, while I appreciate your offer, I want to manage this myself. You've done enough for me over the years. Plus, there's no way on Earth I could repay you. I'm doing well for our family, but not that well."

There was a pause in our conversation. I could tell we both were reflecting on our shared history. "Jack, I see on some things you are as naive as Suzanne. My intention is not to pay him the bribe. Scum like that never goes away when they believe they have an endless well to drink from. However, if I'm forced to, I'll give him the cash. You can look at it as a gift, son, rather than a loan. It won't break me, that's for sure." I couldn't help but inquire, "Dad, what do you intend to do if you don't plan to meet his demands?" "Let's put it this way, Jack, most saints are named after they've died. That's usually because we all have bones buried. No one cares about those bones when you're cold and six feet under. That is, unless there's an inheritance involved," Clayton remarked. He chuckled and went on, "If Ridder Jones were truly a decent guy, he would've gotten your case reopened and attempted to put you behind bars. Instead, the man has resorted to extortion. He's got bones, Jack. I plan to find his dead bones, and when I do, we'll bury them for him together.

"By the way son, I've always admired tenacity. Your life exemplifies the results of perseverance. Know that, whatever happens, we're behind you and your family. I'll be in touch in the morning. I've got a bloodhound on the trail as we speak. Rest easy tonight, Jack. Tomorrow we begin the hunt."

For the first time in two weeks, I slept without nightmares. Yet, I still awoke to a tight neck and tense shoulders. I was unwilling to go to Capitol Hill until I heard from Clayton. My nerves were strained to their limits. I could hardly deal with the Capitol Hill gang on top of everything else. I phoned Joan and told her to clear my schedule. "Is everything alright, Senator?" Joan asked in a distressed tone. "Yes, Joan. I just need to take care of a few personal matters." I hated to give partial truths to one of my most loyal employees, but I thought it best. There was nothing she could do to help me. *Why worry her?*

It was 10:30 A.M. when Clayton Montgomery called. By this time, I was pacing the room and on my second cup of coffee. "Hello, Dad," I said in a relaxed voice I didn't feel. "Jack, I'm glad I caught you on your cell. I was afraid you went into the office and I wouldn't catch you." Clayton's tone was unreadable. "Dad, actually I decided not to go in until I heard from you." "Good, let me call you on your hotel line. It's more secure. With your life being so public, I don't exactly trust your cell phone." The phone went dead. Thirty seconds later the hotel room phone rang.

"Jack, sorry to get back to you so late. The private investigator needed more time. However, once I tell you what he found on our Mr. Jones, I'm sure you'll think it was worth the wait." As I listened to Clayton, my ear became one with the phone. I would not have believed his statements if it were not for my own surreal life. I pulled the telephone over onto the bed and sat there too mesmerized to move.

At the end of our conversation Clayton said, "Son, call Ridder and tell him you want to meet with him. Tell him I'll be accompanying you." "Won't he be curious regarding that, Dad? What if he says I have to come alone?" I questioned. Clayton was quiet for a moment. "Tell Mr. Jones I have agreed to give you the money only if I'm present. He's the one that suggested you hit me up for it, so he should be more open to it than not." "That makes sense. I'll call him as soon as we get off the phone," I responded. I was beginning to feel empowered. *No wonder Clayton Montgomery is one of the most powerful attorneys in the country*, I ruminated, feeling honored to be associated with him. "I'll do all the talking when we meet with him. Is that okay with you?" I could tell Clayton was used to giving orders. I suspected he added the last line because he reminded himself I was his son-in-law and didn't work for him. "Dad, that's perfectly fine with me I rather prefer it that way. I'll keep you abreast of the conversation with Ridder. Wish me luck." Clayton responded, "Better yet son, I wish you God's blessing." "Thank you Dad. That means even more to me." We said goodbye and hung up. I dialed Ridder's number with steady hands.

"Ridder, this is Jack Montgomery," I said, with an authentically commanding voice. "I know who the hell this is, Joe. What took you so long? I've lost my patience with you. Do you have my money?'" Ridder's tone was menacing. I was unnerved by the experience, in spite of my resolve. *You're not going to intimidate me,* I thought, unwilling to alter my course. Ridder was the type of guy that got under your skin and ate at your flesh. He was a parasite, a predator stalking his prey with unrelenting precision. I despised him at a primal level. "Yes, I do," I said unequivocally, "However, there is one stipulation." Ridder interjected, "Don't play games with me, Joe." I continued as if he had said nothing, "I'd like to meet with you to give you the funds rather than drop the cash at the agreed location. Clayton Montgomery will be joining me."

"Hell no!" Ridder said screaming into the phone. "Do you think I'm playing with your ass? There's absolutely no reason to meet with you. We have nothing to discuss." He mellowed slightly, "When are you planning to drop off the cash, Senator? I'm ready to get the hell out of town." I started to panic. I concentrated so I could use my head. My mind was galloping at lightning speed. "Ridder, as you suggested, I went to Clayton Montgomery to get the funds. However, to tell you the truth, he thinks the amount you're demanding is rather minuscule, and because of that, you will be back. Clayton wants this entire matter to disappear. He wants to meet with you to determine if it's truly enough to pay you off, for good. I guess I shouldn't be telling you this, but frankly, I have more to lose than he does."

I could tell by his hesitation, Ridder was soaking it all in. I held my breath. Ridder spoke, "Well, Clayton Montgomery is correct. I went light on you because I wasn't sure you had the balls to go to your father-in-law. Now that I know there's more to you than I gave you credit for, I'd like to discuss a real amount. Yes, let's meet. Tonight at 7:00 P.M. I'll meet the two of you at Ronnie's restaurant in Southeast D.C. Do the two of you remember that low-income black neighborhood?" I ignored Ridder's sarcasm. I'd be damned if I would give him the satisfaction of a response. "Fine, we'll see you then," I said curtly and hung up.

I called Clayton. "Dad, it's on for 7:00 P.M. tonight. Can you make it?" I gripped the phone until he responded. "Good job, Jack. I wouldn't miss this for a date with Tina Turner and Halle Berry on the same night." I smiled. How Clayton Montgomery found humor at a time like this was remarkable.

. . .

Clayton came to my hotel two hours before our meeting time with Ridder. We went over every possible scenario. Clayton was as astute and cunning as ever. I was glad I was not his target. We left the hotel at 6:30 P.M. and made our way to Ronnie's Restaurant. Ridder sat at a table near the back on the east side of the dimly lit restaurant. He was sipping a glass of red wine. He didn't readily acknowledge our presence when we came to the table. "Hello, Ridder," I said in a controlled voice. The sight of him sickened me. "Let me introduce you to Clayton Montgomery," I said. Ridder looked up not to meet my gaze, but to size up Clayton. "Nice of you to come, Mr. Montgomery," he said flatly.

We sat down without an invitation. We were ready to get down to business. As the caramel-colored, stout waitress approached our table, I waved a hand and shook my head to let her know we wouldn't be having anything. Ridder looked surprised by my motion. I turned to him, "Ridder, this meeting should be relatively quick. Plus, I'd rather discuss matters in an open space with few ears to overhear. After you finish your wine, we can walk out to the parking lot." Ridder's eyes were filled with rage. He said nothing, but gulped down his wine and placed a ten-dollar bill on the table. He then stood up sharply and put on his coat. He walked toward the door without uttering a word. We were in astonishment. Ridder abruptly stopped and turned to say, "Let's go gentlemen. Time is wasting." After regrouping, Clayton swiftly caught up with Ridder. I followed closely behind. Ridder's actions were sure to give Clayton a taste of what he's in for. I felt uptight. I prayed our 'meeting' would go according to plan.

We stood in the rear parking lot of the restaurant by Clayton's black 7-series BMW. I could tell Ridder was subtly inspecting the vehicle with a critical eye. *Maybe he's planning to obtain one with his new-found fortune,* I contemplated bitterly. Once Clayton determined that we were not being observed, he began the 'negotiation.' "Mr. Jones, this is how I see things." Ridder was taken aback by the forcefulness in Clayton Montgomery's voice and his direct, authoritative manner. Ridder was about to interject when Clayton put up his hand to stop him. He went on at an equal clip. "Like I was saying, you have two choices. You can take $50,000 as a token for your efforts and leave with your dignity intact, or you can leave with nothing at all." Ridder was about to lunge toward Clayton when I stepped in between them.

Ridder backed off and poked his head around me to meet Clayton's gaze. Ridder's own eyes blazed like a wild cat. "Are you out of your mind, old man? You better at least come up with the money the senator and I agreed on, or your precious son-in-law will be going to jail. Worse yet, Mr. Montgomery, your family name will be dragged through the gutter. The only reason why I met with your stinkin' ass is Joe said you wanted to evaluate whether you should increase the sum. Let me state for the record the payoff is now set at $1 million." Ridder was pointing his finger in Clayton's face. Clayton stood motionless staring back at him, completely unruffled.

"Mr. Jones the only potential jail time we should be discussing right now is yours. You know, extortion is against the law." Clayton continued, "You see, we also did a little tinkering around in your past. It appears you should be the last one blackmailing a person." Ridder exploded, "I don't know what the hell you're talking about. I do know I want my damn money!" Clayton went on with his agenda as if Ridder hadn't spoken.

"Mr. Jones, do you remember the day your partner got killed in the line of duty? It was approximately twenty-seven years ago. I believe his name was Tony Newburn. Well, according to witnesses, it turns out you're largely responsible for the perpetrators getting away. As the story goes, you went after the kid's brother, but got distracted by a sack he dropped accidentally while running from the scene. Of course, twenty-five thousand dollars of drug 'paper' is hardly anything to sneeze at, is it Mr. Jones?" Ridder stood frozen. His face showed shadows of remorse, but he was too shrewd to respond to the accusations. Clayton went on, "I was able to locate the gentleman from whom you confiscated the money. He's locked up in a penitentiary in Lima, Ohio. He's eager to sing in order to obtain a shorter time for an unrelated crime. You see, Mr. Jones, I have friends in many places."

Ridder appeared to be ready to lose control once again, but thought better. His hands balled and his eyes squinted as if ready for a brawl. He replied, "I don't know what you're talking about, Mr. Montgomery. Even if I did know, you don't have a shred of evidence. No one is going to believe a dope dealer, locked up punk." "Now there's where you're wrong, Mr. Jones. While I concur his credibility is not the highest, there are those that will easily corroborate the story. Remember, you had a number of spectators who observed the scene. When you went to see about your partner, you probably thought that the bag by his side went unnoticed, but, unfortunately, it didn't."

Ridder was visibly shaken by Clayton's words. I could tell by the twitch in his clenched jaw. His eyes also displayed poorly cloaked terror. Clayton had no other witnesses to the crime. The tale by the prisoner was all that he could gather in the limited time. Clayton threw out the bait on pure speculation that the story had merit. Ridder devoured it with greedy abandon. It was the beginning of his demise.

Clayton went for the jugular, "It will be interesting to see how your daughter, Adelle, feels about her daddy being caught in such a tangle. I wonder Mr. Jones, did you pay for her college tuition with a portion of those funds? Of course, she is your daughter, isn't she?" Clayton paused to allow Ridder a moment to absorb his words. "The paternity test you took some twenty-six years ago may not agree with your assessment. However, back then you were more focused on saving your marriage than accepting the fact your wife sought relief from her loneliness and your drunkenness in another man's arms. You never told her you had the test performed, did you? Some ghosts are better left in the dark, don't you think? You of all people should understand this. Take the fifty grand and be gone, Mr. Jones," Clayton said in a commanding voice. The words were brutal, but effective. I almost felt compassion for the detective. Ridder's frame twisted in convulsions with each blow.

Once the ramifications set in, Ridder realized he had been outwitted. One thing I had learned was, when you're playing with the big boys you have to be prepared for anything. Ridder was not close to Clayton Montgomery's league. Ruthlessness was a skill necessary to rise to Clayton's station in life. Clayton took Ridder's left hand and placed the stack of hundred dollar bills in it. "If we have a deal, Mr. Jones, I'll bring the remainder of the money over to your car. The deal is for you to crawl back into the sewer hole you came from and never return to our lives again," Clayton uttered with distaste. "If there is a hint of this story entering the press, we will sniff you out, and you'll wish you never heard of the name Joe Baker or knew of a Clayton Montgomery."

Clayton's threats sent chills down my spine. I knew Ridder had to be reeling from them as well. Ridder appeared defeated. He stared at his hand with the 'greenbacks' in it. "You have a deal, Mr. Montgomery," he said begrudgingly. Hatred was plastered on his countenance. Ridder, trying to recoup his dignity, straightened his back and walked toward his car. Clayton got the briefcase filled with cash from his car trunk and brought it over to his vehicle. Ridder's vehicle screeched as he pulled off. He did not look back.

$$\approx \ll$$

Chapter 20:

Quiet Moments

The drive back to my hotel was short, and we traveled in total silence. It was like we had been emerged in rot and were attempting to regain an optimistic view of the world. Life had taken a very revolting twist, and it was nearly successful. As my father-in-law pulled up to my hotel, I turned to him, "I don't know how to thank you for saving me, Dad. I could never have managed Ridder without you." I was feeling the weight of a debt I could never repay. I owed him my life.

Clayton Montgomery looked straight ahead at the city lights, "The best way to demonstrate your appreciation is to take care of my daughter, Jack. I know I've said this before, but she's the pulse of me. You have so much power over her. Her sun literally rises and sets on you. It has since the day she met you. Jack, you have the capacity to make her immensely happy. Live up to that potential, son." There was no response that sufficed. I didn't respond. I got out of the car and was about to shut the door when Clayton met my eyes. He grinned wickedly, "It was my pleasure, son, to put that low-life back in his place. He should be the ardent advocate of second chances, go figure." Clayton again peered straight ahead of him. "Take care, Jack. Remember what I said about Suzanne." I shut the door, and Clayton pulled off into the night.

Not a minute later, my cell phone rang. It was Clayton. "Hey, Dad," I said. "Son, there was one more thing." I stood by the hotel elevator, too curious to press the button. "What's that, Clayton?" "Jack, I meant to convey to you that if you want to breathe air back into your political life, I could help you. It is salvageable, despite what critics say. The public needs only time. They still love you, Jack. Otherwise, they wouldn't be so disturbed by your actions." Clayton continued, "Many people owe me favors in Washington, from Congress all the way to the White House. I could twist a few arms to encourage them to give you one more chance. You would make a fine President, Jack. We could hire someone on your behalf for public relations. We'll have the masses eating out of your hands again in no time."

I was touched. "Dad, you're too good to me. It isn't enough you just saved my 'hide.' Now you're turning to rescuing my career. Thank you." I smiled into the phone. I took a deep breath, "Thank you, Clayton, but I'm going to pass on your offer. I've been giving a lot of thought to the direction I want to take with my life. I plan to mull it over with Suzanne. I know I'm ready for a change. Politics is such a vicious business. It's filled with ferocious individuals, protecting their delicately drawn turfs. I want to be of service to mankind, but in a kinder environment." Clayton responded, "I clearly understand, son. Just let me know if there's any way I can help you. The world needs your talent." "I will, Dad. Thanks again. You're definitely a second father to me, sir." Clayton was silent. His voice was heavy when he uttered goodbye.

Once in my hotel room, I phoned Suzanne. She answered the telephone on the first ring. "Hello Suzanne, its Jack." Exhaustion filled my voice as my muscles relaxed and I let the weight of the past two days envelop my being. "Darling, you sound fatigued," she said, "Did it go okay with Ridder?" Suzanne's voice was trembling. I wondered once again why this magnificent woman loved me so much. "Suzanne, there's no need to be concerned. The meeting went well. It just took a lot out of me. I tell you, I don't see how I would have managed without your father. In hindsight, I'm glad you had enough sense not to listen to me about his involvement. I think my ego, not my head, was speaking when I said I wanted to handle matters on my own." Suzanne giggled, "Jack, I've only intermittently listened to you in the past, why would I start now?" I could only respond to her in laughter. I knew she spoke the truth. Her voice became focused, "Come home, Jack. I miss your warmth at night. I miss you." My heart skipped a beat. "Honey, you don't need to tell me twice. As soon as I can collect my things, I'll be on my way. Suzanne, I've missed you also, more than you can ever imagine."

I was euphoric. I drove the familiar streets home, singing to myself. No amount of traffic, weather or anything else could spoil my journey back to my 'sanctuary.' The time on the road gave me time to reflect on my past, present and future. I'd learned lessons the arduous way, but they were lessons well taught. *I'm ready for changes in my life,* I ruminated, as I glided through the usual thick D.C. maze of automobiles. Life was too short and valuable to waste even a minute of it.

Before I could fully form a mental map of my next steps, I was pulling into the driveway of our home. *It was like slipping into an old pair of slippers,* I reflected, as I stepped out of the car. I grabbed my bags from the back seat and headed to the door. I picked up pace as I visualized Suzanne's willowy figure waiting inside to greet me. Before I could find my key, the door swung open and Suzanne's arms wrapped around my neck in a fierce grip. She got on her toes and landed a kiss squarely on my lips. After several lingering kisses, I reluctantly pulled away.

"Whoa, Suzanne! What will the neighbors think of us out here smooching on the doorstep like teenagers?" Suzanne put her hands on her hips in a sassy pose, "Do I really care what these snobby suburbanites feel about you and me? Let's face it, Senator; we've been the talk of the town for quite a while. Why not give them more to speculate on?" she said, making me smile. "You have a point, Ms. Montgomery, a very solid point indeed," I said in a low sexy voice. Suzanne took my hand and guided me inside.

Once inside, all my pent up yearning was released. I took Suzanne in my arms and we 'necked' for at least five minutes. My hands were groping her everywhere. With each touch of her silky supple skin, my desire rose. Suzanne whispered as we both sought to catch our breadth, "Jack, I made you a wonderful dinner, your favorite. It's roast beef with baked carrots and potatoes, with salad and cornbread." I replied as I nestled her neck, "Suzanne, it smells fabulous, but right now I'm interested in dessert."

I scooped her up and carried her to the master suite. We made love as if our lives depended on it. In many ways, it did. Suzanne had been my sustaining source of energy, even when I wasn't aware of it. I, in turn, brought Suzanne alive like no one else. We needed each other like the sun and moon need each other to keep the pace of time. *How could I have been so foolish not to realize this sooner?*

We remained in bed in the aftermath of passion. Suzanne, being her usual practical self, rolled over and said, "Jack, I better turn off the food before the house burns down." "Okay, baby, but come back to me. I'll get cold here all by myself." Several minutes later, Suzanne crawled back under the blanket. Her skin was inviting as it melded into mine.

"Suzanne, I've been doing a lot of thinking of late," I said, snuggling up to her once more. She turned to face me, giving me her undivided attention. "Yes darling, about what?" she said in earnest. "Well, about a lot of things, but primarily regarding my future, our future," I said, correcting myself. We were definitely in this together. I continued, "I think I want to finish my Senate term and then retire from politics. How would you feel about that? I know you had your heart set on being First Lady." I tried to make light of the question, but her answer would seal my fate. Whatever Suzanne desired, I would deliver on it. She had more than lived up to her end of the bargain. It was about time I started living up to mine.

I squeezed Suzanne's shoulder to let her know that whatever she wanted would be all right. Suzanne peered into my eyes and smiled. "Jack that's the most wonderful news I've heard since earlier today." We laughed at the short time reference. "I wanted to be 'First Lady' because you wanted so much to be President. None of it matters to me in the end, only you. With all that has happened lately, I'm ready for a more mundane life."

I pulled Suzanne to me with immeasurable gratitude. "How did I get so lucky? You're the rarest of jewels, sweet cakes. Though are you sure about this, Suzanne? I mean, I don't want you saying these words just to please me." Suzanne lay on her back and gazed up at the ceiling. "I'm absolutely sincere Jack." Her voice filled with uncertainty when she asked the next question. "Jack, what will you do if you're no longer in politics? Will you go back to law? I know you weren't exactly enthralled with it when you first came out of school, but you might enjoy it more now." I propped up my head to meet Suzanne's eyes. I knew I needed to quiet her anxiety. "I'm mulling over heading up a foundation focused on the economically disadvantaged or perhaps a think tank on urban affairs. What do you think?" Suzanne jumped off the bed and came to my side of the room, "That's a fabulous idea! I would love to help you run it or be involved in some form."

I was delighted with her enthusiasm. "Honey, your involvement would be welcome, if not essential. I've always relied on your smarts." I made my way out of the bed and found my robe and slippers. I turned to Suzanne who was sitting on the bed watching my every movement with a look of unadulterated admiration. *If she weren't my wife, I'd believe she was a groupie,* I thought with amusement. I turned to her, "Then it's settled. One more year of political fancy, and I'm out. Ms. Montgomery, I'm famished. Let's head to the kitchen, shall we? I want some of that delectable dinner you fixed." I patted Suzanne on the butt as we headed to the kitchen. She giggled in response.

I sat at the kitchen table, and Suzanne served me dinner. It was nice to have a home cooked meal again. "Thanks, honey," I said, and licked my lips for effect. My mouth was watering. Suzanne's eyes twinkled as she went to make her own plate. I poured us red wine to complete the meal. "Let's toast to the future," Suzanne suggested in her naturally melodic voice. We clicked our glasses. "To a future filled with adventure, charitable spirit and passion," I remarked. Suzanne smiled and shook her head in affirmation. We drank in silence.

Suzanne put down her glass. "Jack, since we're keeping no secrets, I feel compelled to tell you Nicola called me today." I nearly toppled over my wine glass in reaction to her statement. "She did what?!" I said in a harsher tone than intended. Suzanne continued, "She wants us to talk. She said it was important to apologize to me in person. She said she owed me that much." Suzanne narrowly observed me for feedback. I was too immobilized to give her a response. Suzanne went on, "At first I was unsure about it, but I eventually agreed. To be honest, Jack, I'm not quite sure why I finally decided to meet with her. Maybe it was something in her voice."

Suzanne detailed the exchange with Nicola in a far away voice. I was extremely unnerved, but there was nothing I could do about it. This was between the two of them. I didn't feel I had the authority to stop her from meeting with Nicola. I replied, "Do what your heart is leading you to, Suzanne. I hope you get what you want out of the encounter." Suzanne leaned back in her chair and stared at me as if seeing me for the first time. "That's just it, Jack, I'm not sure what I expect to achieve."

• • •

Nicola and Suzanne sat at the café table, not knowing what to say to each other. Nicola set the meeting, so Suzanne decided to let her speak first. Nicola sipped on her cappuccino and finally met Suzanne's eyes. Suzanne looked into Nicola's exotic, tantalizing and dramatically glamorous face with a pool of emotions. She resented Nicola for sleeping with her husband, she admired her dignity in handling all the attention, and she felt sorry for her. She too had her heart broken by Jack. Suzanne had been in her shoes on several occasions. None of those times were fun.

Nicola spoke up, "Suzanne, I appreciate your agreeing to meet with me. I'm sure this isn't any easier for you than it is for me." Suzanne listened with curiosity now. Nicola continued, "Above all, I wanted to say I'm sorry. I deeply regret the humiliation and pain I caused you and your family. I would like to justify or rationalize away my actions, but I know better. What I did was wrong. It was selfish and in no way depicts the behavior of a Christian. I've asked the Lord to forgive me. However, I beg for your forgiveness as well." Nicola looked away. Her hands were clasped together in a fierce grip.

Suzanne didn't know how to respond. These words of repentance were the last words she expected to spew forth from Nicola's mouth. Suzanne assumed she was going to provide an explanation for what happened, blame Jack or her or someone besides Nicola herself. Suzanne found herself admiring Nicola's forthright confession. *If she weren't intricately involved in the saga*, Suzanne thought, *she would almost find Nicola endearing.* It was a strange and unsettling predicament Suzanne found herself in.

"Nicola, it takes two to tango. Jack has just as much responsibility for what transpired between the two of you. In some ways, he has more. Jack had a wife and two adoring children depending on him." Suzanne was surprised by her own candor and acknowledgement. She continued, "I cannot say I have come to terms with what the two of you did, but we must move forward with our lives. Healing is a process. I do hope you find someone who is truly available to give you his love." Nicola stared back at Suzanne, obviously tormented. Suzanne had been more abrupt than planned, but she was also human. Nicola replied, "That's fair, Suzanne. I'd just like to say before leaving, that Jack is a very lucky man to have someone of such a caliber by his side. Take care of yourself, Suzanne."

"Thank you," Suzanne said softly. It was becoming increasingly difficult for her to maintain her dislike of the woman. "I wish you all the best, Nicola," she continued in a flat voice. Nicola stood. She picked up her purse and jacket and practically ran out of the place. Suzanne visually followed her until she was out of sight and then sat at the table a moment longer to mentally review what had just transpired. She got up and made her way out of the café.

• • •

The remaining year in office flew by. Once I announced that I was retiring at the end of my term, the 'heat' was instantaneously removed. I was no longer a threat to anyone inside or outside my party. And as expected, the public's memory was short lived. As soon as the next scandal broke, I was history. My reconciliation with Suzanne also took the wind out of things. People love a happy ending. Suzanne and I were glowing with our love for one another. It didn't take a marriage 'expert' to tell we were in synch. The public rallied behind us as they had in the past. I realized then I truly was their advocate.

I agreed to have lunch with Dirk at 'Barclay Lounge' ten days before my transition out of political life. Our relationship was back to normal. *It hadn't always been the case,* I reflected. Our relationship became awkward after I learned about his and Nicola's new life together. Fortunately, the bond between us was sufficient to survive the strain. Still, Dirk and I limited most conversations to legal affairs and his political advice. It had been approximately four months after Nicola confessed their relationship to me when Dirk invited me to golf as an attempt to reconcile matters.

"I'm elated you could meet me, Jack," Dirk said, as he swung at a golf ball on the driving range. We shook hands and sized each other up. "No problem, Dirk. These days my schedule is wide open." I smiled at the thought of the difference a chain of events had made. "Do you want to go someplace where we could focus on each other rather than our skills? I don't know about you, but I cannot help but take this game serious." We both laughed, recalling how competitive we were with each other on the golf course.

"Actually, a more relaxed environment sounds like a good idea." Dirk then suggested the D.C. Zoo. "Wonderful idea, I've been sitting at a desk all day. I could afford to stretch my legs," I said. We left the golf course for more sympathetic surroundings. The zoo met our requirements perfectly. Nature has a way of quieting the spirit, I decided, as we drove over and found a place to park. We walked at the zoo in silence for several minutes before Dirk stopped at the gate of the elephants. He leaned on the rail and watched the large majestic creatures move within their tiny space. "Magnificent creatures," he said in an airy voice. It was clear his mind was concentrating on other matters.

Dirk turned to me. "Jack, I know things have been awkward between us since I got with Nicola." I stood there not facing him, but continuing to look straight ahead at the mammals. "I would like to say I wish it had never happened, but that wouldn't be true. I love Nicola. She ignites my soul. I do regret that it created a wedge between us. You're like a brother to me. In so many ways, I look up to you. In the beginning, you were a way of holding on to a part of Jack. Over the years, our relationship has taken on a life of its own. I guess what I'm trying to say, is that I need you, and I want you to be in my life. Anyway, I wanted to let you know that I have asked Nicola to marry me, and she has accepted. For quite some time, I've been gathering the nerve to ask you to be my Best Man at the wedding. It would mean a lot to me."

Suddenly, all that had placed a rift between us became insignificant. I was affected by his words. I knew it took a lot for Dirk to express himself in this manner. He rarely spoke of his feelings for fear of exposing a 'softer' side. In Dirk's mind, tenderness meant vulnerability and that led to victimization. For the first time since we had met on the golf course, I met his stare. Dirk appeared like a younger brother, waiting for his older brother's approval. "Dirk, I admit things haven't been great between us. A large part of it has been my ego, even though I had made the choice to stay with Suzanne anyway. In truth, you're a better person for Nicola. Yet knowing this hasn't made it easier to accept. Anyway, Dirk, I would be honored to be your Best Man."

Dirk turned and put his arm around me in a fashion typical of deep male bonding. "Thanks, man," was all he said as he slapped my shoulder. Dirk's expression tempered once more as he turned to look at me. "How did Suzanne take learning about me and Nicola?" he asked. I searched for the right words. "If I had to sum it up, I'd say, relieved." We both laughed. I continued, "I believe Suzanne remained slightly threatened by Nicola, even after our reconciliation. Knowing that she's no longer 'on the market' was a very good thing. Plus, you know how fond Suzanne is of you, Dirk. She was ecstatic to hear that you had finally found someone to make you happy. The two of them meeting turned out to be a good thing also. They appear to have come to terms with one another." Dirk seemed pleased.

I forced myself back to the present. It helped that Dirk asked me a question. "Sorry, Dirk, I was lost in thought. What did you ask me?" Dirk observed me with a look usually reserved for his legal probing. "Jack, are you alright? I asked you if you were going to be able to make it to the tuxedo fitting next Saturday. Bo and Shelton are going to be there. So far, Drew is the only one that can't make it. He's got a conference to attend in New York that weekend. You seem distracted, Jack." As usual, Dirk didn't hold anything back. I actually enjoyed his candid style; it kept me on my toes.

The world I'd lived in was filled with phonies and pompous 'wannabes.' Dirk was all that he appeared to be. I smiled, "Dirk, I'll be there. And I'm fine. I have a lot on my mind these days. You can definitely count me in for the fitting Saturday though. How could I be the Best Man and not attend? Speaking of the wedding, I need to plan your bachelor party. We only have three weeks before the big day." I laughed, "Dirk, this will be a bachelor party for the books." Dirk responded with equal humor, "Just keep it mild enough that I don't make the front page of the newspapers on my wedding day, dude."

We paused to look at the menu before our waiter returned with our orders of coffee. After a few minutes, Dirk closed his menu and sat it on the table. "Have you decided what you're having?" Dirk asked in his unaltered well-bred New England accent. Before I could respond he went on, "I was thinking about a big juicy steak. To hell with cholesterol and fat, sometimes a man has got to be a man." We laughed. "Dirk, you better enjoy it now because once you're married these types of eating luxuries are few and far between. Soon you'll be munching on alfalfa sprouts and drinking green tea" Our laughter became more robust. I put my menu down. "Now that I think about it Dirk, I better enjoy this moment as well. Let's make it two steaks, with potatoes and a beer."

Dirk became serious, "Jack, do you have any regrets about leaving political life? You'll be sorely missed. There's 'talk' some in the Democratic Party are hoping you'll reconsider and even still run for the presidency. It's not too late. None of us have much hope of regaining the White House with the candidates that have thrown their hats into the ring." I stared at Dirk with reflection I hadn't done for quite some time. It was like Dirk was reading my mind. "Dirk, it's odd that you say that. As I get closer to my 'retirement' from political life, I'm starting to feel an enormous, inexplicable loss. Maybe it's because I've spent my life striving to make a difference through political means. I think I have been tremendously successful at it. My political career has been the one shining point in my life, where I've done it right. It's been a source of pride for me. In many ways, I feel like I would be a better leader because of all I've been through and learned along the way.

"I'm not so sure giving it all up is the right thing to do. Yet, I've set this 'Urban Economic Think Tank' in motion and to back out now may be unfair to those involved, especially Suzanne. On top of that, Suzanne revealed to me shortly after we got back together, she was burnt out with political life." Dirk looked me squarely in the eye, "Jack, as I said earlier, it's not too late to change your mind. I probably shouldn't be saying this, but personally I think you're making a grave mistake. Our country needs you. You have the chance to shape this nation in a way you've never done before. It's almost heady to think about it. As for Suzanne, my guess is, Jack, she would support you in whatever you do. You've got that kind of woman by your side. Plus, Suzanne probably made those comments at the height of the scandal. Maybe you should feel her out once more on the subject. Time does bring changes." After the waiter gave us our coffee and took our order, we sat at the table in silence. I mulled over Dirk's words. Dirk appeared lost in thought as well. "Dirk, thank you," I finally said, "I will discuss it with Suzanne tonight. Based on the outcome, I'll phone Clayton and Bo for political advice on how to get back into the race with both feet running."

. . .

"Hello, Jack," Clayton said warmly over the phone. "Dad, I've got to be brief, because Suzanne and I are heading out to a charity event. However, I wanted to phone you before we left. Clayton, I've talked it over with Suzanne, and I want to get back into the presidential race. Politics is in my blood, Dad. This is where I need to be. My questions to you are, whether you think it's too late to jump back in and if not, how best to do it?" Clayton's voice sounded elated when he replied, "The answer to your first question is absolutely not. The second one is a little trickier, but far more tantalizing. Let's talk as soon as you get back in from your function. Better yet, son, I'll book a flight to come in town this weekend to talk to you in person. Some matters merit face-to-face conversation, this is one of them."

I was feeling energized though cautious. "Thanks, Dad. I really appreciate your support and willingness to be inconvenienced on my behalf," I said with deep gratitude. "Son, this is no inconvenience at all. I've envisioned your inauguration from the day you entered politics. Let's make it come to fruition, shall we? If we can get you selected to head the democratic ticket, I think we are on our way to the gates of the White House. Oh, by the way, see if your old campaign manager, Bo Elison, can join us. He's one shrewd individual. We have so much to discuss, even the selection of your Vice President."

"Will do, Dad. I'll get back to you soon."

. . .

The campaign went without a hitch. The public had not forgotten me. It was now the day of reckoning. We sat in the den of our home in Massachusetts. The intensity in the air was simply stifling. All of us - Suzanne, Papa, Clayton, Bo, Dirk and Nicola, our two children and me, sat glued to the television. My heart was racing with each US state declaring the tally of their votes once the polls closed. One MSNBC political analyst commented, "The race is too close to absolutely call, but so far, with three-quarters of the electoral votes counted, it appears Jack Montgomery may be our new president. The night is still long ..."

Suzanne looked at me. "Jack, I can't take much more of this," she said softly. I squeezed her hand. She curled her delicate fingers around mine and moved closer. "It will be all right Suzanne, whatever the outcome," I said, "We both know we ran a solid campaign and gave it our best." Suzanne's eyes shined at me. "I know one thing, Jack," she said as she leaned to whisper in my ear, "You will always be a winner to me."

Epilogue

I reflect back on my life with varied emotions. So much of it was the ride of a lifetime. Other aspects were equivalent to plunging into the deep blue sea with no lifejacket to protect me and no compass to point me in the right direction. I wasted so much time on the nonessentials. Blind ambition was the worst of them all. I contemplated these things as I sat on my deck bench, eating grilled catfish and listening to the sound of my grandchildren playing. It was the time of year I always relished most, my annual Labor Day family picnic. Being President of the United States was the ultimate public position. This was one of the few occasions I set aside to spend solely with family and close friends. *It was my time.*

I peered down to see my youngest granddaughter, Miranda, tugging at my sleeve. "Grandpapa, are you going to jump rope with us?" I laughed. "I don't think it will happen today," I said with feigned remorse, knowing that these weary bones of mine couldn't carry out those duties, even if my brain instructed them to do so. I picked her tiny frame up and sat her on my knee. Her ponytails on each side of her brown cherub face flopped up and down from the movement. "Honey, Grandpa would love to be able to do a lot of things that I can't do these days, but I'll watch you all with a fervent passion." I patted her on the head, "Now, go have fun kiddo." Miranda seemed satisfied with my response, "Okay Grandpapa. Don't forget to watch me." She bounced off my knee and ran to play with the other kids.

I took in my surroundings with a satisfaction I didn't think possible. There was Suzanne, looking older but more refined and still stunning. Papa and his wife were both barely getting around these days, but still kicking. I was grateful to still have Papa with us. Clayton Montgomery and his 'sweetheart' Naomi were there and continued to show signs of being madly in love, even after all the years. It was very touching. Gabriella and her husband, Rolin, of seven years came late, but came with a handsome amount of food, so they were forgiven. The two had supplied us with three incredible grandchildren. Max and his fiancée were snuggled in the corner. We were glad to see him finally settling down. Both Gabriella and Maxwell were successful attorneys, which made us extremely proud.

Nicola and Dirk stopped in with their two kids, Riley and Brianna. Bo and his third wife, Mitsy, also came by to say hello and have dessert. Erin Rody, my former Legislative Aid and now my Chief of Staff, also joined the festivities. Aunt Sadie and her 'friend' had surprised me and flew into town for the occasion. She arrived in grand fashion. Aunt Sadie was never one to be outdone. She conveyed that Aunt Eulie and Aunt Jean sent their love.

Suzanne's old high school buddies, Roslyn and Shelby, and their families joined the festivities. Roslyn lived in Atlanta. She was a pediatrician and had married an oncologist. They had one son. Shelby's dreams had come true as well. She had married a stockbroker who made a fortune off the market. They lived in New York and were blessed with three children. As a surprise for Suzanne, I had arranged to have both of them, along with Suzanne's friend, Maxine, join us. I wished I could have had her mother join us as well, but she had mentally stopped existing twelve years earlier. However, Suzanne was so moved to see her friends she couldn't stop crying. "Jack, I can't believe you did this! I've been trying to get us all together for I don't know how long." She held me tight and kissed me warmly, in front of everyone. I was very pleased. *It was a good time,* I reflected, not only the day, but also this time in my life in general.

By anyone's standard, my presidency was a success. I was in my third year in office and I had consistently maintained a job approval rating of 60% or better. The Democratic Party even urged me to run for a second term. I was strongly considering the idea. The job of President was enormously stressful at times, especially given the world unrest and economic concerns at home. Yet, I wouldn't trade places with anyone. My chest tightened with emotion. To have this much influence over human plight is truly a gift from God. I would never take my position or impact for granted. I was making a difference. Most of all, life was spectacular because I had the love of my life by my side. What more could a man ask for? I gazed up at the crystal blue sky, "Thank you, Lord," I said under my breath, "I couldn't have done it without you."

Breinigsville, PA USA
05 April 2010
235557BV00002B/12/P